The new Ze[...]
cover is a p[...]
fashionable[...]
satin or ve[...]
nosegay. Us[...]
in design from the elegantly simple to the exquisitely ornate.
The Zebra Regency Romance tuzzy-muzzy is made of alabaster with a silver filigree edging.

FIRELIT MAGIC

"Have you received many of these—massages—before?" he asked.

"No. I learned how to give them, but I've only had one, myself. She was a licensed therapist who gave lessons at our local hospital. As you saw this afternoon, there is nothing necessarily—seductive—about it."

That seemed to appease him. "How do I begin?"

Under her direction, he knelt at her head, poured lotion in his hands, and warmed it by rubbing it between his palms. He hesitated only a moment, then rubbed it along her bare back with long strokes of his powerful hands. His fingertips reached her hips, then slid down her sides, sending ripples of pleasure through her as they brushed her flesh with feather-like strokes on their return trip.

Desire flared, burning hot and uncontrollable. "That—that's not quite the way you're supposed to do it," she managed.

"I thought you said this wasn't seductive." His voice wavered. "It wasn't when you did it."

"It's all in the touch. I didn't mean it to be, so it wasn't. You—" She looked up, and her reproach turned to yearning.

"I didn't mean it to be, either. Until now." His husky voice sounded near her ear.

The firelight sparked and flickered, illuminating the features in the face so near her own, clearly revealing the torment and desire which mingled in his expression. Her will power melted. She rose up on one elbow, slipping her arm about his neck, and drew his head down to hers.

REGENCIES BY JANICE BENNETT

TANGLED WEB   (2281, $3.95)

Miss Celia Marcombe's dark eyes flashed with righteous indignation. She was not a commodity to be traded or bartered to a man
as insufferably arrogant as Trevor Ryde, despite what her high-
handed grandfather decreed! If Lord Ryde thought she would let
herself be married for any reason other than true love, he was
sadly mistaken. He'd never get his hands on her fortune—let
alone her person—no matter how disturbingly handsome he
was . . .

MIDNIGHT MASQUE   (2512, $3.95)

It was nothing unusual for Lady Ashton to transport government
documents to her father from the Home Office. But on this particular afternoon a gust of wind scattered the papers, and suddenly an important page was lost. A document desperately
wanted by more than one determined gentleman—one of whom
would murder to get his way . . .

AN INTRIGUING DESIRE   (2579, $3.95)

The British secret agent, Charles Marcombe, had done his bit
against that blasted Bonaparte. Now it was time to nurse his
wounds and come to terms with the fact that that part of his life
was over. He certainly did not need the likes of Mademoiselle
Therese de Bourgerre darkening his door, warning of dire emer-
gencies and dread consequences, forcing him to remember things
best forgotten. She was a delightful minx, to be sure, but it would
take more than a pair of pleading emerald eyes and a woebegone
smile to drag him back into the fray!

A Touch of Forever
Janice Bennett

ZEBRA BOOKS
KENSINGTON PUBLISHING CORP.

For Wendy and Adele,
for all their support and encouragement

ZEBRA BOOKS

are published by

Kensington Publishing Corp.
475 Park Avenue South
New York, NY 10016

First printing: June, 1992

Printed in the United States of America

Chapter One

She clung to the wooden seat, terrified, as her mother raced the lurching wagon through the darkened street. Ahead, flickering torches revealed the gathering crowd, the angry men waving their pitchforks and guns. Deep voices shouted French words unfamiliar to the vocabulary of a twelve-year-old child.

Her mother's scream blotted out all else as the woman struggled to control the snorting, rearing horse. The reins tangled in her silk shawl, dragging it from the ruffled lace of her bedraggled ballgown. The girl reached to help, but her long skirts wound about her legs and she fell to her knees on the floorboards. She barely regained her seat as they careened around a sharp corner.

An ill-clad ruffian lunged forward, throwing his burning torch into the back of the wagon. It rolled into a pile of debris, beyond the girl's desperate reach. For a moment the dried wood and rags smoldered, then flames burst to life about her.

A man, his garments torn and bloodied, his wild eyes those of a madman, grabbed her mother's arm, half-dragging her from the blazing cart. A metallic gleam flashed in his hand as he swung at her, and the woman slumped to the seat, a dagger embedded in her breast.

For one horror-filled second the girl stared at the chased silver handle, inlaid with an odd blue stone that had a glowing star within it. Then she grasped it, trying to pull it

5

free. An eerie, tingling sensation raced from her fingers up her arm.

With a groaning crack, the wagon shaft broke. The horse veered away but the wagon careened on, slamming into a wall and overturning . . .

Alexandra Anderson bolted upright in bed, trembling, her brow and palms clammy with perspiration. A scream reverberated through her ears, agonized, terrified . . .

She buried her face in her hands. Oh, God, let it have been in her dream. She *couldn't* have screamed out loud, not again, not like last time, or even the terrible time before.

One by one, she forced her fingers to unclench, prying them away from her eyes which remained squeezed shut. It wasn't real. Only her bad dream—again. She repeated that phrase, over and over, chanting it like a mantra to still the raging beat of her heart, her gasping breaths. Only a bad dream.

At last her pulse rate steadied, and she dragged open first one eye, then the other. The hazy, dim light of approaching dawn illuminated the inn's cozy bedroom. No dangers, no waking horrors hovered over her. Lexie shook the shoulder length waves of her dark hair from her translucent blue eyes and drew one more deep, controlling breath into her lungs. Her raw nerves refused to calm.

Throwing back the down coverlet, she swung her bare legs over the edge of the mattress and found her sheepskin slippers. She shivered, even though only a moderate chill hung about the room. Forced air heating, the brochure proclaimed, had been one of the first improvements implemented by the inn's current owners.

She drew on her blue fleece robe and huddled into it, unable to shake off the lingering terror. She needed coffee— hot and sweet and strong. Belting the robe tighter about her slender waist, she crossed to the mini-brewer which sat on the antique dresser. With hands that still shook, she sloshed in the carafe of water she had set out the night before and shoved in the filter basket filled with the rich-smelling grounds.

She turned away, hugging herself. The floral print of the wallpaper took form as the seeping sunlight warmed to a soft glow. Enlarged photos and watercolors of the English countryside hung at intervals above vases of flowers and dried arrangements. The general aura of hominess, though, did nothing to dispel her fear.

Paris. The Reign of Terror. Her research had identified the costumes, the details of which stood out vivid and exact in her mind. Too vivid. Every time she saw another sketch or painting of the time, especially of a similar mob scene, it filled her anew with the sick anguish which haunted her.

She drew back the lace curtains at the multi-paned window and stared out, unseeing, over the rocky Kentish cliffs and the icy gray waters of the English Channel beyond. The nightmare had come more often lately. Four times, in fact, in the six days she'd been in England.

Her internal quaking increased. Lord, she should have grown accustomed to that dream by now. It had haunted her for as long as she could remember—twelve of her twenty-four years. Yet usually it plagued her on a less constant basis.

She cast a longing glance at the coffee pot, but only half the potent brew had dripped into the glass decanter.

Her hand strayed to the oval gold locket on its chain about her neck. She wore it even in that dream. Or rather the young girl, whose living—or dying—nightmare Lexie inherited, wore it. With shaking fingers, she unclasped the chain and hurled the locket from her, onto the bed, where it landed amidst the rumpled covers.

The image of the blazing wagon rose in her mind, and she covered her face once more with her hands, trying to block it out. Unshed tears burned in her eyes as she fought for control. She couldn't give way to terror; there was no point, she was safe. Only a bad dream.

The hiss of the last drops of water dripping from the heating chamber of the coffee maker penetrated her cocoon of horror. She poured some, stirred in two heaping spoonfuls of sugar and another generous one of powdered creamer, and gulped down a scalding mouthful of coffee.

She finished her second cup before her hands no longer shook.

The locket. . . . She set the empty mug on the dresser and scrambled among the covers, searching until she once more held the golden oval, clutching it in her hands, afraid to let it go. That nightmare burst into her consciousness in too much vivid detail, far too often, not to have been real—for someone, for the girl who wore that necklace nearly two hundred years ago. And somehow, now, it possessed Lexie, bringing her those last desperate, tragic moments of the girl's life.

Her gaze focused on the engraved flowers on the front, so familiar—then she turned it over. On the back, a flowing hand had engraved the name "Alexandra." Her name. But only because of the locket. When she'd been found wandering the streets of Paris, a child of twelve, badly burned by the explosion of a terrorist's bomb, her memory too deeply recessed into her subconscious to re-emerge, it had been assumed by the authorities that the name was hers.

Lexie doubted that now. The locket—and the name—belonged to that little girl almost two hundred years ago. Through the long, futile years of trying to reconstruct her own past, Lexie had come to believe the locket had taken her over, erased her memory at the same age the earlier Alexandra had been when she died.

All chance of sleep had vanished; she might as well get to work. At least that would give her mind a more positive turn. She picked up the notebook in which she had jotted down the final ideas she needed to follow up on in order to complete her doctoral thesis, and leafed through to the last page.

She had spent yesterday interviewing that sweet old man, the ninth earl of Wyndham. However, they had rapidly gotten off their topic of Napoleon's aborted invasion of England in 1805. The earl's own troubles with a persistent and unethical land developer had quickly taken precedence.

That must have been what brought on her nightmare, that louse Geoffrey Vaughn's attempts to buy up the park land surrounding Wyndham Priory, and the poor earl's buckling under the pressure brought to bear. Lexie would have given a great deal to have been able to help.

But she hadn't accomplished anything toward her thesis yesterday, and she couldn't stay in England indefinitely. Her limited funds were dwindling quickly, airfare from Seattle to London wasn't cheap, and even the inn's discounted rate seemed exorbitant. She'd run herself pretty deeply into debt to take this trip in pursuit of original documents.

Lexie poured a third cup of coffee, sweetened it, and returned to the window. So far, it had been worth it. That little museum in Rye had been a windfall, especially their treasure—a diary kept by a Miss Hester Langley, governess at Wyndham Priory at the beginning of the nineteenth century. If it hadn't been for Miss Langley's taste for gothic adventure, Lexie never would have given much thought to the ancient abbey, destroyed during the reign of Henry VIII, located a mere five miles from the Wyndham estate. She certainly never would have heard of the secret passage which descended from the ruins, leading to a cavern which had been used by smugglers. Somewhere, it let out into the rocky cove below, where they had landed their boats.

Lexie thoughtfully tapped her pen with her finger. That cavern might have nothing at all to do with the traitorous conspiracy that tried—and failed—to smuggle information to Napoleon to pave his way to London. But then again, it might. Lexie wanted to find it, just in case something—anything—remained within.

She peered into the icy gloom of the January morning. Low tide. Now ought to be an ideal time to explore. It would be cold, but at this early hour she couldn't think of any other line of research she could pursue.

Heartened by this determination, she exchanged her robe and nightgown for a pair of jeans, a warm bulky sweater and a wool scarf, and pulled on socks and her Adidas. To this she added a windbreaker and a pair of gloves. Boy scouts didn't have any monopoly on being prepared.

Dark, roiling clouds filled the sky as she hurried down the

outside staircase of the guest cottage and ran across the garden to the main house. Grass, damp from the overnight sleet, soaked through her shoes and the wind penetrated her clothing. She was going to freeze.

The cook had yet to officially open the inn's kitchen, but a maid, who had just begun to set tables, offered to bring her some of the croissants fresh from the oven. Lexie stuffed one in her pocket and, munching the other, headed toward the converted stable where she had parked her rented car.

A couple of miles' drive along the winding cliff road brought her to what little remained of the abbey. Tumbled rubble met her searching gaze—except for a portion of the main building which still stood tall and proud, as if in defiance of King Hal's edict of disbandment and destruction. Lexie pulled onto the verge, switched off the engine, and climbed out.

It must have been beautiful once, a sprawling arrangement of buildings connected by courtyards, probably gardens. Now grass-covered mounds indicated the outlines of the vanished walls, and weeds and vines clambered over fallen gray stones. Shrubs and small trees encroached on what once must have been expanses of lawn. Only an occasional partial wall remained, jutting upward at a rakish angle.

She locked her purse in the trunk and clipped her keys to her camera case. This she slung over her shoulder and strolled forward, past the collection of wooden picnic tables and the line of trash cans. The abbey rated as a tourist attraction of only minor importance; her guidebook awarded it no more than four lines. She would have given it about the same, had it not been for Miss Hester Langley and her diary.

Following a weed-encrusted path, she circled around to the near side, at last emerging onto the promenade along the cliff. The icy Channel breeze whipped her dark hair behind her, tangling it in a salty, clinging mass about her neck. She wiped stray strands from her eyes, pulled her scarf up so it covered her ears, and took an uneasy step forward.

Fortunately, an iron railing offered the acrophobic a measure of security. Lexie clung to it, not looking down, and inched along the path until she reached the wooden stairway leading to the beach below. She descended with care.

At the foot, standing safely on sand, she paused, gazing along the rocky curve of the sheltered cove, frowning in concentration. Somewhere along this half-mile stretch, well-concealed either by chance or design, lay the opening to that mysterious cavern. It wasn't going to be easy to find. She would have limited searching time down here; the tide, when it returned, would cover the beach, the waves would slam high into the rocks, and she had better be long gone.

Which meant no time to waste. She clambered over the boulders, scanning the craggy surface, seeking any gap or space that might indicate an opening. Nothing.

Retreating to the waterline, she gazed upward at the cliff, trying to gauge how far along the cove she stood in relation to the ancient abbey. If only she knew how the passage behaved, whether it twisted and curved through the rock in a series of switchbacks or proceeded along a steady straight course. She didn't even know in which direction it started out. Miss Langley had been less than specific in her details; her writing had contained a great deal of romanticized embellishment but few actual facts.

An hour later, frustrated, she withdrew once more to the encroaching tide-line. So far, she had detected no trace of this elusive lower entrance. Of course, if it were obvious, someone would undoubtedly have discovered it long ago and opened it as a tourist attraction. As it was, none of the local residents she had questioned remembered hearing of its existence. It would take careful searching out.

The scrape of boots on rock startled her, and she spun about to see a tall, fair-haired man dressed in a bright green windbreaker, light green sweater and charcoal slacks, hands thrust in pockets. He stood only ten feet away, staring at her, his lined face and jutting chin clearly visible in the partial profile he presented to her. So, too, were the soft body lines of self-indulgence. He smiled, displaying a good many teeth.

Capped, she thought, uncharitably. He tried to dazzle her—had even taken pains to present the best angle of his face to her. It hadn't helped.

"Miss Anderson, isn't it?" His cultured accent spoke of years at either Oxford or Cambridge. Carefully copied. "We met yesterday at the Priory."

"So we did." Lexie eyed the developer without enthusiasm—though without open hostility, either. "Good morning, Mr. Vaughn. What brings you here so early?"

"Planning, just planning." Geoff Vaughn gazed across the gray water of the cove, with its occasional white caps and wavelets splashing against the rocks. "I'm going to turn this into a private harbor, with a tidy little fee for each boat."

"You don't own it," she pointed out. His sweater must be cashmere, she decided; his carefully cultivated image demanded no less.

"Only a matter of time." He smiled, turning the full force of his charm on her.

It left her cold. She'd learned about self-centered men the hard way. She'd put up with Randy's ego one semester too long. Even so, six months later he'd still called to see if she'd like company on this trip. This man looked as difficult to discourage.

She tried anyway. "Lord Wyndham doesn't want to sell. I thought he made that pretty clear yesterday."

Mr. Vaughn laughed. "My dear Miss Anderson, he can't stand in the way of progress. He'll be brought to see that, never you fear. No, this is the perfect location for a luxury development."

Cut-rate development, he meant, to be sold at luxury prices. At least that was what the elderly earl had told her—and looking at this epitome of the worst of Yuppiedom, she believed it. Geoff Vaughn must be pushing forty, and she was willing to bet a good fifteen years of mildly dishonest deals lay in his wake. Unless he started as a teenager, which seemed likely. His type started conning as soon as they could talk.

He awarded her his oiliest smile. "And what brings you to Kent?"

12

Did he think her a rival? The idea revolted her. "I'm working on my doctoral thesis. Napoleon's aborted invasion of England in 1805. One of Wyndham's ancestors—the third earl—was supposed to have played some part in preventing it. I'm looking for original documents to try and determine what really happened."

He shrugged. "Never had much interest in history. No, it's the future I find fascinating. The immediate future," he added. "Something I can *build* on." He chuckled at his own feeble joke.

Lexie bristled. "I find Lord Wyndham's future interesting, and I think it's rotten of you to keep upsetting him."

Vaughn shook his head, his face reddened by the icy breeze. "You've got that wrong, Miss Anderson. Wyndham will go along a great deal more easily without all this extra land to worry about and a solid bank account to support that great barrack of a house."

"I doubt he sees it that way."

"Not yet, perhaps. But a place like that requires a lot of upkeep. If he can't afford it, he'll have to sign it over to the government as an old age pensioners' home, or sell it as a posh sanatorium or some such thing. His family's lived there for too many generations for him to take kindly to that. Really, I see my offer as doing the old fellow a favor."

"Only if he agreed with you."

"Don't worry, he will." He glanced at his watch, and a frown creased his brow as his gaze strayed to the cliff above them. "You haven't seen anyone about, have you?"

"Only you." Which she could easily have done without.

He nodded absently, as if thinking. "Are you staying down here for a while longer?"

"Yes." And what business was it of his? Unless he wanted to be certain of her whereabouts—but why?

He glanced at the stairs. "I suppose I'd better see—" He broke off. "If you will excuse me, Miss Anderson? It's been a pleasure. Enjoy your beachwalk."

She managed a sweet smile and watched him stride off over the soft sand. Who was he meeting that he didn't want her to see? Some member of the planning commission he intended to bribe? She considered the possibility of finding out, but decided it could serve the old earl no useful purpose. She'd be better off using Geoff Vaughn's absence to continue her search in private. She certainly didn't want *him* sharing in her discovery—if indeed she made one.

She waited until he had mounted half way up the rickety stairs, then turned her back on him and walked on. He'd destroyed her carefully cultivated peace, brought back the uneasy tension of the early morning which she'd striven so hard to put from her. She tried to banish it again, with no success.

She glared at the rocks, reflecting that their appearance might be considerably improved by having the cut-rate developer spread out over some of them, his skull bashed in . . .

An unsteady laugh escaped her. She'd been reading too many murder mysteries of late. But Vaughn would make such a perfect victim, the greedy developer with an unsavory reputation, keeping mysterious meetings and using unknown threats to force the sweet old man to sell. . . . Only she'd hate to see the poor earl a suspect.

With a sigh, she returned her attention to the cliff face. Boulders tumbled together, piled high, washed clean by the pounding waves of high tide. The few cracks between them revealed nothing but more rock behind. Had the story of a secret passage been nothing more than a bored governess's romantic fantasies? That would explain why no one ever had heard of it.

She glanced at the stairs, but Vaughn had disappeared from sight. Satisfied, she concentrated on the rocky expanse, once more scanning the way she'd come, almost a half mile to the wooden landing with its iron rail. No, she wouldn't give up. She must have missed it, walked right by it. She started back, still studying the cliff. Perhaps she'd been looking too low, and the opening was above the high tide mark.

She stopped, peering hard at a crack in the boulders she

14

had passed when coming from the other direction. From here, it almost looked as if someone had stacked the rocks to seal off an opening about five feet high and two feet wide. And that smoothed mark, could it have been made by a chisel, by someone forming the heavy stones to make a detection-proof seal? She caught her breath, her excitement growing, and checked for the heavy bulk of her flashlight in her pocket. Nothing to stop her . . .

She grasped a boulder and with a groaning effort she dragged it away, revealing only another behind it—but one of similar size, placed with such care as to make her stare in increasing certainty and elation. This one she also lugged out of the way. Two more followed, then she had to collapse, panting. She almost wished Geoff Vaughn hadn't left; she could use an extra pair of hands.

But not his, she reminded herself. She might not be masochistic, but she wasn't foolhardy, either. It didn't strike her as a good idea to let the unethical developer in on the secret of the existence of a cavern. He'd probably turn it into an apartment complex by throwing up a few cheap walls, then rent it out at astronomical prices as "environmental housing."

She sighed. Enough rest. Standing once more, she rubbed her sore hands on her jeans and set to work with a vengeance, dragging away rock after rock with increasing enthusiasm as an empty space began to take form. Despite the frozen air, perspiration beaded on her brow from her labors, but she paid it no heed.

After another ten stones, she examined the widening opening which emerged from the pile of debris. Not a doubt remained. She'd found the cavern.

She dragged away more rocks—smaller now—in a fervor which grew as she continued to enlarge the once invisible entrance. After another twenty minutes, she cleared enough away to permit her to slip inside. Her hands trembling, she pulled out her light and shone it within.

Damp cavern walls glistened in the beam. The space extended back, beyond her sight, disappearing into darkness. It beckoned her . . .

She glanced over her shoulder, where the tide slowly returned. Already the waves lapped the shore only feet below where she stood. She shouldn't enter—but she probably had a good hour before the ocean would roll over the boulder doorstep and into the cavern beyond. A whole hour, in which to explore this treasure she'd searched so hard to find.

She could go in . . .

She *had* to. Unfamiliar urgency filled her, which she didn't even try to understand. An eerie tingling crept up her flesh and she shivered. Just the cold and damp, she told herself. Taking a deep breath, she plunged inside.

The back wall came into immediate focus as her flashlight illuminated the cave; it could be no more than eight feet deep. She took a tentative step forward and put her foot in a puddle of water. One of many small pools, she discovered, as she cast her light over the uneven cavern floor.

After finding drier footing, she cast the beam about the walls once more. A rocky passage led upward from the far end. Trying to ignore the flutter of nerves in her stomach, she headed for this. As if she had any choice. Something compelled her to go, drawing her, luring her on like the promise of a fix to an addict.

Her camera scraped the wall of the narrow passage. Her five-foot-five frame cleared the ceiling by an inch, allowing her to walk erect—barely. Her foot slipped on the slimy rock of the floor, and she stubbed a toe as the angle of ascent steepened.

She ran a hand along the dank, surprisingly regular wall. It had been chiseled, she realized. She focused the light on the tool marks. Yes, someone had formed this passage, perhaps widened an existing one to make it suitable for some particular purpose—like transporting smugglers' cargo?

A thrill raced along her spine, and she shone the beam ahead. It caught the glint of metal on the wall. Metal, a real artifact—someone really *had* used this passage. She hurried forward to examine the bracket, in which rested the moldering remains of a wooden torch.

16

Touching it, a sense of awe enveloped her. It had hung there for nearly two hundred years, undisturbed. As if it waited for her . . .

She shivered again, unsettled by the rush of tingling sensations that assailed her, and turned away. Her foot slipped in a patch of loose stones, but she caught herself on the slick wall and continued upward. Her sense of urgency increased, and her heart pounded so hard it filled her chest, building a pressure in her ears. She *had* to go on, as fast as she could, she had to reach . . . what?

Blind, unreasoning fear surged through her. She swallowed, her throat dry. Every instinct screamed at her to run, to get out of there, to escape—but an inexplicable desperation to continue drove her on.

She negotiated a turn, and after another twenty faltering steps, the walls opened up about her. She moved forward and emerged into a wide cavern well above the tide level. She froze, then against her will she advanced deeper into the stone chamber, her steps dragging, as if something compelled her. She had no choice . . .

Her light picked up the flicker of metal on the stone wall again—this time an ancient lantern in a bracket. Several wooden chairs clustered about a table at the far end; one lay overturned. A thrill raced through her again, this time more intense, and a prickly sensation danced along her skin. A wave of dizziness washed over her. Trembling, she took another step deeper into the cavern, and perspiration dampened her chilled flesh. Yet she had no reason for fear. No one could have been in here for nearly two hundred years.

"What a place this is!" Geoff Vaughn's whispered words sounded from the opening behind her, echoing in the still confines.

She spun about, startled, shining the light on him. She hadn't heard his approach, hadn't realized he'd followed. "I thought you'd gone . . ."

He joined her, barely sparing her a glance as his avid gaze moved around the rocky walls. "A *cavern*. I wonder who

17

used this place?" He shot her a calculating look, his eyes glinting in the beam of her flashlight.

"Smugglers." Well, there was nothing she could do to keep him from it now. "I thought you had a meeting."

"I did. Quite a long one, too. Then I thought I'd better see why you hadn't come back up yet. Here, give me that thing." He reached for her light.

She kept it from him but pivoting away, allowing the narrow beam to illuminate the walls in a slow-moving arc. That seemed to satisfy him, for he made no further move to take it.

At the opposite end of the chamber from the furnishings, something else gleamed as it caught the beam. The glow wavered, quavering, and it took her a moment to realize her hand shook. Vaughn started toward the object, and forcing her unsettled sensations under control, Lexie followed.

A tarnished chased silver handle, set with a star sapphire, protruded from a tear in a shrouded heap. Lexie trembled, hit by wave after wave of dizziness and fear as she stared at this dagger which had haunted her sleep for as long as she could remember. As if caught in her nightmares, she reached out and touched the handle. Her flesh tingled, her breath came in short gasps, and the world spun about her as consciousness ebbed . . .

Geoff Vaughn knocked her fingers aside, grasping the handle himself.

"No!" Lexie lunged, oblivious to reason or logic. She grabbed his arm, tried to push him away, but he wouldn't let go of the dagger.

His wide eyes gleamed with an almost insane determination in the faint light. With a sweep of his arm he knocked her aside. She fell to her knees on the rocky ground, and her flashlight flew from her hand, rolling away, plunging them into darkness as the beam came to rest pointed in the opposite direction.

Another tingling wave of dizziness engulfed her, and she fell forward, colliding with Vaughn, bringing him down with her. She could see nothing, but she heard his boots scrape on the rocks as he scrambled toward the knife. She caught his arm, pulling him back, desperate to keep him from it. . . . Her own hand closed over the hasp.

The world spun. Thought, even sensation, faded. She clung to the dagger as if it were her world. It glowed, even in the darkness of the cavern, as if alive with an inner flame . . .

Flickering light flooded the chamber, where a moment before there had been darkness. Lexie, still gripping Vaughn's arm, sat up, startled, and looked about in disbelief. Five men, dressed in ragged period costumes of the lower classes from the Napoleonic war era, stared at her and Geoff Vaughn, their expressions indicative of patent amazement.

With a growling challenge, two started toward them, menace in every line of their stances.

Chapter Two

Lexie's startled disbelief merged into panic. A cry of alarm broke from her suddenly dry lips as she drew back, and the men leaped upon them. One grabbed her arm before she could roll away and dragged her, struggling, to her feet. Behind her, another, taller man captured Vaughn in a strangle hold.

"And what 'ave we 'ere?" A gust of onions and garlic exploded into Lexie's face as her captor peered at her, his nose barely an inch from her own.

She blinked, and stared back in open-mouthed terror at the stubbly, grizzled face with the eagle-like beak. His loose clothes, ill-kept and liberally smudged, stained and torn, gave him the appearance of a poorly maintained scarecrow. The pungent odors clinging to him sent her back a pace, repulsed. His rough, callused hand tightened on her wrist, allowing for no hope of escape.

A third man, the top half of his face hidden beneath a shiny black mask, stepped forward, and Lexie cringed. A low-crowned hat of some curly, furry material covered his head, and his eyes glinted at her through narrow slits in the material. Those eyes . . .

She struggled against the panic which rose within her, and tried in vain to convince herself it was unfounded. The mask terrified her, that was all—that, and the fact that for whatever reason, the wearer wished to keep his identity secret.

He wasn't as disreputable in appearance as the others. He dressed far more neatly—the way she'd imagine a gentleman might appear. His imposing height and broad shoulders added to the threatening effect. So did the knife he gripped in his hand.

Lexie focused on it. A knife with a chased silver handle. The flickering light from the lantern danced off the star in a dark stone.

She stared at it, and the horror of her nightmares filled her once more. What was going on? How many of these knives *were* there, anyway? She swiveled about to look over her shoulder, but nowhere could she see that blanket-shrouded heap—or any other knife.

"Who are you?" The gentleman's voice, medium-pitched and well-modulated, contained a bored drawl.

Lexie didn't make the mistake of thinking he merely indulged in idle curiosity. His gaze brushed across her face, then lingered on her bulky sweater, her jeans, then settled at last on her sneakers. She opened her mouth, but no sound came out.

"What the hell is going on?" Vaughn's voice quavered, and his carefully cultivated Oxford accent slipped. "Where did all you people come from? How did you get in here without our noticing?"

"Silence!" The man flicked a contemptuous glance over him, then returned his attention to Lexie. "Who the devil are you?" He raised her chin with one finger. "A female, dressed like a boy." His lip curled.

A scruffy-looking man who lounged at the table snorted. He waved a thin arm, which could barely be seen in the recesses of a much-patched coat several sizes too big for him. "Let's get on with it. The tide's a-comin' in."

"All in good time, Sam, all in good time." The gentleman held Lexie's chin a moment longer as his gaze once more traveled over her. He released her with a push that thrust her head sideways, and his lip curled in a sneer as he turned away. "Tie them up, Cocking." His voice held nothing but disinterested contempt.

"You can't—" Vaughn began, but Cocking's hand clamped over his mouth.

"And gag them," the gentleman added.

The man with the onion-breath shifted his grip and dragged both Lexie's arms behind her. Sam at the table searched through a pile of oddments—why hadn't Lexie noticed those barrels and crates before?—and tossed him a short length of rope, which he used to lash her wrists. The coarse fibers cut her skin, but she bit back her cry and gritted her teeth.

Sam burrowed once more in his corner and this time produced a handful of greasy rags. With sick certainty, Lexie realized what he had in mind. Grinning—exposing several gaps in his unpleasant mouth—the man advanced on her, and she tried to lock her teeth together.

No luck. He shoved a foul-tasting cloth into her mouth. She choked and gagged, but he held it in place while her captor wrapped another about it, knotting it behind her neck. A lock of hair caught, and several strands were pulled out by their roots.

Sam turned his attention to helping Cocking with Vaughn, and her own captor shoved her forward. She took several stumbling steps toward the far corner, where he thrust her down and bound her ankles with another rope provided by the grinning Sam. All the while, the gentleman sat at the table, legs crossed before him, dagger in hand, examining his fingernails with a complete indifference to the actions of his minions.

Cocking, the tallest of the men, pushed Vaughn down at her side. The developer landed first on his knees, then fell onto his elbow. He rolled over, and the meager light flickered in his frantic brown eyes. A moaning sound escaped him, but he could manage nothing more through the grimy cloths.

A bundle in the shadowed recess behind them moved, and Lexie's scream caught in her throat. It moved again, inching forward to where the light caught it, and the shapelessness dissolved into the figure of a very frightened looking boy of about thirteen. He stared at her, wide-eyed, from over the thick folds of his gag.

The poor kid. How long had he been here? Lexie drew a steadying breath and studied him. She couldn't see much, just those terrified eyes and a shank of what might be auburn hair, now sadly mussed. His clothing—the same strange old-fashioned garments the other men wore—might once have been as good as the gentleman's. Now they were crumpled and filthy, smeared by the cave lichen. They gazed at each other, both gagged, unable to speak. Lexie longed to ask him a few questions.

The men—five of them in all, she realized—held a low-voiced conversation which did nothing to set Lexie at ease. Three of them—the scroungiest—punctuated each of their comments by casting darkling glances in their direction. Cocking's expression, whenever he looked at her, left her ill.

At last the gentleman nodded, and strode over to tower above them. "I will take my leave of you for a little while. Pressing business, you must understand. But have no fear, I shall return as soon as I can, and then we will become better acquainted, I promise you. We shall look forward to a comfortable coze. And a very enlightening one, I make no doubt. Alfred?" He jerked his head toward the prisoners. "I leave them in your hands."

With an unpleasant chuckle, the gentleman turned on the heel of his polished boot and ducked to enter the narrow passageway which led downward. Cocking, Sam, and a third man who had taken no part in their capture followed him, leaving Alfred—Lexie's particular friend—to plop himself down on a rickety wooden chair. He drew an antique pistol from the depths of the cavernous pocket of his overcoat, propped his feet on the table, and rested the gun across his lap—pointed at his three prisoners. He awarded them a broad smile, made hideous by the number of teeth either rotted or missing.

Lexie shuddered. He looked to be the type to quote "make my day" in all seriousness, and think himself clever rather than corny. She wondered at his restraint.

The scraping booted footsteps, and accompanying curses and grunts, faded as the other men retreated down the passage. At last, silence filled the cavern except for the low roar of the ocean without. This slowly grew. The tide must be filling the entry chamber below. Lexie could only be glad they were so high up.

For a long moment she contemplated the picture her captor made, and decided she'd be a heck of a lot more comfortable with her back to him. She squirmed around to lean against the cold cavern wall, and found herself staring at the barrels. It was a vast improvement.

She still tingled all over—and with more than the cold and damp. *What had happened?* Her mind whirled, refusing to steady, to provide reasonable explanations, sending shivers through her very being.

They must have stumbled across some sort of secret society, she decided at last—one that loved dressing up and behaving in an obnoxious manner. If these men had known the stories of the smugglers, they might not have been able to resist playing the roles when they stumbled across the cavern's upper entrance. Halloween-style makeup—or standard theatrical—would account for the seemingly missing teeth.

Of course, that hypothesis would be easier to accept had they all been younger—university students, for example. Whatever they were, though, they'd undoubtedly tire of their game in a little while. The men would probably return in about an hour, drive them deep into a forest and turn them loose. At least, that was the general scenario for the frat stunts with which she was fairly familiar.

And this had to be something similar—hadn't it?

She managed to turn her head enough to see her companions. Vaughn had been shoved some six feet away from her, the boy a little farther. She sat up to ease her cramping shoulder muscles.

"Get back." Alfred waved his pistol at her, with every appearance of knowing how to use it.

Lexie sagged against the wall. Apparently they were not to

25

be permitted to come close enough to each other to attempt any sort of mutual untying. She shifted again, this time to stop the numbing of her feet, but the bite of the rope proved too strong. She wished she had a chair. At last she achieved a position not quite as uncomfortable, and leaned back to await events. They couldn't be too long in coming, she assured herself.

Yet as the minutes ticked away, and nothing continued to happen, uncertainty returned to plague her. It didn't take long for it to build into a renewed fear. And still no one returned, nor did their guard show any sign of freeing them and announcing the joke was over.

Her stomach grumbled, and she wished she hadn't eaten the second of her croissants in the car. She could do with a snack. Or a meal, for that matter. A seven course dinner held certain appeal at the moment. But even if someone presented one to her, she'd have to get her hands free in order to eat it.

Hours slipped by. She must have drifted into an uneasy doze, for a sudden icy rush of air against her cheek brought her fully awake. The single lantern cast a dim glow about the cavern, not penetrating the shadows, yet she had the distinct sensation someone—or something—hovered just beyond her sight. She strained her ears, but could hear nothing but the heavy breathing of her companions and the dull roar of the ocean.

That seemed to be coming from a greater distance now, hushed, as if the tide once again receded. That thought startled her, sending a renewed *frisson* up her spine. It had only been coming in when she'd entered the cavern. How much time had passed? The breeze might be caused by the emptying of the lower cavern entrance as the water seeped out . . .

A scraping sound reached her, quickly muffled, and her breath caught in her throat. She tried to move her hands, but they were numb, as sensationless as the lumps of flesh that were her feet. She couldn't move. Even if she weren't tied, she would be helpless. . . . Real panic welled within her.

In the blackened recesses of a side passage, a light

flickered, only to be extinguished at once. Or had she imagined it? It had been so brief . . .

The scrape sounded again, and her throat went dry. Someone was coming. But on whose side?

The guard's head jerked. Lexie caught her breath; then a raucous snore escaped the man, and his chin lowered to his chest once more.

Lexie returned her intent stare to the opening where that light had glimmered for a fraction of a second. Something moved in the darkness, a shadow detached itself from the depths, then separated into two dim shapes which together rushed the guard. Alfred's pistol fell to the rocky floor with a clatter as his chair—with him still in it—tumbled over.

In one smooth movement, the guard rolled to his feet, lowered his head and charged, knocking down one of his attackers. The other threw himself upon Alfred, but the guard heaved him off, sending him crashing against the table. Momentarily free, Alfred dove for the lower passage, and the first man he had thrown off struggled to his feet and set off in pursuit.

The other, with a groan, picked himself up from the floor and hurried to the boy. From his pocket he drew a knife and sawed at the bonds. His hands freed, the lad tried ineffectually to rub them while the man set to work on the ropes that secured his ankles. Next, he cut free the gag, pulled it from the boy's mouth, then helped him to his feet. A sharp cry escaped the youth, and he swayed, unsteady.

"Are you all right, Kester?" The deep voice trembled from the exertion.

The boy nodded, albeit with care. "I—I think so. Lord, I was beginning to think I'd never get away. How did you find me?"

"We've been keeping a watch on the more likely taverns ever since you disappeared. We thought this old passage had been blocked up years ago, though, or we'd have been here sooner. Can you walk?"

"Let me sit a minute. What about them?" The boy Kester

27

sank once more to the floor and gestured toward Lexie and Vaughn.

The man, middle-aged and somewhat on the portly side—not at all what Lexie would have expected for a commando-type raid—stared at them. Lexie stared back.

"Who are they?" he asked after a moment.

"I don't know. They appeared this morning. And I mean *appeared*. They were just here, in the cave, after the smugglers had arrived."

"Well, only one way to find out, I suppose." He knelt beside Vaughn.

Before the knife had freed the developer's wrists, sounds emitted from the lower passage and the other man strode back into the cavern. "He got away," the new arrival said, his tone curt—betraying self-anger.

The boy rose on shaky legs. "Uncle Charles—"

Uncle Charles crossed the cavern in four rapid strides and caught the boy to him. "Thank God," was all he said.

The boy gave a shaky laugh and returned the hug with enthusiasm.

The next moment, Uncle Charles put his nephew aside. "Who are these two? More prisoners?" He knelt at Lexie's side and pulled out a knife. "Steady, son, we'll have you out of here in a minute."

For several seconds, the coarse rope sawed at her already raw wrists while he cut through the hemp strands. Then her hands dropped, free but useless, to her sides. One moment of blissful numbness followed, then the blood returned with stabbing agony, so she barely noticed the freeing of her feet. The man helped her to stand; she fell against him, unable to support herself.

"The devil," he muttered. "Must they always pick on children?" He tore the gag from her mouth, catching her hair, and a gasp escaped her. For a long moment he stared at her in the wavering light. "You're not a boy," he said at last.

An almost hysterical urge to giggle welled within her. "Am I supposed to be?" she managed.

Vaughn staggered to his feet, rubbing his wrists. "What

28

the hell is going on?" he demanded. "Who are you? And who were *they?*"

Uncle Charles opened his mouth to answer, then froze. A crunching sound echoed through the cavern. The next moment a light wavered from the lower passage.

"Come on." Uncle Charles grabbed his nephew's arm and started for the upper exit, from which he had come.

Lexie took a staggering step, found her feet weren't cooperating, and fell against the toppled table. The elder man caught her by the elbow, steadied her, and urged her forward. Vaughn followed as best he could, lurching with every step.

No light guided their way. Uncle Charles led, dragging the boy, crouching low, half running as he traversed the twisting path. Somehow they wound their way through a network of tiny caves, away from their pursuers. Lexie stumbled, the older man caught her, and they were off again. Light—if their pursuers carried any—had long since vanished in the numerous turns behind them.

A lessening of the darkness appeared ahead, and gasping for breath, Lexie staggered through an opening. She blinked in the sudden illumination provided by stars peeking through a low cloud cover. About them lay the tumbled ruins of the abbey. She turned, disoriented, and saw behind them the section of the main building which stood partially intact.

Uncle Charles grabbed the boy by the elbow, and with his other arm he caught Lexie and guided their uncertain steps toward the trees and shrubs which encroached on the abbey grounds. "We're not safe, yet," he said, his teeth gritted.

The running steps of Vaughn and the other man sounded a bare pace behind her. Together they crashed through the underbrush, entered a copse, and something large and dark moved, then nickered softly. Lexie released the breath she had caught. A horse. No, three, she realized, as the animals sidled uneasily.

Then more footsteps sounded, and a sharp expletive rent the night. The horses stamped and jerked their heads as the sounds of pursuit closed on their party rapidly, making it difficult for Lexie's companions to untie the beasts. A man's deep voice shouted behind them, then all sounds from that direction suddenly ceased and an eerie silence claimed the night. None of their erstwhile captors moved. . . .

Lexie peered back the way they had come in time to see the masked gentleman raise his arm.

A shot rang out, whining all too near, and thudded into a tree behind Lexie. Too stunned to react, she stared at the shoulder of her windbreaker where the bullet had torn a hole. Slowly, in disbelief, she looked up to where the masked gentleman aimed another gun.

Chapter Three

"Couldn't you have brought a car?" Vaughn yelled. He ran to the horses' heads, shouldering the older man to one side, and jerked at the leather reins which had been looped about the branches of the trees.

One of their pursuers shouted again, but Lexie couldn't distinguish the words. Another shot rang out, and a dull thud struck, once more almost at her side. She didn't need explanations to get the drift.

The horse nearest her sidled uneasily, knocking into its neighbor, which swung sideways, nickering in unease. Vaughn managed to free the reins of the third, fumbled with the stirrup, then pulled himself onto the saddle.

The older man freed another of the mounts, swung himself onto its back with surprising agility for one of his years, and held down his hand to the boy. Kester scrambled up after him, surprising Lexie. Apparently more boys rode in England than did in America.

The man called Uncle Charles mounted the last horse and reached down to aid Lexie. She took his hand, only to cringe back as a third shot rang out. The crashing and swearing grew nearer as their pursuers pushed through the underbrush and parted the low branches which shielded the copse.

"Put your foot in the stirrup and swing up behind me," the man's curt voice ordered.

His words galvanized her. She grabbed for his wrist, and his fingers clasped hers with a reassuring grip. With her right hand, she caught the dangling leathers and twisted the stirrup into position. The horse stood nearly seventeen hands, and Lexie a mere five-foot-five, but with the man's aid she wedged her toe into the metal that dangled at shoulder height.

He slid forward, leaning on the horse's neck, to give her room. She struggled with her jump, and he grabbed her elbow and half dragged her up behind him. She swung her leg over and perched just before the cantle, both feet free of stirrups which were too long for her. She barely had time to throw both arms about the man's waist before his heels dug into the frightened animal's sides.

The horse bearing the older man and Kester lunged forward, taking the lead, and Vaughn urged his mount after them. Lexie and Charles passed him in two strides as their mounts raced away, trampling through the tangled growth, dodging trees by a hair's breadth, several times scraping painfully against sharp bark. Lexie kept her head low, pressed against the man's back, her heart pounding so loudly she could hear little else except the explosions of pistol fire.

Then all fell silent except the thundering hooves over uneven ground, the snapping branches and twigs—then at last the muffled hoofbeats on grass. They had lost their pursuers. . . . Pale moonlight penetrated the low cloud covering, illuminating their path. Relief left Lexie weak, and she tightened her grip about the man's waist to keep her tired, cramped muscles from letting her fall.

They didn't slow. The horses continued their careening pace for what felt to Lexie's aches and stiffness to be an eternity. At last, as clouds once more covered the crescent moon making progress hazardous, the man Charles reined his mount down to a canter, then a walk. Their animal's flanks heaved beneath her and it dropped its head as it paced forward.

Lexie drew an unsteady breath. "Thank you," she managed. The words came out in a hoarse croak.

The man's back quavered against her as if with a repressed laugh. "My pleasure, I assure you. Had I anticipated your being there, I would have brought more horses."

"An armored car might have been more practical." Lexie eased her hold on him, somewhat embarrassed at such intimate contact with a stranger. It was a heck of a lot better than falling off, though. She sat up straighter, and allowed herself to sway with their mount's shambling gait. "Why didn't you bring in the police?"

"The—?"

"The constables? Bobbies? Whatever you call them? The authorities?"

"I thought it better to handle this on my own." Cold determination crept into his voice.

Lexie considered this, and her heart sank. Had she fallen in with a couple of rival drug gangs? The guns, the caverns, the outlandish costumes, even using horses instead of cars. . . . Something was going on here, and she had the distinct feeling she'd be better off well out of it. And the less she knew of everything, the happier—and safer—she'd be.

She studied the back of the man's head, but could see very little in the overcast darkness. From the wisps escaping from beneath his strange hat, it seemed he shared his nephew's auburn hair. His heavy coat merely emphasized the breadth of his shoulders. The tautness of his muscles she had experienced herself, pressed tight against his back. And even though she hadn't seen one, she was willing to bet he carried a gun, just like his rivals. She could only be glad he didn't seem anxious to use it.

She swallowed, and recognized the cold, empty pang in her stomach for fear. Hunger must have passed beyond the registering range hours ago. Her shivering began all over again. Her windbreaker and sweater might have been sufficient for her early morning exploration, but they didn't stand up to an icy night which threatened sleet at any moment.

She closed her eyes. She wanted to go back to the comforts of her bed and breakfast inn, away from these maniacs with their horses and guns. Was playing smugglers the local equivalent of cowboys and Indians? Or did they play for real?

She caught herself slipping and shifted her weight to steady herself. She avoided clinging to the man. The sooner they parted company, the better.

"Look," she said when she could command her voice, "why don't you just set us down here? We can find our own way home."

The man shook his head. "I don't think it's safe. They're bound to have mounts tethered somewhere nearby, and they'll be after us if they can."

"Oh." She cast an uneasy glance over her shoulder. "Then if our horses are rested, shouldn't we risk a little more speed?"

His back trembled as his deep, rather pleasant chuckle sounded, and he glanced back at her over his shoulder. "As you wish. Once we reach the Priory, though, we'll be safe. They wouldn't dare make an open attack on it."

"The Priory?" Her spirits lifted. "Wyndham Priory?"

"Yes. My home. I'm Wyndham."

"Thank heavens," she breathed, and tightened her hold on him once more as he urged the horse into a canter. He must be the earl's grandson, she decided—though she'd have thought he'd go by the family name of Penrith rather than the title. Still, perhaps it was something more than a title.

At the moment, all that mattered was that she'd fallen in with the right side of whatever feud she'd stumbled into. She could never believe the dear old earl was involved in something illegal. That meant she'd find a safe haven at his home, and transportation back to her bed and breakfast.

Transportation. What an idiot she'd been! She'd left her rented car at the abbey. They could have used that for their getaway instead of the horses. Only she'd been beyond thinking when they made that wild escape. In the morning, after a solid meal and a good night's sleep, she'd probably find this whole incident pretty ridiculous.

They didn't speak again until they rounded a bend in the road and approached the wrought iron gate leading to the drive, and the low gatehouse she recognized just inside. Antique lanterns hung at either side, illuminating the black rails that blocked their way. Funny, she didn't remember those lights. Probably because she'd visited in the daylight, when they weren't lit.

As they drew nearer, a wizened little man hurried from the cottage, limping slightly. He held another lantern aloft, and peered at them. "M'lord?" he called, a note of anxiety in his voice.

"We've got him," Charles called. "And two others. Let us through, Welkins."

Welkins hung his light below the one nearest him, and dragged back the iron bar that held the gate. With only the faintest squeak, the panels swung wide on well-oiled hinges, and their party rode through. Behind them, Welkins secured it once more.

Lexie glanced at the little man, curious. She hadn't met him on her visit the day before. Perhaps he was a nightwatchman. This all seemed so strange—but under the circumstances, she supposed that wasn't so surprising.

The gravel crunched beneath the horses' shod hooves as they proceeded up the drive. *Gravel?* For some reason she'd thought it had been paved. That just went to show how involved she'd been in her research. An amazing number of details about this place seemed to have escaped her.

Another thought occurred to her. She'd been way off base about what weighed on the elderly earl's mind. Geoff Vaughn's threats over buying the land must have seemed a paltry irritation to him compared to the kidnapping or whatever it was of his grandson—or great-grandson.

Her heart went out to the sweet old gentleman. He'd been so very upset, with such a tremendous worry, and she'd shown up and pestered him with questions about the distant past. She'd apologize as soon as she could.

They rounded a curve, and she looked up at the great stone mansion. It looked different in the dark, though no less majestic. Wyndham—or Uncle Charles, or whatever his name was—urged their horse forward as if glad to reach home, and they turned into the stable yard.

Lexie blinked and straightened up, staring at the cobbled area enclosed by lines of stalls on either side and the carriage house at the far end. Their mount nickered, and was answered by an animal in one of the stalls. She hadn't remembered horses. Only cars.

And speaking of which, the great old Rolls Royce that had stood in the yard like a show piece was nowhere to be seen. It must have been put away in the carriage house for the night, to protect it from the damp, icy weather. She shivered and huddled closer to Charles for a warmth that escaped her.

Three men, also dressed in those weird, old-fashioned clothes, ran forward and took the horses as their party swung down. Lexie lowered herself stiffly, aware of every aching muscle and the stares of two more men who stood near the great barn door.

One must have brought matches, for he went to each of the antique-styled lanterns that hung about the yard and lit them. A warm glow bathed the old stones in a soft gold that defied the freezing night. The grooms—or whatever they were—led the horses into sheltered looseboxes and went to work unsaddling the steaming beasts.

Someone's sense for detail and period recreation deserved applause, she decided. Everyone wore authentic-looking costumes of the same period, the very early 1800's. She couldn't detect a single flaw in either idea or execution. And she considered herself an expert. Her doctoral thesis might deal with just a single historical event, but she'd spent considerable time studying the political and social aspects of the period, as well. It fascinated her.

And if she admitted the truth—which she would only do to herself—she'd indulged in her share of daydreams about Regency bucks, and the exquisite dandies and sporting-mad Corinthians.

But she knew the difference between fantasy and reality. Regency bucks—or smugglers—simply didn't wander the English countryside looking for people to kidnap or rescue. There must be some sort of recreation going on, like the "Happenings" back in the Sixties, or like the Civil War reenactments they held at Gettysburg. She and Vaughn must have stumbled right into the middle of it, and been mistaken for unexpected participants.

And "Wyndham" must be an actor, portraying the very

man she'd come to England to study.

She couldn't see much of the man in the flickering light—only the impression of broad shoulders and a muscular build. In his early thirties, she guessed. His manner—the way he spoke and carried himself—reassured her somewhat. He *was* a gentleman, not just an actor portraying one.

A shaky sigh escaped her. They'd probably never really been in any danger at all—they couldn't have been. At any rate, it seemed they were safe now. Maybe one of the men would give her a lift back to the abbey later, when they called the game for the night, so she could pick up her rented car. She repressed a shiver, and attributed it to the cold.

She reached for the comforting touch of her camera bag, and found it missing. So, too, were the car keys she'd clipped to it. Damn, she must have dropped it in the cavern. And at the moment, though she knew it was silly and there was a logical—and perfectly harmless—explanation for all this weirdness, she honestly didn't want to go back inside that rocky chamber.

The older man and the young boy already strode from the yard, with Vaughn at their heels. She and Charles, or Wyndham, or whatever, followed across the graveled drive to the low steps leading to the porch.

As they reached it, the great oak door swung wide, revealing a portly man with a balding head and an imposing aspect. His wooden face crumpled in relief. "Welcome home, Master Kester."

"I'm devilish glad to be back, Clempson." The lad managed a shaky smile.

"Kester!" Wyndham cast him a sharp glance.

The lad grinned at him, tired but game. "Lord, Uncle Charles, that's as nothing compared to what I've heard you say."

"Certainly," Charles said calmly. "But not, I believe, in the presence of a lady. Bring something to eat to the library, please, Clempson."

The words worked like magic on Lexie. She wasn't in *that* much of a hurry to get back to her B and B. She could easily spare, say, the time it would take to eat a sandwich or two.

37

She glanced back at the butler to thank him, and frowned. He wasn't the same one she'd met yesterday; what had been his name, Walton?

Nor, she realized a moment later, was the vast hall they entered quite the same. She couldn't put her finger on it; it just *felt* different. As if the furniture had all been readjusted. Maybe it had been.

Her gaze moved over the tapestries that hung on the oak-paneled walls, to the fire that roared in the cavernous hearth, to the twin staircases that curved from either side of the hallway to the picture gallery above. A gallery in which several mob-capped women hovered on one side, looking down on them.

She repressed the eerie sensation of having walked onto the set for an historical movie. Or into the past. A tingling sensation crept along her flesh, leaving goosebumps. What she needed was a good meal and a long sleep to banish these crazy sensations. Everything would probably look normal again in the morning. It could hardly look odder.

She glanced at Wyndham, and that prickly sensation recurred. Now, where she could see him clearly, he looked vaguely familiar. She would swear she had seen him—or his picture?—before. His tall, rugged good looks appealed to her romantic fantasies too strongly. She'd always had something for gold-flecked green eyes and thickly curling auburn hair. On him, the combination proved spectacular. And that old-fashioned outfit set him off to perfection. Even the large emerald that gleamed on his finger belonged, not seeming in the least ostentatious or out of place.

She dragged her thoughts from him as they started down a familiar parqueted hallway. At least the way to the library remained the same. Some things, at least, *couldn't* change— and that fact made her feel better.

As they reached the door, a comfortably proportioned woman with steel gray curls escaping her mobcap and a white apron over her black, high-waisted dress bore down on them. Every detail seemed exact, Lexie noted, from the puffed sleeves of the gown to the woman's lack of makeup. They certainly went in for realism here.

"There, Master Kester," she beamed, "you're back. *As* I knew you would be." She enveloped the lad in a warm embrace. "So glad as the young ladies will be. And Miss Langley. All a-flutter they've been with worry for you. Are you wanting anything?" She dabbed at the corner of her moist eyes with a corner of her starched apron.

"Only something to eat," Kester answered. A rosy tint crept into his face and he disentangled himself from the effusive woman.

"Thank you, Mrs. Clempson," Charles said. "Please inform the household of his safe return. And have two extra rooms prepared, if you please."

The woman bobbed a curtsy and bustled off, murmuring to herself.

"There isn't the least need for a room," Lexie said. "I'm staying in Rye, at a bed and breakfast. But I've left my car at the abbey. And Mr. Vaughn, I'm sure, has a home nearby."

Mr. Vaughn said nothing. He stared about the hall, his expression a puzzled frown. Apparently he, too, noted the differences in decor.

Charles glanced at her, an odd look of curiosity on his face. "Come inside, for now. I can think of several things I should like to discuss."

"I wouldn't mind a few explanations, either." Lexie entered the book-lined room, and a comfortable—and reassuring—sense of familiarity settled over her. This, at least, remained much the way she remembered it from her visit the day before.

Or did it? The huge mahogany desk still stood at one end of the room, but the two large sofas were of a different color —weren't they? And a different pattern of brocade now upholstered the overstuffed wing-back chairs. And they surrounded a round mahogany table, not a rectangular one. A fire burned merrily in the hearth, warming the long room, but elaborate branched candelabra, not lamps, provided the illumination.

The tingling sensation grew, leaving her uneasier than ever. Massive blood sugar drop, that had to be the answer. She never was any good at missing meals.

39

Charles strode to a side table, selected a decanter and filled five exquisite crystal glasses with a dark wine. Lexie took one and sipped the sweet liquid, and a pleasant warmth spread through her as it hit her stomach. That should give her a much-needed boost.

The man drained his glass, then poured more for them all. "Now," he said at last. "Introductions first, I believe." He directed a slight bow to Lexie. "You must forgive the impropriety, but under the circumstances we will have to forego the formalities of a mutual acquaintance. I am Wyndham, and this is my nephew, Christopher Penrith. Make your bow, Kester."

The boy did so with a practiced ease Lexie would not have expected. They must be actors—yet to her dismay, a lingering doubt remained. She'd feel better if the sweet old earl would only join them.

Wyndham turned to the older man who had accompanied him on their rescue, who stood near the hearth. "This is my friend, Doctor Falkirk."

Lexie took the man's hand and felt the warmth and gentle strength of his clasp, and experienced an instantaneous liking. Pale blue eyes—almost as pale as her own—smiled back at her from beneath a neatly trimmed head of graying hair.

"Lexie Anderson," she said. She glanced at Vaughn, who had wandered into the middle of the chamber and now stared about, his frown creasing his already lined brow. "And that's Geoffrey Vaughn, the developer. Unless you already know him?"

"I have not the honor." Wyndham took another sip of wine, but his gaze remained on Lexie. "Now, perhaps you will satisfy my curiosity. How were you captured, and where did you get your unusual clothing?"

Gooseflesh crept across her arms again. "I—I don't know," she said after a moment. "We were in the cave—exploring—when suddenly the men were just there. We never heard them come in." She let the matter of her clothes pass. Her jeans might not be designer, but they were comfortable.

She set her empty glass on the table, but shook her head

when he moved to refill it. If she drank any more on an empty stomach, she'd pass out where she stood. She glanced at Dr. Falkirk, who now sat beside Kester on one of the sofas, deep in a low-voiced conversation. Probably making sure he'd suffered no ill effects.

Her turn to get a few answers, she decided.

She turned to Wyndham, but before she could speak, a petite little lady in a high-waisted lavender gown bustled in, satin rustling. A froth of lace and ribbons, fashioned into a cap, covered a fluff of graying ringlets which clustered about her soft rosepetal complexion. The scent of violets clung to her. She completely ignored Lexie and Vaughn as she rushed to the sofa and enveloped Kester in her embrace.

"You found him, Wyndham. Oh, I am so glad. You poor boy, have you had the most dreadful time of it?" She settled at his side, one arm about him.

"It was something like, Aunt Agatha," Kester announced, recovering with the amazing rapidity of youth now that no further dangers lurked. "They kept me tied up and gagged in a corner of their cavern hideout!"

The woman's startled gaze flew to Wyndham. "Did they indeed? Oh, how dreadful. Come, dear, Miss Langley is settling the girls into bed, so we shall not wait for her. You shall have a bath before your fire, which has been kept burning in your room so you would find it comfortable whenever you returned."

Dr. Falkirk rose from Kester's other side. "I leave him in your hands, Lady Agatha."

"You may be sure I shall take the greatest care of him. And thank you, dear William, for your aid. Come now, Kester, you may tell us all about your adventures in the morning, for I make no doubt your sisters will be anxious to hear." She shepherded the boy from the room, and the door closed behind him.

Dr. Falkirk's gaze followed them, and he nodded. "An excellent lady. No fear of the boy's head being filled with a lot of female nonsense, giving him more nightmares than he's already earned."

"Why did they kidnap your nephew?" Lexie asked.

41

Though it wasn't that hard to guess, she supposed. Money provided the motive for most crimes, and this man reeked of wealth and power.

Wyndham's square chin jutted out. "To keep me from uncovering more of their plans," he said, and his voice took on a hard edge. "I know they're aiding Napoleon."

Lexie swallowed hard. "Are they?" A shaky laugh escaped her. "His invasion of England, I suppose?"

Savage anger reflected on Wyndham's face at her intended joke, startling her.

His hands clenched. "Just what do you know about that, madam?"

For a moment, the floor seemed to buckle beneath her feet and a wave of dizziness washed over her. There, before her, on one of the bookcases, she could make out the hazy outline of a television she hadn't noticed before. The channel showed a man sitting at a newsdesk, reading commentary while behind him a screen displayed film footage of a riot in Northern Ireland.

Lexie started toward it, relieved to see something so familiar, but the image wavered, then faded away. Once more, the bookcase held only leather-bound volumes.

Chapter Four

"It—it can't be!" Lexie whispered, then repeated it over and over, her voice rising in panic. "It—can't—be!"

Wyndham stared at her. "What, in the name of all that is holy, happened? You shimmered!"

She turned her frantic gaze on him. "What year is this?"

His brow snapped down. "What do you mean?"

"What year is this?"

Wyndham exchanged a perplexed glance with Dr. Falkirk. "Eighteen-ought-five," he said.

Lexie's knees gave out, she sank onto a chair, and for a long moment she stared straight ahead, unseeing. The impossibility of it all robbed her of coherent thought. 1805 . . . the strange clothes . . . the differences in the house and furnishings . . . the stable with *horses* instead of cars . . . so many unfamiliar servants . . . and this younger Lord Wyndham . . .

No, it was impossible. It *had* to be impossible. Yet that television . . . what *happened* to it?

She raised her uncertain gaze back to Wyndham's face. The concern she saw there appeared genuine. "Eighteen-ought-five?" she repeated.

"It is already three weeks into the new year," Dr. Falkirk confirmed. His gentle smile seemed designed to reassure.

"Miss Anderson!" Geoff Vaughn, who had wandered to the far end of the library, strode up to her, a frown marring his handsome features. "This room doesn't look anything like it did when I was in here yesterday. Have you noticed?"

She turned her fascinated gaze on him. "Yes, I—I rather think I did."

He cast her a suspicious look, as if he thought she teased him. "There's something peculiar going on."

"A—just a bit, yes. I—" An hysterical giggle prevented her from finishing. Her shoulders trembled with a laughter she couldn't control. "I quite agree," she managed at last. "Things are just a little peculiar."

"Here, lie back, Miss Anderson." Dr. Falkirk pressed her into the cushions of her chair. "Send for some hartshorn, will you Wyndham?" He held his hand to her forehead, then checked the pulse that beat light and rapid at her wrist. Frowning, he stepped back.

Lexie closed her eyes and tried to steady herself. She had to *think*. If it were indeed 1805, if these men weren't actors, then "Uncle Charles" must in fact be Charles Penrith, third earl of Wyndham, the man who undermined the plot to aid Napoleon's invasion of England.

Except he hadn't accomplished it yet.

And she and Geoff Vaughn had arrived right in the middle of all this intrigue, where they didn't belong, where their knowledge and actions could make a colossal mess of history.

Her thoughts raced. If they influenced Wyndham, in some way prevented him from fulfilling his role, then the traitorous plot might succeed and Napoleon would receive the needed information.

And the invasion and Napoleon's subsequent domination of England might become the reality she researched for her thesis.

Wyndham's deep voice sounded, giving his orders to Clempson. A moment later the door closed, and the earl's steady footsteps crossed the rich carpet. She opened her eyes to see him carrying a tray of cookies and cakes he had taken from the butler.

He set this on the table beside the decanters. Vaughn, in an excellent imitation of a vulture, descended on it at once, helping himself to a hefty slice of nut cake and another of poppy seed. He sloshed more wine into his glass with a liberal hand.

Dr. Falkirk drew Wyndham aside. "Miss Anderson is badly shaken. She is trembling, and can't seem to stop. A delayed reaction to all she has been through, I shouldn't wonder. One can hardly be surprised." He rubbed his chin and regarded Lexie with a frown. "A delicately nurtured female, in the hands of those murderers, tied up in that cavern—" His hands clenched. "They should be horse-whipped!"

"My sentiments exactly." Wyndham refilled his own and the doctor's glasses.

Dr. Falkirk pursed his lips. "Her heart is racing more than I can like," he added in an undervoice, shaking his head.

Another unsteady laugh escaped Lexie. "Under the implausible circumstances, I'm surprised that's all that's wrong with me."

"What implausible circumstances, Miss Anderson?" Wyndham piled a selection of the cakes onto a smaller plate and carried them to her.

How could she explain it? To gain time, she picked out a piece filled with raisins, cinnamon and apples and took a bite. Maybe food in her growling stomach would help settle her reeling world. At the very least, it would sop up the wine. She finished off the cake and looked up into Wyndham's frowning face.

He waited with at least a semblance of patience for her reply. Inspiration on how *gently* to break her bombshell to him failed, so she plunged right in.

"Remember that shimmering you said I did a few minutes ago? I was shifting between two times—yours and mine. They—they seem to be about two hundred years apart." On the whole, the matter-of-fact tone of her voice surprised her. Not so much as a quaver. Pleased by this accomplishment, she picked out a poppy seed cake and ate it while the two men stared, apparently too non-plussed to respond.

After a moment of stunned silence, during which her meaning apparently sank in, Wyndham's brow snapped down. "You have obviously suffered more than we realized.

Come, lie quietly before the fire where it is warmer until your room is prepared. You will feel much more the thing in the morning."

"And if I don't, are you planning to have me conveyed to—to Bedlam?" She surged to her feet, her hard-won control slipping once more. "I know it sounds crazy, but time just—blended. I was here, in the past, yet I could see things from the future around me. From *my* time. And there isn't one single thing I can say to make you believe me, is there?"

Dr. Falkirk laid a restraining hand on her shoulder, but she shook him off. "Geoff Vaughn and I were born almost a hundred and seventy-five years from now. Yesterday morning I met the *ninth* earl of Wyndham, a very sweet old man who was going to tell me about his ancestor, the *third* earl. I—"

Another wave of dizziness set her staggering sideways into a bookcase. She caught hold of it, and her fingers gripped the wooden shelf to keep her from falling. A man's voice blared out at her, reporting on the American military presence in Europe. Her eyes flew open, and she found herself staring at a television set directly in front of her. Its case shimmered, the picture blurred, but the voice droned on, ringing in her ears.

With a cry of panic, she spun about, only to collide with Wyndham. Strong arms enfolded her and she clung to him, squeezing her eyes closed tight until the voice of the television announcer faded once more into the oblivion of the ages. Gradually, her insubstantial surroundings took solid form again, and her spinning senses settled into the quiet of 1805.

She drew a shaky breath and raised her face from where it had been pressed tightly against the smooth, fine wool of Wyndham's coat. She looked up into his rugged face which towered over her, and encountered an expression of astonishment mingled with horror.

Charles Edward Augustus Penrith, third earl of Wyndham, stared in stark disbelief at the young lady he held.

It couldn't have happened, she couldn't have shimmered, gone transparent. And the strange things he had seen! None of this could be possible—yet never before had he had reason to doubt the evidence of his senses.

He shook his head, but that did nothing to ease his bewilderment. After a long moment, he transferred his gaze to his friend William Falkirk, who stood behind Miss Anderson. Involuntarily, his fingers tightened their grip on the young lady's shoulders.

"I may be as—as *deranged* as is she—" he managed to keep his voice steady only with a concerted effort, "—but when I touched her, I saw the strangest things, a *marvel* the likes of which I never could have imagined. . . ." He swallowed. "A man inside a box. I heard him talk."

The girl nodded. "It will be invented somewhere in the late nineteen-thirties."

"*Nineteen*-thirties." It made no sense, yet there was something about this young lady that denied logic. "After that experience," he said at last, "I'm almost ready to believe anything."

He set her from him, his hands still resting on her shoulders as he studied her clothes with a frantic fascination. Boys garments, yet the likes of which he'd never seen before. There seemed to be some strange fastening on those peculiar blue breeches. . . . Hurriedly, he averted his gaze, looking elsewhere, to the similar metal contraption that bordered the edge of her odd, light-weight coat. The garment felt smooth and slick beneath his fingers, yet not quite like silk. Slowly, he turned to her companion.

That gentleman—what had she said his name was, Mr. Vaughn?—stood a few feet away, staring at Miss Anderson, his mouth agape. His tall, fair good looks seemed too polished for his rough attire. An Exquisite, Charles decided, yet one whose manners and air lacked distinction.

Mr. Vaughn took an unsteady step toward them. "What happened?" he managed, his gaze never wavering from the young lady. "You—you went all hazy! I could practically see *through* you."

Miss Anderson's shoulders trembled. "I saw a television

set, showing the news."

"Where?" Mr. Vaughn spun about, scanning the room. "Damn it, what's going on?"

Charles stiffened. The man might be, as he appeared, under some extreme emotional upheaval, but that did not excuse such language in the presence of a lady. And the worst of it, he realized the next moment, was that the young lady herself did not appear to be shocked. So many odd details about these two he could not explain . . .

He rounded on Mr. Vaughn. "Where did you obtain your clothing? Never have I seen anything like those garments you are wearing."

The gentleman straightened his shoulders. "Harrod's, of course. I always shop in London."

"Harrod's?" Charles cast a perplexed glance at Dr. Falkirk and encountered an equal measure of incomprehension in his friend's expression. Yet Mr. Vaughn spoke the name as if they should recognize it.

Miss Anderson sank once more onto the sofa and covered her face with her hands. "It hasn't been built yet," she explained. She looked up and met Mr. Vaughn's confused gaze. "Gentlemen of this time have their clothes made by tailors."

"*This* time . . ." The man's voice, hollow, trailed off. His gaze flickered across Charles and Dr. Falkirk, lingering on their apparel, then returned to the girl. "You—you're serious, aren't you?"

"Got any better explanations?" she demanded.

He shook his head. "We've really come back through time? *Why? How?*"

"I don't know." She clenched her hands. "It doesn't make sense. Back through time. . . ." Her shoulders trembled once more, and an unsteady laugh escaped her. "Oh, lord, what an opportunity for my research! I was looking for original documents, you know. I hadn't expected to find the original *people,* as well!"

Charles looked from one to the other of them, then shook his head. With an effort, he kept his voice cool and under control. "I am not much in the mood for jests just at the

48

present. I realize something *unusual* is occurring with you, something I admit I cannot explain, but are you seriously making the claim you have come from a future time?"

Miss Anderson considered. After a moment, she said: "I'm very much afraid I am."

She actually claimed the impossible to be true. Charles poured more wine for himself and swirled the deep ruby liquid in the cut-crystal glass. After a moment, he said: "I suppose you have proof of this absurdity?"

She patted the right front portion of her peculiar breeches —a pocket, he realized—then tried other spots. From one in the rear she at last drew out a handkerchief, badly rumpled—and not made out of muslin or cotton, either, he realized the next moment. The torn edges did not appear to be woven, but to be made of fibers pressed together, rather like a paper-thin felt.

"Not much, I'm afraid." She offered him a wry half-smile. "I left my purse locked in the car I rented, and I've lost my camera and car keys."

Mr. Vaughn shoved a trembling hand into his own pocket and dragged out a collection of coins. These he tossed onto the table, then produced a tiny case of folded leather and flipped it open to display a miniature painting of himself surrounded by printing. "My driver's license," he said.

William Falkirk took it from him and studied the picture. "How did the artist manage so realistic a likeness?" he demanded. "The brush strokes are so fine, I cannot even see them!"

Miss Anderson hugged herself. "It's not a painting, it's a technique called a photograph—an exact recreation of an image. It's done with a camera."

Dr. Falkirk dragged his gaze from it to look at her. "And you claim to *have* one of these marvels?"

"Not on me, but yes. Most people in my time do."

Charles took the picture and stared at it for a long moment. "Good God, it's impossible!" Slowly, he transferred his regard to Mr. Vaughn. "Impossible," he repeated, shaken. "Just like that—that whatever it was I saw when I touched Miss Anderson, and she shimmered."

49

"You shimmered, also. The both of you," Dr. Falkirk told him.

Charles drew a deep breath which completely failed to steady him. "You mean *I* supposedly shifted between times, as well? No," he pronounced at last, his tone purely conversational. "It's too fantastic to be true."

"Of course it is." Miss Anderson crossed to the fireplace and huddled near the leaping flames. It did not appear to warm her much. "Mr. Vaughn and I aren't here," she shot over her shoulder. "I fell and struck my head in the cavern, and in a few minutes I'll wake up and you'll all disappear."

Reluctant amusement tugged at Charles. "That might solve *your* problem, but I fail to see where it will help mine." Once more he glanced at the miniature portrait of Mr. Vaughn, then back at her. "If you disappear now, I shall be left explaining to myself where you came from—and to where you went."

She moved a step closer to the flames, as if seeking comfort from them. "I suppose you're trying to tell me we're stuck with each other."

His lips twitched. Whatever else she might be, Miss Anderson certainly was not in the common way. He found her intriguing. Delightfully—and disturbingly—so. "That does not sound a polite way of putting it," he pointed out.

"Have you a better?" Lexie shot back at him, then turned away. Part of her wanted to scream, another part to laugh. Was this the beginnings of hysteria? She glanced at the bookcase, currently devoid of television sets, and shivered. *"Time* travel. It isn't possible."

The earl extracted a bill from the leather folds of Geoff Vaughn's wallet. *"Nineteen-*eighty-seven. Is that the year in which you claim to live?"

"No, the money is several years old." Lexie sank onto a chair and stared at her clasped hands. "How did we *do* it? How—"

She broke off, eyes closed, images from her nightmare casting dark and terrible shadows into the recesses of her mind. "That dagger," she breathed. "Somehow, that dagger is responsible."

50

"What dagger?" Wyndham looked up from his examination of a plastic credit card.

The vision formed in her mind, the bare inch of silver blade protruding from the woman's breast, the child's hand reaching for the chased hilt with the sparkling blue stone, the star sapphire . . . She shivered, shaking off the dead girl's memory which haunted her, and her fingers clutched the chain of her locket which hung beneath her bulky sweater.

"Miss Anderson?"

She opened her eyes to see Wyndham standing at her side, his expression concerned. He held a glass of wine in his outstretched hand. She took it from him and swallowed a large mouthful, then another.

Forcing herself to maintain a matter-of-fact tone, she described the knife. "I've seen it before, in—in nightmares," she added. "Then in the cavern, when Mr. Vaughn and I entered . . ." She took another drink. "It was there, protruding from a pile of old blankets or something. Then *after* we came back in time, it was *still* in the cavern, only in the hands of that man."

"Which man?" Wyndham pressed.

"I have no idea. He wore a mask. I only remember his eyes, their evil glint—" She broke off, then forced a shaky smile. "I doubt if I would have recognized him, even if he weren't disguised. A little before my time, you might say."

Wyndham's lips curved upward. "So I might. Forgive me, I was forgetting. This must be rather . . . unsettling for you."

"That's putting it mildly."

His smile deepened. "It was an old axiom of my governess's that everything looked better after a bite to eat."

"An excellent suggestion." Dr. Falkirk, who had been studying the coins in silence, allowed them to drop back onto the table and crossed to the bellpull.

Before he could tug it, the butler entered to announce that a meal had been concocted and laid out in the breakfast parlor, if they should care to partake of it. Wyndham thanked the man, then ushered the others from the room.

Lexie allowed the others to precede her, then followed them, her awed gaze roaming about the lofty proportions

51

and elegant appointments of the Great Hall. A variety of swords, shields, and tapestries lined the walls. She'd seen it all before, so familiar—yet so subtly different.

Wyndham led the way up one curving side of the main stair. Lexie came last, slowly, trailing her fingers along the polished mahogany of the banister. The subtle aromas of beeswax and lemon oil hovered in air warmed by the blazing fires in the massive hearths.

They reached the wide gallery above, which lay between the twin staircases. Lexie glimpsed a long line of gilt-framed paintings before Wyndham directed them away from it. They headed down a side wing, between walls lined with portraits and landscapes alternating with windows and arched embrasures in which stood tables with statues or vases of flowers.

At last they entered a comfortably sized apartment decorated in a light style with lace curtains at the windows and numerous branches of candles lending a cheery brightness. Here, also, a fire burned merrily, and on the mahogany mantel stood an assortment of china knick-knacks. Probably Sevres, Lexie guessed. The indefinable aura of wealth and taste permeated the atmosphere.

A large sideboard of carved cherrywood rested against the wall opposite the fireplace. On its surface, someone had arranged an elaborate selection of silver chafing dishes with a stack of china and silver flatware beside them. A huge urn stood at one end, and the aroma of strong coffee mingled with other, less easily identifiable but equally delicious and welcome, smells.

Lexie reacted as if to a clarion call. She hadn't eaten a real meal since her early breakfast of croissant rolls—who knew how long ago. Dr. Falkirk gestured for her to precede him, and she grabbed the top plate and began lifting lids at random. She took a spoonful—some larger than others—from every dish, then settled at the table and set to it with a will.

Clempson entered with a tray, on which rested three bottles of wine. These he presented to Wyndham, who approved the selection. While Lexie watched, fascinated, the butler carried them to the side table, uncorked his treasures with loving care, and decanted the contents into crystal containers.

With a good portion of her meal inside her, Lexie felt a little more capable of dealing with her present reality. She accepted a glass of wine from the doctor, sipped it, and savored the flavor. Looking up, she caught Wyndham watching her.

She offered him an apologetic smile. "I needed this. I'm never much good when I miss too many meals."

He inclined his head. "I doubt many of us are. I am delighted—"

The rest of what he said faded from her hearing. The tingling began in her arms, quickly spreading to every part of her. She rose, pushing her chair back from the table, and heard the muffled thud of its fall as if through a heavy fog. Darkness engulfed the room, and silence. Or almost. From somewhere in the distance came the sounds of rock music.

She spun about, panic welling within her. Something brushed her shoulder, more like a breath of air than anything tangible, then it solidified into the grip of a strong hand. An arm wrapped about her, and slowly the music faded and the flickering candlelight returned. Again, Wyndham's arm pressed her against him, burying her face in his coat.

"My God," he breathed. "I touched you when you shimmered, and you weren't solid." With care, he set her from him. "You really *are* from another era. What did you see this time?"

She swallowed, and her hand closed over the sleeve of his coat in a convulsive grasp. "Nothing. It—it was dark in here. It must be night in my time, too. But I heard music."

Dr. Falkirk picked up her chair and pressed her back into it. For a long minute he kept his fingers on her racing pulse, then at last released her. His gaze strayed to Geoff Vaughn, who stood as if transfixed, staring at Lexie. "Does this happen to you, too?" Dr. Falkirk asked him.

Vaughn shook his head. "Whatever is going on, it must be because of her." His tone denied any responsibility for the situation in which they found themselves.

"It's that dagger," Lexie breathed.

"Well, it's not here now, is it?" Vaughn looked from Wyndham to the doctor, then back to Lexie.

"No, it isn't," she agreed. The dagger affected her—and only her—because of her tie to this time period through that poor little girl's locket. Lexie swallowed. She didn't believe in reincarnation. She wasn't too keen on the idea of the locket being haunted, either, but that seemed the most reasonable explanation for an unreasonable situation. She should get rid of it, throw it into the sea where it would sink into oblivion . . . yet how could she bear to part with it? It held her memories—and those of the other little girl, as well.

As for the dagger . . . It had brought both her and Geoff Vaughn back through time. She might be able to get home without it, but Geoff couldn't, of that she felt certain.

And she couldn't abandon him. It was her fault; if it hadn't been for her and her locket, he never would have been dragged into this mess. He'd still be safe in his own time.

Which left her with no choice. She found her wine and drained the glass. "If we're to get home where we belong," she announced, "somehow, we're going to have to get hold of that dagger."

Chapter Five

Charles propped his shoulder against the wall and regarded the young lady before him with a touch of sardonic amusement. Definitely, she was not in the common way. "Obtaining your dagger should present no problem," he drawled. "Since it appears to be in the possession of the conspirators, all we shall have to do is capture them."

"Oh, is that all?" A shaky laugh escaped Miss Anderson.

His lips twitched in a sudden flash of humor. "Until we do, I believe it will be best if you remain here, at the Priory. You will be safe—and seen by as few people as possible." And where he could keep watch over them.

Miss Anderson nodded agreement, though her pale, translucent eyes clouded. "That's very kind of you. But we've got to make every effort to return home, and as soon as possible, before we interfere with history."

Interfere. Good God, could she? Could her mere presence bear any important influence on events to come? With a sense of shock, he realized that the years—even the days—ahead represented to him a future as yet undetermined. To her, they meant a past already recorded, where the slightest alteration might produce an effect rather like the dropping of a pebble into a still pond. The ripples spread outward, generating change upon change upon change. The concept staggered him.

"We've *got* to get home," she repeated, her tone desperate.

"I suppose you must," he agreed, recovering to a degree.

Or did he? If he were once more his sane, logical self, surely he would not experience a touch of regret at the thought of this unconventional young lady vanishing from his life.

She cast him a half-rueful, half-apologetic glance. "You must be anxious to get us out of your hair—and out of a time where we don't belong."

He resumed his seat without answering. As she said, he should be. So why *wasn't* he? It made no sense.

She turned to Mr. Vaughn. "We're going to have to take the greatest care not to do or say anything that could influence events or change anything while we're here."

Mr. Vaughn settled once more in his chair and rocked it back onto its two rear legs. Picking up his wine glass, he turned the stem between his fingers, his thoughtful gaze resting on the deep red liquid. "Must we?" he asked at last.

"Of course! Mr. Vaughn, this is a—a fluke! We shouldn't be here, and at such a time as this. Think of the damage we could do with our knowledge of the course of the war."

Charles straightened. Their knowledge of the war?

"The Napoleonic Wars," Vaughn said, and grinned. "I wasn't thinking of that. No, don't worry, I don't go in for history changing on a large scale. Espionage isn't my style."

She eyed him, her expression suspicious. "What is, then?"

"Oh, come now, Miss Anderson. Don't try to tell me it hasn't occurred to you, too. The *little* things, things that won't change history—but could made life a lot easier for us. You know, *deals* we could arrange. Have you never wanted to be rich?"

Charles's gaze switched back to her. Her expression showed concern—or distress, as if his words caused a deep foreboding within her.

Her pale eyes narrowed. "What exactly do you have in mind?"

Mr. Vaughn grinned, revealing none of her uneasiness. "*Land* deals. We should be able to come up with a little money here if we try. What would you say to buying up a useless acre or two just outside Rye?"

"*Which* useless acre or two?" She spoke through clenched teeth.

A soft laugh escaped him. "I'm thinking of a particular stretch that's going to be developed around nineteen-twenty. Goes for a fortune, then. Worth even more in our time." He cocked his head to one side. "So, what do you say? No one here will care."

"But someone a hundred years from now will." She folded her arms, glaring at him. "You can't do it. Some family will make a fortune out of that property."

"Well, why shouldn't it be me?"

"Because as far as we're concerned, it's already happened! You'd be changing history."

His smile became more ingratiating. "Only a little. Come on, it's not like I'm planning on helping Napoleon or Hitler win their wars, you know. We're just talking about a few stray pounds. Why shouldn't they end up in my bank account?"

"Because they belong in someone else's!"

He laughed. "How do you know? Maybe history as we know it already took our presence here into account. Maybe I'll set up a trust fund for myself, and when I get home I'll know how to collect it."

"Mr. Vaughn—"

"Geoff. If we're going to be business partners, we might as well be on a first name basis. What do you think, Wyndham?" He turned to Charles. "Shall I win myself a little money at cards and wind up with some future prime development property?"

Charles eyed him with disfavor. "It does not sound to me a completely ethical scheme."

Dr. Falkirk shook his head in agreement. "I should think not."

"Like insider trading," Miss Anderson added. "You can't do it."

Vaughn's grin broadened. "Oh, I bet I can. Want to wager?"

"I do *not!*"

He chuckled, mostly to himself. "We shall see."

Miss Anderson turned on Charles with fierce determination. "I must locate that dagger as quickly as possible."

"Yes, I begin to believe you must." Charles's frowning gaze rested on Mr. Vaughn. "I shall be delighted to help you in any way possible, Miss Anderson. I wonder if Kester managed to discover any of his captor's identities?"

"I asked on the ride back," William Falkirk interpolated. "He heard a couple of names—Sam and Cocking. Not much to help us, I'm afraid. Their leader—a gentleman, it seems—remained masked the whole time. They even blindfolded Kester upon occasion." The doctor snorted. "The lad seemed to think that a rare treat, too."

Charles's tension eased. "Young jackanapes. Well, I can't say I blame him. I doubt there's a schoolboy in existence who wouldn't have relished such an adventure—especially now it's ended happily. I don't doubt he had a few uneasy moments while it was going on, though." He crumpled his linen napkin and rose. "I think what we need now is a good night's sleep—at least, what is left of the night. Ah, Clempson," he added as the butler entered with two footmen and began to collect dishes. "Have the rooms been prepared for our guests?"

"Yes, m'lord. If you are ready, Mrs. Clempson will escort the—" He broke off, eyeing Miss Anderson with a touch of uncertainty.

"The lady." Charles kept his tone gentle, but a determined note underlay the words.

"Yes, m'lord. The lady and the gentleman to their chambers." With a slight bow, he exited the apartment.

Charles returned his gaze to Miss Anderson, and his sternness melted before a touch of ruefulness. On the whole, he could not blame Clempson for his uncertainty. But neither could he permit any disrespect for the young lady to develop among the servants. He contemplated her with an assessing frown. "I can see we'll have to do something about your clothing if you are not to have my staff in an uproar. Do ladies actually wear such garments in your time?"

"Yes, and we find them every bit as comfortable as men do. And practical. I could hardly have gone scrambling over rocks and searching for a cavern in a skirt."

"No, I shouldn't imagine you could." The vision thus

58

conjured made him smile. "Well, we shall have to see what we can do for you."

Mrs. Clempson, who must have been waiting nearby, entered the parlor, curtsied to Charles, then turned her disapproving regard on Lexie. The woman's chin rose a fraction, and she gave an audible sniff.

Charles's brow snapped down. "This is Miss Anderson, Mrs. Clempson. She has played an important role in rescuing my nephew. She will be visiting my aunt for a few days. And as she has lost everything she owns, perhaps you will be kind enough to locate her the things she needs?"

The housekeeper melted at his words. "Saved the young master, did you now, miss? Well, don't you worry none about losing your trunks and bandboxes. We'll take care of everything, we will. Sir?" She turned to include Vaughn. "If you'll come this way, please?"

With a sense of unease, Lexie followed the housekeeper and Geoff Vaughn. She'd rather remain with the other two men, she realized. She'd felt safe with them.

No, that was just being ridiculous. Her exhaustion played tricks on her. She'd feel her usual capable self after she'd had time to recover. *Time travel,* of all things! No wonder her world still spun.

They retraced their steps to the wide picture gallery overlooking the Great Hall. At the other end, they proceeded down another corridor and up a flight of steps. Vaguely, Lexie wondered how she'd survive the search for breakfast in the morning. Until she had at least two cups of coffee inside her, her brain didn't function—certainly not well enough to navigate her way through this great barrack without a map.

At last they entered a low-pitched chamber decorated in tones of pink. "The Rose Room, Miss," her guide said. With that, she left Lexie to look around while she saw Vaughn to his quarters.

Lexie strode into the apartment, looking about in interest. Yes, little painted roses did indeed sprig the wallpaper, and exquisite renditions of the flower buds also patterned the heavy silk curtains about the bed. Did people actually pull these before going to sleep? She'd get all claustrophobic. Like being in a tiny tent.

What she really wanted was a bathroom, but she had the distinct feeling she wasn't going to find one. Plumbing, after a rudimentary fashion, she knew to be in existence. But not all houses indulged in that luxury.

A brief search, during which she discovered a washbasin and a chamber pot—both decorated in rosebuds, of course—assured her Wyndham Priory had not jumped on the bandwagon. A pitcher in a matching pattern containing hot water stood on the stone hearth, and she carried it to the basin. Over this hung a large oval mirror flanked by double branches of candles. She lit these, discovered the ingrained dirt on her face and neck, and set about scrubbing with the rose-scented soap.

A light tap sounded on the door, and Lexie mopped her damp skin on the provided towel. A glance at her reflection made her abandon any attempt to straighten her dark hair; it would take too long. With a fatalistic shrug, she answered the knock.

A slightly built young woman in her mid-thirties, wearing a plain long gray dress, stood before her. She had pulled her smooth brown hair back into a chignon, but a few wispy strands escaped to cluster about her ears. Her plain face, brightened by a pair of large hazel eyes and a tentative smile, gazed back at Lexie. In her arms she clutched a small assortment of gowns.

"Miss Anderson? Forgive me for intruding. Mrs. Clempson has told me you have nothing with you." The woman's gaze brushed across Lexie's bulky sweater and jeans, and delicate color tinged the pale cheeks.

"It's been dreadful," Lexie assured her cheerfully. She made a pretty rotten female of this era, she reflected. She was quite used to being without anything, and managed very well.

"Oh, I cannot imagine not even having a *gown!*" the woman declared. She took a tentative step into the room.

"If you do not think it the most shocking piece of impertinence, Mrs. Clempson thought perhaps you might be able to wear one of my nightdresses, only for this one night, of course. . . ." Her voice trailed off and she looked up, eager to please but obviously afraid she might instead offend.

Warmth rushed through Lexie. "It is very kind of you. I—I don't think I'll be here long, but I would be very grateful to be able to borrow something."

A shy smile hovered on the woman's lips, and she deposited her burden on the counterpane. "I have this." She held up a gown of fine lawn. "And in the morning you will need a chemise and gown. I thought perhaps—?" She held up a plain high waisted dress of cream-colored muslin, sprigged with tiny pink flowers, with small puff sleeves and made high at the neck with a ruffled gauze inset. "We are much of a size, I think."

Lexie touched the gown, and a pang of guilt assailed her. These must be the woman's best things. "It is very kind of you," she said. With a sinking sensation, she realized she had no way to repay her. "Miss—?"

"Langley. Hester Langley. I am governess to his lordship's nieces."

The governess who kept the diary. . . . Lexie regarded her with renewed interest. "And his lordship's nephew?"

"Oh, no, Master Kester is at Eton, now. And he had tutors before, of course." She glanced at a clock and a slight frown creased her brow.

"Have I disrupted your schedule?" Lexie asked.

"No." The woman raised her large eyes to Lexie's face, then looked down as color once more crept up her cheeks. "Oh, no. It is only that—but I must stay within call of Master Kester, in case he should have nightmares."

Lexie caught the play of emotions across Miss Langley's expressive countenance. "Is there somewhere else you are supposed to be?"

"No, oh, no." The woman bit her lip. "I—I had intended—that is, it is not of the least importance. I merely had thought to go for a walk."

"But it's freezing outside!"

The woman's color burned brighter. "You are right. It was naught but a silly fancy. Pray, do not let it disturb you." She turned toward the door.

"Wait!" Impulsive as always, Lexie caught her arm. "You are being so very nice to me, let me do something for you in return. I'll sit within call of Master Kester while you go out."

The fine lines about Miss Langley's bright hazel eyes deepened, revealing her indecision—and longing. "I couldn't ask you—"

"You aren't," Lexie interrupted. "I'm offering. Now, go get your coat and tell me where to go. Is there a book or something I could read? I'm too wound up to sleep, anyway."

In a short while, Lexie curled up in an overstuffed chair before a blazing hearth in the schoolroom, a woolen shawl over her legs. Behind her stood the partially opened door to Master Kester's bedchamber. If he so much as moaned in his sleep, she would hear him. Across the long chamber stood his sisters' rooms. Lexie picked up the book—the first volume of the suitably gothic *Castle of Otranto* by Horace Walpole—and settled down to unwind.

Her strategy proved remarkably effective, for she not only relaxed, but drifted off into a light doze before reading more than a half dozen pages. Not until the door into the corridor opened did she awaken.

Miss Langley slipped in, shivering, and went to stand before the fire, which had burned low. Lexie stretched and yawned, then noted the governess's lined face.

She straightened. "Has something happened? You look worried."

"Do I?" Miss Langley managed an artificial laugh. "Only tired and cold. Has all been quiet here?"

Lexie assented, then stared at the clock, which showed the time to be almost three-thirty in the morning. The governess had been gone for over three hours. Her cheeks were abnormally pale, with the color brought by the wind and cold standing out as if painted, artificial.

Miss Langley looked away and murmured her thanks.

To Lexie, it seemed as if the governess hurried her from

the room, and shut the door as soon as she was in the hall. Lexie turned and stared at the closed panel. Where had Miss Langley gone after midnight, then stayed until three in the morning? If her memory served, there were few houses nearby—at least, only a few in her own time. She doubted it was different now. So where had the governess gone? Or perhaps more important, whom had she gone to see—and why?

Chapter Six

Lexie stretched, easing her stiff muscles, then snuggled deeper into her down-wrapped cocoon. The bed cradled her in comfort, the pillow so soft, the covers so warm . . . so unfamiliar . . .

Her eyes flew open, and she bolted upright, staring about in rising panic. Roses enveloped her, from the coverlet over the bed to the canopy above, even to the curtains that hung about each of the four posts. The color of the roses flecked the wallpaper, a china basin, everywhere her frantic gaze roved.

She clutched the blanket, her hand trembling. Her hand? She trembled all over. Why wasn't she at the bed and breakfast—or better, in her own room at her apartment in Seattle?

Because, a niggling voice in her mind warned her, her familiar Seattle might not yet have been settled, nor her apartment built.

In which time did she currently exist? Her own, or 1805?

She scanned the room, her sense of foreboding deepening, and spotted a tray which rested on the bedside table. Two flaky rolls sat on a plate, and dark brown liquid filled a cup. Coffee! She grabbed for it with aching gratitude, gulped down a swallow—and her hopes collapsed. Not coffee, but hot—or rather cool—chocolate. With a sigh of regret, she sipped it.

By the time she'd drained the cup, her mind had kicked in

and begun to function. The chocolate was cold, but not *that* cold. The presence of a breakfast of sorts meant someone knew she was here. And that blew any lingering hopes she might have had about having returned to her own time while she slept.

Her own time. She closed her eyes. Somehow, she'd been caught up in her nightmare, and this time the terror wouldn't disappear with her waking. She actually had spent the night in the Rose Room at Wyndham Priory, almost two hundred years before she visited the house for the first time—only two days ago. The logistics of that one gave her a headache.

She fell back against the pillow, then grabbed another and buried her face under it. No, hiding would do her no good. She rolled over and stared up into the silken canopy, then about the room. It looked much the same as it had last night, except the illumination came from the windows where the drapes had been dragged back. From the warm depths of the bed she could just glimpse the edge of an icy lake and two swans huddled together on the snowy bank.

She'd need her down jacket today.

Except she'd left her down jacket in her room at the bed and breakfast. And if she went there, what would she find? The inn had already been built, and so had the guest house where she stayed. But the current landlord would never have heard of her, and her luggage would not yet be in the room. It wouldn't arrive, in fact, for almost another two centuries.

And she shouldn't have, either. She didn't belong here, she had to get home, before she did anything that affected history.

The blood drained from her face, leaving her as clammy as if the burning wagon had once more raced through her subconscious mind. What if she already *had* altered the course of events? What if her watching Kester last night enabled the governess—the Hester Langley who kept the diary, who knew about the smuggler's cavern—to go out and see someone to whom she otherwise would—*should*—not have spoken?

With a groan, she dragged herself out of bed. A pitcher of water stood once more by a hearth filled with glowing embers. She tested it, and found it tepid. With a sigh, she set about washing her face once more with the soap that undoubtedly clogged her pores. What she wouldn't give for some toner to clear away the scummy residue.

A glance at the clock warned her the hour already advanced on ten. That's what she got for staying up so late—and probably playing havoc with history. She'd better find Lord Wyndham and Geoff Vaughn and discover if either of them had come up with a plan for locating the dagger. She certainly hadn't.

The chemise loaned to her by Hester Langley fit her well enough, though the gown hung a little loose. Still, it reached her ankles, putting her right in fashion for the time. Her fascination with this era paid off, it seemed. She'd thought her forays into social quirks and customs to be frivolous, window dressing to her serious pursuit of political history. Hopefully, her carefully culled information would see her through.

She sat down on the edge of the bed, reached for her shoes, and grinned. Sneakers and knitted wool sports socks with a high-waisted, puffed-sleeved, sprig-muslin gown? The ultimate in chic it wasn't, by any means.

She had a shrewd suspicion that going barefoot, though, would not be considered proper etiquette. Well, she had better pay Miss Langley a quick visit.

She slipped out of her room and padded down the carpeted hall, retracing her steps of the previous night. Even before she reached the schoolroom door, lively, high-pitched voices reached her, raised in querulous tones. The muffled but determined sound of Miss Langley's soft voice reached Lexie, and the other two silenced.

Lexie rapped gently, then entered. Two girls, one about ten, the other eight, sat at adjoining tables facing their preceptress. The elder, a mischievous urchin with a freckled nose and copious amounts of gleaming auburn hair like her uncle, eyed Lexie with candid interest. The other, a pale, frail child with dusky curls, regarded her through huge green eyes that promised to be languishing in far too few years. Both wore gowns of a light, warm-looking wool of a soft blue color.

"She hasn't any slippers on," the older girl cried in delight.

"Miss Langley, may *I* go without snoes?"

"Only if yours are ruined." Lexie threw a look of mute apology at the harassed governess.

Miss Langley frowned upon her charge. "That was shockingly impertinent, Marianne. You will copy out the next page in your reader as a lesson. And mind, use your neatest hand, or you will do it again."

The other child rose and bobbed a curtsy. "Please, are you the lady who saved Kester?" She slurred her words slightly, as if trying out the effect of a lisp, but not quite having it down right.

"Don't talk so, Sukey," Marianne told her. "You know how Uncle Wyndham hates it when you put on those die-away airs."

Sukey sniffed, but otherwise ignored her sister. "Are you?" she persisted.

"Actually, your Uncle Wyndham saved us both." Lexie turned back to Miss Langley. "And the other girl was quite right. I haven't any shoes. I was wondering—?"

"Of course." The governess hesitated, and cast her charges a distrustful glance. "If you would mind staying with them a moment? I don't know why I never thought of slippers. Is there anything else you need?"

"No—at least, I hope not. This is very kind of you. I only hope I can make it up to you."

Soft color crept into the woman's cheeks. "Nonsense. It is a pleasure."

Miss Langley hurried across the long chamber and through a door at the back. Marianne turned her considering gaze once more on Lexie, her expression speculative. Sukey studied her covertly, as if seeking any mannerisms worth copying, and ran a thoughtful hand through her dark curls. Lexie realized her own hung loose, unconfined. She'd have to do something appropriate with it in a hurry, if she didn't want to attract disapproving attention.

Miss Langley returned a moment later, before either girl had advanced to the question-asking stage. The governess directed a searching look at them, and apparently their enthralled expressions satisfied her. She handed a pair of white slippers to Lexie, then a pair of stockings and garters.

After thanking her, Lexie retired to her bedchamber once more to figure these out. To her immense satisfaction, she soon had the garters tied below her knees. The slippers, though, proved too small, unable to stretch sufficiently to accommodate her twentieth-century feet. The sneakers would have to do, as incongruous as they might appear.

Her footwear settled—however unsatisfactorily—she turned her attention to her thick dark hair. Only a few minutes, though, proved sufficient to let her know that coming up with a suitable style was beyond her capabilities. Hopefully she wouldn't be here long enough to corrupt the Misses Marianne and Sukey Penrith with her unconventional appearance.

She gave herself one last critical appraisal in the mirror. The result wasn't quite right—even aside from the fact she bore not the least resemblance to any of the women in the BBC productions of Jane Austen's works. Something was missing— She froze. Her locket. . . .

No, it hadn't fallen off, she remembered in a flood of relief. She'd been so tired last night when she returned to her room, she'd taken it off, hoping to prevent a return of the nightmare. She'd set it on the bedside table.

At first glance, she could see no sign of it. Frowning, she lifted the tray, then pulled back the covers, shook out the pillows, then crawled on the floor looking under everything. The locket simply wasn't there.

A stabbing sense of loss shot through her, agonizing. No, she must have just missed it. Perhaps she'd grabbed for it in her sleep, lost it under the sheets.

She tore the bedclothes off, layer by layer, shaking each out. Nothing gold and glittering fell to the floor. Nothing. . . . She searched once more, going over every inch of the room, even looking inside the pitcher and a vase.

Could the maid—or whoever brought the chocolate and rolls and made up the fire—have picked it up? If she had, she might be in for a dreadful shock if that poor, long-dead girl's nightmares began haunting *her*. No, a servant in this house would not have taken something deliberately. It must all be a mistake or a misunderstanding. Yet the sooner she saw Wyndham, the easier she would be.

She set off at once. After only one wrong turn, she found her way back to the wide picture gallery between the stairs. She ran down the carpeted steps, then paused in the Great Hall, looking around. Where would he be?

For that matter, where would *anyone* be? A small army could probably hide with great success in this rabbit warren. She shivered and rubbed her bare arms for warmth. It must take a whole forest to heat this place, too. Damn the prevailing fashion for Grecian drapery instead of real clothes. She should have put on her sweater. It would have looked ridiculous over the gown—but it would at least match her tennies.

But that didn't help her find anyone. She considered a moment, then decided to try the bookroom. At least there might be a fire in there, and she'd seen a bellpull so she could always summon someone and ask. She hesitated, re-oriented, and headed down the correct hall. The second door she opened proved to be the right one.

Lord Wyndham, resplendent in a russet shooting coat, looked up from his seat behind the huge mahogany desk. The flickering flame from the candelabrum at his side glinted off his dark auburn hair and set a light dancing in his wide-set green eyes. His puzzled gaze rested on her a moment, then he slowly rose to his feet. "Miss Anderson? I didn't recognize you for a moment. You look—quite delightful."

"I have Miss Langley to thank for that. But Wyndham, my locket is missing. I've looked everywhere in the room and can't find it."

His brow snapped down, giving him a thunderous—and dangerous—expression. He came around the side of the desk and half sat on the corner, his steady gaze holding hers. "You are quite certain you did not lose it earlier? In the cavern, perhaps?"

"No, I took it off just before going to sleep. I know I had it."

He drew a deep breath, nodded to himself, and crossed to the embroidered bellpull. "We will have Clempson in, I believe."

The butler, when Wyndham told him of the missing locket, appeared outraged. He turned to Lexie, and an expression that might have been mortification flickered across his impassive features. "Such a thing has never before happened in this house, miss," he informed her. "I am deeply grieved. The matter shall be righted at once, I promise you."

"I didn't mean to imply someone *stole* it." Lexie glanced at Wyndham's stern features, then turned back to the butler. "I must have been careless, but it means so very much to me."

Wyndham nodded, though his features did not relax. "Please have a couple of the maids go over Miss Anderson's chamber. They will most likely find the locket behind the dresser."

"Very good, m'lord." The butler, mollified, bowed and took his leave.

"I hope that's the case," Lexie said as the door closed after him. "I couldn't bear to lose it. But right now, we've got to concentrate on getting Mr. Vaughn and me out of here, back to our own time before anything happens."

Wyndham's lips twitched into a wry smile. "I doubt your Mr. Vaughn shares your concern."

It was a very pleasant smile, lessening the harsh lines of strain etched into his features. It even touched his eyes, warming them to liquid pools. . . .

Good grief, she couldn't go all fanciful. She dragged her thoughts away from him, back to his words. "He is not *my* Mr. Vaughn, thank heavens. But you're right, I've got to get him out of here before he acts on any of his frightful schemes. Do you know where he is?"

"Riding. I loaned him some clothing this morning and escorted him about the estate. When I had to come back to meet with my bailiff, he asked if he could continue on his own."

"Well, I doubt he can do much harm riding. What are we to do now? Go to the authorities?"

Wyndham paced to the hearth, then swung back to face her. "That will do no good. I have already been told by them that my story is nonsense."

"But—what about your nephew's being kidnapped? They can't dismiss *that*."

71

He shook his head. "I didn't dare go to them when he was abducted, for fear he'd be killed. And now no one will believe me."

"But why on earth not?"

His wry smile returned. "Because you have fallen into quite an adventure, Miss Anderson. Quite the material for a gothic romance, I fear. When I first went to the Customs Land Guard with my story, they investigated and decided I was either making it up or well on my way to being incarcerated in Bedlam. I might add that when I went to our intelligence people, it was the dam—dashed excisemen's account of the matter that bore weight. It was believed I made too much of my brother's unfortunate death, and it had affected my judgment."

"Your brother's death?"

He strode to the window, then turned back to her. "Forgive me, I should not be troubling you with my problems."

"On the contrary, since they apparently affect my ability to return to my own time, I think you'd better. How did your brother die?"

"He drowned, just over fourteen months ago. A tragic boating accident, it was determined."

"But you don't think it was?"

He shook his head. "I am very certain it was not. Vincent had left a note, you see, telling me he suspected a traitorous conspiracy but could not prove it."

"Didn't *that* weigh with the authorities?"

Again, Wyndham shook his head. "I was out of the country when he died, you see, visiting a cousin at Jamaica House. By the time I returned, my bailiff and our solicitor had gathered his papers together, and it was not until some six months ago I discovered his note."

His face clouded, as if in remembered pain at going through his brother's things. For a long moment he stared at his hands. "I took the paper to the authorities at once," he said at last, "but they had had no notion any such conspiracy might be afoot, and nothing had occurred during the eight months since Vincent's death to lead them to believe he was

72

correct. They ran a few patrols, of course, just to be safe, but on the whole they simply dismissed it all as a flight of fantasy."

He drew a small enameled box from his pocket and tapped it lightly with one finger. "They seem to believe the Penrith family is given to seeing hobgoblins, that we are obsessed by fear of a possible invasion because of the location of our estate."

Lexie digested this. "So you were forced to let the matter drop."

He had started to open the little box, but at this he snapped it closed once more. "Of course not. I began my own investigation."

"And?"

"And it resulted in Kester's being kidnapped to keep me from continuing."

"But that's got to convince the authorities. Hasn't it?" she added as he scowled.

"I didn't dare go the Land Guard during the four days Kester was in their hands. By the time I found him—" He shook his head.

"Do you have any idea who these conspirators are?"

"They're British, of that I'm fairly certain. Kester's account—and yours—seems to confirm it."

She worked her lower lip between her teeth for a minute, thinking. "What will you do now?"

"I'm going to have to find out who they are, and stop them."

"How?" This was exactly what she had wanted to research, the subject for her thesis for which she had found no documented evidence so far. If she were to remain for any length of time, it would seem she would learn firsthand. This put a whole new meaning to the term "original sources." But who would ever believe her footnotes?

Wyndham flipped open the box and took an infinitesimal pinch of the powder within. Snuff, she realized, fascinated, and watched as he closed the box and restored it to his pocket.

"How," he repeated. "As Hamlet would say, there's the

73

rub. The authorities aren't going to believe in Kester's abduction any more than they did in his father's murder. But I'll find a way. You may count on that."

She did. Not so much because she knew the invasion attempt came to nothing, but because of the sheer power and determination of the man. Unless . . .

"Unless our presence ruins everything," she said, voicing the fear that nagged at her.

She joined him at the window, and stared out over a landscape dark and brooding enough to delight the most romantic of artists. Snow hung heavy in the clouds, as if it merely awaited a signal to begin covering the icy ground with a fresh layer of soft, drifting flakes. She shivered, and returned to the warmth of the crackling fire.

"You should have a shawl," Wyndham said.

"Or my sweater. But that would look somewhat incongruous with this dress, wouldn't it? Don't you like the shoes?"

His brow furrowed. "Do you always wear those—those men's garments you wore last night?"

"Most of the time. They're comfortable, you know. I wear skirts and dresses, too, though—when I have to." She stared down into the flames. "And speaking of things I have to do, I've got to get back, get out of here before we do any damage."

Even as she spoke the words, regret flickered through her. She wouldn't mind staying a little while—just to further her research and understanding of the period, of course. She glanced at Wyndham's frowning profile and looked quickly back to the fire. The sooner she left, the better for her piece of mind. She found him a little too attractive for comfort.

To take her mind off him, she concentrated on the "how." "That dagger," she said at last. "It's got to be the key. Our being thrown into the past must have been a fluke that would have been rectified by now if we'd stayed in its vicinity."

"I suppose you're going to blame me for trapping you here?" A slight, ironic smile softened the firm line of his mouth.

She inclined her head. "Well, you have to admit, if you hadn't rescued us, we'd still be near it—or possibly even home already."

He burst out laughing. "If that isn't just like a female to never appreciate anything a man does for her. If you would like, I will be delighted to tie you up and put you back in that cavern."

She gave an exaggerated sigh. "No, it's too late. There wouldn't be any point in it, now. Your conspirators won't return to that spot, because they'll know it won't be safe for them anymore."

"You must allow me to apologize for making this all so very difficult for you. You must admit, though, you were glad enough last night to come with me."

"I didn't know I'd been dumped in a different time, then. Good grief, this all feels like some silly science fiction plot. Dr. Who and the Invasion of England, with the tardis controls in the hands of the aliens so we can't go home."

"What?" He stared at her, blankly.

"Never mind." She waved her facetious comment aside. "We've got to concentrate on finding that dagger. So far, the only thing we can be certain of is that some of your conspirators are from around here."

"Yes, that really narrows down the possibilities, doesn't it?" He smiled at her with false affability.

She shook her head. "The one with the dagger had a cultured voice—he was probably a gentleman. I might recognize him if I heard him speak again."

"Are you suggesting I hold a party and invite every gentleman within a twenty mile radius, so you may listen to them? I doubt our villain would come."

She grinned. "No, I'm very certain he wouldn't, not to your house, at least. It would help, though, if you knew of someone who had such a dagger."

"We could make inquiries. If he lives locally, it is possible someone has seen the knife and remembered it—if it's as unusual as you say."

She shivered again, though this time she wasn't cold. "It is. Where would a gentleman be likely to bring out a dagger?"

"In polite society? Only if he showed it to someone, I would assume. I suppose I can make inquiries at the taverns." He frowned, as if already working out a campaign for discovering the knife's owner. After a moment he apparently came to a decision, for he nodded to himself. "I believe I will go into Rye at once, Miss Anderson. Pray excuse me to your companion when he returns. I should be back around dark." With a slight bow directed at her, he strode from the bookroom.

Which left her with nothing to do but wait, and do and say nothing that might change history. She'd feel better if Geoff Vaughn came back, though. She didn't trust him to watch what he said.

She emerged from the bookroom, found her way back to the Great Hall, then hesitated. She was hungry, but had no idea how to go about getting food. Perhaps Miss Langley could tell her what to do. She started up the stairs, just as the butler emerged from one of the several corridors which opened off the vast entry.

"Excuse me, miss." He waited for her to turn and acknowledge him, then strode up to her. "Lady Agatha's compliments, miss, and will you join her in the breakfast parlor for a nuncheon?"

"Thank you, I'd be very glad to." One problem solved, at least. "Where—"

"You partook of a supper there last night, miss. The next floor up, to the left of the Picture Gallery. And about your locket, miss. I very much fear it has not turned up."

With difficulty, she kept her dismay from appearing too obviously on her face. She forced herself to merely nod. "Thank you for trying."

She made her way up the stairs, turned to the left, and with surprisingly little difficulty found the breakfast parlor. She opened the door, and the cheery, elegant little lady she had seen the night before looked up. On a plate before her rested wafer-thin slices of cheese and ham, a roll, and an apple.

Lady Agatha Penrith beamed at her. "There you are, my dear. I am so sorry I did not properly greet you last night. Pray forgive me. I was deeply concerned for my poor great nephew, you must understand, and I didn't quite realize—" She broke off.

"You thought I was one of the men who had helped Lord Wyndham?" Lexie supplied for her.

"Well, yes, I did." A twinkle lit her bright hazel eyes. "You

76

were not dressed quite in the ordinary way, you see."

"No, I gather I wasn't. But thanks to your Miss Langley, I hope I look better today."

"Indeed, you do. Have you nothing of your own?"

"No, I—I seem to have lost everything."

The little lady exclaimed in dismay. "How dreadful for you. Do not concern yourself, we shall rectify that presently. Indeed, I do not know what Wyndham could have been thinking of. I should have taken you into Rye this morning."

"No, I—I won't be staying long enough for that to matter." Or at least so she hoped.

"Not matter? Wherever you go, you will need luggage. Now, not another word, my dear. We will go into Rye as soon as you have eaten something. We are quite close, you must know."

"I'm without money, also," she said bluntly. "And I won't take any, so please don't offer it."

"I wouldn't dream of it. I shall simply have the bills sent to Wyndham. Gentlemen are always much better at handling such matters, do you not agree?"

Lexie bit back her emphatic "no." Instead, she shook her head. "I can't leave the estate today. I'm waiting for—for the man who came with me. We have a few things to discuss."

Lady Agatha's disappointment showed clearly on her expressive countenance, but she did not press the matter further. Instead, she satisfied herself with a long, surreptitious scrutiny of Lexie's figure, which she obviously hoped went unnoticed. It left Lexie in little doubt that some article of clothing would appear in her chamber before the end of the day.

After the meal, which she made a generous one, Lexie felt considerably better. She went downstairs where she again encountered Clempson, and asked him to let her know the minute Mr. Vaughn returned. She then made her way to the bookroom where she browsed through the shelves until she discovered a section that must belong to Lady Agatha. She selected Maria Edgeworth's *Castle Rackrent* and settled by the fire to wile away the time. Well, it was a *sort* of original document.

Not until the dimming light made reading difficult did she

lay down the volume. She rose and went in search of anyone. At last she located a maid, who directed her to Clempson.

The butler, though, had no word of Mr. Vaughn's whereabouts. Lexie, her worry growing, returned to the library and stared out the window. The full darkness outside defied her attempts to see. Only the whiteness of a few falling flakes greeted her searching gaze. For a long while she remained where she stood, watching crystals form and melt from one of the panes, her book forgotten.

Behind her the door opened abruptly, and Wyndham entered. "Vaughn hasn't returned," he declared by way of greeting.

Lexie hurried over to him, barely preventing herself from holding out her hands for his comforting clasp. Whatever spell this man cast on her, she had best ignore it. Gathering herself together, she asked: "Do you think we should search for him? If he fell off his horse, he could be out there, anywhere."

Wyndham cast a frowning glance into the icy darkness beyond the window. "I wouldn't have thought he could come to grief. The farms are all tenanted, anyone could—and would—have given him aid or directions."

Her heart lurched painfully in her chest as a possible explanation occurred to her. "Unless it was someone who didn't want him to get back."

Their gazes met. He looked away first. "Let's not assume the worst. I'll call out the grooms. If we ride out singly, we should be able to cover most of the estate in little more than an hour. Then if we still haven't found him—"

"It might be because he's been recaptured," Lexie finished.

Chapter Seven

Mr. Geoff Vaughn riding beyond the boundaries of the estate, recognized by one of the conspirators, captured again . . . Charles drew a deep breath and wished he could assure Miss Anderson of the impossibility of that thought. But he couldn't. Nor would false words of platitude ease the distress he read in her expressive countenance. Only definite action and tangible results would serve with this young lady, unless he was much mistaken. He didn't think he was. He turned on his heel and strode to the door.

Before he reached it, Miss Anderson was after him. "Where are you going?" she demanded.

He looked down at her intent face—her *arresting* face, with the straight little nose, the generous, determined mouth, and the willful chin, all surrounded by that shoulder-length ruff of dusky curls. The desire to see the strain melt from her lovely eyes struck him like a physical blow to the stomach.

"Where—" she began again.

He recovered. "To start the search parties."

"Right." She pushed past. "I'll change and be with you in a minute."

"You'll do no such thing." He caught her arm. "It has started snowing again."

She freed herself from his loose grasp. "What has that got to do with anything? If Geoff Vaughn is out in it, the sooner we find him, the better. If he's not—" she swallowed, and fear flickered in the depths of her pale eyes, "—the sooner we know, the better."

He reached past her, opening the door, but positioned himself in her way. "We will search, and diligently, I promise you that. But there is no need for you—"

"Oh, quit arguing." She glared at him, her anxiety patent. "I'm not about to sit here like some useless idiot along with the 'womenfolk' or whatever you call them. I'm going to help."

Charles froze. "Is there an attachment between you?" he demanded.

"An *attachment?*" She stared at him, obviously startled. "Good grief, no! I barely know the man, and what I *do* know, I don't particularly like."

A satisfaction he didn't bother exploring replaced his budding anger. "Then why—?"

"Because he's probably in this mess because of me. Look, shall I meet you back here or at the stable?"

His last remnants of irritation vanished. He could understand—and approve of—her sense of responsibility. But he would not subject her to the rigors which lay ahead. Gently, he said: "You really should not go out in this. We'll be riding, you must know. There is no point in taking a carriage, for if he had stayed on the roads he would have found his way back by now."

"I know how to ride a horse—astride, at least. Don't you dare have them give me a sidesaddle. And I'm not likely to melt—or freeze—with a little snow." She hesitated, and a rueful smile just touched her lips. "I don't suppose you could loan me a warm jacket, though?"

"If I refuse, will you remain indoors?" He fought back an answering smile.

She directed a scornful look at him. "We're wasting time."

She was right—in spite of the fact he found arguing with her to be an enjoyable pastime. His narrowed gaze rested on her willful expression. If he left her behind, he had a shrewd notion she would find a way to follow. It would be better to have her with him, where he would know her to be safe. He nodded. "Very well. Can you be ready in fifteen minutes?"

"Try five." She took off at a run.

He watched her bound up the stairs two at a time, both amused and disconcerted. Her behavior shocked him—yet intrigued him at the same time. What other oddities of manner and opinion would she betray? And how much would be due to the differences in the eras in which they were raised, and how much to her unorthodox personality?

He summoned Clempson, and within minutes the menservants, both inside and out, prepared themselves for the search. Charles went to his own chamber to obtain warm coats, then made his way back to the library.

Miss Anderson met him on the threshold of this apartment, and swooped down on the heavy overcoat he carried. "It only took me seven minutes," she announced with pride.

He stopped short, his gaze resting on the blue breeches which clung to her hips and legs in the most unseemly—and provocative—manner. The heavy knitted shirt she wore outlined her generous curves. "Good God," he muttered. Yet his gaze lingered on her in a flagrant denial of the disapproval he had inserted in his tone. He had seen her dressed like this before, only yesterday—but at that time he had not yet seen her demurely attired in a gown. He turned abruptly about. "Let us get started."

They reached the Great Hall to find a selection of warmly clad menservants standing in rank, receiving their orders from the capable Clempson. An upper housemaid, who watched the preparations, let out a scandalized shriek at sight of Miss Anderson. The butler glanced up, and his jaw dropped. His minions' gazes zeroed in on her garments, and a startled but appreciative whistle escaped the cheeky boots, a lad not yet out of his teens.

Charles's jaw tightened as Clempson rounded on the boy, and the butler's scowl set the youth shaking in his shoes. Clempson's challenging glare traveled across the others, and they hastily wiped all expression from their faces.

"Put on your greatcoat," Charles ordered Miss Anderson.

She cast him an apologetic look and struggled into it. "I know—intellectually, at least—that what I'm wearing must be shocking for a woman of this time. But I'm so much at home like this, I can't really *believe* it."

He adjusted the folds of the cavernous garment—cut for his generous height and breadth—so it covered her tiny frame completely, all the way to the tops of her peculiar shoes. "That should do," he announced, and took her elbow. "Let us go. You are going to be sorry you came," he added as he led her out into the icy night air.

"Most likely," she agreed.

Already, large flakes of snow drifted past their faces. He half expected her to try to catch some on her tongue, and found himself surprised—or was that disappointed?—when she did not. This was hardly an occasion for levity, though, not with Mr. Vaughn missing, possibly lying somewhere injured and unprotected from the elements.

He cast the young lady at his side a frowning glance. "This is going to be rather uncomfortable for you."

Some two hours later, Lexie decided the earl had erred in that comment—but on the side of optimism. They rode in dejected silence across a fallow field, their knees and lower legs brushing with the swaying steps of their mounts as the horses hugged close to one another, as if seeking warmth. Not so much as a single star remained to be seen in the snow-laden sky. How could there be so much left up there when so much had already fallen—*still* fell?

The shrouded moon reflected off the clouds and ground, surrounding them in a dim glow which did little to illuminate their way. Lexie shivered and huddled deeper into the inadequate coat. She would swear an icicle formed on her nose. Her weary horse stumbled, and as he regained his balance, she caught her reins to steady his head. At least, she thought she did. She could see the thin strips of leather there, even if her fingers were too numb in their leather gloves to actually feel them. She couldn't remember ever being so cold.

"I thought there was a chance, back at that hedgerow in the south pasture, near that ditch." Wyndham spoke for the first time in almost twenty minutes.

Lexie nodded and concentrated on keeping her teeth from chattering. "We're not going to find him out here, are we?" she asked through jaws clenched against the cold.

"He could have ridden farther afield," Wyndham pointed out.

"But you don't think so. You think those—those conspirators—recognized him and captured him again, don't you?"

He drew a deep breath, then exhaled it slowly. His cloudy breath hovered before him, then dispelled among the flakes that drifted through the dark. "I wish I could be certain," he said at last.

"You—don't suppose they could have taken him back to the cavern?"

He looked at her, his eyes no more than a flickering gleam in the darkness. "There's only one way to find out." His voice held a note of challenge.

Lexie reined in her mount. "If they did, it might only be to set a trap for you, you know."

"Possibly," he agreed with maddening calm.

Lexie nodded. "Which way?"

He turned his horse, and she followed. The road seemed wholly unfamiliar in the enveloping cocoon of drifting snow, yet she had driven it—even ridden it in the dark—before. Strange how ghostly everything now appeared.

The thick carpeting of white muffled their horses' hoofbeats, and Lexie set her chin to keep her teeth from chattering. If Vaughn were indeed in the cavern, then one or more of the conspirators probably would be, as well—even if this weren't a trap. She refused to consider what they would do if it were. Instead, she concentrated on the owner of that dagger, willing him to be present. If she could just get her hands on that knife, perhaps she and Vaughn could return home at once.

She kept her head lowered, relying on Wyndham and her horse to carry her to their destination. Flakes continued to swirl about them, landing on her hands, melting, only to be replaced. On either side of them, looming shadowy shapes

83

faded into the vast darkness of woods filled with the silence of winter. Definitely not a night to be out without one's woolies.

A tingling sensation crept up her arms, flickering along her flesh, and her horse sidled uneasily. She clutched the reins as a silence even more complete than before engulfed her. Wyndham, at her side, seemed so hazy, as if the snow drifted right through him. . . .

A low rumbling started, then grew in intensity until it filled the night. Through the darkness ahead, two bright pinpoints of light formed, growing larger, illuminating the painted line on the asphalt road beneath her shimmering horse's hooves. A huge lorry—a moving van—barrelled toward them.

Lexie screamed, digging her heels into the flanks of her startled mount as she swung his head toward the side of the street. The animal lunged forward, then stopped, trembling beneath her, at the edge of a deep ditch. The massive lorry faded, leaving only Wyndham in the middle of the dirt lane.

"Miss Anderson?" He brought his horse up to hers. "What happened?"

"Nothing. We nearly got run over by a lorry, that's all."

"A what?"

"A lorry. A huge truck. A—oh, never mind." A shaky laugh escaped her. "It probably couldn't have hit you, you weren't there."

He watched her, his expression unreadable in the darkness. She managed a smile he probably couldn't see. "No, I'm not ready for your Bedlam—yet. I shifted between times, into a—a rather dangerous situation, that's all. I nearly got run over by a—a giant carriage that moves at a tremendous speed."

"Good lord, no wonder you screamed." The furrows in his brow deepened. "Perhaps I should take you back to the Priory before I go on."

She shook her head with more conviction than she felt. "No, I—I've got to find that dagger."

"But you are in no fit state."

"Yes I am. I—I'll be fine. Let's go on." She stroked her

84

horse's neck, and felt even through her gloves the heat and dampness not caused by their exertion. She'd terrified the poor beast.

Wyndham started off at a steady trot, and Lexie kept pace with him. At last he slowed, and Lexie peered ahead. She could just make out the towering shape of the ruined abbey through the trees.

A chilling fear crept through her, but she forced it down. She had to go back into that cavern. Even if Vaughn weren't there, they might discover some clue to the conspirators' identities. And she needed to know who they were. *Wyndham* needed to know.

They circled the perimeter with care, then dismounted and led the horses into the sheltered depths of a copse where they tied their reins to a snow-laden branch. From his saddle Wyndham unstrapped a lantern, which he did not light. It wouldn't be safe, Lexie reminded herself; yet she could wish for both the guidance and comfort of the flame.

They left their shelter and crept across the exposed stretch of rock-strewn grass and weeds that had once formed a courtyard. Now snow covered all. Toward one side of the wall that still stood, near the rocky cliff edge, a massive oaken door hung crookedly on its hinges across the passage entry, its bolt broken. Wyndham set his shoulder to it and inched it aside enough to allow Lexie to slip within. Someone had closed it since their flight last night.

"How has the door lasted when everything else is in ruins?" Lexie whispered as Wyndham joined her.

"It was put in only a century ago, to keep the neighborhood children from wandering through the caverns," he said.

"Offhand, I'd say it needs to be replaced."

"No one had come here for so long, it didn't matter. Before."

Inside, the blackness was complete, impenetrable. Wyndham inched forward, carrying the unlit lantern in one hand, the other feeling the rocky wall for guidance. Lexie caught his sleeve and shuffled along after him, following the downward-leading passage.

After about forty paces, it turned abruptly back the way they had come, only still heading lower with every step. Lexie's shoulder brushed the lichen-covered wall; the clammy dampness left no part of her unchilled. Her toes in her woolly socks and leather shoes had lost most of their feeling.

Abruptly, the air closed about her, still and stale. Wyndham continued, though, and she realized they had merely reached a smaller chamber. She would love to light the lantern and see what lay about them. But if someone waited, not far ahead . . . Her fingers tightened on the thick fabric covering Wyndham's arm.

They rounded another corner, and the earl stopped. Lexie bumped into him, and experienced no desire whatsoever to move away. She huddled close. Not that she was afraid—precisely.

The next moment, a distant arhythmic pounding reached her ears. Her heart stopped, then lurched back into full gear, sending the blood surging fast and rapid through her veins. She pressed even closer against Wyndham.

"What—?" she whispered.

"The ocean," he breathed. "The main cavern is just ahead. Take the lantern and the tinder box." He pressed a small metal container into her hand, then followed it with the heavy lantern.

"But—"

His gloved hand covered her mouth, and the smell of damp leather filled her nostrils. Somehow she found it comforting.

"Let me go ahead," he murmured.

The briefest scrape of loose pebbles sounded, the merest breath of air stirred, and she stood alone. She stared through the complete blackness at the objects she held, but could see nothing. And even if she could make out their shapes, how on earth did one strike a fire from a tinder box? And if one managed that feat, how did one then go about lighting a lantern? Her Coleman used white gas. She balked at thinking what this one needed.

"Bring the lantern," Wyndham's voice reached her.

"There's no one here."

Lexie started forward, only too happy to comply, running her hand along the wall to find her way. She stubbed her toe, swore softly, then stumbled as the solid rock vanished from beneath her searching fingers at her next step. A cold draft wrapped about her, and the hollow echoing of the surf below warned her she stood in a vast chamber.

"Where are you?" she called, her voice still hushed.

"Over here. Why don't you light the lantern?"

"I don't know how."

An irritatingly masculine chuckle drifted through the darkness.

"Quit sounding so disgustingly superior. I've never had to deal with one of these contraptions before. I'm from a more civilized time, I'll have you remember."

"I beg your pardon." A soft laugh still sounded in his voice.

Though she couldn't be certain, she had a shrewd notion he accompanied the words with a bow. She stuck her tongue out at him, and knew the gesture wasted. Then he was beside her, taking the box. She heard scraping sounds, probably as he opened the tin and removed whatever he needed, then the lantern door creaked.

A moment later fire sprang to life in the waiting compartment as he thrust his hand inside. The wick flared, and a comforting glow filled the cavern, banishing the blackness from about them. Eerie shadows danced on the fringes of their isolated little island of light.

Lexie took a step closer to Wyndham. "What now? Has he been here?"

"We'll have to see."

To her dismay, he carried the lantern across the vast expanse of darkness to where another hung from a bracket hammered into the stone wall. In another minute this, too, blazed with light, dispelling the threatening shadows even farther.

Hugging herself against the cold, Lexie glanced around. It looked all too familiar—and all too devoid of any clues. The rough-hewn table still stood on the far side, with four rickety chairs arranged about it. A deck of cards—greasy and stained, she noted—lay scattered across the wooden surface as if something had interrupted a game. Nothing else, no personal items, no clothing. . . .

Instinctively, she turned to the corner where she and Vaughn had seen that pile of old blankets with the dagger protruding. It stood empty now, without even a barrel or crate to fill the space. She shivered.

Wyndham, still carrying his lantern, strode about, poking into corners, running his hand along the underside of the chairs and table. At last, he shook his head. "Nothing."

"What were you hoping for, labels?"

He grinned, suddenly. "A calling card or two might have been helpful. Well, wherever else your Mr. Vaughn might be, it isn't here."

"Then where?" Exhaustion and tension finally got the better of her, and her throat burned. She fought the tears which filled her eyes, but found it a hopeless task. One slipped down her cheek. "Wyndham, it's my fault if he's in trouble. I've *got* to get him out of here."

The earl set his light on the edge of the table and took a step toward her, only to stop short. "You must not blame yourself," he said after a moment. "I should not have let him ride out alone."

She shook her head, and another tear followed the first. She covered her face with her hands. "I wish I knew where he was. I wish I knew what *happened* to us. I wish we were home."

"So do I."

He spoke with a sincerity that drew an unsteady chuckle from her. "I'll bet you do. This is the second time in as many nights you've been out in the freezing cold in this stupid cavern, isn't it? I'm sorry we've complicated your life. We'll get out of it as soon as we can."

"I know you will." Abruptly, he turned on his heel and crossed to the lantern which hung from the bracket. He extinguished it, plunging the rocky chamber back into dancing shadows. "Come, it's time we returned to the Priory. Perhaps one of the others has had some word of him."

88

"And if no one has?" She bit her lip, waiting.

"Then in the morning we'll go to the authorities." He picked up his own light and strode out of the cavern by the narrow pathway leading back to the abbey entrance.

"And just how much good will that do?" Lexie asked softly of the thin air, then hurried after the vanishing glow.

Chapter Eight

Lexie roused from her fretful doze to a dim, gray light and a dull throbbing in her temples. For a long minute she fought the desire to bury her head under her pillow like an ostrich. None of the search party, which straggled in freezing and miserable in the early hours of the morning, had found so much as a trace of Geoff Vaughn. Lexie's worry left her stomach hurting.

Maybe—just maybe—word had been brought in during the few hours she'd been in her bed. When the farmers trudged out to their fields to tend their animals in the pre-dawn gloom, perhaps one of them found . . . something. Or better, perhaps Vaughn had ridden too far afield, and sought refuge at some hospitable house rather than try to return in the growing dusk with the threatening snow at last starting to fall. And if he'd reached an inn, he would only have had to mention he was a guest of Wyndham's to assure his credit. Clinging to these hopes, she dragged herself from the warmth of the covers.

After pulling on her chemise and gown, she checked her woolly socks which hung over the back of a chair before the fire. Still damp. With a sigh, she put on the stockings and garters borrowed from Miss Langley, and laced up her incongruous but practical sneakers. Water once more waited by the hearth, as did a pot of chocolate and a covered plate containing rolls. Now, that had been thoughtful of the maid, to make her delivery in such silence. The girl must have been advised of the lateness of the hour Lexie went to bed.

Eating the light meal restored her normal equilibrium, and in a more positive frame of mind she went in search of the earl. She found him in the breakfast parlor, staring out the window over the snow-covered landscape. He held a mug of ale, still nearly full, and his creased brow betrayed his uneasy thoughts.

She hesitated just over the threshold. "I take it there has been no word, yet?"

He looked up, then shook his head. "I'll go into Rye as soon as my curricle is brought around. There's a chance—"

"I know. But what if he's *not* there?"

Wyndham drew a deep breath. "Then I must go to the authorities."

"And what are you going to tell them? They thought you were crazy before, remember? How do you think they're going to react to your latest story—that a man who won't even be born for nearly a hundred and fifty years has been misplaced? Or possibly kidnapped?"

A slight smile eased the tension in his face. "No, I think he's my distant cousin from America. As are you, by the by. That will be the easiest—or at least the most acceptable— explanation."

"They will help this time, won't they?" Her fingers crept to where her locket no longer hung, and clenched on empty air.

He met her gaze. "I don't know," he said at last. "They have been remarkably uncooperative, so far."

"I wonder—" She broke off, her eyes widening as a new and very disturbing thought occurred to her. "What if there's a reason for that? What if someone *in charge* is part of this conspiracy? Do you realize, it was never recorded who was involved? What if it's because it was someone important, whose name was being protected?"

He lowered his mug to the table, an arrested gleam in his eyes. "It would explain a great deal," he declared. He stood and paced about the room as if new energy infused him, only to stop abruptly before her. "If you are correct, it must be someone fairly highly placed, probably in government circles."

"Which doesn't sound like it's going to make it any easier for us to find Geoff Vaughn."

"No." Wyndham stared in pensive silence at the Aubusson carpet beneath his feet. "I believe," he said at last, "it will be best if we do not go to the authorities after all."

"And concentrate on locating the owner of the dagger—and hope that leads us to Geoff?"

He nodded. "It's not going to be easy, but at the moment I don't see any other course open to us."

"Rather like looking for a needle in a hay stack, isn't it? I don't suppose you learned anything about knives yesterday?"

"This one does not appear to have been purchased locally—at least it did not sound familiar to any of the shopkeepers to whom I spoke." He cast her a rueful glance. "It would have been easier to describe it if I had seen it myself."

"How many daggers are there around here with heavy chased silver handles set with star sapphires?" She fell silent as she filled a plate at the sideboard. "Can I set myself up as a collector, do you think? Say I have come to England looking for unusual knives?"

"That might work. We would certainly be likely to learn if there are other collectors in the area. But I doubt someone involved in a conspiracy of this magnitude would permit himself to be diverted by so inconsequential a matter."

Lexie pursed her lips. "It's not as if his plans would take up every minute of his time, you know. If he's a collector, he might well be delighted to show off his treasures to another."

Wyndham lounged back in his chair, a slight smile playing about the corners of his mouth. "If you're a collector," he shot at her, "what are you doing in Kent? You'd be far more likely to accomplish your purpose in London."

"Why, that's not the only reason I'm in England." She opened wide, innocent eyes. "I also hope to persuade my distant cousin Lady Agatha into presenting me this Season. I'm in no hurry."

"It might work." Wyndham nodded slowly, but the beginnings of a frown creased his brow. "Unless, of course, our villain recognizes you."

She stared at him, aghast.

"You said he wore a mask," he pointed out. "But you did not."

Lexie sank her chin into her hands and stared with unseeing eyes at her breakfast plate. "I looked very unusual for a person of your time when he saw me," she said, her thoughts racing. "Do you think he noticed *me* so much, or just the picture I presented—my clothes?" She looked up and met Wyndham's steady gaze. "I think I look quite different, now. Maybe if I change my hair, too?"

He shook his head. "Your connection with me will make you instantly suspicious."

"Damn, of course it would. Unless . . ." A new idea formed.

"Yes?" He raised politely inquiring eyebrows.

"He wouldn't make the connection if I'm not already here, would he?"

His eyes narrowed. "What are you suggesting? That you be seen to 'arrive?'"

She nodded, her enthusiasm for this scheme growing. "You could have someone take me to an inn, not too far from here, and I could rent a carriage to bring me back—or better, to Rye, where people would see me arrive. Then I could play my part of cousin/collector, and no one would suspect me of already having been here. You don't like the idea?" she added at his frown.

"Yes, I do, actually. I'm only worried about Vaughn. They wouldn't have captured him again if they didn't think him useful in some way. What is he likely to tell them—about you, about the immediate future?"

"He wouldn't *dare,*" she breathed. "They'd think he was crazy if he told the truth. Wouldn't they?"

"Unless he showed them those peculiar artifacts he carried with him."

Lexie's jaw dropped. "His wallet—" She started for the door. "Where did he sleep?"

Wyndham passed her, and she ran after him, along the hall, up a flight of stairs, then down another corridor. The bedchamber Geoff Vaughn had occupied stood in another wing from the one allotted to Lexie. They entered the large, airy chamber and Lexie glanced about, then pounced on the bedside table. In the top drawer lay a leather wallet. She pulled it out, dragging it open with trembling fingers, and stared down at his driver's license.

A shaky sigh escaped her. "It's all right. He left it. And all his money. If he was wearing your clothes, he shouldn't have anything on him to prove he's from the future."

Wyndham nodded. He took the wallet from her, glanced at it once more as if to reassure himself he hadn't been mistaken before, then returned it to the drawer. "Now to set about finding him before he tries too hard to convince them."

They made their way to the bookroom, where the earl tugged on the bellrope, then paced the length of the chamber, scowling in silent thought. Lexie watched him, while her own mind desperately recalled every fact of regency-era life her reading—both research and leisure— had provided. She could probably carry off the act of being a young lady of this time period—especially with the excuse of being from America to carry her through. When the butler entered, Wyndham rounded on him at once, giving him the gist of their plan.

Only a flicker registered on the man's impassive countenance. "Very good, m'lord. When are we to expect Miss—?" He broke off.

"I'd better have another name," Lexie declared. "Geoff may have told them mine."

Wyndham nodded. "Use Penrith, then. She will need a trunk brought down, and a dressing case, I believe. I'll leave the details to you. Do we have a maid who could accompany her?"

At that, a shadow of doubt crept into Clempson's magnificently bland features. "Not one that isn't known in this neighborhood, m'lord. If I might make so bold as to offer another suggestion?"

"Yes?"

"I have a niece, m'lord, who has recently moved to Dover

from Nottingham. If miss were to carry a letter to her, I am certain she would oblige."

"Then write it at once." He dismissed the butler to arrange for the luggage and send for the traveling chariot to carry Lexie by backroads to Dover. Then he unlocked the bottom drawer of his desk and brought out a large pouch. From this he drew a number of bills. "You will need some money. I'll give more to my groom to arrange for the hire of the chaise and your accommodations for the night. I wish I could send a more proper courier, but we must arrange this as quietly as possible."

Male chauvinism dominated this time, she reminded herself—even for someone so otherwise intriguing. A spark of irritation ignited within her, which she couldn't quite extinguish. "I'm not helpless, you know," she pointed out, her tone as condescending as she could manage. "I'm quite able to make my own arrangements. There's no need to send anyone with me."

A gleam—of surprise? Of a challenge acknowledged?—lit the depths of his bright green eyes. Yet he shook his head. "You're in my time now, not your own."

"Yes, so I am." And despite the chauvinism, she realized with a sense of shock, she liked that idea a bit too much. She had to go home, where she belonged. She rushed into speech to cover her confusion. "I shouldn't need any money, though."

"I want you to purchase some clothing. You can hardly wander about Rye pretending to be my eccentric American cousin—"

"Eccentric?" In spite of herself, she grinned.

"Any young lady who collects daggers is bound to be considered eccentric. But as a Penrith, you will also be expected to present a creditable appearance."

"But won't it take days to have dresses made up?"

"Not if you find ones finished except for the final fitting. We'll order more for you here."

"But I can't let you buy me clothes. I'll only be here for a few days—"

"If you help me find those conspirators, I will owe you a

96

debt I can never repay. Allow me to do this little thing for you in exchange."

She started to protest, changed her mind, and merely nodded. "You *do* find them, according to history, you know. *And* louse up their plans. I'll try to make certain Geoff Vaughn and I don't alter that."

A gleam lit his eyes at her words. "At least you give me hope."

Wyndham's head groom, summoned to his master's bookroom a few minutes later, listened to his orders in thoughtful silence. Twice his gaze flickered across Lexie. What he thought of her—who she was and where she came from—she had no idea. But the simple fact she intended to help find the men who abducted Master Kester and "done in" Master Vincent seemed to prove sufficient to the little man. He promised to have the gig ready in under half an hour.

"The gig?" Wyndham snapped. "She'll freeze."

"That's as may be, y'lordship, but are you wishful to 'ave 'er jaunterin' all over the countryside an' inter Dover in a carriage bearin' your crest?"

"Oh, the devil! Thank you, Huggins. Miss Anderson, I very much fear this will be an uncomfortable journey for you."

"Oh, I'll manage. Just loan me a robe or two. And I demand a hot brick for my feet."

He grinned suddenly. "You're incorrigible, Miss Anderson."

"My disgraceful upbringing."

"Lamentable, I believe, is the adjective you want," he murmured. His gaze lingered on her for a moment, assessing. "No, you will do very well, I make no doubt," he added, and approval warmed his words.

She departed a bare twenty minutes later, driven by the capable Huggins. For the first half hour, neither spoke, the groom concentrating on the road made slippery by the melting snow, Lexie wondering what she had gotten herself into. In the reticule borrowed from Lady Agatha rested a considerable amount of money. More, she felt certain, than she could ever spend. She would have to have a few items, though, if she were to convince Clempson's niece she actually belonged in this time period. That must be a secret only Wyndham and Dr. Falkirk could be permitted to share.

"Where do we go first?" she asked at last.

The groom spared a glance from his horse. "Dover, miss, so as yer can do some shoppin'. If'n you think you'll be all right, I'll leave you with a seamstress, then go and find Mr. Clempson's niece. When we gets back, we'll sees your trunk packed all right 'n proper, then finds an inn for the night. I'll arrange for a post-chaise to bring you back on the morrer."

"Thank you, Huggins." This all seemed such a round-about way of doing things, but she had to cover her trail, or the first time she appeared anywhere in public with Wyndham, the conspirators would realize who she must be—and recognize her as a potential danger, one who might be able to identify them.

She closed her eyes and leaned back against the surprisingly comfortable seat, huddling in her blanket. Already, the bricks had begun to cool. Oh, well, it couldn't be helped. At least the gig had fairly good suspension, all things considered. If only the road weren't so rutted, the ride wouldn't be bad. She dug under the seat for the picnic lunch prepared for them in the Priory's vast kitchens.

Darkness closed about them long before they reached Dover. Huggins stopped the carriage to light the lanterns which hung on either side, and Lexie huddled deeper into the robes, shivering. Her bricks had long since turned into giant ice cubes.

"Not much farther, miss." Huggins urged the horse forward once more—not the same animal they had started with. They had changed three times so far.

At last they drew up before a signpost. Huggins got out and held a lantern aloft, studying the inscribed arms. "Maybe it'll be best, miss, if'n we fetch the young person first after all," he called back to her.

Lexie, tired and frozen, agreed.

They turned onto a winding lane and followed it for perhaps a mile or two, then slowed at a sign on which the lettering "Ruddimere Farm" could just be made out. They traversed the pot-holed and scarred drive to where the lights of a cottage gleamed through the drifting snow. Lexie took the reins from Huggins.

After a moment's considering glance at her, he jumped down. "Won't be long, miss. Thankin' yer kindly."

He strode up to the porch and thumped on the door. It opened, and the interior light silhouetted a woman of considerable girth. The groom handed her Clempson's letter, she ushered him inside, and the door closed, leaving Lexie shivering outside.

Barely five minutes passed before the groom appeared once more, alone, and retrieved the reins from her. "Rebecca Meeker, 'er name is, miss. Just run up to pack a few things, she did."

The large woman, wrapped in a voluminous robe, emerged from the cottage and hurried over to the gig. She clasped a mug of steaming coffee in her hands. With a clumsy curtsy, she presented it to Lexie. "If you would like, miss, to step inside to wait? Dreadful cold, it is."

"Thank you, but it will be quicker this way, I'm sure. If I went inside a warm room, I don't think you'd ever get rid of me."

The woman beamed, pleased. "Well, miss, it'd be an honor to have you stay with us, though I misdoubt me there's a room in the place suitable to a lady like yourself."

Lexie, on the point of correcting her on this mistaken belief, caught herself up. Instead, she said: "It's very kind of you to let your daughter assist us like this. I don't know what I would have done without her."

Her glow increased. "It's an honor, miss, our Becky being able to do somethin' to help his lordship. She's a good girl, she is. She'll hold her tongue, of that you may be sure."

Two more people emerged from the house, a girl of about nineteen and a young man not much older. The youth strapped a small case to the back of the gig.

Lexie slid over on the bench, making room for the girl. In the uneven light, she seemed somewhat plain and rather shy, though little of her features or coloring could be seen beneath her hood and cloak. She bobbed a curtsy, accepted meekly her mother's objurations to be a good, obliging girl and do just as she was told and make her uncle proud of her, then climbed up beside Lexie. Huggins started the gig forward.

"Thank you for coming to my aid," Lexie said as they turned once more onto the road.

"Oh, yes, miss," the girl breathed.

"I suppose it's so late now, we'll just have to find a place to spend the night, but in the morning I'll need to do some shopping. What time should we start back to the Priory?" she added to Huggins.

"Well, miss, if'n it's your intent t'be seen comin' inter Rye, yer'd best set forth right early of a mornin'. Day after tomorrer will be best, I'm thinkin'. I'll make the arrangements afore I go."

Lexie thanked him once more, then fell silent.

Some half hour later, they pulled into the yard of a brightly lit inn on the outskirts of Dover. Huggins jumped down to the snow-covered cobbles, tossed the reins to an ostler, and strode into the building. By the time Lexie, with the wide-eyed Becky trailing after her, joined him, Huggins was well launched into a story of a carriage accident, and how his mistresses had sent him to convey Miss and her abigail to the safety of the inn.

The landlord, a comfortable looking soul with a round, jovial face and a cleanly pressed apron showing only a single smudge, called for his goodwife, and promised Lexie a large chamber with a roaring fire and a private parlor so she could dine in comfort without being disturbed by the inn's patrons. Huggins then arranged for the post-chaise and, amid Lexie's thanks for his assistance, took himself off ostensibly to his mistress's home, but actually to another inn where he might spend the night before beginning the long journey back to the Priory.

Lexie, enjoying the adventure hugely, her avid gaze taking in a multitude of details, followed a chambermaid up the uneven stairs to a low-pitched chamber at the end of the hall. If miss could fancy a braised chicken, a venison pasty, and a fine dish of baked squash, the woman assured her, the covers would be laid out for her in the parlor in half an hour's time. A truckle bed would be set up for her abigail, the woman promised, and hurried away to take care of it, leaving Lexie facing the curious Becky.

The girl eyed her with uncertainty. "Do you wish to change, miss?"

"I would love to, but I haven't anything. Not so much as a toothbrush."

The girl's jaw dropped. "But your trunks—"

"Empty. I told you, I have to spend tomorrow shopping. You will advise me, won't you? I brought very little with me from America, and I consigned it all to a courier, and they have not yet arrived."

If the explanation didn't satisfy the girl, she at least made no further demure. She stripped off her cloak, revealing a head of strawberry blond curls, a pale complexion liberally sprinkled with freckles, a pair of friendly gray eyes and a generous mouth inclined to smile.

She set to work at once, satisfying her sense of duty by taking Lexie's gown and subjecting it to a stiff brushing, all the while bemoaning the fact she could not remove the wrinkles. She then helped her back on with it and turned her attention to Lexie's hair. After only three unsuccessful attempts, she achieved a becoming style.

"We should trim the front, miss," she said with a sigh. "It would look much more the thing, it would."

Lexie studied her reflection in the mirror. Already, she looked very different. Amazing the change to her face, just by pulling up the hair from her neck. Reckless, and knowing the need to disguise herself as much as possible, she directed Becky to cut at will. The girl produced a pair of sewing scissors from her bag, and with a few deft snips shaped the curls about Lexie's face, then teased the thick waves into a fluffy fuzz.

Lexie stared at herself, amazed. She looked exactly like the fashion plates she'd seen—not at all like herself. Immensely pleased with the whole picture she made, she went down to her waiting dinner.

The shopping expedition on the morrow proved satisfying in every way. At their first stop, the establishment of a fashionable modiste, Lexie selected a traveling gown of blue grenadine, a matching pelisse of Gros de Berlin, a dinner gown of peach-colored gauze, and a pale green merino round dress, all of which required only a final fitting and a few hours with a seamstress to make them ready. They would be delivered to the inn late that afternoon, the modiste promised.

Smug at having carried off her act so well thus far, Lexie next asked for the location of a cobbler able to provide her with a pair of slippers and boots suitable to the snowy ground—and large enough for Lexie's feet. In her own time, she'd considered them tiny. Here, they were on the large size.

Her shoe problem solved with surprisingly little difficulty, she then turned her attention to the innumerable other necessary items. Her new abigail advised her on the selection of corsets, chemises, and garters, and Lexie laughingly chalked up her ignorance to the inferior quality of merchandise in America. This Becky seemed to accept. In a very short time, Lexie also owned a toothbrush, soap, a bottle of Milk of Roses, a comb, several pairs of stockings, a reticule, a warm shawl, and a muff. Lexie added to her pile another shawl—a gift for Miss Langley. One becoming bonnet completed her purchases, and they headed back to the inn.

That evening, Lexie went down to her meal in the beautiful peach-colored evening gown with its low scooped neck and tiny sleeves, worn over a white gauze underdress. White slippers covered her feet, and Becky had draped the warm shawl over her shoulders. She could hardly wait to show this finery to Wyndham.

Would he approve of the way she blended into his time? She caught herself up on that thought. He might—but she had better think no more wistful thoughts about him. Damn him for being so exactly what she liked in a man—and damn herself, for allowing this impossible attraction to threaten her normally good sense.

As she reached the door to her parlor, a deep voice rose

from the floor below. "What the devil do you mean, man? You always save that parlor for me."

The landlord's response rumbled forth, too indistinct for her to make out.

"An unaccompanied lady?" the other man exclaimed. "Damme if this don't turn out to be a better evening than I thought." He started up the stairs, only to stop dead at sight of Lexie standing at the top.

She stared back. A tall, lithe gentleman stood just below her, with waving blond hair and bright brown eyes characterized by an innocence belied by his rakish air. A multi-caped overcoat trailed behind him, open to reveal a rust-colored coat and brightly patterned waistcoat, buckskin breeches and topboots glossy in spite of the slushy conditions outside.

He swept off his shallow beaver, awarding her an exaggerated bow. "Well met, lovely lady."

"I doubt that." Prudently, she turned toward the parlor.

He chuckled. "A damsel with spirit. How delightful. Allow me to introduce myself. Grenville Stoke, and very much at your service."

He did not bear the appearance of one who would be easily discouraged. She wished she had a fan to hide her face, it must reflect her growing unease. Time to invoke the magic of Wyndham. She turned her haughtiest expression on him. "I am—Miss Penrith. Perhaps you are acquainted with my cousin, Lord Wyndham?"

The man froze, and his knowing smile melted from his face. "Wyndham?"

"Yes. I've just come from America to stay with my cousin, Lady Agatha Penrith, at Wyndham Priory."

Visibly, he retreated. "Then I am sure we will meet again. My brother's home is not that far distant from there." He swept her a bow, then for one moment met her gaze squarely.

Lexie froze as he turned and descended the stairs, and for a very long minute she stared after him, chilled. Those eyes. . . . Had she seen them before, gleaming from behind a mask in the flickering light of the cavern?

Chapter Nine

"No, I'm not *certain.*" Lexie paced to the crackling fire in the bookroom at Wyndham Priory and stared down into the dancing flames. "I don't think I slept at all last night, trying to make up my mind."

"But you don't think Mr. Grenville Stoke recognized you?" Wyndham demanded.

Lexie shook her head. "Either he didn't connect me with the person in the cavern—or he had honestly never seen me before. I *do* look different, don't I?"

He stared at her for a long moment, and a light sparked to life in the depths of his sea-green eyes. It faded the next moment, and he turned away. "Very. That new way you have with your hair—it suits you. No, you do not look at all the same." He strode to the long, multi-paned french windows and stared out into the blackness of the night. "Did you make your arrival sufficiently obvious in Rye?"

At that, she smiled. "I most certainly did. I made the postboy stop in the middle of town and Becky and I asked everyone where we might purchase flowers to bring to Lady Agatha. The whole town must know by now you have a very peculiar cousin coming to stay with you."

His lips twitched, easing the lines of tension in his face. "Then we've accomplished our purpose, and the delay may be all to the good. Tomorrow we will go into Rye and you may start dropping hints about knives."

She cast him a sideways glance. "I don't suppose you

know anything about them, do you?"

"I've never made a study of them," he admitted.

"Well, I'll just have to wing it, then."

"'Wing it?'"

"Make things up as I go along. I'll never fool a *real* enthusiast, though. So I'd better concentrate on being a collector rather than on knives, themselves." She frowned, her fertile imagination supplying details. "Yes, I think I inherited the collection from my uncle—my mother's brother, of course, not a Penrith—who was a sea captain. No boys to follow in his footsteps, so he left it to me. I keep it up solely in his memory."

A gleam of amusement warmed his expression, and he nodded. "Do you know, I almost begin to believe we'll discover that dagger. And Mr. Vaughn."

She caught the subtle alteration in his voice as he spoke the name. "What's wrong?" she demanded.

Wyndham hesitated, met her worried gaze, and seemed to come to a decision. "Vaughn. I can see why our conspirators might have recaptured him, but they must have realized fairly soon afterward he would do them little good."

Lexie swallowed to ease the sudden dryness of her throat. "Do you think they've killed him?"

"Not necessarily."

His response came a little too quickly for Lexie's liking. "You think it's possible, though, don't you? Oh, for heaven's sake, don't treat me like a baby. I feel responsible for him, I'd rather know the truth."

He crossed to stand before her. His steady gaze rested on her, his expression unreadable. "Guesses are hardly 'the truth.'"

"Neither is patting me on the head and telling me everything is going to be all right."

"Is that what I was doing?"

After a brief struggle with her innate honesty, she admitted: "No."

"You're tired." He moved away from her, toward the fire, then cast an unreadable glance back at her. "Why do you not

106

go to your room? I'll have your dinner brought up on a tray."

Disappointed, she went. They knew so little, guesses proved so frustrating and unsatisfying. And on top of everything else, she'd been looking forward to hearing what he'd say about her new dinner gown. She latched onto that thought as preferable to contemplating Geoff Vaughn's possible fates. A definite appreciation had lit Wyndham's expression when he'd seen her in that blue traveling dress and bonnet. Perhaps tomorrow she'd find out if she passed muster in the peach-colored gauze.

As she started up the great stair, the bell jangled at the front door. A footman standing at attendance opened it, and the flickering candles illuminated the solid figure of a gentleman of medium height. He stepped inside, took his curly beaver from his graying head, and dragged off his benjamin.

"William!" Wyndham came forward to greet Dr. Falkirk. "What brings you out here?"

Lexie turned, but did not go down.

The doctor clapped his hands together, warming them. "It's a cold night," he said. "Demmed cold."

"Come into the library. There's a very tolerable sherry, unless you'd prefer brandy."

"Sherry is most acceptable." He glanced up and saw Lexie. His eyes narrowed, then a slow smile lit his entire countenance. "Miss Anderson. I hardly recognized you."

"It's Miss Penrith, now." Lexie came down to join them. "I'm posing as Wyndham's cousin from America."

The doctor took her hand, smiling. "You'll do very well. Even your friend Mr. Vaughn is managing to carry off a creditable performance."

"Vaughn!" Wyndham exclaimed.

"What do you mean?" Lexie gripped the doctor's hand. "Where is he?"

Dr. Falkirk blinked. "In Rye. Did you not know?"

"Rye? Do you mean he's all right? He's not in trouble?"

Dr. Falkirk's astounded gaze swiveled from her to Wyndham. "You *didn't* know?"

Wyndham drew his snuff box from his pocket. "We did not. We even went back to that dam—dashed cavern, in the mistaken belief our conspirators might have taken him prisoner once more."

The doctor shook his head. "Rum business, that. He should have told you."

"What is he doing?" Lexie demanded. "It's been three *days* since he disappeared. He didn't have any money with him, nothing he could sell. How is he living?"

"He had something to sell, all right." Sadness flickered across the doctor's countenance, and a hint of moisture clouded his eyes. "This." He drew a golden locket on a long chain from the pocket of his coat, and ran a loving finger along its rim.

"You found it!" Lexie breathed, and caught it from him, her fingers tightening on the beloved object. It might give her nightmares, it might even be haunted, but it was all she had of her unremembered past. And now she had it back. Emotion choked her, and she raised her tear-blurred gaze to Wyndham. "Vaughn must have taken it while I slept, so he could get some money."

"Then he must have planned running off like that before he ever asked me to show him about the estate. I suppose I must be grateful if we find he has not sold my horse, as well."

Dr. Falkirk, a puzzled frown creasing his brow, stared from one to the other of them. "You say this locket is yours?" he asked Lexie.

She nodded, and brushed her fingertip over the familiar engraving. She blinked back the moisture that brimmed in her eyes. "What did he tell you, that he found it? I wouldn't put that beyond him. How did you get it?"

"I saw it in the window of a pawn broker's."

"I wish I could repay you. You can have no idea how glad I am to get it back—what it means to me." Her voice broke on a quavering sob, and she averted her face, feeling ridiculous. Wyndham pressed a handkerchief into her hand, and she took it with gratitude.

"But—how *can* it be yours?" Dr. Falkirk asked.

"What do you mean?" Wyndham glanced at the footman, who appeared to be watching them with avid interest. With a muttered oath, the earl ushered Lexie and his guest down the hall toward the bookroom once more.

Dr. Falkirk remained silent until the door closed behind them. He sank into a chair and took the sherry the earl offered him. "It belonged to my daughter," he said at last. "I purchased it for her when she was born—had her name engraved on it. Alexandra." His gaze traveled to Lexie.

"What happened to her?" Lexie asked, her throat painfully tight.

"She was killed, along with her mother, during the blood bath in Paris twelve years ago. Just days before her twelfth birthday."

Lexie clutched the locket, and this time the tears slipped unheeded down her cheeks. "Her mother was stabbed, by that dagger we're trying to find. She—Alexandra—I think she was killed when their wagon slammed into a stone wall."

Both men stared at her. "How—?" Wyndham began.

"The locket. I've had that nightmare, where I see them both killed, for as long as I can remember—possibly as long as I've had the locket."

Dr. Falkirk closed his eyes and leaned back in the chair. His hand trembled as he raised his sherry to his lips.

"Where did you get it? The locket, I mean?" Wyndham asked.

Lexie shook her head. "I was wearing it when I was found—wandering in the streets of Paris, badly burned. I—I can't remember anything before that, just the hospital where I was taken, the woman who found me. The doctors thought I must have been in an explosion. There was a lot of terrorist activity in France at that time." Her left hand touched her right wrist where the scars remained. "The woman was an American—she took me home with her, and raised me. She called me Lexie, because of the locket." She bit her lip to control her quavering voice. "Now I know how I got my name."

Dr. Falkirk shook his head slowly. "I can only wonder

how the locket survived for almost two hundred years, until it came to you. I wonder—" He broke off, staring hard at her. "Yes, there's a definite resemblance. Can you see it, Wyndham?"

"Her eyes, do you mean? They're even paler than yours."

Dr. Falkirk nodded. "My own little Sandra's—" He broke off, then continued. "My sister's are the same, too. And her son. Well, I suppose you're descended from my nephew, then. But how he—or his descendants—obtained Sandra's locket, is a mystery."

Lexie used the handkerchief, then managed a shaky smile. "Perhaps you or your nephew goes to Paris after the war ends and finds it?"

"Yes," he brightened. "Perhaps we do. It had best stay in your possession, then, my dear, since it's yours, now—or in the future, or whatever." His gaze rested fondly on her. "I can't say I mind discovering a great niece. Well, my dear? Will you have me for an uncle?"

"Gladly," she managed to say before bursting into tears.

Lexie woke in the morning to a warm sense of well being she had never before known. She had a family, not just one that accepted her out of kindness, but *real* kin, someone to whom she actually belonged.

Not for a moment did she question the relationship with William Falkirk. The locket *might* have been found or purchased in an antique shop, but that didn't explain her eyes, those strange translucent blue eyes. They belonged to the Falkirk family, and the doctor wanted to acknowledge her as his own blood.

Unfortunately, their little family reunion, as wonderful as it was, could not last. Before she remained long enough in this time to risk contaminating history, she had to locate Geoff Vaughn, find that dagger, and get back where she belonged. Which meant all too soon she would have to say goodbye to this distant great-uncle she had barely met.

Considerably subdued, she rose and stared out the

window. A clear, crisp morning greeted her. Pale sunshine filtered through the scraggly oak and yew branches; the swans basked in a patch of its feeble warmth.

With Becky's help, Lexie donned the blue traveling gown once more, and experienced a spark of pleasure at her appearance. Definitely, the high-waisted dress suited her, as did the up-swept hairstyle with the curls about her face. She felt *pretty*—an unusual occurrence for her. Normally she lived in denim and sweaters. She adjusted the warm folds of her shawl about her shoulders and made her way downstairs.

Lady Agatha sat in solitary state in the breakfast parlor, spooning lemon curd and strawberry jam onto scones. She looked up at Lexie's entrance, and her lined face brightened into a welcoming smile. "You are back at last, my dear." She caught Lexie's hand and drew her down to kiss her cheek. "I understand I have developed a new cousin," she added, a twinkle in her hazel eyes.

"I'm afraid so. I'll do my best not to impose on you too much, though."

"Nonsense, my dear, I shall enjoy myself no end. Am I really to present you in London?"

"No, that you won't have to do. I won't be here long enough. We just needed a plausible story."

"Well," she patted her hand. "I should be only too delighted. Just bear that in mind."

Wyndham entered, looking even more handsome than usual in a riding coat, buckskins and gleaming black boots with their white tops turned down. He greeted his aunt, then his gaze traveled to Lexie. He nodded in approval. "I will have the carriage brought round in half an hour. Will that be convenient for you?"

"Will it be an open one? Your curricle?" she asked.

"Wouldn't you rather travel in a covered vehicle?"

She shook her head firmly. "I've always wanted to ride in a curricle."

"Very well, then." He appeared amused. "Half an hour." He strode out to give his new orders.

Lexie applied herself to her breakfast with a will. They

would find Geoff today, perhaps gain a clue about the knife. And then she might be able to go *home.* . . . That prospect should please her more than it did.

At the appointed time, Charles strode into the Great Hall, drawing on his driving gloves. Running footsteps sounded on the carpeted stair, and he looked up to see Miss Anderson, bonnet and pelisse on, muff in hand, ready to go. He nodded approval of her punctuality—and of the charming picture she presented. He would not mind in the least claiming her for a cousin—though perhaps she should have taken the Falkirk name.

Warmth surged through him at memory of the happiness this young lady had given his old friend. But would the good doctor grieve for her when she returned to her own time? For that matter, would he, himself? With a touch of dismay, he realized he had already come to welcome her presence in his house.

Banishing that thought from his mind, he escorted her outside, then helped her to mount into the low-slung sporting carriage. A footman placed two hot bricks at her feet, and Charles pulled a robe from beneath the seat and spread it over her. Taking his place at her side, he gathered the reins. Huggins let go the horses' heads, then jumped up behind as the curricle swept forward.

The sun, now bright, warmed his shoulders. Miss Anderson raised her face to it, though the chill breeze whipped becoming color into her cheeks. She didn't appear to mind.

The snow on the exposed patches of road had melted, leaving a muddy slush in its wake. They drove in silence for perhaps twenty minutes, with the young lady alternately watching the scenery and his driving. Once when he looked up, he caught her intent gaze resting on his hands, then transferring to the frisky pair. Without having to ask, he knew what thought dominated her mind.

"They have been too long in their stalls without exercise,"

he told her, not bothering to hide his smile. "They should be on better behavior by the time we come home."

"I *did* wonder if it might be safe for me to try driving them," she admitted.

"Yes, I suspected as much. We shall see. At the moment," he drew in rein and slowed as they reached a side lane, "this is the way to Sir Thomas Stoke's home."

Miss Anderson leaned forward, peering down the tree-lined way. Nothing of interest presented itself to their sight. "I wonder if his brother has returned," she said.

Wyndham frowned as he urged his horses into a trot once more. "We are not upon close terms, or I might invite them to a card party. We shall have to think of another way to ask them about knives." He fell silent, his thoughts wrestling with this problem. Unfortunately, no obvious solutions for finding it sprang to his mind.

Miss Anderson shoved her hands deeper into their fur-lined muff. "How are we to convince Geoff Vaughn to leave Rye and return to the Priory with us?"

He glanced down at her. "We will find a way."

She nodded, though as one not convinced. "I only hope he hasn't done anything yet to endanger history."

He caught the strained note in her voice, and barely prevented himself from reaching for her hand. "As you said yourself, he wouldn't dare," he assured her.

They entered the outskirts of Rye, and his companion leaned forward, looking about with fascination. She caught him watching her, and smiled. "I still can't get over how much it looks the same as it does in my time. There are differences, of course, but I can pick out historical buildings I've already visited."

"Streets aren't often moved," he reminded her. "A town's layout will remain very similar as the years pass."

She nodded. "I suppose so. The outskirts grow, but the central parts can't change much."

Charles drove to the far end of the town, then down a side street. At last he drew into the crowded, dirty yard of the dilapidated inn specified by Dr. Falkirk. A carved wooden

113

sign over the door, creaking in the wind, proclaimed the establishment to be the Crown.

He regarded it with disfavor. Mr. Vaughn must have selected it for its inexpensive price, not for any elegance of feature. Several broken-down carriages stood within the walls, and a pack of ill-assorted dogs growled and fought for a bone. Three youths in scroungy garments cheered them on, shouting bets as to the possible outcome.

Huggins jumped to the muddied cobbles and ran to the horses' heads. "Beggin' your pardon, m'lord, I could walk 'em till your done 'ere."

"An excellent suggestion. Twenty minutes?"

"Aye, m'lord." The little man took his place as his master stepped down.

Charles came around to Miss Anderson's side and held out his hand. "You will muddy your gown, I fear."

She shrugged and jumped to the ground—though she held up the hem. "Can't be helped. Let's just find him and get out of here."

Huggins gave the horses the office and turned the curricle neatly out through the gate. Charles watched until they disappeared from view, then took Miss Anderson's elbow. He assisted her over the uneven stones, and she dodged the worst of the mud.

They entered a gloomy common room and paused just inside the doorway. A burly man in a filthy apron stood behind the bar, a greasy rag in his hands. His beady eyes watched them, unblinking, from beneath a shock of grizzled hair. Miss Anderson shivered, and Charles's hand closed over hers where it rested on his arm. He shouldn't have brought her to such a place.

Well, it was too late to return her to the curricle. They might as well get on with the business at hand. He led her forward a step, his gaze circling the dingy chamber. Except for one lanky old farmer who sprawled across a table, snoring, the remaining motley assortment of occupants—all six of them—sat about a table at the far end, near a window so covered with grime that only a meager light shone through.

Miss Anderson hung back, as if she didn't care for the feel of the place. He couldn't blame her. This was not the sort of establishment to which one brought a lady. Nor did the appearances of the men please him, either. One, an unkempt sort with stubbly whiskers, bleary eyes, and clothes badly creased, turned to stare at them. From the looks of him, Charles guessed the fellow hadn't left the table all night. His coarse features settled in a leer directed at Miss Anderson, and Charles's jaw clenched.

Then he glimpsed Geoff Vaughn's thatch of fair hair. Relief struck him, only to vanish the next moment beneath anger. That damned scoundrel had no business distressing Miss Anderson so deeply, when all the while he obviously had been enjoying himself.

He cast an assessing glance over the man. His chin bore signs of needing a shave, and his clothes—Charles's actually—appeared rumpled. He probably hadn't changed out of them since he disappeared three days before. A large pile of coins and vowels lay before him.

Vaughn looked up, and his gaze fell on Miss Anderson. His dissolute features broke into a grin, and he waved.

Charles could almost hear her temper snap.

She stormed away from his side, up to the table where she stood glaring at her erstwhile companion, arms akimbo. "I want a word with you, Geoff."

"Do you?" He turned his enigmatic smile on her. "In a moment, then. We have a hand to finish."

Charles joined them, touching Miss Anderson's shoulder, silencing her before she rushed into ill-judged speech. He directed his cool gaze on the miscreant. "I will see if there is a private parlor in which the lady may sit, Vaughn. This is obviously no place for her. You will join us in five minutes."

For a moment, Vaughn looked as if he would protest, then he merely shrugged. "All right. Five minutes. That should give us time for another hand. Gentlemen?"

Miss Anderson drew a ragged breath. "I wanted to wring his neck," she muttered as they headed for the bar.

Charles fought back a smile. "I may well spare you the effort. I wouldn't mind doing it myself."

She clenched her teeth. "We spent a miserable night searching for him in that rotten, freezing cavern, I've been suffering the worst guilt, and I've worried myself sick. And over nothing! There he sits, looking like he's been having the time of his life. And to top it off, he's been winning a fortune!"

"Do not be concerned. We will not let him use it for the purpose he intends. Ah, my good man," he added as they confronted the surly individual with the greasy rag. "Has this establishment a private parlor?"

It had, or at least what passed for one. The bartender escorted them up a narrow flight of rickety stairs and opened the first door off the dark corridor. Charles ushered Miss Anderson inside, then looked about the chilly, low-pitched chamber with disfavor. None of the furniture matched, and most appeared to have been repaired at least twice. No fire burned in the grate, nor did the bartender make any move to start one. Miss Anderson ran a finger across the seat of a lopsided chair, examined the dust, and wrinkled her nose.

"Coffee, if you please," Charles told the man. "And a cloth with which we might make the furniture fit to sit upon. Also a fire, I believe."

The man cast him a darkling look and slouched out, grumbling to himself.

Miss Anderson held up the hem of her gown to keep it out of the dust, and strolled to the window. Charles followed. Thick grime covered the cracked panes, but he could see down into the yard below. It was deserted now, even the dogs having abandoned their fight, probably for more promising activities.

The man returned with a tray and an ill-favored maid, who swiped at the seats of the chairs with a well-used rag. This done, she laid a fire in the grate, lit it, then beat a strategic retreat. The next moment, smoke gushed forth from the hearth.

Miss Anderson gagged and dove for the window. Charles beat her to it. It creaked in protest, but on the second attempt he managed to fling it wide.

"No wonder she left so fast," Miss Anderson gasped. "She might have warned us."

"A definite mistake on my part to ask for it," Charles agreed. "I should have known the chimney wouldn't draw. Would you care for your coffee over here?" He brought the tray to the window seat.

She had barely poured them each a cup when the door opened and Vaughn strolled in, very much at home. "Well, Lexie." He smiled. "Are you enjoying yourself?"

"It is Miss Penrith, if you do not mind." Charles's voice held a note of reproof tinged with determination.

"Why should I?" Vaughn raised his eyebrows and glanced at the young lady. "What's going on? Why the alias?"

"Because of *you*," she exclaimed. "Good heavens, Geoff, didn't you think your disappearance would worry us? We thought you'd been taken captive by those—those conspirators again."

"Taken captive?" He stared at them for a moment, then burst out laughing. "What a ridiculous idea. Why would they want me?"

"What *did* happen, then? And why did you take my locket?" She returned to the most grievous point.

"Oh, that. Just to get me started, you know. I meant to buy it back, but with one thing and another, it just slipped my mind. Then I ran into Falkirk in the shop, and he'd just gotten it, so I figured it would get back to you eventually."

"You didn't even bother telling him it was mine!"

He shrugged and grinned. "What a time I've been having. Do you know, people actually gamble around the clock? I mean it! I think I've only been to bed twice, and then it's been after dawn."

"What are you playing?" she demanded.

"Piquet and hazard. Getting pretty good at them, too. I've won enough so far to pay for a room here and set a tidy little sum aside, as well. I think I'll get some clothes, next, then look into a little land purchasing. By the end of the week I should be able to buy up a tidy stretch on the edge of town." He winked at her. "I think I'll leave it in trust to myself, in the

117

hands of some bank or law firm that'll still be in business in a couple hundred years."

"You can't." She slammed her cup down on its saucer and came to her feet. "For heaven's sake, Geoff, you've had your fun, but you can't change history. Someone else owns the land when it's turned into that expensive development. Someone *else* makes the money."

"Well, why shouldn't it be me?" Vaughn asked, his tone infuriatingly reasonable.

A frustrated exclamation escaped Miss Anderson. "We've already gone over this. Because you'd be changing history! What if a marriage is made, based on that land as dowry? You might prevent someone's being born!"

He chuckled as he leaned back in the chair and stretched his booted ankles before him. "Don't be so dramatic. I'm not hurting anything. In fact, I'm having a pretty good time. I like this era. A man can win himself quite a tidy fortune. I just might stay."

She stared at him, aghast. "You can't!"

"Why not? It's not like I need papers or ID or anything. It's a hell of a lot easier to set up a new identity here than it is in *our* time. Give me a couple more days, and I'll have enough money to set myself up comfortably."

"No!" She clenched her hands as if to prevent herself from throwing something at him, and drew a deep, steadying breath. Her voice remained calm, though with an obvious effort. "No, you can't stay. Every minute we're here, we're contaminating history. We've got to get out of here, and as fast as we can."

He shook his head. "I think I'm going to stay. For now, at least."

That did it. Charles rose to his feet in one smooth motion and glared down at Vaughn. "The lady said you are going."

Vaughn tensed, but otherwise betrayed no alarm. Only the knuckles clutching the arm of his chair whitened. After a moment, his lip curled. "What are you going to do, knock me out and drag me back to your place? You'll have to keep me locked up if you do. And you might have a slight problem

118

carrying me out past my friends down there. They won't take it kindly if they think they're not going to get their chance to win their money back from me." He shook his head, a sly smile just touching his mouth. "It really wouldn't be smart to try, you know."

Miss Anderson laid her hand on Charles's elbow. "He's right, there's no point in our taking him now, not if he's going to make it difficult. You'd have an awful time keeping him locked up at the Priory. And we can't risk a fight. What if something happened to you—or one of the others—because of us?"

He turned to face her, stung. "You think me incapable of handling myself in a fight?"

"I think you capable of just about anything," she responded, her tone exasperated. "But if you get into a brawl, it will be because of us, which means if anything happens to *anyone*, it will be our fault. We can't risk even *slight* changes to history."

"I'll take that chance," he said through clenched teeth.

"No, please." Her fingers tightened on his arm. "What if you seriously hurt one of those men down there? Try, just for a moment, to think of the long term ramifications. What if he can't work? What if he loses a job? What if—"

"What if you ruin my coat sleeve?" He caught her hand and pried her grip loose. "All right, I will agree—but on one condition. We'll leave you here, Vaughn, until we find the dagger—providing you promise to do nothing and say nothing that might alter the way things are."

Vaughn considered, his countenance lined in a frown. "I'll tell you what. I'll agree to that for three days. If you don't have that knife back by then, the deal's off and I'll do as I like." He stood. "Enjoy yourself, Miss—Penrith." He strode to the door. "Three days," he repeated, and went out.

Charles glared after him. "Perhaps I had better take him with us after all."

She shook her head. "No, I—" She broke off.

"Is something the matter?" He watched as she raised an unsteady hand to her brow, and concern replaced his anger.

"No, just a dizzy spell." She shook her head and managed a smile. "We can't take Geoff, no matter how tempting. We promised. But you can be ready to do whatever you have to at the end of three . . ." Her voice trailed off. She took an unsteady step as if to catch her balance and extended her hand toward him. "Not now," she breathed. "Not without Vaughn."

He was beside her in a moment, catching her elbows to support her, but his hands closed over insubstantial flesh. She shimmered, barely with him, as she flung her own arms about his shoulders, hanging on with her desperation to remain. For a split second she faded, then resumed solid form within his grasp.

Now it was the room that seemed transparent, swirling about them as he clung to her, holding her with him—or did he follow her? Loud raucous music filled his ears, and laughter reached him from the floor below. A small blonde girl sat in the corner of the brightly lit room on a quilted bed, playing with a stuffed doll. Thin volumes of brilliantly colored cartooned pictures lay scattered on the floor.

He had to bring Miss Anderson out of this spell, bring her—them both—back to his own time. He stooped, scooping her up in his arms, holding her against his chest. She turned her head, burying her face against the wool of his coat with a soft cry. Brown curls pressed against his face, tickling his nose, and the tantalizing aroma of violets filled his nostrils.

Slowly, the alien surroundings faded and the dismal parlor once more took shape about them, as unappealing as ever yet amazingly welcome. Still she clung to him, not looking up. He found it difficult to object.

He carried her to the window seat and set her down on the bare boards. Gently he disentangled himself from her grip. She still seemed so shaken—he found her forgotten cup of cold coffee and pressed it into her hands. He had to help raise them to her mouth. She swallowed a mouthful, then took another at his insistence.

"Are you all right now?" he asked as he at last took it from her.

She nodded, though her muscles still trembled. She grasped his hand, and with an obvious effort brought herself under control. "I dragged you *between* times with me, didn't I?"

"Yes."

Her hold on him tightened. "I might be drawn back at any time. Do you realize what that could mean?"

He'd never see her again. That realization left an empty sensation within him.

"If that happens," she continued, apparently oblivious to his silence, "if I actually go *home,* then Mr. Vaughn might be left here forever. I don't dare think of the damage he'll do if he knows he's here to stay. We've got to find that dagger, and quickly. Before it's too late."

Chapter Ten

Wyndham and Lexie lunched at a very different sort of inn on the other side of Rye. Although she had visited the establishment during her own time, Lexie was not in the mood to search out the subtle differences in structure and decor. She sat in the private parlor, gazing into the blazing fire, feeling adrift in a sea of time.

"It's so eerie!" she said at last, after the waiter had removed the covers and departed. "I can see things from the future, yet I don't seem to be really part of it. No one there sees *me*. I don't know if I could really get back that way, or if I'm just going into some limbo between two times."

Wyndham turned from the fire, the poker still in his hand. "Do you mean there is a possibility you might get lost there? *Between?* Not in either one?"

She nodded. Somehow, voicing that fear didn't make her feel any better about it.

He gazed at her for a long minute. "Let me take you to Dr. Falkirk."

Her lips twitched. "Uncle William? That was sweet of him to claim me, whether there's any truth in our being related or not."

"Come." He set the iron rod aside, dusted his hands, and picked up his high-crowned beaver.

"No." She shook her head. "There's nothing he can do for me." Except make her realize that here, in the past where she didn't belong, someone welcomed her, was willing to acknowledge a relationship with her that no one in her own time could. It was enough to make her want to cry at the rotten unfairness of life. Fighting back tears, she surged to her feet. "The sooner I get back to my own time, the better!"

Wyndham's expression remained solemn as it rested on her. "The best I can offer at the moment is the Priory."

Unwanted tears filled her eyes and she turned from him, leading the way to the courtyard. That would do—and all too well.

Wyndham drove in silence. Lexie huddled beneath the carriage robe he spread over her knees, and stared with unseeing eyes at the trees and fields they passed. Slowly, her gaze rose to the sky where dark clouds gathered once more. There would be snow before nightfall—again. What was the weather like in her own time?

No, she reminded herself. Her own time did not yet exist, nor did any of the intervening years. Which meant events *could* change. . . . Damn, she'd been over and over this already.

At last, Wyndham turned down the gravel drive of the Priory, then into the stableyard. Lexie took the blanket from her lap and folded it with care before returning it to its place beneath the seat.

"We are home." He took her hand as she jumped down to the cobbled ground.

"We—oh!" Her gaze flew to his face—so far above her own. "We forgot to look for the dagger."

Wyndham's lips twitched. "Not forgot, precisely. You did not appear to be feeling quite the thing."

"No," she agreed, "not for a few minutes there, at least." She started for the Priory, craving its welcoming fires and warmth. And a stiff drink. Wyndham strode silently at her side, his mere presence a comfort.

"Why isn't Geoff Vaughn affected like I am?" she asked suddenly. She stopped and turned to Wyndham, searching his face for the answer she knew he didn't have. "Why doesn't *he* shift between times?"

For a long moment, the earl said nothing. "You must be more sensitive to it," he answered at last. "Perhaps because of your long association with the locket."

"The locket." She started forward again, and they fell silent once more. As they reached the door nearest the stable, she asked: "Do you think I should *try* to go back the next time I'm pulled like that?"

His eyes clouded, and concern lined his brow as his gaze rested on her upturned face. With one finger he touched her cheek; then he lowered his hand to his side. "No. You don't know where you might end up. What if you didn't make it—and couldn't return here, either?"

A shudder ran through her, and she turned away. "Let's go inside. I'm cold."

She made her way to her room, still shaken. She needed something soothing, some familiar routine, something mundane like washing her hair. In fact, that sounded like a good idea. She rang for Becky, announced her intention, then waited until the hot water arrived.

The procedure required the maid's assistance for pouring while Lexie leaned over the basin. Becky provided her with an aromatic soap and a rinse distilled from rosemary and violets, but the latter, Lexie suspected, wouldn't do a darned thing for tangles.

She was right. And to make matters worse, the contemporary equivalent of a hair dryer proved to be sitting in front of the fireplace with a brush. The concept might appear romantic on the surface, but it took a long time for her thick mane—especially since her wayward curls loved to tie themselves in painful knots.

Despite all her studies of the politics of this era and her fascination with the social aspects, she hadn't realized the full extent of the day-to-day tortures faced by ladies. No cream rinse, no eyeshadow or blush, not even any foundation. At least there were definite advantages to having naturally dark lashes. Lexie didn't need mascara.

But oh, for the rest of it, especially some powder! Her vehemence against using the white lead available at the shop in Dover had startled Becky. At least she had a marvelous lotion of strawberries with which to cleanse and moisturize her face—thanks to the maid's guidance. If she were to remain here many more days in this icy weather, though, she would have to investigate lip salve. Hers were chapping badly.

She dressed with care that evening; it gave her something on which to concentrate, other than her problems. It also resulted in a very creditable achievement. The peach gauze over-robe hung about her in graceful folds, lending her slender figure a grace to which she was not accustomed.

While Lexie watched with awe, Becky set about the difficult task of arranging her freshly cleansed hair. The heavy tresses tended to curl on their own, generally refusing to cooperate without benefit of styling mousse, hair clips, and a blow dryer. Becky, though, wrought wonders, brushing the dark mass until it gleamed with reddish highlights, then coaxing it to the top of her head and arranging it in becoming ringlets.

With the locket clasped once more about her neck and her shawl wrapped warmly about her shoulders, she made her way downstairs. These flimsy gauze gowns were probably all well and good in the blazing heat of summer—or in the Mediterranean climate where the inspirations for these wispy creations had originated two thousand years ago. In the drafty halls of a rambling manor, in the depths of an English winter, they left much to be desired—such as a couple yards of good, warm material right where it mattered.

She reached the main hall, then paused in uncertainty. She should have asked someone where to go, but it never occurred to her. She took a step forward, and in relief saw a door open.

Clempson emerged from a room, and behind him she glimpsed the crimson and gilt decor of a salon. The butler bowed to her, then stood back to allow her to enter. Apparently this was where the family gathered before dinner. She stepped inside and came to a hesitant halt just over the threshold.

Only Wyndham occupied the salon. He stood by the hearth, and the flames glinted off his auburn hair, setting it afire as if with a life of its own. His coat of rich mulberry velvet seemed molded to him, as must be the black satin knee

126

breeches and white stockings. He looked up and smiled, and the light flickered in his green eyes, filling them with a glow that held her mesmerized.

She couldn't be reacting this way, the hazy warning drifted through her mind. Not to a man of a different time. Not, at least, if she had any sense.

Apparently, she didn't. But this was only a physical attraction, she assured herself. Only chemistry. Chalk it up to his sexy air of determination and command, and those blazing eyes . . .

She came forward an unsteady step. His smoldering gaze rested on her face, then roamed over her, taking in every detail of her appearance, lingering at the point where she clutched her shawl just beneath the low scooped neckline. Her heart rate shot off like a rocket, pounding as if she'd jogged a marathon, and she found it difficult to breathe.

Slowly, his gaze returned to her face, burning into her. He raised one hand—then allowed it to drop to his side. He spun on his heel and crossed to the side table where several decanters and an assortment of cut crystal glasses stood.

"Would you care for some ratafia?" Without waiting for her response, he poured a dark red liquid into a glass. The subtle aroma of almonds wafted through the air.

She could only hope it wasn't too alcoholic—the heady intoxication of his presence already bemused her brain, dulling her reason, filling her senses with only him. He held out the glass; as she took it, her fingers brushed his, then somehow his hand closed over hers on the crystal stem. A wave of pure desire washed through her, unfamiliar in its intensity, desperate in her knowledge there could be so little time for them to share.

The fire in his eyes owed nothing to the flames that warmed the room. His thumb trailed across her fingers, and she surrendered to her longings. She swayed against him, and with a groan he gathered her into his arms. One hand closed about the nape of her neck as he drew her face toward his, covering her mouth with his own. His other hand slid under her shawl, caressing her back through the flimsy fabric.

127

She gave herself over to pure sensation. She wanted nothing more than to make love with him. Right now. With the last vanishing traces of her rational mind, she realized the attraction could not be so great—so all consuming—if it were merely physical. She had come to care for him deeply in just a couple of days.

He released her, pushing her away, putting several feet between them as rapidly as possible. He grabbed up his glass and drained it in one swallow, then drew an unsteady breath. "I must apologize." His words sounded as stiff as his bearing. "My behavior was unforgivable. I have never conducted myself in so unseemly a manner."

"If you dare say you don't know what came over you, I'll—I'll pour the decanter over your head."

He turned back, his expression surprised but wary.

Damn the man, did he have to be so devastatingly masculine—and tender at the same time? "And don't blame yourself. I think I've wanted you to kiss me since the first time I really saw you, in your library that night you rescued us."

He strode to the hearth and gazed down into it as he ran an unsteady hand through the russet waves of his hair. "To take advantage of you in so unseemly a fashion is not the act of a gentleman."

"Who's taking advantage of whom?" she demanded.

"Miss Anderson—"

"For heaven's sake, call me Lexie," she snapped. "We're supposed to be cousins, after all."

He kept his back to her. "Lexie." He spoke her name with a caress. "I don't know what is considered proper behavior in your time, but any lady of my acquaintance would have swooned had she been subjected to such treatment."

"Would she? Have you kissed many ladies like that?"

She fancied she heard his teeth grind.

"Not like that." His voice sounded tight. "At least, not *ladies.*"

Her chin came up in irritation. "And just how am I to take that? That you don't consider me a lady?"

"Confound it, that's the point!" He spun about, his

expression haggard. "You are a lady, yet I'm treating you like some common courtesan."

"Only because I asked for it. And oh, how I wanted it. Wyndham—" She took a step toward him, but he held up his hand, stopping her. "Things are very different in my time. *Not* to have acknowledged what we—what we seem to feel for each other would be considered unnatural."

His eyes narrowed. "Have *you* kissed many gentlemen like that?"

That stopped her. "No," she admitted, as remembered sensation washed over her anew. "Not like *that.*"

Fortunately, he didn't press that point. Now, she suspected, would not be the time to admit an affair lurked in her past.

He turned away once more and stared into the fire. "We've acknowledged we feel something for each other," he said, repeating her earlier words. "Where does that leave us?"

She took a reviving sip of the heady liqueur she still clutched, grateful now for its strength. "I don't know. A cross-time love affair is doomed from the start, isn't it? We'll have so little time together."

His hand tightened on his glass, his knuckles whitening, though his lips twitched into a reluctant smile. "A love affair. This is hardly a fit topic, Miss—Lexie. It should bring a blush to any lady's cheek."

"But isn't it much easier to have it out in the open? To be able to talk about it?"

He turned and gazed fully on her, his expression troubled. "I don't know. It makes it far more difficult to behave as I ought. Confound it, the sooner you go back where you belong, the better it will be for me."

The door opened, and he started guiltily. A dull flush darkened his complexion as if he had been caught with her still in his arms. Lexie averted her face, giving herself a moment to recover.

Lady Agatha swept into the room, a petite, comfortable figure in trailing blue silk. She went to her nephew, offered her smooth cheek for his salute, then turned to Lexie. "Well, my dear, you look quite the thing. That niece of Clempson's has definite talent. Doesn't she look delightful, Wyndham?"

"Indeed." He busied himself at the side table, then handed a glass of ratafia to his aunt.

Lady Agatha laughed. "Men. Don't mind him, my dear. He never was one to do the pretty. Not at all a ladies' man, I fear. Tell me, did you have a pleasant day in Rye? Did you learn anything?"

"We found Vaughn," Wyndham said. Briefly, he told her what had occurred—leaving out only Lexie's disturbing experience.

Lady Agatha shook her head as he finished. "Do you know, I can't quite think his behavior is all one could wish. Not that I would care to speak ill of him, you understand, my dear, for if he's a friend of yours—"

"He's not," Lexie broke in. "We—arrived—here together because we were fighting about something."

Lady Agatha clucked her tongue. "There, now if that just doesn't go to show. A gentleman should *never* fight with a lady."

Lexie bit her tongue. If Lady Agatha guessed Vaughn had had her in a hammerlock or half-Nelson, she'd probably have a heart attack—or go off in palpitations or spasms or whatever it was ladies of this era had. Damn, why couldn't she remember more of what she'd read about customs and figures of speech?

They ate in the "small" dining room, a chamber that appeared capable of seating twenty. Lexie didn't ask if there were a larger one; that went without saying. The country seat of an earl undoubtedly had a full complement of state apartments—large, lofty chambers designed for the maximum of pageantry, pomp, and discomfort.

Afterward, they retired to a drawing room where Kester, his two sisters, and their governess awaited them. The two girls eyed Lexie with critical interest, then returned to their game of jackstraws, which Kester appeared to be refereeing. Miss Langley sat in a corner, darning a stocking. Wyndham strolled over to watch his nieces, offering a word of advice to young Miss Marianne, who accepted it with alacrity.

"Miss Anderson—Cousin Lexie, I suppose I should call

you," Lady Agatha laughed gently. "Dear me, pray do not consider it an impertinence. But if I am not to make the mistake in public, I must grow accustomed to it in private, must I not?"

"Please, calling me 'Miss Anderson' sounds so formal and unfriendly. I much prefer Cousin Lexie."

Lady Agatha beamed at her. "I'm so glad, my dear. Do you play?" She gestured to the pianoforte.

Lexie stared at it. "No."

"Miss Langley could play for you, if you'd care to sing," her hostess pursued.

Lexie laughed. "I *don't* care to sing—and if you ever heard me, you'd be begging me to stop. No, I'd much rather listen to someone else."

Lady Agatha coaxed the governess to take a seat at the bench, and Lexie leaned back in her chair, eyes closed, listening to what she supposed to be a Handel sonata. It drew to a close, and the young woman began a second piece with a haunting melody. Her soft voice rose in the first verse of a ballad unfamiliar to Lexie.

Awareness grew in her, and slowly she opened her eyes. Wyndham sat in a chair beside his nieces, but he watched *her* with a steadiness that brought warm color creeping up her cheeks. She stared back, their gazes locking. It was difficult to tell in the candlelight, but she could have sworn his eyes darkened, then blazed with a smoldering need that found answer in herself.

He surged to his feet. "There are some accounts I must go over," he informed his aunt. "If you will excuse me?"

"Of course, dear Wyndham. Do you join us later for tea?"

"I'll take it in the library. I wish you all a good night."

His departure was delayed as first Susan, then Marianne, flung their arms about him in enthusiastic hugs. Lexie fought the urge to follow suit; she couldn't trust herself to let him go if ever she touched him again. At last he left, but a sense of his presence lingered, haunting her, filling her with a desire that refused to be quenched. When she finally retired to her room, it was with a frustrated yearning and darkling thoughts about exasperating men who held their instincts

131

too closely in check.

In the morning, much to her surprise, she found she could face him over the breakfast table with some measure of composure—at least on the surface. By concentrating very hard on the chafing dishes on the buffet, she kept from reaching out to him. Of course, it helped that he gave no sign of wanting her touch.

She seated herself beside Lady Agatha and steadfastly avoided looking at Wyndham. That would only lead to more frustration. Instead, she listened to his aunt's description of the ball her cousin Mrs. Rimbolden intended to hold to relieve the winter doldrums.

At last, Wyndham emptied his tankard of ale and stood. "Do you accompany me to Rye this morning, Miss—Cousin Lexie?"

Lexie stopped with her forkful of ham half-way to her mouth. "When are you going?"

"As soon as you can be ready."

Lexie swallowed her bite whole, washed it down with a last gulp of tea, and bolted for the door. "Let me get my coat."

"Pelisse," he corrected as he caught up with her on the stairs. "And don't forget your bonnet."

She wrinkled her nose. "Why do ladies wear them all the time? They make such a mess out of my hair."

A reluctant smile played about the corners of his mouth. "But you look so charming in it."

With an effort, she matched the teasing note in his voice. "Do I?"

His expression closed and he withdrew once more into himself. "Put it on, then you may see for yourself."

With an exasperated sigh, she ran up the stairs. Wyndham was not a man to be rushed. Nor was he one to lose control of himself. How he had ever come to kiss her last night remained a mystery. How she would get him to repeat it was an even bigger one.

Outside, a light covering of snow lay on the ground, and a crisp breeze ruffled Lexie's curls and flattened her skirts about her ankles. A pity long flannel underwear hadn't been

132

invented yet. She stuffed her hands deeper into her woolen muff. This was a good day for curling up in front of a roaring fire with a rousing good murder mystery or a poignant love story. It was definitely *not* one for braving the elements.

Yet for her peace of mind—for the safety of history as she knew it—she had to begin her search, find that dagger and return to her home time as quickly as possible. And the worst of it was, she *liked* it here, in this simpler time without cars or pollution or the too-fast-paced lifestyle of her own era.

Wyndham, though, standing silently at her side watching his curricle drive up to the door, was the best reason she could think of to rush proceedings along. If she weren't careful, guarding her wayward yearnings every minute, she might distract him from his purpose. Already she longed to lure him into a delightful interlude—and while he was thus occupied, she doubted the conspirators would be idle. They would be able to advance their plans to their hearts' content, free from the earl's historically important hindrance.

When the carriage pulled to a halt before them, Wyndham assisted her to the seat, took his place at her side, and they moved forward with care. Icy patches spread across the road, and more than once the wheels skidded. Lexie gripped the edge of the carriage. All right, maybe she wouldn't mind a car. Especially one with four-wheel drive and an efficient heater. By the time they reached Rye, she was beginning to consider the virtues of using an ice pick to remove herself from the open carriage.

They stabled their horses at the inn where they had lunched the day before. Lexie climbed stiffly down from the seat, cast one longing glance at the flickering light within the windows indicating a roaring fire, then turned resolutely to Wyndham. "How do we begin?"

"With the first pawnbroker we reach," he decided. He offered her his arm, she took it, and they started off.

How *did* one conduct a search of this nature? The question ran over and over through her mind, uselessly, producing no new answers. They strolled down streets almost emptied by the icy breeze, except for those few whose errands forced them out of doors. Lexie huddled closer to Wyndham's side

133

and lovingly contemplated thoughts of the fire they would soon enjoy.

"Here," he said at last.

She looked at the window of the shop, and her gaze met a startling array of mismatched items. Definitely a pawn shop. The proprietor stood behind his display, eyeing them with hopeful interest.

Immediately she went into her act, and laughed in what she hoped was a natural way. "Well, why not?" she demanded of Wyndham.

He mastered his surprise admirably. "Why not, indeed?"

"It will only take a moment. Come on." She dragged him toward the door and pushed it open.

A jingling bell hanging above it announced their arrival, and sent the stoop-shouldered man scurrying behind his counter. He peered at them through thick spectacles perched on his narrow nose. "May I be of assistance?"

Lexie threw a broad smile at Wyndham, as if they shared a joke, then turned back to the thin little man. "I'm looking for knives."

The shopkeeper blinked. "Knives? Have you tried a cutlery shop, miss?"

Lexie shook her head. "I'm looking for something special. Different. It's for a collection."

"I see." The man lifted a key ring from a hook on the wall, then with deliberation unlocked a display case. He sorted through this and at last emerged with three knives which he laid on a cloth spread on the counter.

Lexie picked up first one, then another, turning them over with pretended interest. "What do you think, Wyndham?" She lifted the last, a steel dagger set in a chased silver handle.

Wyndham took it from her, then nodded. "This one, I think. Unless you have more?" He turned his inquiring gaze on the shopkeeper.

The little man shook his head. "Nothing that would interest a collector," he apologized.

"Are there any here? In Rye, I mean?" Lexie managed a fair imitation of ingenuous delight.

"I wouldn't know, miss." He replaced the rejected two into

134

the case, locked it, then informed Wyndham they owed him seven pounds. Wyndham handed over a number of bills.

"Don't you have any regular customers for knives or daggers?" Lexie pursued, determined to get their money's worth of information.

The man cast her a curious glance. "No, miss. Not something as folks usually collect."

"It appears your uncle's collection may be unique," Wyndham informed her. He accepted the package from the shopkeeper and steered Lexie toward the door.

"What a waste!" she declared as soon as they were outside once more.

"It appears this will shortly become an expensive search."

Impulsively, she laid her hand on his arm. "I'm sorry, Wyndham."

He gave a short, derisive laugh as he tucked her fingers more comfortably through the crook of his elbow. "This is my search as well as yours. I'd give a great deal more than that paltry sum to get my hands on the people responsible for my brother's death."

On their necks, she guessed he meant. She couldn't blame him.

They proceeded as fast as they could along the street, avoiding slippery stretches, until they reached another pawnbroker's. Here they repeated their performance, and for ten pounds Lexie found herself in possession of a Turkish dagger set with what she strongly suspected to be a phony ruby, but no useful information.

"Why did you buy it?" she demanded as they emerged onto the frozen flagway. Tiny flakes of white drifted through the sky, settling on their clothes. She wiped one from her nose.

Wyndham unwrapped his new possession and turned it thoughtfully over in his hands, studying it. "You said the one we're looking for is set with a star sapphire, did you not?"

"Yes, but—" She broke off, her eyes widening. "I see. You're going to casually brag about this one, aren't you?"

He folded the paper about it once more and slipped it into his pocket. "Someone is bound to tell me they've seen a

135

better one with a more distinctive stone—don't you think?"

She drew a deep breath, then let it out. It hung in a fog before her face, then slowly dissipated. "Why don't you join Mr. Vaughn in a card game? You might meet some interesting new people."

His lips parted in a broad smile, and the lines of amusement at the corners of his eyes deepened. "Exactly what I had in mind. The Crown has been rumored to be a gathering place of freetraders."

"Free—oh, smugglers. Of course. And possibly some of the men who know the gentleman with the knife." Lexie cast him an uneasy glance. "Are you sure you won't just get mugged and robbed?"

He glanced down at her, and the glint in his eyes took her aback. A touch of danger hovered about him.

"Just let them try," he said with a cheerfulness that did nothing to disguise the threat of his determination.

They were in luck—as far as their purpose went, at least. As they entered the Crown they caught a glimpse of a group of men playing cards in the corner of the tap room. A selection of tankards stood on the table amid the piles of coins.

Lexie lowered her muff, eyeing the tableau with misgivings. "At least it's warm in here."

Vaughn looked up, smiled, and raised a hand in casual acknowledgment as if they had parted yesterday on the best of terms. One of his companions leaned over and said something to him which didn't carry. Vaughn nodded.

"Wyndham," he called, gesturing for the earl to join him.

Lexie shot an uneasy glance at her companion. "I don't trust him," she murmured.

"I thought this was what we wanted. Would you care to wait in the private parlor? I imagine I'll be a little while."

Lexie shook her head. "I'd rather watch."

She eyed Vaughn's five companions, a motley assortment in a variety of garb. One appeared to be a tradesman, another a farmer. Two she couldn't fathom a guess, but doubted sincerely they indulged in any honest work. Certainly their disreputable clothes placed them in the lower orders of society. The last man bore that slick, polished air of a professional gambler. Dress him in black with a white ruffled shirt, and she might be staring at Bret Maverick—only a lot less amiable.

Vaughn didn't bother performing any introductions. He merely invited Wyndham to join them. The earl settled Lexie at the next table, ordered coffee for her, then drew up a chair and took his place. Lexie, uneasy, settled back to watch proceedings.

Three hands of whatever they played passed, and still Wyndham made no move to bring out his dagger. What on earth was he waiting for? She tapped a finger against the side of her chipped cup in growing impatience. Or did he fear looking too eager? It had to be done in a casual manner, she supposed.

She drained the last muddy dregs, then went to the tap where the bartender—wearing the same soiled clothes he had the day before—ran a dirty cloth over the bar. "More coffee, please. And do you have another pack of cards?"

He produced both for her, she told him to put it on Wyndham's tab, and retreated once more to her table where she shuffled and dealt out a game of solitaire.

Nothing new happened at the other table. Wyndham appeared to be losing heavily, for the pile of coins before him had dwindled to almost nothing. Nor did she like the way the gaze of the gambler—gamesters, they were called in this time—rested on the earl. Was it just speculative, or was it something more? He eyed Wyndham much as a child might eye the last cookie in a jar.

The man's lips twisted into a slow, oily smile. "Not your game, m'lord?"

Wyndham laughed easily and tossed down his cards. "Perhaps not my day."

"Maybe your luck will change at something else. Piquet, perhaps?"

Wyndham inclined his head.

"Would you care to join me in a hand?" The gamester rose and signaled the tapman, who hurried over with another deck.

Interesting, that. Had the man been watching the players,

waiting for just such a summons? Pluckable pigeons must be a main course around here.

Wyndham and his dubious new friend retired to another table. After an overly polite exchange involving the stakes and who should deal first, the gamester—Mr. Jessup, she caught the name—shuffled, Wyndham cut, and the man dealt. Each declared points, sequences, and sets, then followed a rather mystical exchange Lexie couldn't quite see. Really, she was going to have to learn the game. Perhaps she could talk Wyndham into teaching her this evening.

At the moment, though, this Mr. Jessup interested her more than the cards. She couldn't shake off the feeling she'd seen him before. Had he been one of the conspirators? Perhaps the man in the mask—with the dagger? No, he didn't seem tall enough. *Had* he been in that cavern? Or was she so desperate to find that knife she was creating familiarity where none existed?

The game continued. When the last card had at last been played, Wyndham appeared to be the winner. Mr. Jessup laughed smoothly and insisted on another hand. This, also, Wyndham won, and they embarked on a third.

By the fifth, the gamester glowered across the table, watching Wyndham's every move as he dealt. He ran a finger along the edges of his cards, then threw them down. "You've notched them!" he shouted.

Abrupt silence filled the taproom as the men at the other table turned to stare.

Slowly, Wyndham lowered his cards, his brow deeply furrowed as he watched the gamester through slitted eyes. "You will explain that statement, if you please."

His voice, dangerously soft, sent a shiver through Lexie. She started to rise, then hesitated.

"You will be the one to explain, if you please, my lord." Mr. Jessup surged to his feet. "You have won every hand, and now I find the cards notched. What am I to think? What is anyone to think? In a word, my lord, you are a cheat!"

Lexie gasped. In her own time, such a statement would provoke a fight. In this era—no, Wyndham wouldn't—couldn't!—allow himself to be dragged into a duel.

138

The earl rose slowly, his complexion unnaturally pale, the rigidness of his mouth betraying his careful control. "Perhaps you would care to reconsider that statement." He spoke through gritted teeth.

The gamester's lip curled. "I would not. I think it portrays the situation very well. If my meaning is not clear to you, perhaps this will be." He reached over and grasped a fine leather glove that lay beside his place at the other table. Lightly, he flicked it across Wyndham's cheeks.

A dangerous gleam lit the earl's eyes. "If you were a gentleman, I would call you out for that."

"If *you* were a gentleman, there would have been no need for my action."

Wyndham's hands twitched with his effort of control. "Your friends will hear from mine."

The man shrugged in an offhand manner. "Why not settle the matter here and now? No need to involve others—who might involve the authorities." He glanced at the disreputable men who watched them, some grinning openly. "Mr. Vaughn can act for you." He gestured toward the tradesman. "You, Mr. Walling. Set it up for the morning. Pistols at twenty paces?"

Chapter Eleven

Lexie stumbled as she scrambled to her feet, knocking over her chair. She reached the earl in three running strides. "You can't do this, Wyndham." She clutched his sleeve.

Gently he freed himself from her grip. "I cannot draw back."

"When did you step forward?"

His inscrutable gaze rested on her face, then turned back to the other men who now stood in a huddle, conferring. "This is an affair of honor, Miss—Cousin Lexie. I cannot expect you to understand."

"You're right about that. Your stupid rules shouldn't apply in a situation like this. It's a set-up, can't you see it? That man notched those cards himself! And you're walking right into his trap."

"Am I?" His eyes gleamed. "Very well, then."

She seethed in exasperation. "They're setting this up to murder you!" she hissed at him.

His unnerving gaze returned to her face. "Have you that little opinion of my abilities?"

"Quit being so damned—*macho!* Chauvinistic. Whatever. Can't you just be reasonable for a moment?"

His jaw clenched. "I said this is an affair of honor. Go upstairs to the private parlor. I will call for you when this matter is settled."

"Oh, go to—the devil!" she exclaimed, borrowing from his vocabulary. She turned on her heel, grabbed up her muff, and stormed out of the inn. Men were such damned, stubborn fools! He'd go and get himself killed just because of some ridiculous obsession about not losing face. It made no sense.

And it would be because of her, and Vaughn. She couldn't let him die—she couldn't allow history to be altered. He had to stop the conspirators from aiding Napoleon to invade England. He had to live. . . .

She halted in the courtyard, stricken. He had to live. Not just for history, but for himself. She wanted him to have a long, wonderful life—even if she couldn't spend it at his side.

But what could she do to save him? He'd made it obvious she didn't have the least shred of influence over him when it came to an affair such as this. So who did? Not any mere "female," that much was certain. Men didn't seem to consider the fairer sex to have any sense of honor. So who . . .

Dr. Falkirk. Uncle William. The briefest warmth eased the chill in her heart at thought of him. She would tell her new-found relative everything, and he'd convince Wyndham to see reason. He'd probably be at his house, unless he were out on a call. She'd try his home. . . .

Except she didn't have her car. She might be able to hire a carriage—if she had any money. Her troubled gaze fell on Huggins's liveried figure, standing aloof from the ill-kempt ostlers and stable lads.

She forced her features into a calm smile and walked over to him. "Could you take me to see Dr. Falkirk, Huggins? His lordship will be busy for some time, I believe."

The groom eyed her, as if assessing her request. "Certainly, miss," he said at last, and turned to his horses.

If only Huggins would hurry. She cast an uneasy glance over her shoulder toward the inn's door. Wyndham might reappear at any moment, his business settled. She had to reach Dr. Falkirk . . .

Huggins swung onto the seat of the curricle, turned the matched bays, and brought them abreast of her. As she grabbed the side of the carriage and jumped up, an all-too familiar footstep sounded on the cobbles behind her.

142

She froze for a split-second, then took her seat and managed a false smile for the earl. "I thought you'd be longer than that," she said with forced brightness.

The groom threw her a suspicious glance, then handed the ribbons to his master.

Wyndham, his brow thunderous, took his seat. "Where were you going?" he demanded.

Hot color crept into her cheeks, and she looked down, not meeting that piercing glare. She could lie, of course, but he'd have the truth from his servant. "Dr. Falkirk. I thought I'd pay him a visit."

"The devil you did," Wyndham muttered. He gave his pair the office, and they bounced forward over the uneven stones through the gate. "I'll thank you not to meddle in my affairs."

"It wouldn't be your affair if it weren't for me!"

He gazed down at her, sparing his attention from his mettlesome pair. "You do not understand the rules governing the conduct of a gentleman."

"What about the ones governing the conduct of traitors and conspirators? Please, Wyndham." She caught his arm, causing him to jerk his ribbon and set the off horse's head shaking in vigorous protest. "That gambler—Jessup—looked familiar to me. I'm fairly sure he wasn't the man in the mask, but he might have been one of the other men in the cavern."

A grim smile just touched his lips. "Yes, I suspected as much. Interesting, is it not?"

"Interesting! And I suppose you'd describe being murdered as fascinating? If you guessed, why did you agree to this crazy duel?"

"I didn't see any alternative."

She stared at him, nonplussed. *"Don't* meet him."

Infuriatingly, he shook his head. "I cannot draw back from a meeting."

"He wants to kill you. And if you hadn't been playing cards—because of Geoff Vaughn—he wouldn't have such a marvelous opportunity."

He kept his head straight, but cast a sideways glance at her through his lowered lids. "Are you afraid of changing the course of your precious history?"

"No! I mean yes. I mean I don't want you killed."

His hands tightened on the ribbons, this time causing both horses to protest. "You seem quite certain he has only to aim a pistol at me for me to be dead," he said, his voice cool.

"Quit being such a little boy about this," she snapped. "I'm not implying you're not the world's greatest shot. For all I know, you're another Dead-Eye Dick! But what makes you think he's going to play fair? If he's one of the conspirators, then he means to see you killed, one way or another."

He nodded. "Exactly what I thought. Who, by the by, is Dead-Eye Dick?"

"A sharp-shooter. Never mind that. If you *knew* this was a set-up, why did you walk into it?"

"I was offered no choice. And now that I think of it, it seems a better chance to find our conspirators than wasting days asking around after knife collections."

She bit her lower lip. "Look, you don't have to fight him, do you? Can't we just watch him? He's bound to report in to their leader sooner or later."

"But this way, I am aware of the nature of my danger. They have been at such pains to assure it will not look like a simple murder. Which means they will make no attempt on me until the morning."

"And if they fail then?"

His brow furrowed. "I do not believe they will risk anything—such as killing me outright—which might give credence to my tales of conspiracy. No, even another 'accident' such as befell my brother might raise suspicions. A duel is their best chance."

They fell silent for some time while the earl maneuvered the bays through the street crowded with carts and wagons. When they reached the main road that would take them back to Wyndham Priory, though, he turned down a side lane.

"Where are we going?" she asked.

His gaze rested on her fleetingly. "You said you wished to pay a morning call on Dr. Falkirk."

"Oh, thank heavens! You *will* tell him. I was afraid you'd go out there tomorrow alone."

"I desire a witness to the proceedings. And it is customary for a doctor to attend affairs such as this."

She swallowed. "What are we going to do?"

"*I* am going to meet Mr. Jessup in the morning, of course. And see who else turns up."

"*I* see. And then you and Uncle William are going to surround them all—by yourselves—and place them under arrest?"

He cast her a withering look. "I admit the situation is not all one could wish."

Nothing more could she get out of him. Nor, to her further distress, could Dr. Falkirk offer any helpful plans. He would come, he promised, and could only hope his presence would deter any blatantly murderous activities.

A strangled cry of frustration escaped Lexie. "Can't we at least go to the authorities?" She looked from one to the other of the two men, pleading.

Wyndham and the doctor exchanged glances. "It would do no good," the earl said.

Dr. Falkirk pressed her into a chair, assuming his best bed-side manner. "The Horse Guard has already dismissed the matter, as have the Customs Land Guard, my dear."

"But this duel—"

Wyndham paced to the window of the cozy salon. "I lack proof of a conspiracy. This would be treated as a common meeting, and both Mr. Jessup and I would find ourselves under arrest."

Lexie clenched her hands in her lap. "That would be better than dead, wouldn't it?"

"And preferable to being forced to flee the country for killing my man," he agreed. He returned to stand before her. "But I would be equally unable to stop the conspirators' schemes."

Her eyes widened. "Do you think that's their plan? To lay information against you—or whatever it's called?"

He considered a moment, then shook his head. "I believe they would prefer a more permanent solution to the problem I present them."

She glared at him. "Yes, I'm sure they would, so why fight

it? You just run along tomorrow and let them shoot you. I'm sure that'll make everything much easier for everyone."

He stormed to the hearth, then spun back to face her, his expression thunderous. "That is not my intention."

"Well, how are you going to prevent it? Call in the marines? But you said they won't come."

"I said—"

"Charles." Dr. Falkirk laid a restraining hand on his shoulder. "My dear great-niece, this is a meeting from which it is impossible for Wyndham to draw back. As a female, you cannot be expected to understand—indeed, it is most improper you should have heard anything about it at all. But rest assured, they will count upon this Mr. Jessup's marksmanship. My presence will prevent anything untoward."

She bit her lip to prevent herself from uttering further protests. They would do no good. These two suffered from a terminal case of chest-beating masculine mentality, which to her mind equated with an opossum's determination to waddle across a freeway. Common sense just didn't measure up.

She rose and followed Wyndham back out to the waiting curricle, her heart heavy. He shouldn't *be* in this position. This was all *her* fault, for she had brought Vaughn—and the denizens of that disreputable inn—into Wyndham's life. If anything happened to him . . . She couldn't bear that possibility. Even the thought of him injured caused a pang of anguish to lance through her.

To her further distress, the earl spent the remainder of the day setting his affairs in order. Lexie alternated between pacing about the bare-branched rose garden in the icy air and popping into the library to remind him to include some ridiculous item in his will. Her attempts failed; he seemed oblivious to both her sarcasm and her fear.

She did, though, succeed in exasperating him. Upon hearing her suggestion that his second footman would undoubtedly be grateful to be remembered with a shoe horn, he grasped her shoulders and gave her a gentle shake. "I can do very well without your assistance."

"Can you? Look what you're doing! Writing out instructions for the spring planting."

"I am merely preparing for any contingency. I have no intention of being killed tomorrow, I assure you."

"It's a set-up! He won't be taking any chances!"

His eyes narrowed. "Do you think I lack courage?"

"No, brains!" she shot back.

A sudden gleam lit his eyes, her only warning. He spun her about, marched her through the door, then slammed it behind her. The tell-tale sound of a key turning in the lock reached her.

Dinner proved a strained affair. Only Lady Agatha, in blissful ignorance of the impending disaster slated for the coming dawn, chatted happily. When at last the silence of her two companions brought home to her that all was not well, she rounded on Lexie.

"There, my dear, you don't look at all the thing. You're tired, I make no doubt. All this walking you do in such dreadful weather. Why do you not go up to your chamber immediately after dinner, my love? I'll have Mrs. Clempson bring you a warm brick for your bed."

"I can always use it to hit Wyndham over the head," Lexie muttered, too softly for her hostess to hear. Yet she knew herself too sick with worry to remain in the woman's vicinity without arousing her suspicions, so when Lady Agatha retired to the drawing room, Lexie climbed the stairs to her bedchamber.

The hot brick proved not to be Lady Agatha's only offering. That motherly woman arrived shortly, interrupting Lexie's agonized pacing. With her, Wyndham's aunt brought her abigail and an assortment of remedies including laudanum, a vinaigrette, pastilles, and several feathers which it appeared the maid intended to burn and wave under Lexie's nose. Lexie thanked them but declined their proffered aid, and escorted them firmly out of her room.

She wanted to be alone—no, what she really wanted was Wyndham there so she could tell him what a fool he was. She wanted him safe, the duel over—or better, canceled. If he were killed . . . emptiness welled within her, an aching void

147

which she could not fill.

Restless, just to give herself something to do, she changed into her nightrail, but did not get into her warm bed. What would be the point? She would never sleep, not with the duel hanging over her like a razor-sharp sword of Damocles. She curled into a chair, drew a comforter over herself against the chill, and tried in vain to think of some way to prevent the coming meeting.

She passed an uncomfortable night, dozing briefly, during which times nightmarish images of Wyndham, wounded and dying, filled her mind with distressing clarity. Just before three o'clock she woke fully, and rose to relight her fire—and every candle the room possessed. Light flooded the chamber, driving back the physical shadows. It failed to touch the ones which lurked in her heart.

One of the many things Wyndham hadn't told her was the exact time of his meeting. Dawn would come late during these short winter days, she assured herself, but it would take a while to get to whatever field they would use. At least they'd have to wait for the rising of the sun before they could begin their deadly game. Floodlights wouldn't be invented for many years, yet.

She dressed quickly in the blue gown and pelisse, then went down to the bookroom. This showed signs of the earl's having made a late night of it. A glass with the dregs of brandy stood on an occasional table by an armchair, which had been positioned before the hearth. The smoldering remnants of the fire remained, though it had mostly been reduced to ash. Lexie added more sticks, fanned it into a blaze, then sat on the edge of the chair, her hands clenched in her lap, fighting back her rising panic.

Almost an hour of intolerable strain passed before the door opened behind her and someone entered the room. She hunched down into the upholstered cushions, her desire to delay the impending confrontation outweighing her need to see him. Heavy, booted footsteps crossed the Aubusson carpet, then paused by the desk. Paper rustled against paper as he picked something up. Lexie peeked around the edge of the high wing-back. He held a single folded sheet in his hand, staring at the inscription above the wax seal.

"Your will?" she asked.

He looked up, startled, and a muscle twitched in his cheek. "What are you doing up?"

"I'm going with you."

He dropped the sheet. "You're *what?*"

"Going with you. No, don't yell at me, you'll wake the house. I know you don't approve, but I want to see if I can identify anyone from that cavern."

He appeared to have been winding up for a monumental tirade, but that stopped him. He glared at her, bereft of any scathing comment.

She managed a tremulous smile. "Don't worry, I'll stay well in the background. You might even want to drop me off before we reach the field so I won't be seen. That way I can keep an eye out for anyone else who shouldn't be there."

"I haven't room for you in my carriage. I'm picking up Mr. Vaughn."

She rose, but kept her gaze focused on the fire. "Isn't your second supposed to call for you? I thought that's the way they did it in books."

"My *second* hasn't a vehicle."

She nodded. "Then Dr. Falkirk can take him. I'm riding with you. I don't want anyone shooting you from behind."

"They would not dare make this an obvious murder. I can manage this very well on my own, madam."

"Only if you could identify the men from the cavern. Which you know very well you can't. I'm sorry, but I'm coming. I've got a dagger to find." And an idiotic, infuriating, and wonderful man to protect, but she left that unsaid.

To her relief, he made no further protest, merely stuffing the paper out of sight into a drawer. He lit a taper, and with this to light their way, they traversed the corridor to the kitchens where they obtained a lantern. This cast a bright swath, illuminating the stone path across the herb garden toward the stable yard, where lights indicated Huggins was already awake and preparing the bays. Small carriage lamps hung on either side of the curricle, throwing a dim glow

149

around the yard.

Huggins stared at Lexie in amazement, cast a dis-approving look at his master, but continued his work in silence. Lexie huddled in her pelisse and wished again she'd been wearing her down jacket that morning so long ago when she went wandering along the bottom of the cliff.

"Cold?" Wyndham asked. Only polite solicitude sounded in his tone.

She nodded, trying in vain to keep her teeth from chattering.

"Why don't you go back to your room, then?"

"What, and miss all the fun?" She looked up, met his look, and a flood of emotion washed through her, filling her throat and burning her eyes. He *had* to be safe . . .

His expression softened, then grew more intense as his gaze burned into her. He touched her cheek, allowing his finger to trail to her lips. Yet when he spoke, he kept his tone stern. "A lady should know nothing about such affairs as this."

"I—I thought you'd decided I wasn't a lady." She found it difficult to command her voice, and knew more than her fear for him lay behind this.

Huggins came forward, and Wyndham drew his gaze from Lexie as if with a tremendous effort and went to meet his groom. They drove through the pre-dawn chill in a silence neither seemed anxious to break. With every step the bays took, Lexie's sense of dread grew stronger, until it was all she could do to keep from screaming.

They reached Dr. Falkirk's neat little house and found him on the point of departure. His eyebrows rose at sight of Lexie, but he refrained from comment, thereby winning her fervent gratitude. He acquiesced to her suggestion that he be the one to collect Vaughn, and, that detail settled, Wyndham headed toward the field on the outskirts of Rye where the meeting would take place.

No light yet eased the blackness of the sky as they approached the town. The earl slowed his pair, searching through the darkness for the turnoff, and Lexie touched his elbow.

"Let me out here. You don't want anyone to see me, do you?"

His lips twitched. "Do I have a choice in the matter?"

"I'll be careful. Through there?" She jumped down as he drew to a stop. She hesitated, then reached back, catching his arm. "You be careful, too."

"It would be more to the point for me to be accurate."

She bit her lip and shook her head. "If I see anyone lurking in the bushes with a pistol, I'll warn you."

He grabbed her hand as she released him. "Don't stand where *you* might get hurt. The only possible place for another man to stand will be *behind* my opponent. They will have to fire at the same time, or risk the good doctor's raising a hue and cry about murder."

A painful dryness rasped at her throat, and she turned her hand in his, welcoming his clasp. "Is the risk you're taking really worth it? Is there really *no* other way?"

His fingers tightened over hers. "We're both convinced this is a plot by the conspirators. What better chance will we have?"

She nodded. For a long moment she stared through the darkness into the deep gleaming pools of his eyes, their smoldering glow unmistakable. His pressure on her hand increased, and gently he drew her toward him.

With a soft cry she threw her free arm about his neck, pulling his head down to meet hers, her mouth seeking his with a desperation that overruled all else. Sensation shot through her, and for one blissful minute all thought, all worry, ebbed from her mind. Only Wyndham—Charles—existed for her.

Gently he removed his hand from hers, and reality returned, hitting her like an unwelcome nightmare. His fingers brushed her cheek, his gaze seeking hers once more, but the magic had faded, replaced by her fear for him. With reluctance she stepped away from the curricle, and he drove on.

He wouldn't be harmed, he *couldn't* be. Chilled to her very soul, she turned away and trudged along the snow-covered lane until the approaching dawn made it possible—and

151

necessary, if she were to arrive unseen—to cut across a muddied field and proceed through a spinney.

She had barely reached the sheltering cover of a row of high shrubs when a closed carriage turned down the road, then pulled up near Wyndham's vehicle. Two men climbed down and Lexie peered through the still-green branches of an elm. The gambler Mr. Jessup and his second—the Mr. Walling who looked like a businessman. The newcomers studiously avoided looking at Wyndham, merely retreating a few paces to wait in silence.

If they tried something, Lexie didn't know what she could do to help. She held her breath, her heart pounding, her nerves raw.

At last, the doctor's gig joined the others. As soon as it drew to a stop, Geoff Vaughn jumped down. Even from her distance, Lexie could see the avid excitement on his face. Like a little boy getting a rare treat.

At that moment, she hated him. Didn't he realize his crazy idea to win money might be about to get Wyndham killed? He had no business in any of this!

Apparently, someone had instructed Vaughn in his duties as a second. After exchanging a few words with Wyndham, he went to the curricle and drew a wooden box from beneath the seat. They had ridden out with the dueling pistols, Lexie realized, and felt sick at the thought.

Her wave of nausea passed, and she looked back to see Mr. Jessup holding one of the deadly guns and Vaughn watching Wyndham load the other. Next Vaughn and Mr. Walling paced off the field, and Wyndham and the gambler took their positions. Now, if this were a trap, a third man must also take his place . . .

Lexie crept to the side, her intent gaze searching. No one had driven up, no one seemed to be lurking in hiding except herself . . . *Could* this be a straight-forward duel? Had Wyndham placed himself in danger for *nothing?* A dull pain in her hand penetrated her consciousness, and she eased her grip on the biting bark of the tree behind which she huddled.

Both Wyndham and his opponent had buttoned their coats to their throats and now stood facing sideways. No jewelry or buttons gleamed on either of them, nothing that might afford their opponent a target. Lexie forced herself to resume breathing. The seconds consulted, Dr. Falkirk turned his back, and the businessman raised his arm. A white handkerchief fluttered in the icy wind, gripped between his two fingers.

Lexie scanned the brush behind Mr. Jessup. No one lurked there . . .

Light glinted among the leaves as the rising sun touched a metallic object several yards to Mr. Jessup's left. A dark shape—a man enveloped in a voluminous coat, a hat pulled low over his face—straightened from a crouch, emerging from his cover. He clasped a pistol in his hand.

As the businessman released the handkerchief, Lexie screamed, breaking the stillness of the dawn.

The shots—all three—rang out.

Chapter Twelve

For a long, paralyzed second, no one moved. Then the pistol fell from Mr. Jessup's slackened grasp. He stared at Wyndham, mouth open, for a full four seconds before clutching his right side and dropping to his knees, his eyes wide with shock.

Lexie recovered. The other man. . . . While she just stood there, he escaped, crashing through the underbrush, his need for silence past. Lexie dove after him, determined to get at least a glimpse of his face. Wyndham must not have gone through this for nothing.

Before she could cross the dueling ground, a horse, its rider crouching low in the saddle, broke free of the entangling branches and galloped across the field beyond. Lexie slowed, panting, a silent scream of frustration welling in her. She'd failed. . . . Depressed, she turned back.

Dr. Falkirk knelt by Mr. Jessup, but he stared after the rider. Geoff Vaughn and Mr. Walling remained as if rooted to the ground. Her gaze narrowed on the latter; Mr. Walling did not appear in the least surprised. He'd expected this— had waited, in fact, to give the signal to fire until that other man had taken aim.

Wyndham hadn't moved, either. He still stood in his place, the pistol hanging in the loose clasp of his right hand. He transferred it to his left and walked to where the two seconds stood.

Vaughn, abnormally pale, accepted the gun into his

trembling grasp, then stuffed it into its case. Mr. Walling retrieved the other, gave it to Vaughn also, then returned to stand beside his principal while Dr. Falkirk examined the wound.

"The pistols should be cleaned," Wyndham said.

Vaughn turned a blank stare on him, then held out the case.

The earl took it but made no move to open the cherry wood box. He stared at it as if unable to make up his mind, then simply replaced it in his curricle. For a long moment he stood beside the carriage with his head bowed. As Lexie reached him, his left hand came up to clasp his right arm just below his shoulder. Vivid scarlet seeped between his fingers. The stain showed dimly against the black fabric of his coat.

"Charles—" Panic welled in her, and she barely prevented herself from throwing her arms about him.

The graze stung abominably. Flesh wounds frequently did, Charles reminded himself. He managed a tight smile for Miss Anderson's benefit.

The blood drained from her face, leaving her pale and stricken. "Your arm—"

"The merest scratch, I assure you. My coat, however, has been ruined."

"Your *coat?*" Tears started to her eyes. *"Damn* your coat. *You* might have been ruined. I mean killed." She choked back a sob and turned away, groping through the reticule dangling at her wrist.

"Here." He drew a handkerchief from his pocket and pressed it into her hand. The pain had lessened, he noted—probably a result of his slowing heart rate and easing tension. Having to remain calm for Miss Anderson's sake provided certain benefits, it seemed.

She drew a shuddering breath and gave a final dab at her eyes before handing back the cloth. "Where is Dr. Falkirk? We'd better get your arm looked at. It must be hurting like mad." She looked over her shoulder. "Doctor! Uncle William!"

The doctor knotted his bandage and abandoned his patient with a curt order for his second to take him in charge. After gathering his equipment back into his bag, he strolled toward them. "Well, I must say—" He broke off. "So one of them did hit you. I thought you stood there too long." He shook his head. "Let's have a look at this."

Miss Anderson's worried gaze rested on the torn, bloodied fabric. "I wonder which one did it?"

"Let us hope it was Mr. Jessup," Charles said, "and he is now incapacitated for a while."

"Bad business, this." William Falkirk shook his head. "That fellow Jessup will be unconscious for a while, I fear. We can see what we can learn from Walling, though. Now, my dear great-niece, if you will help me?" Murmuring encouraging phrases, he directed Miss Anderson to help him ease the exquisitely tailored cloth from Charles's shoulders.

Charles glanced at the fine-pointed scissors the doctor drew from his bag. Clenching his teeth, he turned to Miss Anderson. He could not as easily blot out the sound of the blades cutting the soft linen, nor their pressure so near his raw flesh.

"There is no need to fold my coat," he pointed out as she smoothed the garment with care. It gave him something on which to focus, at least.

She shrugged and continued her occupation with painstaking concentration, as if she found a measure of relief in such a mundane pastime.

William Falkirk pulled back the tattered flaps of shirt, revealing a nasty scratch along the top of Charles's arm. He grunted with satisfaction. "This should heal quickly."

"Will it?" Miss Anderson shoved the coat onto the carriage seat, then eyed the wound with trepidation. "How deep is it?"

"The merest scratch, I promise you." The doctor gave her a reassuring smile. "He'll be stiff for a day or two, but I shouldn't think it will trouble him after that."

She nodded. "He got off easily—this time."

Charles winced as the doctor dusted the wound with

basilicum powder. "We will have to make sure this is also the last."

She glanced to where Mr. Walling and Mr. Vaughn carried Mr. Jessup's inert form to his waiting carriage. "If you had been killed, because of Vaughn and me . . ."

"I wasn't," came his sharp response.

"And for that we may be grateful for your shouting as you did, my dear," the doctor said. "That warning of yours probably saved his life. There." He fastened a bandage in place. "That should hold you for now."

Miss Anderson grabbed his greatcoat and held it up to him. "Here, ease your arm into this. It's too cold to be out here in your shirt sleeves."

"Or what is left of them," Charles agreed. "And now," he stood, and was pleased to find himself steady on his feet, "there is a little matter I believe we should clear up. Before they depart," he added, as Mr. Walling swung into his carriage.

He started toward the vehicle. Mr. Walling gave his horses the office, but Charles caught the near ribbon, pulling the chestnuts to a halt. "There is something we still have to discuss," he said, keeping his tone mild.

Mr. Walling licked his lips, and a gleam entered his eyes. "Indeed there is, my lord, but I had not expected you to approach the subject. Who was that man you positioned behind my principal? Was his purpose to shoot Mr. Jessup if you missed?"

Dr. Falkirk gave an audible gasp. "So that's what they will be about," he muttered.

Charles's grip tightened on the leather. "You know perfectly well he was not there at my bidding. On the contrary, in fact."

Mr. Walling straightened. "Do you mean to imply *I* would stoop to such a trick? If we were not already on a meeting ground, my lord, I vow you would hear from my friends."

"I should like that very much. Who are they?"

Suddenly wary, the man cast him a sideways glance. "Mr. Jessup will be in no state to act for me for a while. Now if you will excuse me? I wish to see him safely into the hands of a *competent* doctor."

Still, Charles held the horses' heads. "Where may I find you?"

A sneer settled on the man's face. "I fail to see why that information would interest you."

Mr. Vaughn, who had watched the interchange with a frown, spoke up. "They have rooms at the Crown Inn."

Mr. Walling opened his mouth, then shut it with a snap. "Will you release my cattle?" he demanded through clenched teeth.

Charles hesitated. To hold them now, without tangible proof that would satisfy the excisemen, would do him little good. If these two did not return to their lodgings, he had a shrewd suspicion someone would lay information against him—anonymously, of course—for abduction. He would not so play into the conspirators' hands. Instead, he would set a watch upon the inn at once and discover where they went and who called upon them. He would learn the names of their "friends" soon enough.

Stifling his desire to beat answers out of these two, he released the horses and watched them pull forward. Mr. Walling turned his pair with more speed than finesse and urged them into a trot. As they drew away from the field, the man cast a rapid glance over his shoulder as if to assure himself no one intended to shoot him in the back.

As the carriage pulled out of sight, William Falkirk clapped Charles on his good shoulder. "What you need now is a shot of brandy. There's an inn not far from here."

Charles shook his head. With Vaughn there, it didn't seem wise to speak freely of his plans. "I want to get back before we're missed. Cousin Lexie? Mr. Vaughn, do you accompany us?"

"No." He eased a step away from them. "If the doctor will just give me a lift to the inn?"

"How can you go back there?" Miss Anderson demanded. "They're murderers!"

"They're not friends of mine," Mr. Vaughn protested.

159

"They've just been useful in getting me established. Maybe it's time I moved on to greener pastures." He turned to the waiting carriage. "Remember, you only have until tomorrow to find that dagger, or our deal's off."

Miss Anderson's jaw set and her lovely pale eyes sparkled, but she made no reply. Instead, she stalked to the curricle and pulled herself onto the seat. Charles followed, and her expression softened to concern. "Can I help you up?" she asked.

"There is no need." Or at least he wasn't about to admit one. He joined her with a semblance of ease for which he offered himself silent congratulations.

Dr. Falkirk watched while he settled himself in the vehicle and took the ribbons. "I'll see if I can find out anything more from Mr. Vaughn. And don't forget, I'll be by this evening to see how you go on. My dear Lexie, see to it he remains quiet this day."

"Count on it. Good luck with Vaughn."

Smiling, the doctor stepped back and allowed them to proceed. Wyndham started his pair, and Miss Anderson leaned back against the cushion.

They drove in silence. Once he felt assured of his ability to control his mettlesome cattle in spite of his injury, his thoughts returned to the recent meeting.

He had learned nothing for his efforts. That irritated him more than did the grazed arm. He had felt so certain he would see the hidden assailant, learn some fact of importance— Well, he had. One of his enemies, he now knew, was a damned excellent shot. How fortunate he was Miss Anderson had shouted her warning, allowing him that split-second to move.

And now that he thought about it, he had learned something else, as well—that the conspirators considered him a serious threat, as serious as his brother Vincent had been. But why? Because he had discovered their cavern meeting place? Or because he had visited the Crown Inn? Or perhaps they merely tired of his attempts to interfere. *Feeble* attempts, he reminded himself. So far, he had achieved

160

nothing but the rescue of Kester.

And the sooner he packed his nephew off to school once more, the safer the lad would be. He would set about it as soon as he reached home.

That decision made, he returned his thoughts to Mr. Jessup and Mr. Walling. Neither, he was willing to wager, would prove to be more than pawns, or they would not have revealed their involvement so easily. But pawns might know more than their masters realized, and might be induced to tell. He would try once more this afternoon, when Mr. Jessup would have regained consciousness—and before any of their cohorts had a chance to hatch any new— and deadlier—plots.

They reached the Priory at last. With a sense of relief, Charles handed his pair into the capable hands of Huggins. He then drew aside Jem, a young stable lad who had upon more than one occasion shown considerable presence of mind. After dispatching the boy to observe the comings and goings at the Crown, Charles escorted Miss Anderson inside the house.

His aunt, he learned from Clempson, had not yet come downstairs for breakfast, which gave him time to make himself presentable. He accompanied Miss Anderson up the stairs, parted from her at the second landing with assurances he went on very well, and made his way to his own elegant apartments overlooking the back lawn and shrubbery.

As he entered, his valet rose from an overstuffed chair before the hearth, worry patent in every line of his angular face. His thick brown hair, normally slicked back in impeccable neatness, showed signs of agitated hands having run through it. His avid gaze scanned Charles from head to toe. "Is all well, m'lord?"

"I am neither dead nor forced to fly the country, Seddons." Charles eased the greatcoat from his shoulder. "But I fear my coat and shirt are ruined."

A spasm crossed his man's face. "Indeed, m'lord." He hurried to Charles's assistance. By the time he had gently stripped off the shirt, as well, the valet had recovered his normally impassive countenance. "If I may be permitted to say, I have never liked that particular coat above half. A vastly inferior garment, I have always believed."

"It certainly is, now," Charles agreed. "What, may I ask, are you about?"

The slightest of smiles tugged at Seddon's lips as he produced a tray bearing lint, various bottles, and a bowl of water from the dresser. "Preparing to cleanse your wound, m'lord."

"Falkirk dressed it already."

"The good doctor is, as I am well aware, a most excellent physician. But I believe the bandage is in need of changing. And now if you will be seated, my lord?"

Charles glanced at the pad, now soaked with blood. "Oh, the devil," he muttered, and submitted to his man's ministrations.

Seddons worked with swift precision, and in a short time knotted a new wrapping about Charles's arm. He set the remaining lint aside, and while Charles pulled on a fresh shirt, the valet disappeared into the dressing room, from where the sounds of cupboards opening drifted through the doorway. Seddons returned and with a flourish presented his master with a glass containing an evil-smelling concoction.

Charles regarded it with undisguised distaste. "What in heaven's name is that?"

"A potion, m'lord. It has been handed down in my family for generations."

"What, this same glassful?" Charles asked.

The valet permitted himself a prim smile of reproof. "It has long been revered for its healing abilities, my lord. I believe you will find it efficacious."

"You do, do you?" Charles sniffed it and recoiled. "Good God, what is in there?"

"Laudanum, m'lord. And a concoction of herbs. My great-grandmother was renowned for her receipts."

"Was she?" Charles asked, fascinated. "Has anyone in your family ever been burned as a witch?"

"No, m'lord. If you will drink it?"

In the firm knowledge his valet would allow him no peace until he did so, Charles manfully swallowed the potion. It tasted a little less vile than it smelled—though he hardly considered that a recommendation. He drained the contents, and to his surprise experienced a general sense of well-being rather than the stomach-lurching reaction he had expected. Encouraged, he allowed his man to assist him into a fresh coat.

By the time he had arranged his neckcloth to his satisfaction and brushed his hair into its usual windswept style, the pain in his arm had lessened considerably. He was able to go downstairs feeling much more the thing.

As he started along the corridor leading to the breakfast room, Miss Anderson emerged from a darkened salon. "There you are," she exclaimed. Her anxious gaze searched his face. "I've been waiting for you forever! Are you all right?"

"As you see. My valet insisted upon changing the dressing. Is my aunt within?" He took her elbow and guided her toward the room from which tantalizing aromas wafted. Miss Anderson went with him, though her clouded expression warned him she was not yet convinced as to his well being.

Aunt Agatha smiled her greeting as they entered. "You are up late, Wyndham. I had expected you to be out hours ago."

"I was." He crossed to the sideboard and lifted a lid. A twinge in his upper arm caused him to replace it at once.

"Is something wrong?" His sharp-eyed aunt watched him, frowning. "Your shoulder—"

"A fall from that young colt. Cousin Lexie, would you care for a slice of ham?" He served her without waiting for a response.

"There, if that beast has not the most disagreeable temperament." Aunt Agatha set down her tea cup. "I wish you will consign him to the sales at Tattersall's."

Charles inclined his head. "I shall give it some thought."

To his relief, his aunt let the matter drop. He applied

himself to his breakfast and found his appetite had returned with a vengeance. Apparently duels in the pre-dawn freeze agreed with his constitution.

Miss Anderson seemed intent on keeping him indoors and quiet for the remainder of the morning. In this he indulged her, allowing himself to be persuaded to teach her some of the various games of cards. Piquet she announced to be fascinating, and she concentrated on this pastime with a will. He discovered in her an apt pupil, and long before nuncheon she had mastered not only the fundamentals but a number of the more subtle nuances.

By early afternoon, though, restlessness drove him outside. He was never one to sit idle when the crisp air and snowy landscape beckoned. Miss Anderson, to his pleasure, went with him to stroll through the straggly winter shrubbery.

Fear for his safety, though, made her an uncomfortable companion. She clutched his good arm, nervous, scanning the area with worried eyes, apparently seeking any sign of an unwelcome intruder. Charles bore with her jumpiness for twenty minutes, then acquiesced to her pleas and returned indoors.

What he intended to do next, he decided, would be best done without her. A certain measure of danger lay in this venture, and he did not want her involved.

They strolled into the Great Hall, and Miss Anderson took off her pelisse and handed it to Clempson. "Now what?" she asked.

Charles shrugged off his greatcoat and winced as the movement jarred his wound. "I believe I will go to my bedchamber to rest for a while."

"You will?" She regarded him in alarm. "Should I send for Uncle William?"

He fought back his twinge of guilt for worrying her, and dissuaded her from summoning aid. His valet, he assured her, was well up to the occasion. He saw her into the care of his aunt, who mulled over the latest fashion plates that had arrived in the morning's post. Satisfied Miss Anderson would not soon escape, he reclaimed his greatcoat, hat and gloves, and slipped out of the house.

The drive into Rye barely troubled his arm at all. He would have to tell Dr. Falkirk about his valet's potion, he decided. He actually felt ready for the coming confrontation.

He went first to the doctor's home. The housekeeper greeted him warmly and ushered him into the study, where he found his old friend pouring over his accounts. These the man was easily persuaded to set aside, and before Huggins had time to walk the bays more than twice down the lane, they were ready to depart.

The yard at the Crown contained its usual motley assortment of occupants when they pulled in through the open gate. Charles glanced around and spotted Jem lounging on a crate, his hat pulled low. The lad's bulky coat protected him from the chill wind as well as providing an ample disguise—if one were needed.

As soon as the curricle drew to a halt, Jem sprang to his feet and ran over to grasp the vehicle's side. His eager young face looked up into Charles's. "No gen'lemen 'as come, m'lord, savin' only yourselves jus' now. And no one dressed as you said 'as come out, nor no one as is injured."

"Thank you, Jem." Charles swung down. "Continue your watch until we come out again, if you please. William?" He handed the ribbons to Huggins as the doctor descended to the cobbled stones.

They entered the dingy common room and paused to allow their eyes to grow accustomed to the comparative darkness. No card game took place at the corner table, Charles noted. Nor did he recognize any of the patrons. Frowning, he approached the tapman—a younger person than the one he had seen before, dressed with a neatness that seemed out of place with his surroundings.

The man put down the box he carried, dusted his hands on his breeches, and came forward a step. "May I help you, sir?"

"I have come to see Mr. Walling and Mr. Jessup. If you will tell me where I may find their rooms?"

"Walling," the man mused. He ran a hand through his

shock of sandy blond hair. "Can't say as I can place the name, sir. Nor the other—what was it again?"

"Jessup." Charles rocked back on his heels, fighting the sensation that something was very wrong. "You are not the man I saw in here yesterday. Where is he?"

"Left, sir. First thing this morning, it was. Just up and packed his things and walked out without a by your leave. The owner was that angry, he was. Sent me over here to do what I could."

Charles glanced at the doctor. "Packed his things," he repeated. "Could you check the records to see if there ever *was* a Mr. Walling or a Mr. Jessup registered here?"

A search of the inn's books produced no such entries. Charles, about to close the volume in frustration, fastened on a name he did recognize. "Mr. Vaughn. Is he here, at least?"

"Oh, aye, that he is, sir. Saw him this morning, I did. Didn't look none to well. Took a bottle up to his room with him."

Charles swore. "Where is he?"

The tapman escorted them up several short flights of rickety stairs and along a number of uneven halls to a room overlooking the yard. The best bedchamber, Charles guessed. Mr. Vaughn had moved himself up in the world. He knocked but got no answer. The new landlord, on Charles's insistence, opened the door to admit them.

Mr. Vaughn lay on the bed in a disheveled heap. For a long moment he stared at them through bleary eyes, then smiled. "Wyndham," he pronounced with care. "Pull up a chair and have a drink."

It came to Charles the man was three parts disguised. "Where is Jessup?" he demanded.

Vaughn squinted at him and shook his head. "Not in his room?" he asked, slurring the words.

"Why don't you show me where it is?" Charles grabbed one arm and Dr. Falkirk took the other.

Vaughn straightened up with what little dignity he could muster. "I can walk by myself," he insisted, and nearly fell.

166

The room to which Vaughn took them stood empty if not clean. The landlord muttered in dismay and began stripping the sheets and linen while Charles and the doctor looked around, examining the remaining litter. After opening every empty cupboard and drawer the chamber possessed, Charles pulled the mattress off the bed and searched the frame.

Vaughn, who had collapsed on a wooden chair, now sat with his head lolled back, snoring. Charles looked about the room in rising frustration. Walling, Jessup, and the barman, his only definite ties to the conspirators—his brother's murderers—all neatly removed from his grasp. Piqued, repiqued, and capoted. They had left him with nothing.

Chapter Thirteen

"What do you mean they're gone?" Lexie demanded. "How do you know?"

"I went to call on them." Wyndham strolled to the hearth in the bookroom, then turned back to face her.

"You—" She glared at him. "And you told me you were resting. Why didn't you take me?"

"I feared it might not be safe."

"And what if it wasn't for *you?* What if they'd tried to kill you again?" She clasped her hands, fighting back her fear. Would she feel this sick dread every time he went outside?

"It wasn't likely," came his calm response.

"Oh, maybe not today, not till they get organized again. But what about tomorrow? And the day after?" She paced the length of the library. How much of his danger did she cause, and how much would he face anyway? The duel should never have taken place. For the sake of history—of everything as she knew it—she had better return to her own time as quickly as possible, before she did any more damage.

Yet her departure depended on finding that dagger.

She stopped her restless walking in front of him. "You haven't any clue at all where they've gone? Where do we look next?"

A grim smile tugged at his lips. "I fear we must resume our search for a knife collector."

She sank onto a chair in dismay. "What fun."

As promised, Dr. Falkirk arrived in the early evening, then remained for dinner. He induced Wyndham to swallow another of Seddon's remarkable draughts, this one containing considerably more laudanum. After that, the earl made only a few desultory cracks about their overprotectiveness and retired early to his chamber.

Lexie, sighing in relief, accompanied the doctor back downstairs from where they had seen Wyndham into the capable hands of his valet. "He's not really going to be safe until we find these conspirators, is he?" she asked.

Dr. Falkirk shook his head. "I wish I knew where to begin."

"That horrible inn." Lexie paced to the great hearth beneath the stairs and stared into the crackling flames. "Do you suppose they've abandoned it completely?"

"I fear they have."

Lexie nodded. "That leaves us Geoff Vaughn, then. Honestly, he must be the biggest idiot alive if he never caught on to what he's been in the middle of!"

Dr. Falkirk pulled on his gloves. "I doubt he cares."

She threw a rueful glance at the doctor. "No, he doesn't. I don't think this is real to him. It's like a monopoly game. He's collecting play money and now he's going to buy land so he can put a hotel on Boardwalk."

"Monopoly?" The doctor shook his head. "I fear your allusions escape me, my dear." He strolled over to stand beside her. "Mr. Vaughn was considerably shaken by the events of this morning. It is possible you can convince him to see reason, now."

"Do you think so?" She considered. "Perhaps he's heard something but doesn't realize its significance." A shaky sigh escaped her. "If only he has, then maybe we can settle this, find that dagger, and go home." And leave Wyndham. She fought her regret. It was for the best. "I think I'll go see him tomorrow."

Dr. Falkirk shook his head. "I'm not certain that would be safe—at least for you to go alone. There might still be someone watching the place. Permit me to accompany you."

170

"You don't mind?" She smiled, suddenly much relieved. "That would be great. I didn't really like the idea of walking in there by myself. Though with my luck Wyndham will insist on coming."

The doctor chuckled. "Just you try and keep him out of the action." He patted her shoulder. "Allow him to drive you to the inn tomorrow. I will meet you there at about eleven. And whatever you do, do not enter the place until I am there."

"All right." She caught his hand and squeezed it.

He touched her cheek, a fond smile lighting his eyes, then he crossed the hall to receive his heavy coat from the hands of the butler.

Lexie rose early the next morning, anxious to settle the business. She ran lightly down the stairs to the breakfast parlor, and to her pleasure found Wyndham there before her. Kester, he informed her, had left by post chaise an hour before, accompanied by four well-armed outriders. The prospect of a journey under such conditions had delighted the boy.

Lexie shivered. "Poor kid. At least he'll be safer at school." She selected a piece of toast and a slice of ham. "I've got plans, too. I'm going into Rye to talk with Vaughn."

His brow snapped down. "The devil you are. And just what do you think you can get out of him?"

"I've no idea. But anything will be more than we've got now. Dr. Falkirk is meeting me there."

"Have it all worked out, have you?" He took a long draw on his tankard of ale, then set it down on the table. "All right, I'll drive you in."

"Do you know, he said you'd probably be a stubborn idiot and insist on that."

"Did he?" His eyes gleamed.

Lexie tilted her head. "Well, maybe it was me."

He burst out laughing. "You are incorrigible."

"Right now I'd settle for omniscient." She settled across from him and bit into the cold, crunchy bread. "If only there was someone else—" She broke off and stared at Wyndham.

"That man, the one I met in Dover! The duel put him completely out of my mind. What was his name, Stoke? Grenville Stoke, that was it! Oh, how could I have forgotten?"

Wyndham folded his arms. "Because you said it was never more than an impression, a feeling his eyes looked familiar. That's not much to go on, you know. Particularly when you are dealing with the Stoke family."

His tone gave her pause. "What do you mean?"

"Merely that his brother, Sir Thomas, enjoys somewhat of a reputation as a hero. He aided several French aristocrats to escape from their revolution, you see."

"Oh." Her enthusiasm faded. "He wouldn't be likely to help Napoleon then, would he? But that doesn't mean his brother wouldn't," she added, regaining momentum. "There can be no harm in learning a bit more about Mr. Grenville Stoke, can there?"

"That depends on how you intend to go about it. I don't recommend arriving at his home and asking him if he happens to have the dagger, and by the by, is he perchance part of a conspiracy to aid Napoleon."

Lexie directed a withering look at him. "Don't be ridiculous. But I don't see any reason why I shouldn't ask Vaughn if he's met him. If Mr. Stoke visited *that* inn, then I think we can guess his business."

With that, Wyndham agreed. They set forth for Rye a short while later. Lexie couldn't keep herself from glancing over her shoulder, but no one followed them, nor did any villains leap out at them in ambush.

"Highwaymen!" she exclaimed as that last thought registered.

"Where?" Wyndham's hands clenched on the ribbons.

"No, it's all right. I just realized how they could kill you."

"Did you, now?" He spared her an exasperated glance. "How delightful. What have you in mind?"

"Highwaymen," she repeated. "If you were shot on the road and robbed, the authorities would just assume you had been held up by—road agents, isn't that the term?"

His mouth tightened. "It is. Do you know, I think I even

172

prefer that one to their duel. Far more original. Let us hope they lack your inventiveness."

Fortunately, no such untoward incident occurred. They pulled through the gates of the Crown in safety to find Dr. Falkirk's gig already waiting, with that gentleman himself standing beside it in friendly conversation with an ostler. The doctor came forward at once, smiling his greeting, and helped Lexie down.

Vaughn sat in a corner of the transformed taproom. Gone was the gloomy atmosphere—and the disreputable clientele. Only two other patrons sat in a corner, neither of whom Lexie recognized. Light shown through the newly washed windows, and the floor showed evidence of industrious work with a broom. The fair-haired landlord stood behind the bar on which he had stacked the bottles from the shelves he cleaned.

Vaughn looked up and winced, as if the light hurt his eyes. He waved to Lexie as if nothing had occurred the last time they met. In growing exasperation, she stormed up to him.

"Easy," he said. "You're walking too loud. What's got you all upset?"

She clenched her teeth. "Good grief, have you got a hangover? What did you do yesterday, get drunk?"

He nodded. "Seemed like a good idea at the time. I'm having my doubts, now." He eyed the doctor who stood behind Lexie. "I don't suppose you've got any aspirin?"

"Ignore him," Lexie advised the puzzled doctor. "Let him suffer. Did you learn anything from that duel yesterday?" she demanded of Geoff.

He nodded, which caused him to grimace. "I sure did. I'd always wondered how those things worked."

"I'm so glad you had the chance to find out," she informed him, her sarcasm heavy. "That's not what I meant, though. In case you hadn't realized yet, that was an out-and-out attempt to murder Wyndham."

Vaughn's pained gaze fell on the earl. "It was, wasn't it. Hit squads." He swallowed a mouthful of coffee. "Things aren't that different from our own time, are they? It's as bad

173

as if Wyndham had come up against some drug lord or crime syndicate."

"That's exactly what he *has* done. Only they're spies. Look, you've got to help us."

"I do?" He had closed his eyes, but at that he opened one. "And *you're* the one who keeps telling me we can't get involved."

"I've got to make sure we haven't altered things already," she improvised. Telling him she tried to find the dagger would only make him stubborn. "Have you met a man named Stoke? Grenville Stoke?"

Vaughn frowned. "Name sounds familiar, he might have been here for a game. I can't remember everyone I've played, though. Why? Is he important?"

"He might be," she temporized. She didn't want to give too much away, or Vaughn might well blurt out something if he came face to face with the man. "If he comes here again, will you let me know? Who he talks to? Anything?"

Vaughn's eyes narrowed. "This is your specialty, isn't it? This invasion plan?"

She hushed him. "Yes, it is. So if I can find out about Stoke, I'll know if we've made a mess of history or not. Can you do that for me? Without being obvious about it and making people suspicious?"

"Why not? Sounds like fun. Okay, I'll play spy for you. If I get the chance, I'll get to know him."

"Just send me a message," she said.

Dr. Falkirk accompanied them back to the Priory, where he took the opportunity to examine Wyndham's wound once more—over the earl's protests. The bleeding had stopped completely, he announced, and showed every sign of healing to admiration.

Lady Agatha, informed by the pleased doctor of her nephew's improving condition, nodded approval. "I'm so very glad. Such excellent care as you have given him, I make no doubt. Though the sooner we are rid of that wretched colt, the better I shall like it. I must say," she added, turning to her nephew, "it is most unlike you, Wyndham, to permit

174

yourself to be thrown."

The earl's lips twitched. "A most unusual set of circumstances," he agreed.

His aunt nodded. "But if you are indeed doing so well, perhaps you would care to escort us to my cousin's ball tomorrow night?"

His brow snapped down, the smile evaporating. "Tomorrow night, is it?"

Lady Agatha patted his hand. "To be sure, you've had too much on your mind to remember such a trifling matter. I should enjoy it of all things, though, and of course it would be such a splendid opportunity for Cousin Lexie to try her wings a little in society. Would you not like that, my dear?"

Attend a ball, with Wyndham. . . . Her gaze strayed to his tall, muscular figure, and the vision of waltzing with him rose before her mind's eye, swirling about a glittering hall lined with mirrors and hundreds of candles, clasped close in his strong embrace, gazing up into his mesmerizing eyes. . . . Reality took over and her romantic vision faded. They wouldn't waltz in England for another eleven years.

The earl's gaze rested on her, his expression thoughtful. "It would give you the opportunity to expand your acquaintance," he pointed out.

"So it would." Lexie's eyes widened in comprehension. Impulsively, she turned to Lady Agatha. "Do you know if a Mr. Stoke will be attending?"

"Sir Thomas and his brother, do you mean? I should think so, if they are currently in residence. Why, have you met them?"

"Mr. Grenville Stoke, yes. In Dover." A slow smile quirked up the corners of her mouth. "I definitely think we should go."

The simple decision to attend Mrs. Rimbolden's ball, however, proved more complex than Lexie had expected. She could not, it appeared, attend in her beautiful new evening dress. She had to have a ball gown. This resulted in a return trip to Rye upon the instant, where they were lucky enough to find, at only their third stop, a creation of celestial

175

blue silk and blond lace which had been left at the modiste's when its purchaser had suddenly gone into mourning. The modiste quickly fitted the gown to Lexie's slight figure, pinned it deftly in place, and promised to have it delivered the following afternoon.

Snow fell steadily during their return journey, making progress slow and treacherous. By the time they finally reached the Priory, the dinner gong had long since sounded. Lexie, hungry from the cold, started at once for the dining room, but a shocked exclamation from Lady Agatha reminded her she was in another era where a very different set of rules applied. Formality, it seemed, must take precedence over practicality. Irritated, she ran up the stairs to her room where an anxious Becky waited to help her into a more appropriate gown.

That evening and the following day were devoted to dancing lessons for Lexie, by the end of which time she felt somewhat comfortable with three country dances and a round dance.

"If they'll just play those over and over," she sighed to Wyndham, "I'll be just fine."

Miss Langley, who sat at the pianoforte, smiled shyly. "You have done very well, Miss Anderson. Unlike others I could name."

Miss Marianne, partnered by a giggling Miss Sukey to make up a set, laughed and skipped in a circle about her sister. "Let's do it again."

Lady Agatha shook her head. "Cousin Lexie's gown has arrived. We must check the fitting, then let her rest before tonight."

The latter appealed to Lexie. Dancing was hard work. But between putting the finishing touches on her gown, having her hair arranged in a style which pleased Lady Agatha, and eating a hasty meal, not a moment remained for lying down.

At last, bundled in one of her hostess's fur-trimmed cloaks, she climbed into the closed traveling carriage and sank back against the squabs. From her wrist dangled a borrowed fan, though she couldn't imagine having need of it in the icy weather. Lady Agatha merely smiled and told her not to mislay it, she would find it of use if she wished to flirt. With a sign of pleasurable anticipation, that lady settled next to her.

After assuring himself his aunt was quite comfortable, Wyndham took the facing seat. Lexie tried to catch his attention, but steadfastly he kept his gaze from her. That irritated her. She didn't really need his assurances, of course; she knew she looked her best this night—despite the lack of makeup. Still, she had hoped to win a compliment from him.

Maybe if she had a hint of blusher, and just a touch of shadow—her eyes were so pale, they would vanish in her face if it weren't for her lashes. And a creamy lipstick of a luscious color to moisten and enrichen her chapped lips. Ah, well, no point in wishing for the impossible. And that included any relationship with a man from a different time. Once she had that dagger, she'd return home and never see him again. She found that prospect very difficult to face.

She closed her eyes and leaned back against the squabs. What a cruel twist of fate, that she should meet such a man here, in an alien time and environment, where they could share only brief days together, then only memories. And she had depressingly few of those, at that, for her to treasure over the years.

The carriage jostled its slow, careful way through the lightly falling snow, through Rye, then down a narrow lane just beyond the town. At last they drew up before a stately Georgian manor. Other carriages lined the drive, waiting their chance to set down their passengers on the carpet which descended the front steps. Lexie peered through the window kept closed against the icy cold, fascinated by the cloaked and hooded guests.

At last their turn arrived. Wyndham jumped down, then handed out his aunt and Lexie. At his signal, their carriage moved on, making way for the next in line. Under the earl's escort, they ascended the shallow steps and entered a vast hall which ran lengthwise along the front of the mansion.

On the opposite side another staircase led upward. They

177

released their wraps into the hands of waiting footmen, then joined the procession mounting these carpeted steps. At the top they crossed a gallery, then stepped through an open double doorway onto a landing.

Lexie caught her breath at the splendor laid out below. Candles flickered everywhere, reflected in the long mirrors which lined the walls, surpassing even the brilliance she had envisioned. A dozen chandeliers, all polished to a sparkling gleam, filled the ceiling with hundreds upon hundreds of crystal dewdrops catching the light, competing with the jewels that gleamed about every feminine neck. Lexie touched her borrowed pearls and thought herself underdressed. Her gown, though, made up for it—she hoped.

Directly across from them, in an obvious minstrel's gallery, a chamber orchestra warmed up. A violin ran through a series of scales, paused for tuning, then a flute joined in. She heard their names announced, and Lady Agatha led the way down the steps to where a tall, elegant woman in yards of lilac silk waited in the receiving line.

Lexie focused on Lady Agatha's cousin. Her silvery hair provided the perfect setting for a dazzling amethyst tiara. Good heavens, should she curtsy to her? Lady Agatha, though, swept into Mrs. Rimbolden's arms, brushing cheeks, then presented Lexie.

Lexie stepped forward, hesitant, and thanked her for including her in the invitation. The woman smiled, and the sweet expression reminded her so vividly of Lady Agatha, she relaxed. She turned next to a portly gentleman of jovial mien, assumed correctly she addressed her host, and thanked him also. He patted her hand, gave Wyndham a broad wink, and told him to find her a glass of punch or champagne. They moved on, and more guests took their place. Lexie let out a long breath.

Lady Agatha beamed on her. "There, my dear, you did very well. There is no need to be nervous. Now, shall we see about finding you partners?"

"No!" Lexie forced a laugh. "I don't know if I trust myself."

Lady Agatha laughed. "Really, my dear, balls cannot be that different in America. Oh, Wyndham, there's that dreadful Seaton woman. I must speak with her." With a murmured excuse to Lexie, Lady Agatha swept off to corner her quarry.

For the first dance, at least, Lexie found herself safe from potential partners. No one approached her—not even Wyndham. Convincing herself this was all for the best, and she could take the opportunity to study how she should behave, she watched as two sets formed, each made up of eight couples.

As the music started, and the couples curtsied and bowed to each other, Wyndham strolled over and handed her a card. "May I have the honor of the next dance?"

"Yes, please—if it's one I know. It all looks so different than the way *we* did them this morning, doesn't it?"

He shook his head. "You'll do very well."

"I'm glad someone thinks so," she muttered.

Much to her surprise, she did manage very well—but mostly thanks to the earl's steadying presence. She only made two slight missteps, but nobody seemed to care.

Not everyone danced with flawless grace, she was pleased to note. More than one gentleman approached the movements with more vigor than accuracy, and wound up treading on his lady's toes. At least she didn't have that trouble with Wyndham. The earl performed his part with an elegance that drew upon them the envious gazes of several girls with clumsy partners.

This could be quite fun, Lexie decided as she began to relax. To take Wyndham's hand, to have his arm about her—ever so properly, of course—as they circled, to look up into his encouraging smile and find his gold-flecked green eyes sparkling with more than the reflected candlelight. Dancing really was a very potent and provocative art. Why had her own time abandoned these slow, formal, *romantic* movements?

The music ended at last, but the spell lingered, wrapping her in a cocoon of sensation and awareness. His simple

179

touch, as he transferred her gloved hand to his arm, sent a ripple of desire through her. She followed, uncaring where they went as long as he remained beside her where she could see him, experience the power of his presence.

He raised her fingers to his lips, and for a moment she thought she might melt. With an effort, she commanded her knees to support her as he bowed before her. Then he dropped her hand and turned away.

The spell holding her burst like a bubble. She blinked. What . . . ?

"Join me, my dear." Lady Agatha's voice sounded behind her.

Of course, Wyndham had returned her to her chaperone and gone in search of his next partner. She sank onto the chair, glad of its support, and resorted to her fan to cool cheeks flushed by something far more intriguing than the mere exercise.

After several minutes, her control returned. She hadn't come here to flirt with Wyndham—well, not *only* for that, at least. She wanted to meet Mr. Grenville Stoke once more.

Leaving Lady Agatha to watch the dance in progress, she strolled away, searching the crowd. If she could find him, perhaps she could remind him of their prior encounter, then induce him to ask her to dance. Surely politeness must dictate he do so. Then they could sit it out and she could tell him all about her fictitious uncle's fictitious knife collection.

She went first to the punch bowl, then wandered about the room, carrying her glass in what she hoped was an idle manner. She didn't recognize anyone—but then that was hardly surprising. She hadn't exactly met the upper crust of society while haunting the Crown Inn. And only one of the men in that cavern had been a gentleman, and he had worn a mask.

And what if she were wrong about it being Mr. Grenville Stoke? What would she do if he displayed no interest whatsoever in daggers?

And what if she couldn't find him? Exasperated at her lack of success, she started back toward Lady Agatha, then came to an abrupt halt as inspiration struck. There should be a card room somewhere nearby. She glanced about, then spotted an open door beneath the staircase. Through it she glimpsed several gentlemen. Bingo.

She strolled toward it, then casually glanced into the comfortably furnished chamber.

And froze.

Her heart pounded and a wave of dizzyness sent her reeling backward into the doorjamb. Near the blazing hearth stood two men, one a tall, fair gentleman she recognized. He held an object, which the other man examined.

A dagger, with a chased silver handle. And in the hasp gleamed a star sapphire.

Chapter Fourteen

Lexie clutched the edge of the door and ordered her reeling senses back under control. The occupants of the room shimmered, becoming transparent to her—as she must to them.

No, not here! Panic surged through her, and she struggled to maintain her sense of presence, her hold on this time, these surroundings. Whatever eerie phenomenon assailed her, she couldn't let it happen now, not in the middle of a ball with so many people about.

One thought remained clear in her befuddled mind. She had found the dagger—and, as she had hoped, it was in the hands of Mr. Grenville Stoke. Clinging to this knowledge, half-afraid it would fade into intangibility as did she, she dragged herself away, back into the ballroom, away from that undeniable force in the card room.

Almost at once, the terrifying disorientation began to fade. She could hear again, something other than the pounding of her heart. The elegantly dressed people and the furnishings ceased their ghostly dance around her and settled once more into their normal, solid selves.

And now she knew for certain the identity of the conspirator who had been in charge that night in the cavern.

She drew a deep breath to steady herself, and to her relief her legs supported her. She hurried away, stumbling only once. She needed to find Wyndham.

She spotted him after only a few minutes search. He stood

near the punch bowl, a glass in his hand, in conversation with a tall, broad-shouldered gentleman, elegant in a coat of deep blue velvet and knee breeches of black satin. She started toward them in a rush, then her steps slowed, faltering. Something seemed eerily familiar about that man, perhaps the way his thick blonde hair waved back from his high forehead . . .

The gentleman turned, and the piercing regard of his bright brown eyes fell on her. A slight frown entered their depths, and his finely arched eyebrows rose a fraction. He said something to the earl which Lexie couldn't quite catch, and Wyndham looked up and saw her.

"Cousin Lexie." He held out his hand to her. "Allow me to present you to Sir Thomas Stoke."

"Sir—" She took a hesitant step forward, and the baronet swept her an elegant bow, giving her a moment to recover from her surprise. No wonder he looked familiar. A strong family resemblance existed between the brothers. She hoped it didn't extend to political sympathies. Though if Sir Thomas's history was anything to go by, it would seem it didn't.

She managed a brilliant smile. "I believe I encountered your brother in Dover not long ago."

"Very likely." His gaze remained on her face, and a slight smile played about his lips. "He is forever haring off somewhere or another without any warning."

"But it gives him so many opportunities to add to his knife collection," Wyndham said.

Lexie directed a speaking look at the earl. Yet just knowing who possessed it wasn't sufficient. They still had to get it from him. Reverting to her role, she opened her eyes to their widest. "Oh, does he? Collect knives, I mean? Has Wyndham told you about my uncle's collection?"

Sir Thomas's smile became a trifle fixed. "Indeed he has. I am quite certain my brother will be delighted to hear more of it."

Unlike you? Lexie thought. Prudently she kept the comment to herself.

"She has been all over Rye in search of something unique

184

to add to it," Wyndham declared. The two gentlemen exchanged the long-suffering looks of fellow victims.

Lexie pressed her advantage. "I should so love to meet him again—and see his knives."

Sir Thomas inclined his head. "It will be our pleasure, I assure you." With another elegant bow, he excused himself and drifted off to watch the ending of the current dance.

Lexie bit her lip. "You must have been laying it on thick. He could hardly wait to escape before I began raving about daggers at him."

Wyndham's lips curved into a singularly charming smile. "You have been elevated to the status of an enthusiast, I fear."

She rolled her eyes heavenward. "How am I ever to maintain *that* act? Especially in the presence of a *real* expert? I don't know a darned thing about them."

"From what I've seen of you, you will manage very well." He offered her his arm, which she accepted, and they strolled to the edge of the dance floor. "The next step is to encounter Mr. Grenville Stoke and obtain a look at his collection. I wonder if it contains a dagger with a chased silver handle and a star sapphire?"

"It does."

He shot her a quick glance. "The devil. How do you know?"

"Because you aren't the only one who's been investigating this evening. Mr. Grenville Stoke is at this moment in the card room, showing it to someone."

Wyndham's fingers brushed hers where they rested on his arm, then closed tightly over them. "Are you all right? Did it—"

"Oh, yes, it certainly did. I thought it had me for a minute, but I'm okay, now. I'm not making any guarantees if I actually touch it, though."

For a long moment he stood in silence while the dancers left the floor, intent on finding their next partners. His clasp tightened on her fingers. "Then I suppose there is nothing left for us to do but collect our Mr. Vaughn and get that dagger."

185

"I suppose so."

He glanced down at her. "You don't sound certain."

Steadfastly, she avoided his gaze. "I know I should be, that Vaughn and I should get out of here at once."

"It's for the best!" He bit out the words.

She looked up, straight into his eyes, and her heart wrenched. "I know it is."

He didn't seem able to tear his gaze away. They remained where they were, staring into one another's eyes, and once more sound receded, to be replaced in her ears by the rapid beating of her pulse. Only his eyes remained real to her, deep and burning, as luminescent as the sea sparkling in the sunlight. All else faded to a blur.

Someone jostled her, and with reluctance she recalled her surroundings. Wyndham, once more his usual controlled self, led her onto the floor and into the set that formed for a country dance she had learned. Somehow, with his guidance, she made it through the steps without any glaring errors.

They left the ball early, but though they arrived at the Priory by two o'clock in the morning, the first pink tinges of dawn lit the sky before Lexie drifted off to sleep. She arose late with a lingering headache, and donned her traveling gown and warm shawl before going down to the breakfast parlor. There she found Dr. Falkirk with Lady Agatha, drinking tea together.

"Ah, there you are my dear." The lady extended her hand toward her. "Did you sleep well?"

"Yes, thank you," Lexie lied. On impulse, she stooped to kiss the woman's cheek, and received a beaming smile in response. "Is Wyndham down yet?"

"Down and gone. He has ridden out to inspect some repairs on the tenanted farms this morning."

Lexie tensed, then covered her reaction by selecting a breakfast she no longer wanted. Would he be safe? Would one of the conspirators be lying in wait for just such a chance to spook his horse, to have him thrown into a ditch or against a stone wall? But if she begged him not to ride out alone, he'd just go all stubborn on her and do something dangerous. Men could be such idiots—especially certain earls with dark auburn hair and sparkling green eyes.

The housekeeper entered, requesting her mistress's instructions for the day, and Lady Agatha excused herself to pay a visit to the kitchens. Lexie added a roll to the slices of ham on her plate and turned to find Dr. Falkirk watching her.

"Did you learn anything last night?" he asked as she joined him at the table.

"We certainly did." She took a sip of tea and told him about Mr. Grenville Stoke.

Dr. Falkirk frowned. "You are quite certain?"

She nodded. "There was something familiar about his eyes when I saw him in Dover. Yes, I am quite certain. What do you know about him?"

The doctor drained his cup, then stared at the dregs in the bottom. "He is of excellent family. His brother—Sir Thomas—is well respected, enjoys somewhat of a reputation as a hero."

"The French aristocrats. Yes, Wyndham told me."

The doctor picked up a piece of toast and frowned at it. "I do not believe their fortune is extensive, though."

"Well, that might be a motive right there, then. I don't imagine money is any less important now than it is in my own time. Possibly more so, since 'gentlemen' can't hold down paying jobs."

"But to betray his country—!" Dr. Falkirk shook his head. "I find it very hard to believe of him. Of anyone."

She reached across the table, just touching his hand. "I know. He seemed quite charming when I met him in Dover. But someone killed Kester's father—and kidnapped Kester. And I saw that knife, both in the cavern and last night at the ball. Grenville Stoke," she added as the door to the breakfast parlor opened, "is our villain."

A soft cry sounded behind them, and Lexie turned to see Miss Hester Langley, with Miss Marianne and Miss Sukey at her side. The governess stood immobile on the threshold, her face unnaturally pale, her hazel eyes wide with distress.

187

"What—of what are you speaking?" Delicate color suffused her plain features. "Did—did you just call Mr. Stoke a villain? That—you cannot mean that."

"Why?" Lexie's gaze narrowed. "Do you know him?"

The color deepened. "I—I am somewhat acquainted with him."

Miss Marianne giggled, and the distressed governess threw her charge a pleading look.

"You've been seeing him?" Lexie asked, catching on.

Miss Langley looked down in confusion. "We—we have an understanding," she said at last. "Nothing formal, you must know, for his brother would never approve of the match. But he hopes to come into some money soon, and when he does, he will no longer be dependent upon his brother's purse strings."

Lexie and Dr. Falkirk exchanged glances. "Could someone watch the girls for a few minutes?" Lexie asked. "I'd like to ask you a couple of questions."

"Oh, why must we always be excluded?" Miss Marianne objected, pouting. "We never get to hear anything of interest!"

"Can we not stay?" Miss Sukey chimed in.

"Absolutely not!" Lexie declared. "Unless you want to hear stories that will give you nightmares for months!"

Miss Sukey took a step backward, her delicate features a picture of dismay.

Miss Marianne's eyes brightened. "No, would we really? May we, Miss Langley? I should like it of all things."

"She is teasing you," the governess said firmly. "You would be quite bored, and I will not tolerate you squirming about in the most unladylike manner. Off with you, now. Go find Gladys and have her give you tea and biscuits in the kitchens."

The two girls squealed in delight at this proffered treat and scrambled into the hallway in a way that made their preceptress roll her eyes in dismay. When the door closed behind them, though, she turned with no little trepidation to Lexie.

"What is all this about Mr. Stoke being a villain? Is it some joke? Or is he to take part in a play, perhaps?" Hope lit her large hazel eyes.

Lexie bit her lip at the honest distress on the woman's face. "I wish it were something like that. Have you never suspected he might be in some trouble?"

"Never!" Miss Langley shook her head. "Of what are you accusing him? I—I think I have the right to know."

Lexie hesitated. Dr. Falkirk glanced at her, then leaned forward, clasping the governess's agitated hands in his own. "You know that Kester was abducted by the conspirators who are trying to aid Napoleon."

She nodded, then her eyes widened in horror. "No!" she whispered.

"I was in the cavern when Wyndham and Dr. Falkirk rescued Kester," Lexie said as gently as she could.

Miss Langley turned her anguished gaze on Lexie. "Did you see him?" Her tone begged for a denial.

"He wore a mask, but he also carried a very distinctive dagger. I recognized his eyes, and I saw him showing that dagger to someone last night at the ball."

Miss Langley pulled free of the doctor's clasp and covered her face with her hands. "I don't believe it. Not of Mr. Stoke. He wouldn't. He *couldn't!*" She looked up, and tears slipped unheeded down her cheeks.

"Did you go out to meet him that night I arrived?" Lexie asked. "When I sat with the girls and Kester for you?"

What little color remained drained from Miss Langley's face, and she shivered. She managed the merest breath of a response. "Yes."

"What did he say? You were pretty upset when you returned."

"He—he didn't come, that was all. I had counted on seeing him, to tell him—" She broke off.

"To tell him Kester had been rescued?"

Miss Langley nodded, her expression miserable.

"Was this the first time he failed to keep a meeting with you?"

Again, the governess nodded. "He—usually he sent a groom with a message if he had been called away."

189

"But you've seen him since, haven't you?"

"No."

She sounded so forlorn, so miserable, that Lexie called a mental time out to her questioning. She poured a cup of tea for the governess, pressed it into her trembling hands, and sat down to wait.

Charles strode down the corridor, still chilled from his ride through the snow. So many problems needed his attention, so many repairs on the tenanted farms to be overseen. But the matter of the conspirators occupied his attention above all else.

His comments about Miss Anderson's knife collection last night to Sir Thomas had not as yet produced the expected invitation to view Mr. Grenville Stoke's. He would have to try another way. If they were in London, he could stroll around to the clubs until he encountered his quarry. In the country, though, seemingly accidental meetings were harder to arrange. Perhaps the doctor could help. Clempson had told him his friend had called.

He reached the breakfast parlor and strode inside. "William, I—"

He broke off, taking in the scene before him. William Falkirk and Miss Anderson sat on either side of Miss Langley, who huddled in her chair, her hands clasped about an empty cup, her face tear-stained. Instinctively, he turned to Miss Anderson and raised a questioning eyebrow.

That young lady met his gaze with a slight grimace and turned back to the governess. "Has Mr. Stoke ever asked you about the Penrith family?"

"No, of course not! That is, no more than politeness might dictate. He has asked after their healths."

"Have you ever spoken to him about Wyndham's fears about a conspiracy? Or rather, Kester's father's fears?"

"I—" She broke off on a wail. "I—I did! Oh, do not tell me I gave Mr. Vincent away, that I—" She spun about in her chair to face Charles, her features contorted. "No, I still cannot believe it! I would never do harm, never do anything

190

to hurt Mr. Vincent or—or any of the family, you must know that. And Kester—" Sobs overcame her, and she buried her face in her hands.

Charles retrieved a handkerchief from his pocket and presented it to her.

With a muffled "Thank you" she accepted it. At last, still clutching the embroidered muslin square, she looked up at him. "If—if that is what you think, my lord, pray accept my resignation. I will leave at once."

"For where?" he asked.

She sniffed and dabbed at her eyes again. "You cannot want me to remain in charge of your nieces, not if you believe I have done you such a grievous harm. Nor do I expect a reference. I will pack upon the instant—if you could permit someone just to drive me into Rye where I might catch a stagecoach?"

"You aren't going anywhere." Charles seated himself across the table from the little group. Her confession explained a great deal—but he couldn't blame Miss Langley. Nor could he desire to see her sunk so deeply in self-reproach. "You have done nothing wrong."

"He's right." Miss Anderson caught Miss Langley's trembling hands. "I know you still do not believe it, but whether it is true or not, *you* had no idea he used you. Now, don't upset yourself any more. No one blames you, or—or thinks ill of you in any way. It's only natural to talk about the people who make up your life, especially to the man you care about. The most successful villains *have* to seem nice, or they'd never get anywhere. It would have been surprising if you *hadn't* been taken in."

"I find it hard to believe of him, too," Dr. Falkirk announced.

"There, see?" Miss Anderson said. "Even *I* would have thought him to be a nice guy if I hadn't recognized his eyes. And even then, I doubted myself. Didn't I, Wyndham? It didn't seem possible."

A rush of pleasure, of satisfaction at her gentle handling of the poor governess, eased Charles's tension. He knew he could trust Miss Anderson to soothe the woman. She could soothe anyone with her warm smile and open manner. One felt one knew her—felt *comfortable* with her, he realized. In fact, he would feel very *un*comfortable without her.

Miss Langley sniffed and rumpled the handkerchief in distraught fingers. "I—I still think there must be a mistake, my lord. Mr. Stoke—I cannot believe him capable of doing harm to anyone. I promise you, though, if you are certain you wish me to stay, I shall *never* speak of family matters to *anyone, ever* again."

"I am quite certain, Miss Langley. Where are the girls now?"

"In—in the kitchens, with Gladys."

"Very well. Go to your room and rest. Gladys may tend to them if they need anything for the remainder of the day."

Miss Langley stood and managed a half-hearted, watery smile. "It is very kind of you, my lord. I—I will not fail you again."

"There is no question of that. Now, you are not to distress yourself further. Is that understood?"

She hesitated. "If there is anything I can do—any way I can prove to you Mr. Stoke is innocent?"

Damn the man! Charles controlled his reaction, saying merely: "I should be glad, for your sake, if that is proved to be the case. But until then, you must mention nothing of this to him."

"No, I—I won't." She hurried from the room.

Miss Anderson took a sip of her tea and stared at the closed door. "If a man has to use a woman, why can't he pick on one less vulnerable?"

"A less vulnerable woman would not so easily be deceived." Charles strode to the urn and poured a cup of coffee, and the dark liquid swirled into the delicate china. He sweetened it and swallowed a steaming mouthful.

No *gentleman* would have caused a defenseless female such distress, or would have used her so abominably. His free hand clenched into a punishing bunch of fives. Murder, treason, and now this repellent betrayal of a loving heart. The man deserved no mercy. And Charles would show him none.

Miss Anderson sighed. "So now you know how the conspirators learned of your brother's suspicions."

Charles stared into the cup. "And how they knew enough of his movements so they could kill him and make it appear to be an accident."

She joined him at the sideboard, refilled her own cup with tea, then turned to face him. "Can you go to the authorities now?"

"And tell them what?" He seated himself next to the doctor. "*I* may be certain, but I lack proof. Without some tangible evidence to give my crack-brained story some credence, I won't get any further than I did before."

"So what now?" She settled across the table from him.

"So now," he said, "we must either provide that proof, or ourselves stop Mr. Grenville Stoke and his accomplices from aiding Napoleon."

Lexie took a considering sip. "The plot failed, I know that —or at least it did *before* my interference in history." She looked up, meeting his steady gaze, her own strained. "*Before* the duel and the disappearances of Mr. Jessup and his friends. And *before* I identified a key conspirator. How many changes have I caused?"

"Miss Anderson." He caught her hand.

She shook her head, her pale eyes wide with dismay. "They'll have to adapt their plans, *alter* them to allow for my interference. Don't you see? *Before,* you were able to stop them. But what about *now?* They can no longer follow their original course of action, because *I've* caused things to be disrupted. My simple presence in this time is wreaking complete havoc with what's about to take place!"

Dr. Falkirk drew a deep breath. "She is right. What are we to do?"

Charles leaned back in his chair and stared into the fire. "I don't believe I have any desire to take on a conspiracy by myself. And we have still the problem of Miss Anderson to settle."

She cast him a rueful glance. "Thank you, I'm well aware I'm a problem."

"Indeed you are." And the prospect of her leaving only

193

made it worse. He forced that from his thoughts and instead contemplated the enormity of the plan that had just occurred to him. Yet he could see no other way. "It seems we have two objectives."

"Which are?" Dr. Falkirk asked.

"To find proof of the conspiracy, and to obtain that dagger."

"And how are we to do that?" Miss Anderson asked.

Even upon reflection, his outrageous plan still seemed the best chance. A reprehensible sense of anticipation eased his tension, and he nodded to himself. "We can no longer wait for an invitation to view Mr. Stoke's collection. I fear we must act at once."

"Do you mean call on him? I don't think that'll work," Miss Anderson objected.

His lips tugged into a grim smile. "I am very sure it wouldn't. No, I believe I will indulge in a little housebreaking."

Chapter Fifteen

"My dear Wyndham—" Dr. Falkirk stared at the earl in open-mouthed shock. "You cannot mean it."

"Oh, can't I?" Wyndham's green eyes sparkled. "Can you suggest an alternative?"

For a long moment the two men stared at each other. At last, the doctor shook his head. "Indeed, under the peculiar circumstances, I fear I cannot."

"Neither can I." Lexie leaned forward, intent. "When do you have in mind?"

"Tonight, I believe. Or rather, tomorrow morning. Three o'clock might prove an excellent time."

Dr. Falkirk nodded. "We will set forth at two, then."

Wyndham's eyebrows rose. "You will accompany me?"

"But of course. I cannot permit you to go alone."

Lexie opened her mouth to say that she, too, intended to make up one of the party, then closed it again. Such a declaration would only lead to endless argument. Much better to spring it on the stubborn earl at the last possible moment. Unless, of course, she could think of a way to win—or force—his consent. She'd have to give that some thought.

Wyndham focused his frowning gaze on her, and she rushed into speech, determined to divert his mind from the order he obviously intended to issue. "Then that gives you an entire day to wait before you can do anything." She lounged back in her chair and balanced her cup between her hands.

Dr. Falkirk rose. "Not I, I fear. I have my rounds to make.

I will see you tonight, Charles. My dear great-niece?" He leaned across the table and caught the hand Lexie freed. "Take care, my dear."

"And you." Emotion surged in Lexie's throat. Great-niece. How good that sounded to her, how infinitely wonderful. When she returned to her own time, she would search out the other descendants of his nephew. But the doctor would always remain the most beloved of her newly discovered relatives.

"Join us for dinner." The earl came to his feet also and escorted his friend from the salon.

He returned minutes later, but did not resume his chair. Instead, he stood across the table from Lexie, his penetrating gaze resting on her. "What have you in mind?" he demanded.

"Actually, I *was* thinking of something. Will you teach me to ride? Sidesaddle, I mean?" After all, she never knew when that might come in useful—or become necessary.

"Teach you to ride?" he repeated, obviously taken aback.

"Unless you have somthing more important to accomplish today? I've always wanted to learn, and since there's nothing I can do until you and Dr. Falkirk find the dagger. . . ." She let her sentence trail off.

"You were not thinking of accompanying us?"

"Would it do me any good to argue with you?" she countered. Now, *that* was a neat evasion.

Only the faintest gleam of suspicion remained in his eyes. After a moment, he seemed to accept her comment for acquiescence, for he nodded and said: "You will need a riding habit. Your skirt would be confiningly narrow."

"If Miss Langley has one, perhaps she will let me borrow it."

He took his leave of her, and she finished her breakfast, then made her way to the schoolroom. She found the governess seated before the hearth, gazing into the flames, her mending lying in her lap, forgotten. Lexie hesitated on the threshold, the awkwardness of her request, following the scene in the breakfast parlor, dawning on her a little late. The woman must be angry with her, and terribly resentful of the

196

person who brought such a terrible accusation against the man she loved.

Yet to her amazement, Miss Langley displayed no such animosity. If anything, the governess seized upon Lexie's faltering request with relief, as if eager for even the most minor of distractions from her worries. Lexie's anger flared once more against a man who could so cruelly use such a gentle, innocent woman. She deserved so much better. Maybe Sir Thomas—a far more eligible catch than his younger, deceitful brother—might come to notice her. . . . Matchmaking thoughts drifted in Lexie's mind.

She soon found herself holding a heavy black dress with yards of material in the skirt. Next the governess pressed a demure hat into her hands, assuring her all the while she found it a pleasure to be of even the most insignificant assistance. With a stammered thanks, Lexie made her way to her own chamber to change. Definitely, she wanted this woman to find love and happiness with a good man.

While she changed, she realized, with a sense of shock, she had no idea what became of any of these people, not even Wyndham. Once they played their roles in foiling the plans of the invasion conspirators, they had dropped out of the reports and accounts she had read. She had never even seen later volumes of Hester Langley's diary—if any existed. They hadn't been real to her, these people who now made up her life. Well, that was different, now.

At last, dressed suitably for the occasion—except for her sneakers—Lexie hurried down the stairs. Clempson met her in the Great Hall, where he bowed and informed her his lordship awaited her pleasure at the stable. The butler then escorted her out through the side entrance nearest the cobbled yard, and Lexie hurried through the morning chill across the open expanse, wishing once more for a high-loft down jacket.

She found Wyndham, ruggedly handsome in his fawn-colored buckskins and forest green riding coat, examining the legs of a neat little bay. Yes, he had become real to her, all right. Far too real. With an effort, she dragged her thoughts from this intriguing line and instead focused on the mare. The animal stood quietly while Huggins checked the cinch and fastened a long line to the halter which remained beneath the bridle. Wyndham stepped back, nodding approval.

"What, not taking any chances?" Lexie managed a note of bright cheerfulness. "She looks calm enough."

He nodded, a twinkle in his eyes. "She belonged to my late sister-in-law, whom I fear was not an intrepid equestrienne. I believe you will find her as docile as you could wish."

Lexie laughed. "I *have* ridden before, I'll have you know. Just always astride. If I pass my first tests, will you let me try a horse that can get out of a walk?"

"America must be a very strange place," he said, pointedly.

Lexie glanced at Huggins, but the groom's face mirrored only the wooden blankness that seemed to be the obligatory expression of the serving class. That didn't mean he wouldn't be tempted later to regale his fellows with her oddities, despite his master's obvious trust in him. She'd better watch her tongue.

She offered an apologetic glance to Wyndham. "What first?"

"Put one hand on the pommel, the other on the cantle. Then place your foot in my hands—very good. Now, as I lift you up, turn toward me. You will have to—" He broke off, his color heightening.

"Hook my knee over this thing?" Lexie suited action to words. "That's a bit awkward, isn't it?" she added, settling onto the seat.

He moved away. "Straighten your skirts."

She did, amused. A gentleman couldn't refer to a lady's legs, she remembered. Most highly improper. And Wyndham was nothing if not proper. Poor soul. Thoughts of his impassioned kiss, and his resulting fury with himself, returned to tantalize her. His sense of chivalry was sweet—but definitely misplaced. She'd have to convince him that far from shocking her, his reprehensible behavior pleased her very much indeed. She hoped he hadn't really minded it all that much, either.

The mare shifted her weight, recalling Lexie to the matter at hand. She fitted the toe of her left sneaker into the stirrup, then on inspiration hooked her right foot behind her left calf for added stability. Yes, that felt more secure. Her skirt pulled easily free from where she'd trapped it in the leathers, and she arranged it in graceful folds.

Wyndham handed her a riding crop, took the long lead from the groom, and backed a few paces away. "Now, if you will collect your reins?"

The lesson progressed with surprising ease, once Lexie learned to compensate for being able to use only one leg to signal the horse. The crop, Wyndham told her, provided the corresponding pressure against the animal's other side. After only a few attempts, she achieved an adequate result to direct the placid mare.

Still, she couldn't see the point of inflicting a sidesaddle on women. Riding astride made much more sense, and left her feeling in control. This way, she felt as if she might lose her balance and land flat on her back the first time the horse shied sideways. A riding habit with a split skirt would be far more to the purpose.

Wyndham, though, appeared pleased with her progress. He removed the lead line, then mounted his own Roman-nosed black which Huggins had saddled for him. He sat easily, swaying with a graceful lack of concern to his mount's playful dancing. Yet in the set of his narrowed eyes, Lexie sensed a tense anticipation for the coming events of the night.

Somewhere, she remembered reading that riding a horse while upset only served to distress the horse, as well. Sensitive animals, these great creatures beneath them. Lexie contemplated her own docile bay with the gleaming brown coat and glistening black mane, and patted her reassuringly on the neck.

"Would you care to follow the lane for a ways?" Wyndham brought his stallion under control.

A gallop would best suit both the earl and his mount, but Lexie knew herself not up to it. Instead they set off at a brisk trot, and Lexie seriously regretted the lack of a second stirrup. She'd give a great deal to be able to post as did Wyndham, swiveling from the knees, rising and falling in the saddle with a practiced grace. Denied this relief from the jarring gate, she concentrated on riding it out, then gave up and allowed her mount to break into a rocking canter. If she ever actually *needed* to ride, she could only hope she'd be wearing her jeans and have a man's saddle available.

"Are you quite certain you are ready for this?" Wyndham kept pace at her side.

"Beats trotting," she assured him with forced cheerfulness.

A mischievous light sparkled in his eyes. "Are you up for a little more?"

She caught the teasing twist of his lips, the devil-may-care set of his jaw. No, despite discomforts and awkwardness, she wouldn't miss this expedition for worlds. She loved riding— the chill, crisp wind blowing in her face and filling her lungs, the sense of freedom, of being able to point her mount at any obstacle, clear it flying, and take off across fields and streams with abandon, leaving her cares far behind.

"What have you in mind?" she demanded, suddenly breathless with a growing excitement her saner self knew to be dangerous in this saddle.

"That ditch?" He nodded toward the shallow channel, no more than three feet across, an easy beginner's obstacle. He pulled ahead—but only enough to lure her on.

"Why not?" A spirit of recklessness caught her. Nudging the mare's ribs with her calf, she pressed the opposite side with the crop. The bay responded sweetly, lengthening her stride to come abreast with the great black stallion.

A deep laugh escaped Wyndham. He cast her a sparkling glance brimful of pure enjoyment and pulled ahead, gathering his mount for the low, broad jump. The animal's great haunches bunched, the gleaming black coat shimmered over the rippling muscles, and the horse soared into the air.

And so did Lexie's. She gasped, caught off guard by her admiration of the stallion, and grabbed for the pommel. The mare landed on an icy patch, slipped, scrambled for balance, and landed on her front knees. The jolt threw Lexie forward, free of the saddle, onto the snowy ground. The mare lurched to her feet, unharmed, and trotted to a safe distance where she stopped.

"Lexie!" Wyndham spun the black about.

The high spirited stallion took exception to the frantic tug on his sensitive mouth. As the earl kicked his foot from the stirrup to swing clear of the saddle, the animal reared onto his powerful hindquarters.

With a muttered oath, Wyndham reached the ground, the rein still firmly in his hand. The stallion pulled back, snorting in protest, his eyes wild above his streak of white blaze. Wyndham's booted heel struck another icy patch as he lunged forward to keep hold of his recalcitrant horse. The earl skidded, lost his footing, and landed face down in a drift. The black took off at a trot to join the mare.

A long moment of silence followed. Then Wyndham declared, in a purely conversational tone: "Hell and the devil confound it."

"Well said." Lexie, giggling, dragged herself to her feet and brushed off her habit. "I'm not hurt, Wyndham. Are you?"

He winced and sat up. "Only my pride, madam."

"And your shoulder, by the looks of it. Did you pull anything? Or reopen your wound?"

"No."

His tone sounded too clipped for Lexie to take his denial at face value. At the very least he must have strained something; one didn't try to hold onto about a half ton of rebellious horse without suffering the consequences. He'd be stiff by nightfall.

When he needed to be in top condition for a bit of housebreaking.

The earl stood with care, dusted off his snowy breeches and coat front, and started toward his erstwhile mount. Both horses now stood quietly, cropping the straggly remains of dead weeds as if they had nothing on their minds other than a snack. Wyndham kept up a steady stream of gentle-sounding blandishments and abuse as he approached, and the intelligent stallion cocked a wary ear at him, but condescended to allow his master to gather the lost rein. His own horse secured, Wyndham collected the mare, as well.

"I'm sorry for falling," Lexie said, contrite, as he reached her. She removed the last remnants of twigs and snow from her borrowed dress.

He raised his eyebrows in surprise. "It is not your fault. I shouldn't have suggested the jump, especially here where the ice is patchy. I cannot think what demon possessed me. I can only be grateful you didn't suffer more for my folly."

"But it *was* fun," she assured him as she climbed once more onto the mare's back by way of a fallen tree.

He grinned a reluctant acknowledgement. He mounted with more care than usual, and turned back toward the lane. He *had* been hurt, Lexie realized—only he wasn't about to let on.

"Let's just walk," she suggested.

To this he agreed. Their mounts crossed the shallow ditch with no mishap, and they headed down the quiet lane in silence. Lexie cast a surreptitious glance at Wyndham, noting the tense set of his shoulders, the way he gripped the reins in only one hand. The other rested on the strip of leather, but she guessed he did that mostly for show, for her benefit.

On impulse, she reached across and touched his arm. "I think I can help."

He tensed. "What do you mean?"

"Your arm. And don't pretend you didn't hurt it, I can tell. If we don't do something about it, you won't be in any shape to visit Mr. Grenville Stoke tonight."

He shrugged—albeit stiffly. "I'll use some liniment."

"I have a better idea. Can you sneak me into your room when we get back?

His jaw clenched. "Miss Anderson—"

"Hey, I'm not planning anything improper. Believe me, when I'm done with you, you won't have enough energy for what you're thinking about. Typical male, only one thing on your mind."

She peeked at him from the corner of her eyes and bit back a smile of triumph. She had him intrigued.

"What *are* you contemplating?" he asked, grudgingly, after a moment.

"You'll see."

"And why in my room?" He kept his gaze straight ahead, as if he didn't dare look at her.

"You'll see," she repeated.

No matter how hard he tried, she vouchsafed nothing more. By the time they reached the cobbled yard, she had not a doubt he would admit her into his private chamber just to satisfy his now raging curiosity. She only hoped his too-advanced sense of decorum would permit him to accept her ministrations.

They lingered in the stable while Wyndham and Huggins examined every inch of the two animals. The black, they decided, had escaped injury, but Lexie's bay mare showed a tenderness in her front knees. Agreeing on a course of treatment at last, the earl allowed his head groom to lead the patient into a loose box out of the wind, where poultices would be applied to her legs. He waited until two undergrooms removed saddles and bridles from both horses and began rubbing them down, then at last turned toward the house.

"And now for *my* treatment?" He cast Lexie a challenging glance.

"Certainly. Go get unsaddled and groomed, yourself. And light a fire in your hearth, if there isn't one there. I want to change out of this habit and get it brushed before I give it back to Miss Langley."

He stopped, a frown marring his brow. "What do you mean, 'get unsaddled?'"

Trouble already. She hesitated. "I'd like you to take a bath first," she hedged.

"I fail to see the need."

"No, I don't suppose you would." She fought a smile and lost. "Just for me? It will help loosen up your stiffness."

He eyed her warily. "Very well," he said at last.

"Now, how do I find your room?"

Half-amused, half-scandalized, he gave her directions through the vast house, then promised to leave his door ajar so she should not mistake it. She left him in the hall giving orders for his man, a tub and quantities of hot water to be sent to his chamber, and hurried up the stairs to her own apartment.

To her relief, Becky came quickly in answer to her summons, and very soon she divested herself of her hat and heavy, snow-dampened gown. While the maid set to work brushing the smooth wool, Lexie settled before the fire, untangling her hair.

She would have to dress as demurely as possible, she decided. Wyndham would not take it kindly of her to breeze in wearing something provocative. As if she even had such an outfit, aside from her evening dress. No, her round dress of pale green merino, with the net insert made high at the neck, would set just the right tone. To make certain, she had Becky pull her hair back into a severe chignon which would have done credit to Miss Langley's strict sense of propriety.

She needed oil, of course, for a proper massage. Barring that, she collected the lotion she had puchased. If Wyndham had a liniment, so much the better. They would manage. She only hoped she could convince him to let her go through with this, once he realized the exact—and intimate—nature of her intentions.

She gave him another twenty minutes, then slipped through the corridors, up short flights of steps and along hallways she had not yet seen. The place was a regular rabbit warren, without master plan, added onto over the generations with a haphazard but pleasing result. At last, she found herself in a quiet hall where the elegant decorations and tasteful, almost severe, decor indicated a masculine hand in control. She'd found him.

The second door on the left, which must look out over the back of the great house, stood slightly ajar. For his sake, she didn't want to get it wrong—or get caught. Holding her breath, Lexie tapped lightly, then eased it open and slipped inside.

He sat stiffly in an arm chair before the hearth, dressed with a studied elegance that suited him, a wine glass clasped in his hand. He wasn't letting down his guard by so much as an inch. He rose as she advanced into the room and watched her with a closed expression she finally identified as wariness.

She smiled brightly at him. "Ready?"

"That depends upon what it is you have in mind," he countered.

"Some good old fashioned hands-on physical therapy, known as massage."

His eyes narrowed. "Miss Anderson—"

"Earlier you were calling me Lexie," she pointed out. "I'm not trying to seduce you, so quit looking nervous. This is a form of medical treatment in the future."

"It is?" Suspicion still colored his words.

"It is. Now, I don't suppose you have any loose-fitting clothes? Well, never mind," she added as he returned no response. "Take off your coat. Or I'll do it for you."

A reluctant smile lit the depths of his green eyes. "You would, wouldn't you? I've never met a female like you before."

"How could you? You might say I'm ahead of my time. Here." She took the coat from him and regarded his loose-fitting shirt. "That should do." It would be better if he took that off, too, but she wasn't about to press the issue at the moment.

He appeared somewhat uncomfortable. "It is hardly proper for me to be so unseemly attired before you."

"Are you trying to tell me no female has ever seen you in your shirt-sleeves before?"

The tantalizing twinkle returned to his eyes. "Let us say no *lady*."

205

She wrinkled her nose. "I'll let that pass. Think of me as an associate of Dr. Falkirk's. After all, I am his great-niece. Now, do you have a blanket we could put on the floor?"

For the first time she looked about his vast, high-pitched chamber, and experienced a sense of awe. Again, everything spoke of quiet elegance, from the beautifully carved cherrywood furnishings to the massive tester bed raised high on its dais, to the wine-colored velvet hangings about the canopy and at the windows. A man's room, where excellent taste and an expansive budget had ruled. It suited Wyndham.

She went to work. Under her direction, he drew back the chairs and pedestal table from before the fireplace. Then, while he watched in apparent fascination, she stripped a comforter from his bed. This he helped her stretch out on the rug where the flames warmed it.

The task completed, he stepped back, keeping a careful distance between them. "What now?"

"Now you get rid of your boots, lie down on it and get comfortable. Temporary doctor's orders."

After a moment's hesitation, he complied. He moved with care, not putting any pressure on his left shoulder—the arm with which he had held his rebelling stallion. At last she settled him to his apparent comfort, and she positioned herself on her knees at his head.

"We need to work on the muscles around your neck and down your arm," she said, beginning a gentle effleurage, stroking over his shirt with both hands down either side of his spine, then back up and along his shoulders. She kept this up for several minutes, and gradually felt the tension ease from his muscles.

"You seem to know what you are doing." He sounded surprised. Mildly, though; already he seemed to have relaxed, growing lethargic.

She kept her voice slow, calming. "It would be best if we remove your shirt, so I can work in the liniment. I doubt the muslin—or is it linen?—would benefit from it. What do you think?"

"Is this an order from my 'temporary' doctor?"

206

"What else?" She kept her voice cool, clinical. Yet she didn't quite fool herself. The prospect of his removing his shirt set her pulse racing.

To her surprise, he made no protest. He eased himself onto his good elbow and pulled the long fabric free from his riding breeches. Resolutely she looked away from the sight of his broad chest with the thick, auburn curls covering an impressive set of pectorals. Longing stirred in her, a desire he seemed all too capable of awakening. It wasn't safe, there was no future for what she wanted, all too soon she'd never be able to see him again, no matter how passionate her yearning for him. It wasn't fair; but then, neither was life.

"Lie down again." The words came out curt, but she didn't care. She laid the garment aside, poured equal amounts of lotion and liniment in her hands, warmed them, and set to work once more with the light, long strokes. A contented sigh sounded from him.

Next she began thumb strokes at the base of his neck, drawing her fingers out to the points of his broad, muscled shoulders. His breathing, she noted, deepened with his growing relaxation—the exact opposite of the reaction she battled. By the time she set to work with little friction circles of the thumbs along either side of his spine, he was literally as putty in her hands.

At last, she worked her way up his neck, easing up on the pressure as she reached his scalp. Then she switched once more to the flowing effleurage strokes along his back to finish. The prospect of giving him a full body massage appealed to her strongly, but she resisted. Still her fingers lingered, trailing along his well-defined muscles, until they at last broke contact with his skin.

"Well?" she asked after a moment's silence.

"Mmmm?" He didn't move.

"That's what I thought. Any soreness left?"

He rolled over, testing his shoulders, setting his thickly furred chest into intriguing motion. Lexie gritted her teeth and averted her gaze. In a different era—such as hers— the man could pose for a hunk calendar.

A slow smile lit the depths of his green eyes. "How do I express my thanks?" His voice sounded lazy.

She rose to her feet and picked up her lotion bottle. "What, do I get to ask up to half your kingdom?"

He cocked a wary eye at her. "Let us say any reasonable request."

She'd got it! She bit back her grin of triumph, and instead merely nodded as she moved a step away. "Fine with me. I'm very reasonable. I get to go along with you tonight, on your housebreaking. And with no arguments from you."

"What?" He sat bolt upright, but too late.

She already slipped strategically out his door and broke into a run.

Chapter Sixteen

Moonlight seeped through the low cloud cover, glimmering on the snow, bathing the tree-strewn landscape in a soft, iridescent glow. Lexie huddled into the greatcoat she had appropriated from Wyndham, glad she had exchanged her flimsy skirts for her denim jeans. At least she rode astride.

Her horse sidled as she shifted her weight. "It's freezing!" she said through gritted teeth.

The earl cast her a darkling look. "Why don't you go back to the Priory, then? You could be quite comfortable waiting for us, sitting in front of a blazing fireplace, having a glass of wine. Think how warm you could be."

"Part of the deal was you wouldn't argue about this. Remember?"

"Am I arguing? I merely pointed out the obvious truth, which anyone less stubborn—and devious—than you would see upon the instant."

"At least your're not as stiff as you might be," she shot back at him.

Dr. Falkirk glanced from one to the other of them, uncertain. "It really would be safer for you to return to the house, my dear," he pointed out.

"No, it wouldn't. How do you think you'd find that knife without me? It could be anywhere in the house. I'll be able to tell the moment I get in the same room with it. It'll be much faster this way."

"And what if you're pulled back to your own time?" Wyndham snapped.

"Isn't that what you want?"

"You're forgetting Mr. Vaughn."

"Damn Mr. Vaughn," she muttered, causing Dr. Falkirk to direct a startled glance at her. She relented. "I'll be careful not to touch it. Though very likely since Mr. Vaughn and I arrived here together, it'll take both of us to make it home." Or at least all the way home. She shivered at that everpresent threat of making it only part way, leaving her trapped in some nebulous limbo.

"Let's get on with it. The sooner we get that dagger, get home, and find your Mr. Vaughn, the better." Wyndham dug his heels into his stallion's sides and the animal surged forward into a canter.

Lexie and Dr. Falkirk followed. She just wanted to get into a house—anyone's house, even Sir Thomas Stoke's. At least the temperature inside would have to be above freezing.

A half mile farther, they turned onto a narrow lane which wound through what Dr. Falkirk assured Lexie to be a picturesque landscape with many pleasant prospects and a magnificent stand of oaks. She took his word for it. A flurry of flakes made vision all but impossible, and Wyndham slowed the pace back to a walk.

After perhaps twenty minutes, they reached a wrought iron gate closing off a gravel drive, and Lexie reined in. "What now?"

"Why don't you wait here? We'll just ride a little farther ahead," Wyndham suggested, a shade too eagerly.

"By that, I assume this is the wrong house. You need me, remember," she called to Wyndham's retreating back.

Two miles and three more drives later, Wyndham finally came to a halt and looked back to where Dr. Falkirk brought up the rear. "Let's tie the horses in the spinney over there." He gestured to the other side of the road where several elms could barely be discerned.

Lexie eyed the closed gate. "How are we going to get in?"

"There will probably be a break in the hedge." Wyndham swung down.

The other two followed suit. The doctor took Lexie's reins and led her horse along with his own after the earl. Lexie watched, rife with suspicion, but after several minutes the two men returned, minus their mounts.

Wyndham turned his considering gaze on the fence. "I doubt it continues more than a quarter mile in either direction," he said at last.

"Do you think that far?" The doctor poked his gloved hand into the hedge, then shook his head.

The three of them crept along the line of shrubbery, feeling their way with care, frequently checking the thick, leafy barrier. They had gone about a hundred yards when a short exclamation of satisfaction escaped Wyndham.

"Here," he declared in triumph. "The ironwork has ended. Now look for a break in the branches."

The hedge, though, proved solid. Another fifty yards passed before the doctor paused and dragged stiff twigs apart. Lexie pressed closer, but could see nothing but deeper shadows.

"Do you think you can get through this?" the doctor asked Wyndham.

The earl squared his shoulders. "I can try."

It took several minutes, but he managed to squeeze through the gap. The unmistakable sound of ripping cloth filled the air, unnaturally loud in the stillness of the snow-muffled night. He muttered something Lexie couldn't quite catch.

"Miss Anderson? It might be advisable for you to remain on that side."

"Hah!" She scrambled after him with considerably less trouble than he had experienced.

Both turned to help the doctor, who emerged breathless and panting from the exertion. At last, though, all three stood within the grounds of the Stoke estate.

Lexie eyed their entrance point with disfavor. "You can barely see it. Shouldn't we mark it with something in case we're leaving in a hurry?"

"An excellent suggestion." Wyndham grasped a corner of the torn fabric of his greatcoat and ripped a long strip of lining free. This he hung from a branch, where it fluttered gently in the breeze. Paler than the bush, it could just be discerned if one made a point of looking for it. With a nod of satisfaction, Wyndham turned away and headed toward a line of yew trees.

Through this, Lexie glimpsed a light, and the desire for the warmth of a fire filled her. Not much longer, she promised herself. They would find that dagger, find some proof of Mr. Grenville Stoke's traitorous activities which would enable Wyndham to destroy the conspiracy, then they would be off home to their waiting beds. And then she would be off to her own time, away from Wyndham. . . .

The earl and Dr. Falkirk slipped forward through the dark. Only the slight crunch of their boots on the new-fallen snow marked their passage. Lexie stirred herself from her reverie and followed.

At last they reached the yews, and all crouched low, hiding in the depths of the shadows. Before them, a small Georgian manor stood on a slight knoll, silhouetted in the pale moonlight. One room on the ground floor blazed with light; the rest of the house lay in snug darkness.

"Sir Thomas would seem to be entertaining," Dr. Falkirk said.

Again, Wyndham muttered something under his breath.

"Or perhaps it's *Grenville* Stoke," Lexie suggested. "Could it be a meeting of the conspirators?"

"I doubt it, unless Sir Thomas is from home." Wyndham shook his head.

"We might as well check." She inched forward, found herself in filtering moonlight, and darted toward the cover of a shrubbery. A moment later, the two men joined her. "So far, so good," she said, and made a break for the side of the house—and the lighted window.

A raucous laugh reached them from inside, followed by a comment slurred by too much wine. "Devil a doubt," a higher pitched voice responded.

Lexie stood on tip-toe and peeked in. Four men gathered about one table, and two more sat at another, nearer the hearth. Cards lay spread on the surface before them, as did piles of counters and wine glasses. Five bottles, all empty, stood on a sideboard. The evening appeared to have been a convivial one.

One man waved his cards and said something Lexie couldn't quite make out to his partner, Sir Thomas. The others laughed, and Mr. Grenville Stoke rose and walked a trifle unsteadily to the fireplace to retrieve a bottle of wine which warmed by the flames. Another man, fair-haired, turned to hold up his glass.

Lexie caught her breath. What was Geoff Vaughn doing here? How had he come to know the Stoke brothers—though she thought she could guess.

"Do you suppose Grenville Stoke deliberately made his acquaintance to discover if Mr. Vaughn recognized him?" she whispered to Wyndham.

The earl shook his head, his expression grim. "More like to press him for information. He must be wondering how you turned up in the cavern the way you did."

A knot formed in Lexie's stomach. Oh, the things Geoff Vaughn could tell the conspirators. If he became drunk—as appeared to be his intention—he would reveal such a chaotic story that his companions would either convey him to Bedlam or—Lexie shuddered, unable to complete that thought. Just how much did Vaughn know about the history of the Napoleonic Wars? As much as an American might know of the Civil War or the Revolution?

He probably didn't know details, but even if he couldn't drop hints about the invasion scheme, he might well say something about the other battles. What if he told them about Waterloo? The British originally intended to defend Quartre Bras, didn't they? Then fell back when they realized they were too late and the French forces were too strong? If the French were forewarned of Wellington's schemes. . . .

If events ever reached that point. The entire Peninsular Campaign had yet to be waged, and who knew what details Geoff Vaughn might know of those battles? She had to get him out of here, out of the past, back to where he—and she—belonged. And for that, she needed the dagger.

She glanced at Wyndham, but he appeared to be intent on

the conversation which took place within. It didn't make any sense to her, but he seemed satisfied to remain where he was for the moment, trying to learn what he could. She'd leave him to it. She slipped away.

After a few steps she looked back. Neither of the men had even noticed she'd left them. Dr. Falkirk must be as intent on those within as was the earl. That allowed her a free hand. She walked slowly along the edge of the shrubbery, scanning the house for any further sign of life.

A light gleamed from a basement window near the front door. Probably the butler, maybe also the valets of the two Stoke brothers. It didn't seem likely anyone else would be awake, certainly not any maids. She glanced at her watch, but couldn't make out the time. It must be going on three o'clock, though. They had set forth a little before two.

She reached the corner and left her sheltering bushes, making a dash for the low parapet wall of a terrace. All looked quiet on this side, too. She continued her prowl, and reached the back. And stopped.

A light glimmered, about half way along the house. Not as bright as the room where the men played cards, but she couldn't be certain no one sat in there. She drew a deep breath, then another, trying to steady herself. Definitely, she wasn't cut out for the criminal life. Her nerves would never stand it.

Gathering her remnants of courage, she inched forward, hugging the side of the house. With every step, she expected disaster, but no twigs snapped beneath her feet, no butlers waving fowling pieces erupted from the house in pursuit. At last she reached the window and pressed her back against the stone wall, not daring to breathe, waiting for the sound which would warn her she'd been caught . . .

Nothing. She drew a silent gasp into her aching lungs. Carefully, she leaned closer, standing on tip-toe so she could just peek in over the high sill.

The glow of the dying fire illuminated a small section of a large chamber—a library, judging from the shelves of books which came in her view. The chairs stood empty; no one huddled over a book, reading by the fading flames. No one . . .

Taking a chance, she grasped the ledge and pulled herself up so she could see more, and caught her breath. In the corner nearest her, sparkling in the reflected light of the dancing flames, a display of knives hung upon the wall. Grenville Stoke's collection.

She shivered, more with excitement than with cold. If she could just get this window open. . . . That chased silver dagger with the star sapphire must be in there, somewhere, among the others. And she was so close. . . .

The glass pane wouldn't budge. She tried it again, then stared at it in dismay. Here she was, probably only *feet* away from the dagger, with no one to stop her from getting it, and she couldn't reach it!

She caught herself on the verge of rattling the window in frustration. She wasn't going to let a little thing like a lock stop her. If only she had a glass cutter. She could break the pane, of course, but the noise would undoubtedly bring someone running.

This wasn't the only window on the ground floor, she reminded herself. She shied from considering how many there might be. She'd probably find out by the simple expedient of trying every one of them. Except for the ones bordering the salon where the gentlemen played cards, of course. Aside from not wanting to risk making a noise where she might be heard, an even greater danger lurked. Wyndham would be certain to take a dim view of her un-authorized entry into the house—without his permission.

The back portions, though, offered possibilities. She retreated the way she had come, testing every window. Unfortunately, the butler knew his duty. Not a single one offered entry. Frowning, she returned to the library and tested the windows heading in the opposite direction. No luck there, either.

She withdrew a few paces to huddle beneath the questionable shelter of an oak tree. The intermittent snow drifted down once more; at least it would cover her

215

footprints. She looked up into the sky, but could see little through the thick branches which spread above her, brushing against the side of the house.

Against the side of the house. And right up to a window, at that.

She bit her lip. She hadn't climbed trees since that spruce at her foster mother's house in Seattle, when Danny, their next door neighbor's son, bet her she couldn't. She'd proven him wrong. She only hoped she could still do it. At least she wore her jeans and not those ridiculous narrow skirts. She was going to feel awfully silly, though, if the window was locked.

She studied the limbs, found one she could reach, and pulled herself up. The swing to the next branch proved easier, and she crawled to the third. With arms and legs wrapped about it, she eased herself higher and higher until she intersected with another branch which came within a foot of the window.

She transferred to it. It looked—and felt—solid. Ah, there was nothing like an oak. She continued her slow progress until at last she stared across at the blankness of a curtained window. She'd have a few protesting muscles tomorrow, but she'd made it. Bracing her nerve, she reached for the leaded pane.

It opened without so much as a squeak. For a long moment she sat where she was, too startled to move. She'd expected—or was that hoped?—to have made the gesture, then be forced to climb back down, defeated. She honestly hadn't expected success.

And certainly she hadn't expected the ease with which the sash swung outward. Apparently, someone in the house used this route on a regular basis. Probably a footman, sneaking out to meet a maid on summer nights.

Not that it mattered at the moment. She was now faced with having to either carry out her search or creep down in ignominy to tell Wyndham of her discovery. The thought of the ever-correct earl climbing trees to break into someone's house almost made her giggle. No, she'd better do this herself.

Getting from the tree limb onto the window sill only

stopped her heart for a moment. It started beating once more—with unwarranted violence—as soon as she dragged herself over the edge and into the room. Dark folds of velvet covered her head, and it took her a moment to disentangle herself from the curtain and gently close the sash. She left the drapes parted, allowing the dim moonlight to illuminate her surroundings.

A large tester bed stood against one wall, but the rest of the furnishings blurred into dark shapes. No fire burned in the hearth on the wall opposite the bed; apparently, she had located an unused chamber. So much the better. She took a cautious step forward, bumped into a table, and steadied it before anything fell off.

And what would she have done if something *had* crashed to the floor? Dived out the window before someone could catch her? And what if she made a noise after leaving this room with its handy exit? Good heavens, what a reckless, foolhardy, *stupid* thing to have done. No one in their right mind walked into a situation like this.

And why *had* she? To prove to Wyndham she could do it? All she'd proven was what an idiot she was.

Still, having come this far, she didn't really want to leave empty-handed. She had to get that knife, and she doubted very much Mr. Grenville Stoke would loan it to her just for the asking.

Thoughts of Geoff Vaughn downstairs, telling the conspirator who knew what, solidified her evaporating courage. She had to take this risk.

Speed, she decided, might be in her favor. Acting on this, she searched for the door, then eased it open and peered into the dark hall. Not a sign of anyone. She stepped out, leaving the door slightly ajar. She wanted to be able to find it again.

This wasn't a large house, not like Wyndham Priory. The library shouldn't be far away. Below this room, perhaps a little to the right. What she needed was a staircase.

She followed the hall, staying to the middle to avoid any stray pieces of furniture, and at last reached what was probably the main staircase. Oil lamps burned low, but their dim glow proved sufficient to keep her from breaking her neck. Then she had only to cross the hall and duck down a corridor which ended, to her breathless relief, at the library. She slipped inside, closed the door behind her, and her knees nearly gave way.

After her dealing with the darkness of the house, the glowing coals provided more than sufficient light. She started toward the knife display, then paused, struck by an unpleasant realization. No tingling sensation crept along her spine, no shivers swept through her. In short, no reaction whatsoever assailed her.

The dagger wasn't in the room.

Casting caution to the winds, she ran forward, her frantic gaze searching the gleaming blades arranged in neat rows on the wall. Several, she realized, were missing.

She stepped back, biting her lip, disgustingly close to tears. All that effort, all that fear, and no dagger to show for it. Grenville Stoke must keep it on or near him.

Or perhaps in a safe place? Maybe wrapped in something protective which might prevent it from influencing her? She turned to the desk, not wanting to give up, unwilling to accept she could have failed.

High-pitched barks shattered the stillness of the night, answered a moment later by deeper growls, then a frenzy of canine fury. Lexie froze, then realized the baying hounds headed away from her, around the corner of the house . . .

Right toward Wyndham and Dr. Falkirk. She rushed for the door.

As her fingers closed over the handle, a single shot rang out, followed immediately by a second.

Chapter Seventeen

Lexie dropped to a defensive crouch, then rose, feeling sheepish for her instinctive reaction. How ridiculous could she get! No one shot at *her*.

Wyndham and Dr. Falkirk were another matter, though. Somehow, she had to help them. She eased the library door open a crack and peered out.

A light danced along the corridor, a little too close for comfort—a candle held aloft by a man garbed in solemn black. Lexie ducked back, out of possible sight.

Beyond, a door slammed and heavy footsteps crossed a tiled hall. "Hill! Where the devil are you, man? Hill, I say!"

The man turned. "Sir! An intruder on the grounds. He has escaped. The groom who spotted him says he heard horses."

Lexie let out her breath in relief. Wyndham and Dr. Falkirk had escaped—she hoped. Which left her to get out of this mess and get back to the Priory on her own. She had a sneaky feeling Wyndham was not going to be too pleased when he couldn't find her anywhere outside.

She shut the library door quietly and cast one last look about the room. No, she experienced no reaction whatsoever. The dagger couldn't be in here. She might as well leave, before anyone had the bright idea of searching the house for more intruders.

The window here would be the easiest method of getting out. The fire had faded to embers, but she could still make out outlines and shapes, enough for her to move without tripping over things. Outside, snow fell steadily, blurring the landscape, filling the air with swirling flakes. Fine, that should muffle any slight noise she made. She caught the latch and tugged.

Nothing happened. She tried again, then stopped at the first protesting creak of the hinges. That was no *slight* noise. She couldn't get out that way unless she wanted to bring the whole household down on herself. Gingerly, she let go, then backed away.

A dark figure ran past the window—not Wyndham, but a servant. He brandished a pitchfork.

She swallowed hard. She was trapped. Even if she could sneak through a house now alert for trespassers, she could never cross the grounds without some over-eager footman tackling her.

Or maybe now was the time to go back upstairs, while the hunt was up outside.

She peeked out once more to find the corridor dark. Taking her chances, she crept down the hall, reached the stairs, and ran up them as fast as she could. She paused for only a moment at the top to re-orient herself, then dove for the shelter of the unused bedchamber like a fox going to ground.

The window formed a pale rectangle in the fastness of the room. She crossed to it and peered down, only to see two men meet at the base of the tree directly below her. One glanced up and she drew back, her heart pounding so loudly it seemed impossible those two didn't hear. She was going to have to wait until the hunt was called off. Hopefully, no one would think to climb that tree. The new-falling snow must have covered any traces she'd left at its base by now, leaving no clue.

The bed looked too tempting. She could just imagine what would happen if she curled up on it to wait, or even borrowed the comforter to wrap about her shivering shoulders. Instead, she sank down to the floor, drew her knees up to her chest, and concentrated on being invisible.

Shouts drifted up from outside as the searchers reported their lack of success. Then came the sound of carriages pulling up as the guests prepared to depart, followed by the slurred but amiable goodbyes. As the last one pulled away, the servants resumed their search, and Lexie closed her eyes in despair. Would they never give up and go inside?

The realization of complete silence startled her, jarring her fully awake. It must have been quiet for several minutes while she drifted toward a doze. Alert now, she dragged herself to her feet and peered out the window. Snow fell heavily, turning the sky gray, muffling noises and covering footprints. Now, if ever, was the time to make her escape.

She eased the casing wide and sat on the ledge. Funny how it didn't look quite so high when she was climbing *up*. Steadfastly she avoided looking again at the ground, which seemed a terribly long way down. Stealing her wavering nerve, she grasped the thick limb and swung herself over.

For a long, heart-stopping moment she dangled in space, then her flailing feet caught the limb below and she found solid footing. Pausing only to calm her gasping breaths, she began her cautious descent. Long, tense minutes passed before she dropped the last three feet to the banking snow below.

She straightened at once, and her gaze darted around. No one, though, came running to waylay her. She had escaped detection . . . so far.

She hesitated only long enough to figure out which direction to take, then crouched low and ran for the line of trees. These she followed to the corner of the house, then she made her way through what sheltering growth she could find to where she caught a glimpse of the pale piece of lining from Wyndham's greatcoat. She pulled it free and squeezed through the gap, then swore as a sharp twig drew blood on her cheek.

Her horse wasn't where they'd left their mounts. Well, she hadn't really expected it would be. Wyndham and Dr. Falkirk could hardly have abandoned it to be found when they escaped themselves. Hopefully they would be waiting for her somewhere on the road home—unless they'd given up by now and decided she'd been caught. Hugging herself for warmth, she tramped along the verge of the snowy lane.

A little over a mile later a rustling noise reached her, and she stopped, alert for danger. The sounds repeated, louder, then two horsemen emerged from between the trees, leading a third mount. With a cry of relief, Lexie ran toward them.

Wyndham swung down from his saddle and caught her arms. "Are you all right?" he demanded. "We've been searching everywhere for you. We were about to return to Stoke's and try to break in to find you."

A rush of warmth flooded through her at the anxiety in his tone. "I'm fine." She attempted to return the embrace, but he held her just away from himself. "I had to stay hidden until they called off the search."

"You must be frozen. William, you'll have a look at her when we get back to the Priory."

Lexie felt the color rise in her cheeks. "It's not necessary. I—I was inside."

Wyndham stiffened. "Inside?" he repeated, his voice as icy as their surroundings.

She managed a casual smile. "It wasn't any big deal. I saw the knife collection through the library window, so I—I found a tree and got in on the upper floor. I'd just discovered the dagger we're after wasn't with the others when the shout went up for you two. All I had to do was go back upstairs and wait until everyone went to bed, then I climbed down and—" She broke off and winced as his fingers dug into her arms through the heavy cloth. "I was perfectly all right," she protested.

"Of all the idiotic, addlepated, *corkbrained* stunts—!"

"Why do we not continue this discussion indoors?" Dr. Falkirk's amused voice sounded above them. "In case it has escaped your notice, it has begun to snow harder."

With a half-shake, Wyndham thrust Lexie from him and swung into his saddle. Lexie followed suit, then wished she'd brushed the snow from the leather seat before settling on it. Cold penetrated her jeans.

The journey home they accomplished in complete silence, though she feared she had not heard the last of her escapade. She was right. After they reached the Priory, turned their mounts over to the sleepy grooms and entered the house,

Wyndham bade Dr. Falkirk a curt goodnight. The doctor cast his host an appraising glance, then started for the stairs and the guest chamber he would occupy.

Lexie, prudently, hurried after him.

"If you please, Miss Anderson?" Wyndham spoke through gritted teeth.

Lexie's heart sank. She turned slowly, and managed a strategic yawn. "Yes? I'm tired. Can't this wait 'til morning?"

"It cannot. In my library, if you please?" Grasping her elbow, he marched her down the hall into his private sanctuary. A fire still burned within, and he kindled a punt from it and lit several candles.

Lexie tossed on another log. "It's quite comfortable in here, isn't it?" she remarked.

He wasn't to be distracted. Planting himself squarely in front of her, he glared down his aquiline nose until she retreated a step. Her reaction seemed to please him, for his mouth twisted into a tight-lipped smile. "How dare you pull off such a ridiculous stunt! Have you any idea what might have happened to you if you had been caught?"

"I didn't think about it," she admitted. She met his gaze, and her own anger sparked at the fury reflected in his eyes. "And what right do *you* have to yell at me?"

"You had no business taking such a risk."

"Of course, I did. I had to try for that dagger. I couldn't let Geoff Vaughn tell them who knows what about the battles over the next few years."

"You should have stayed here." He turned away. "I never should have let you come on so dangerous an undertaking."

"You *let* me come, did you?" Her eyes narrowed, and her voice dropped to a dangerous pitch.

"Of course. I—"

"Just who the hell do you think you are, dictating what *I* do? I'll thank you to remember I only asked you to agree not to argue! I went on my own accord."

He spun back, the furrows in his brow deepening. "A lady is not suitably—"

"Damn it, Wyndham, I'm not helpless! I'm every bit as able to take care of myself as you are. Don't women of your

223

time ever get to do *anything* interesting? Or do you just expect them to sit home with their needlework and select your dinners?"

"I expect them to submit to my orders."

"Your *orders?* What is this, a male dictatorship? What are your orders *now,* my lord and master?" She sank onto one knee in a sweeping curtsy.

"Confound it, Lexie!" He dragged her back to her feet.

For one long, furious moment he glared at her, then swept her against himself. One arm fastened about her waist, molding her against him, while the other encircled her shoulders. His fingers entwined in her hair as he forced her face to his, and his mouth covered hers in a kiss that robbed her of breath. Her lips parted and she pressed closer, running her hands up his back to clasp his shoulders in a far more sensuous stroke than the effleurage.

He thrust her aside and took an unsteady step away. "My behavior with you is enough to give me a disgust of myself. I thought I was a gentleman."

She swallowed, but it did little to still her trembling. "Well, you're not. You're a stubborn, pig-headed, chauvinistic—spoiled—" She broke off, unable to think of a word suitable to the situation.

"Thank you, madam. You have said quite enough." He turned on his heel and slammed from the room.

Lexie seethed, wishing he'd come back so she could hurl more insults at him, yet knowing what she wanted to hurl was herself, right into his bed. Damn him, for being so infuriatingly old-fashioned, and damn herself, for wanting him to the point of distraction.

She made her way to her bedchamber, slammed her door and dragged off his greatcoat. She hadn't said nearly enough. She should have told him about equal rights and Margaret Thatcher and the women's army corps. She should have kissed him until he admitted she could be a desirable woman and still be a lady. She should have made him admit how much he wanted her.

She stalked farther into the room, only to stop short. Before her roaring hearth stood a huge tub filled with water from which a delicate, sweet scent rose. That must be Becky's doing, anticipating Lexie's cold upon her return. Her muscles ached, too, from all that unaccustomed tree climbing. A bath would be very welcome indeed, and might calm her temper.

The water was even comfortably warm. Her normal equilibrium returning, she pulled off her clothes and tossed them over the foot of the bed. Towels lay in a pile on the carpet, and she arranged them over the back of a chair to heat, then climbed in. This was going to feel good.

She closed her eyes, controlling her breathing, allowing the fatigue and stiffness to seep from her body. Violets, that's what she smelled. Becky must have added the distilled essence with a liberal hand. She'd thank the girl tomorrow.

A light knock sounded on her door, and a slow smile touched her lips. She could thank her now. The poor maid, she must have waited up for her! She called for her to enter, then turned to chide the loyal Becky for allowing herself to miss so much sleep.

Not her abigail, but Wyndham, stood on the threshold, wrapped in his deep green dressing gown, a chamberstick clasped in one hand and two tiny bottles in the other. He stared at her, immobile, as if unable to drag his gaze from her glistening damp shoulders which just emerged from the high-sided tub. Slowly, as if against his will, he came a step nearer.

"I should go," he breathed, but made no attempt to do so.

Her own breath caught in her throat. The flickering flames of her roaring fire danced off the thick auburn waves of his hair, burnishing them to copper. His eyes glinted like the reflections on a pool in a shady glen, echoing the glittering emerald on his finger.

Slowly, his hand unsteady, he set his candle on the edge of a table and advanced another step. "I came to see if you were all right."

She swallowed, but couldn't find her voice.

His gaze moved slowly over the length of the tub. He might not be able to really see her, but the imagination could be very vivid in filling in details if it chose. A noise sounded in her ears, and she recognized it as the pounding of her heart.

"You said you climbed a tree. I thought perhaps you must have become as sore as I did this morning. I brought you the liniment and the lotion you left in my room. . . ." His voice trailed off.

A peace offering. Guilt flooded through her for her earlier, angry words. It wasn't his fault he was the product of an age that treated women like china dolls. He was thoughtful, generous, so infinitely dependable and caring. Emotion welled in her, an unsettling realization of just how much this man meant to her.

She crumpled. "I'm sorry. That *was* pretty dumb of me tonight, and I didn't mean to worry you. I promise I'll warn you next time."

Her words seemed to break the spell which held him, and he looked away from her, staring instead into the shadowed recesses of her room. "You were quite correct, though. I have not the right to dictate your actions."

"After all you've done for me, perhaps you do."

He turned back, and a slow smile lit his eyes. "Are you in need of a—what did you call it, a massage?"

"I—yes." To refuse his offer would be unthinkable; but to feel his hands smoothing over her skin would be sweet torture. She wondered if she could bear it.

His gaze strayed to the darkened waters, then switched to the flames. "Should I clear an area for you to lie?"

"No need, there's room." She bit her lip. "If—if you'll turn around for a moment while I get out?"

He complied. "I could leave," he offered, yet he made no move to do so.

"Don't bother." She stood, and the water, alive with the flickering light, cascaded down her skin. She scrubbed herself off, then spread the towel on the floor. After a moment's hesitation, she stretched out on this, face down, then discreetly arranged a dry one over her hips.

"Okay, I'm ready."

He turned, then abruptly spun about again. "Will you not put on your dressing gown?"

226

"The lotion. You had to take off your shirt, remember?"

"The lotion," he repeated. He drew a long, steadying breath, then positioned himself at her head and stared down at her. "I don't believe I thought this through," he admitted. "I had envisioned you dressed."

It would be safer if she were, she realized. She didn't want him uncomfortable—yet an awareness of the full implications of the intimacy of massage sent an aching need through her.

"Have you received many of these—massages—before?" he asked.

"No. I learned how to give them, but I've only had one, myself."

"From a man?"

She tilted her head up to look at him, and caught an assessing look—could it be jealousy?—lurking in his eyes. "No," she reassured him at once. "An older woman—the one who taught me. She was a licensed therapist who gave lessons at our local hospital. As you saw this afternoon, there is nothing necessarily—seductive—about it."

That seemed to appease him. "How do I begin?"

Under her direction, he knelt at her head, poured lotion in his hands, and warmed it by rubbing it between his palms. He hesitated only a moment, then rubbed it along her bare back with long strokes of his powerful hands. His finger tips reached her hips, then slid down her sides, sending ripples of pleasure through her as they brushed her flesh with feather-like strokes on their return trip.

Desire flared, burning hot and uncontrollable. "That—that's not quite the way you're supposed to do it," she managed.

"I thought you said this wasn't seductive." His voice wavered. "It *wasn't* when you did it."

"It's all in the touch. I didn't mean it to be, so it wasn't. "You—" She looked up, and her reproach turned to yearning.

"I didn't mean it to be, either. Until now." His husky voice sounded near her ear.

The firelight sparked and flickered, illuminating the

features in the face so near her own, clearly revealing the torment and desire which mingled in his expression. Her will power melted. She rose up on one elbow, slipping her arm about his neck, and drew his head down to hers.

He gathered her to him, fitting her body against his. His arm encircled her waist and his mouth held her captive and hungering for more.

His lips broke away from hers, then brushed her cheek, her eyes, then trailed down her neck to the pulse which beat erratically at her throat. His fingers traced along her bare shoulders, and he buried his face against her neck.

"You smell of violets," he murmured. His gaze drifted downward from her face, over her body from which even the towel had slipped. "Lexie."

His burning regard left her in no doubts of his feelings. Or her own. With a hand that trembled, she unfastened the sash of his dressing gown. The rich velvet fabric fell away, revealing his shirt, complete with neckcloth, beneath.

"I don't think you need this anymore," she whispered. She met his gaze, and neither made any attempt to look away. Her breath came shallow and rapid, and her pulse rate soared to new heights as she unknotted the intricate folds of the cloth, then reached for the buttons of his shirt.

He joined her on the towel before the hearth, stretching out full length at her side, drawing her into his arms to lay her head against his shoulder. The firelight danced off his hair, throwing his face into shadow. The green stone glowed on the hand that brushed her cheek.

She touched it. "I think emeralds will always remind me of you, of your eyes."

He hushed her with a kiss. "Don't think of that now, not while we're still together. Let's savor what we have."

"Charles—"

"My dearest love." The words were no more than a breath.

His mesmerizing gaze enveloped her, drawing her in, sharing with her an understanding that encompassed their very souls. Time seemed to stop as all else faded from her mind. Only he mattered, only the warmth of love that flooded through her, of knowing herself both cherished and cherishing.

As his mouth sought hers again, dizziness swept over her, leaving her disoriented, adrift in a shimmering, intangible nebula. Not now! She couldn't be torn from him, not at this moment. . . .

She struggled against it, then the sensations caused by his expert hands brought her back. She clung to him, kissing him with desperation. She could—would!—stay, she would be his, if only for this little while.

Once more, the two times shimmered about her, neither solid—neither claiming her. Wyndham faded in her arms, and with a cry of anguish, she grasped his hazy form, trying to hold on. Her hands closed over nothingness. . . .

Then the solidness of his bare, warm flesh returned, and she wrapped herself around him with a passion so intense she scarcely recognized it as her own.

Chapter Eighteen

Lexie awoke to an aching body. Every muscle protested from her tree climbing as she stretched and snuggled deeper into the warm bed. Only there'd been more to the night than that; there had to have been, for such contentment to suffuse her. A warm glow lingered, and her skin retained the memory of a gentle, sensuous touch.

Memories flooded back, of Wyndham's—Charles's—exquisitely unbearable tenderness and passion—and of the unwanted tug from the future. She had clung to him, to the love that filled her, fighting against the call from her own time, struggling to remain with him for just a little longer.

Yet that other time remained her own. One day soon it would succeed in claiming her.

And when it did, how could she bear to be parted from this man she loved, but with whom she could never have a life? She reached for him, desperate for the reassurance only he could give, and her hands encountered an empty pillow.

Her eyes flew open and she sat up, panicking. Where was he? Oh, God, in what time was she?

The room was hers—or was it just another empty guest chamber? *Where was Charles?* She threw back the comforter and jumped from the bed, wincing as her muscles complained. Her jeans, sweater and underwear lay where she had discarded them when she'd climbed into her bath the night before. Surely, if she'd been pulled back to her own time, her things would not have come with her.

Her gaze fell on the still-full tub lying before the hearth. Towels lay scattered about where they'd dropped, and a faint scent of violets lingered in the air. A sigh of relief escaped her. She was still with Charles—though for how much longer?

She shoved her futuristic clothes out of sight in a drawer, then turned to her meager Regency-era wardrobe. Slipping on her green merino, she experienced a strange sensation, a pleasurable anticipation to wear the high waisted gown again after such a short time back in her own clothes. She frowned, running her hand along the soft fabric. She'd give a great deal to know if her liking for this feminine style lay in Charles's preference for it, or in her own.

Becky arrived in answer to her summons, bearing a tray with rolls and a cup of hot chocolate. While Lexie ate, the maid set about arranging Lexie's thick dark hair in a becoming style, pulling it back from her face. Lexie thanked her, grabbed a shawl as she left, and wrapped it about her shoulders as she headed for the stairs. She had to find Charles. She needed to be near him.

And after last night, that need had grown a hundredfold.

He wasn't in his library, nor in the estate room. A tentative query of the butler informed her his lordship had not yet gone outdoors. Encouraged by this information, she made her way to the breakfast parlor.

She found him standing in front of the bow window of this apartment, staring across the snow-covered landscape. His commanding figure drew her gaze, and the emotion she experienced at just the sight of him filled her, making it difficult to breathe. Here, in this one man, lay her happiness. She had to relish every moment with him as if it were their last—for it might very well be.

He turned, even though she would swear she had made no sound. He must be as atuned to her as she to him. His solemn gaze rested on her, and the glowing embers in his eyes fanned to flame. He held out his hand.

She ran to him, her satin slippers making only the veriest whisper on the carpeted floor. His warm embrace closed about her, holding her tight, wrapping her in a cocoon of security and happiness. Here she belonged—and here she could never stay.

She drew back. "Charles—"

He touched her lips with one finger, silencing her, then his mouth claimed hers in a kiss that demanded a response from the depths of her being. For a long moment she gave herself over to it, and the unpleasantness of reality faded from her consciousness.

"Good morning, my love." A smile softened the firm lines of his mouth as he released her. "Did your bed grow lonely without me?"

"You know it did. I suppose propriety dictated you shouldn't be caught there. Or was it practicality?" she added, dragging herself with reluctance out of the hazy mists of "if only's."

For a long moment he stood before her, his hands caressing her shoulders. Slowly they trailed down her arms to her elbows, then dropped away. His voice, when he spoke, sounded dull and flat. "I should not have permitted it to happen."

"We didn't plan it," she pointed out. "And I tried to tell myself we couldn't, but it didn't work." She turned away, staring out the window, her throat constricting. "I don't believe in casual affairs. Yet even knowing this couldn't last, I've longed for it. What are we to do?"

He dragged her against his chest, his arms clasping about her as he held her close. With a muffled sob, she turned to bury her face in the soft green superfine of his coat. Her hands locked behind his back, returning the demanding pressure of his body. As if trying to imprint this memory of the *feel* of him in her mind forever, she realized.

After a long silence, he said: "We can either put this from our minds and forget it happened, or we can try to compress a lifetime of love into the hours we have."

She leaned back, just enough to look up into his beloved face. "It's odd, isn't it? We're from such different worlds— yet I'm only whole when I'm with you."

"And you'll be gone all too soon." He rubbed his cheek against the top of her curls. "Almost, I would delay

233

uncovering this conspiracy if it would keep you with me for a little longer."

"Almost," she repeated. "But you can't let my presence interfere with—" Her eyes widened, and she backed away from him. "Oh, no. Charles, you mustn't let me even *influence* you. Not in *anything!*"

"What do you mean?"

"Oh, what a fool I've been!" She strode to the window, then spun back to face him. "I thought the little things wouldn't matter, that I could stay here, *be* with you, that as long as I didn't tell you anything of historical importance I wouldn't do any real harm. But I was wrong!"

His brow furrowed. "What the devil are you talking about? We hurt no one by being together."

"But what if, instead of standing here talking to me this morning trying to sort out our fouled up love life, you had gone into Rye and learned something about the conspirators? My very presence here, *loving* you, may interfere with your role in history! Maybe my even telling you that you *have* a role in history has done the damage."

"Loving me." He ignored the last words of her speech and focused on these earlier ones. For one moment, his every feature reflected raw desire.

She caught her breath and fought an answering response in herself. "Do you understand what I'm saying?" she managed at last.

He shook his head. Step by slow step, he closed the space between them and gazed down at her, his eyes as cloudy as if someone had stirred their deep green waters. "How can you ask me to behave as if you aren't here, when every part of me responds to your mere presence—even to just the thought of you?"

Somehow, she had to resist, or she would be back in his arms, forgetting the conspiracy, thinking of nothing but her all-encompassing and ill-fated love. The temptation to delay her return to her own time loomed far too great. Already the voice of longing whispered in her ear, telling her one more week wouldn't make that much of a difference, that no harm could be caused by allowing herself so brief an idyll with this man she loved.

Yet if she and Charles wrapped themselves away in their own little world, Napoleon's invasion would proceed without Wyndham's interference—and probably reach a successful conclusion in London. The whole course of the war could so easily be changed—and the course of history as her time knew it.

Behind them the door opened, and Lexie turned away, trying to compose herself. Charles muttered an oath, and a wistful smile tugged at her lips. It was just as well, or they'd have found themselves back upstairs in her bed, their good intentions a victim of their love.

"Good morning." Dr. Falkirk's cheerful voice sounded from the threshold. He advanced into the room, stifling a cavernous yawn. "Lord, what a late night. How can you two be up and about so early?"

"It's gone on ten," Wyndham pointed out. Only the slightest tremor in his voice betrayed his emotion.

Dr. Falkirk waved that aside. "Irrelevant, my boy, quite irrelevant. I can only hope no one has been sending urgent messages for me. Have you told my dear great-niece what we overheard last night?"

"You heard something?" Lexie demanded, startled out of her unhappiness. She looked from Wyndham's solemn countenance to the doctor, who inspected the contents of the chafing dishes. "What?"

Wyndham seated himself at the table. A touch of strain lingered in the fine lines about his eyes, as if he closed his emotional upheaval away deep within himself before turning to this new topic. "Your friend Mr. Vaughn appeared to be about three parts disguised, Lexie," he said. "We had the dubious pleasure of hearing him regaling his hosts with tips on how to make the invasion of England possible."

"Oh, no!" Lexie stared at him, aghast. "Oh, how could he?"

"Quite easily, apparently." A sardonic smile flitted across his face, only to vanish the next moment. "We also heard there is to be a meeting with the smugglers who carry their information to France. Tonight, in the cavern."

"To—" She sank onto a chair. "Why didn't you tell me? Charles, we've got to stop them! What else did he say?"

"Steady, my dear—Lexie." Dr. Falkirk took the seat next to her, and his calming hands closed over hers. "I thought you would have told her last night," he added to Wyndham.

"I was—otherwise occupied." The earl frowned at the empty tankard before him.

"You're really sure about this meeting?" Her gaze rested on Charles's face. "Did Geoff have anything to do with setting it up, or was it all Grenville Stoke?"

The two men exchanged a glance. "It was Mr. Vaughn who spoke of going out to the cavern tonight," Wyndham said. "We deduced the meeting. As to who set it up—" He shook his head.

"We don't know for certain if it has been," Dr. Falkirk explained. "They might be making the arrangements today."

"But a meeting will take place." Lexie clenched her hands in her lap. "We have to stop him."

"Rather, I believe we'll do best to spring a trap."

Her eyes widened. "You're right. This might be your only chance! Do you think the authorities will listen to you now?"

His expression hardened. "I wish I could be certain."

She leaned forward, intent, her thoughts racing. "If Grenville Stoke is there, then the dagger probably will be, too. And if Geoff Vaughn is with him, all I have to do is *get* that knife, then latch onto Geoff. Then he won't be able to cause any more trouble." She bit her lip and lowered her gaze. "And neither will I."

Wyndham rose. "I believe I will go into Rye and visit the Land Customs office."

Lexie sprang to her feet. "I'll go with you. Just let me get a coat."

"No. You will stay here."

"Don't be ridiculous. They never listened to you before, so why should they now? I might be a different case, though."

"I thought you were worried about changing history."

"That was before you told me what Geoff Vaughn's been up to. His helping the conspirators changes everything. Now

236

I've got to help you, to equalize things again. Please, let me try!"

Dr. Falkirk looked up from his plate of rare roast beef. "She's right, my boy. It certainly can't hurt, at any rate."

Wyndham stared at her, his expression a cross between a caress and a frown. "And what if it hurts *her?*" he asked.

Lexie shook her head. "I'm not some poor female from your time who has to be protected from everything, remember."

His steady gaze rested on her. "You may have come from an era that allows you more freedom, but that does not mean you are necessarily prepared for the dangers your freedom brings."

She opened her mouth, then closed it again. Irritatingly, he had a point.

He nodded and turned toward the door. "I leave as soon as the carriage is brought round."

Lexie excused herself to the doctor and hurried after Wyndham. The earl wasn't likely to wait for her.

He did, though, take time to assure her comfort. As she joined him at the front door, a closed carriage with the Wyndham arms emblazoned on the panels pulled up before the great old house. A footman hurried from the kitchens bearing several towel-wrapped parcels which radiated warmth as he passed Lexie. Heated bricks. Another footman followed, bearing an assortment of carriage blankets which, by the feel of them, had been hanging before a fire.

After they had seated themselves comfortably within the vehicle, and he had arranged the robes about her and the bricks at her feet, Charles turned to stare out the window. He must be concentrating his thoughts on the coming interview with the authorities who had rejected his story already. She couldn't blame him, but she'd much rather they took what might be one of their last opportunities to concentrate on each other.

She slid her hand through the crook of his elbow, and he turned to look down at her. "I may be gone before midnight," she said.

237

He drew her against him, holding her tight, vouchsafing not a single word. There was no need. For a few delightful minutes she contemplated the possibilities of seducing him right there in the carriage, then with regret abandoned the idea. It would be too cold, far too hurried, and as uncomfortable as anything. Resting in his arms would have to do for now. But somehow, before they left the Priory for that fateful meeting tonight, they would have to find a couple of hours alone. They had so little time . . .

All too soon for her taste they entered Rye, and Wyndham set her from him with a regretful comment about proprieties. Eventually they pulled up before an unprepossessing building, which Lexie regarded with a fluttering of nerves in her stomach. Well, here went nothing, she reflected—then hoped sincerely that trite old phrase would not prove to be true.

She jumped down from the carriage behind Wyndham and shivered in the icy wind. He gave her an encouraging smile, which she tried to return. Still without speaking, he took her arm and guided her up the shallow steps and inside.

Two rooms flanked the dark entry hall. Wyndham went to the door on the right and flung it wide, revealing a small chamber holding two desks, a blazing hearth, and several chairs. Lexie loosened the top button of her pelisse as the heat washed over her.

The only occupant, a small bespectacled man with neatly trimmed grizzled hair, looked up from his work, then laid aside his quill. After a moment's hesitation during which time he examined his visitors, he stood. "My Lord Wyndham. You visit us again. What may we have the honor of doing for you this time?"

"Listening—and acting, *this time.*" The earl stalked forward, drawing Lexie with him. "Good morning, Captain Doring. I have learned there is to be a meeting this night of several conspirators against His Majesty's government."

"Indeed, my lord?" The captain eyed him without enthusiasm. "And how, may I ask, did you learn this?"

"*I* learned it," Lexie declared, rushing into speech before Wyndham could reply. She faced the captain, and wished a note of challenge hadn't crept into her voice. She didn't need to antagonize the man. Oh, well, it was too late to repine. Instead, she tried a tentative smile.

The man's eyebrows rose, and his critical gaze swept over her. "And what, precisely, did you learn, miss?"

Lexie glanced at Wyndham, who nodded encouragement. "I am a visitor to this area, from America. A man who—who traveled with me has been behaving in a very odd manner, and last night when I saw him he said something about Napoleon's plans to invade England, and having to meet several people tonight." Well, that was close enough to the truth. At least it got the idea across.

The little man tilted his head, and the candle light glinted in his narrowed eyes. "I see, miss. And you're the young lady who is visiting Lady Agatha Penrith, are you not?"

Lexie blinked. "Yes."

A slow smile just touched the man's lips. "Very set on this conspiracy idea, are they not, miss? I daresay you've heard a lot of talk about it since you came?"

Wyndham stiffened, but Lexie's fingers closed over his elbow. To her relief, he kept silent. She managed a puzzled frown and directed a questioning look first at Wyndham, then back at the captain. "What do you mean? The first I heard of it was last night, when Mr. Vaughn and Mr. Grenville Stoke seemed so very pleased about something. It worried me, so I told . . . his lordship, who brought me to you."

The furrows in the captain's brow deepened. "Is that so, miss? And you've never heard so much as a whisper about such a conspiracy before?"

Lexie turned toward Wyndham, hoping her expression presented a picture of perplexity. "What is he talking about? *Should* I have?"

A contemptuous smile just touched the earl's lips. "I warned you they were not likely to take your fears seriously, Cousin Lexie. If time allowed, we could go to the Horse Guards. As it is, I see we shall have to handle this matter ourselves. I only wonder what your superiors will say, Captain, when they learn you knew of this meeting and did nothing to prevent it."

The harassed captain glared at them. For a very long minute he remained silent, his eyes flashing as if with a reflection of the thoughts that must whirl in his mind. At last he nodded, and a satisfied smile replaced his irritated expression.

He strode to the door. "Very well, my Lord Wyndham. We shall see. I'll send a man with you. But if nothing comes of this, I warn you, I will seek action against you for laying false information."

"There won't be the need," Wyndham snapped.

"Crewe!" the captain called through the doorway. "Come in here." He returned to his desk.

A minute later, a thin young man of medium height with an unruly shock of light brown hair entered. "Sir?" He cast a nervous glance at the two visitors.

"My Lord Wyndham, this is Lieutenant Crewe. Lieutenant, are you familiar with the earl's previous complaints?"

The young man's eyes widened. "Indeed I am, sir. I read his reports with the greatest of interest when I first came."

The captain nodded. "Well, you may now have your dearest wish. He claims there is to be a meeting this night of his conspirators. You may accompany him, and if the situation arises, you may take whatever action you deem necessary under the circumstances."

The man's gray eyes positively glowed. *"Thank* you, sir. My lord!" He turned to Wyndham. "Tell me what you know. Everything!"

"Perhaps in the other room?" the captain suggested. He turned back to his work, as if he had already forgotten the matter of Wyndham and his unsubstantiated fears.

Lexie glared at the man in barely contained indignation. No wonder Wyndham had been reluctant to approach these men. His refusal to believe them she found as insulting as his abrupt dismissal. He obviously thought the earl crazy—or at least obsessed with a mare's nest. Well, they'd prove him wrong.

Lexie followed Wyndham and his newly assigned assistant across the hall to a long room where several men worked at desks. Lieutenant Crewe led them to the far corner, where someone had positioned several chairs around the hearth. The lieutenant gestured for Lexie and Wyndham to be seated, then settled across from them.

"Tell me everything," he begged. He leaned forward, arms resting on his thighs, his expression enthralled.

They could have desired no more eager an audience, Lexie reflected. She could only hope this would compensate for his youth and inexperience. Wyndham repeated their story of what they had learned, and the lieutenant's innocent gray eyes widened with every word. His mouth formed an ecstatic "Oh," then he swiveled to his desk, dipped a quill into the ink well and took rapid notes.

"Tonight?" he breathed at last. "Don't worry, my lord, I've waited my entire career for a chance like this! They won't get away."

"His entire career," Wyndham muttered some fifteen minutes later when they at last escaped the effusive lieutenant, "being possibly six months in duration."

"He's probably a little older than that," Lexie temporized. "A whole year, maybe."

Wyndham humphed. "All I need is some Johnny Raw recruit with delusions of glory to go rushing in and give us away. He'll be more trouble than he's worth!"

"He's an official, that's what matters. If we aren't able to capture all your conspirators, at least we'll have someone along whom the authorities will believe."

"We?"

"Of course. I have to be there because of the dagger. You know that."

His gaze rested on her, his expression unreadable. "You do not." He brushed a stray tendril of hair from her eyes, and his fingers lingered in her curls. "I will bring you the dagger. And Vaughn. No," he added as she opened her mouth to protest. "I'll have no arguments from you. Is that understood? This might prove very dangerous tonight. I'll not have you in the middle of it."

"The devil you won't," she informed him, borrowing from his own vocabulary. "Will you quit treating me like a child?

241

I'm able to make my own decisions."

"Then make a sensible one, and remain at the Priory."

"I will not!" She clenched her fists at her side. "Charles, I'm involved in this. That dagger actually transported me through *time*. Do you have any idea how impossible a concept that is? Yet I'm here, where I don't belong. Maybe it's because of my locket, and what happened to Dr. Falkirk's daughter when *she* wore it in the vicinity of that dagger. Or maybe there's more to it than that. Maybe I'm here to fulfill some role Alexandra Falkirk would have filled if that dagger hadn't brought about her death. Maybe I'm supposed to be there."

"I will not have you along." Maddeningly, he shook his head. "I will not risk your life."

"Damn it, Charles, *you* aren't risking anything! *I'm* the one making the choice. It's my life to risk if I want to. I make my own decisions."

He rocked back on his heels, his eyes glinting as his gaze rested on her face. Warm color rose in her cheeks in response. He wasn't accustomed to a woman making decisions on her own, she reminded herself. A pity they didn't have more time together for him to grow used to the idea.

"I make my own decisions, as well." His eyes hardened. "And I choose not to take you. Make of that what you will, madam."

She clenched her teeth. There would be no talking reason to the man. She'd have to handle the matter in her own way. And she would, too, to her own satisfaction. What he didn't know wouldn't hurt him—and it wouldn't hinder her plans.

Without another word, she allowed him to lead her to the waiting carriage, then subsided against the cushions and pointedly stared out the window. Let him think he had the final word. He'd learn differently soon enough.

He sat beside her, tense, staring straight ahead, obviously deep in plans for that night. Lieutenant Crewe would come to the Priory, then he and the earl would ride to the spinney near the abbey ruins. Lexie would follow them—though the men didn't need to know that.

Lexie glanced at Wyndham, at the hands he clenched tightly together. The emerald gleamed from his finger. What if something happened to him? What if, because of her, because of Geoff Vaughn's interference, things progressed along a different pattern? They had so little time together, maybe less than either of them knew. She didn't want them to spend what could well be their last hours together in anger or argument.

She waited until they returned to the Priory, then followed him to his library. As soon as the door closed behind them, she laid her fingers on his arm. He looked down at them, then into her face. "Charles," she whispered, her longing clear in her voice.

His hand closed over hers. "No, Lexie. You won't cajole me into agreeing." One by one, he pried her fingers loose from his coat sleeve.

"This has nothing to do with tonight. We have several hours before you have to begin preparations. And there might only be this afternoon for us . . ."

He raised her hands to his lips. "There will be tonight, my love. *After* I return. I will bring you the dagger and your Mr. Vaughn, and I will see this conspiracy brought to naught. And *then* we can discuss how soon you must leave me."

"Charles—!" That sounded so perfect—and so impossible. "I'd give anything to stay, for even *minutes* more with you, but you know I can't." She pulled back, frustrated, fighting the tears that burned in her eyes. "I *must* leave, as soon as possible, you know that. Any minute I might let something important slip. And Vaughn might reveal things on purpose."

His brooding gaze rested on her face. "Is it your tongue you don't trust, my love, or your desire to remain with me?"

She blinked. "What do you mean?"

He retained his hold on her hands. "You are so eager to leave. Do you miss your own time?"

"No," she said, somewhat surprised to discover she didn't.

"Then why—"

A knock on the door interrupted him. He muttered something under his breath, and called: "What is it?" over his shoulder.

The door opened, and Miss Hester Langley stood on the threshold, regarding him in uncertainty. "My lord? If you have a moment?"

He drew a deep breath, and let it out slowly. "What is it, Miss Langley?"

The governess took a hesitant step into the room. "I—I saw Mr. Stoke this morning. He rode over for a brief visit—I thought you couldn't mind, the girls were never out of my sight."

Wyndham waved that aside. "What did he want?"

"Only to see me. He's been away, you must know, visiting friends. He has been, since *before* those dreadful men took Master Kester. That's what I wanted to tell you. Grenville—Mr. Stoke—*cannot* be behind this conspiracy as you believe. He wasn't even here!"

"Or so he says," Wyndham responded, though gently.

"Oh, no! But—he *wouldn't* lie to me. Would he? It *cannot* be him. You must have it wrong, Miss Anderson. It could not have been Mr. Stoke whom you saw."

Lexie took a step forward, but the agitated governess strode to the hearth. "There is the dagger," Lexie reminded her.

"The dagger," Miss Langley repeated. Tears filled her eyes. "No, I cannot believe it. I'll prove to you, you are wrong!"

"I know he has that dagger," Lexie said at last. "I *saw* it at the ball. I only wish it wasn't true."

A shaky sob broke from Miss Langley and she ran from the room, leaving Lexie and Wyndham to stare at each other in dismay.

"That poor woman." Lexie shook her head. "Probably the first *gentleman* to pay attention to her, and he did it only to learn about your family. She must be crushed."

"You may stay this night and comfort her."

She'd do something far more constructive than that. She glared at him but held her tongue. The less he knew of her plans, the better for her.

244

Chapter Nineteen

Lieutenant Crewe, Lexie guessed, would arrive at the Priory shortly after the ladies withdrew from the dining room. Alert for this event, she settled in a chair near the drawing room door. Only part of her attention focused on Miss Langley and her two young charges.

While the girls regaled Lady Agatha with a lively tale of their day's doings, their governess sat quietly in a corner, her head lowered, her expression strained. Lexie wished there might be something she could say to ease her unhappiness. Men were such louses. Or was that lice? Either way, they shouldn't romance a woman just to get information out of her. Not innocent and tenderhearted governesses, at least.

The poor woman was defenseless, alone in the world, living out her life in other people's houses, caring for other people's children. It was only natural she should grasp at the hope of a family of her own—and be all the more easily taken in by a smooth talker with no scruples. At that moment, Lexie could easily wring Mr. Grenville Stoke's neck—except she didn't want to deprive Wyndham of that pleasure, for the murder of his brother.

Lexie glanced at the clock. Eight. And Wyndham and Dr. Falkirk, who refused to be left out of this adventure, had not yet joined Lady Agatha. Perhaps that meant Lieutenant Crewe had arrived.

Lady Agatha appeared completely absorbed in the two girls, which suited Lexie exactly. She rose, then slipped out of the room. Just before she closed the door, she glanced back—and caught Miss Langley's woebegone gaze following her. Quickly, Lexie turned away.

The men would probably be in the library. That seemed to be where all momentous decisions were made in this house. She hurried down the stairs to the main hall, then slipped along the corridor leading to the earl's sanctuary.

As she inched open the door enough to hear, Wyndham's deep voice reached her. "—can't take them all, with only the three of us."

Her hand tightened on the brass handle. Captain Doring had not relented at the last moment and sent any additional men. The possibility that he might hadn't consciously occurred to her, yet the confirmation he had not left her shaken.

The door pulled wide, almost yanking her off her feet. Wyndham stood before her, an ironic smile twisting her lips. "You may come in, Cousin Lexie."

"Thank you." She straightened up with what dignity she could muster. To her irritation, her heart pounded in her chest.

"Listening at key holes can be very unsatisfying," he added.

She inclined her head. "It sure is. It makes it hard to make comments. Why don't you bring your grooms or the footmen with you? They'd be willing to help, wouldn't they?"

"They most certainly would, which is why I have no intention of asking them." He returned to his seat behind his desk. "They are not trained soldiers, and I will not risk their lives. Any more than I will risk yours."

She shook her head. "We've already had that argument. I take my own risks."

The earl's brow snapped down, but before he could speak, Dr. Falkirk cleared his throat. "I don't believe it would be wise for you to go, my dear. You are well aware of your reaction to the dagger. What if it affected you at a critical moment?"

"I won't let it." She turned to Wyndham. "You can't leave me behind."

246

"I can and I will. This is no place for you. We will capture Mr. Vaughn, if we can, and Mr. Stoke. I doubt the others will be much of a problem."

The lieutenant glanced uneasily at the earl. "That's as may be, your lordship, but I doubt that just three of us, against we don't know how many, can be of much use."

"Then you should have brought reinforcements," Wyndham snapped.

The lieutenant lowered his gaze to the desk. "Well, my lord, Captain Doring thought it might be best if we just had a look around tonight."

"Hah!" Wyndham surged to his feet, setting his chair rocking. "He thinks we're chasing mare's nests. If he suspected for even a moment what we're going to be up against tonight, he'd have sent his entire contingent of men. This isn't going to look very good on his record, you may be very sure of that."

Lieutenant Crewe cleared his throat. "Only if we fail, my Lord."

Wyndham turned to look back at him. "If we fail, Lieutenant, his record will no longer be of any moment whatsoever, to us or to him."

Lieutenant Crewe sat back, dismayed. "You really think they'll succeed in this invasion scheme?"

"I don't see anything to stop them. We've been expecting the French to try, but there have already been so many false alarms, no one is willing to act until it's going to be too late."

Lexie broke the silence that followed this statement. "So what is your plan?"

Wyndham swung his quizzing glass by its riband and turned his thoughtful gaze on her. "My plan, such as it is, will be to enter the cavern after the conspirators are already gathered, and hear what we may. Once we know how many we're up against, we'll have a better idea how to proceed. If there aren't too many, we might be able to capture them as they try to leave—unless they go by the ocean."

"You mean—direct to France?"

Wyndham raised a sardonic eyebrow. "Why else would they risk returning to the cavern now that their use of it has

247

been discovered? Stoke's smuggler acquaintances must be planning a run tonight." His gaze held the lieutenant's, then moved to Dr. Falkirk. "I believe it is time we set forth. Cousin Lexie? You may await our return in here, if you wish."

He ushered the other two men from the room, then turned back to her and held out his arms. Now wasn't a moment for arguments, she reflected. She went to him, holding him tight, raising her face to his for the offered kiss.

"Don't worry, my love," he said when he could speak again. "I will bring you both Vaughn and the dagger."

Her hands slid to his shoulders. "And yourself in one piece. Take care."

He kissed her once more, then followed the others.

She shook her head. Men. He *let* himself be fooled, because he couldn't conceive of her defying his commands. He had so much to learn.

The three men departed for the stables twenty minutes later, garbed in their heavy greatcoats and armed with both pistols and knives. Half way across the yard, the tallest—Wyndham—paused and looked back at the house. Lexie, staring through the frosted pane of her bedroom window, drew back into the shadows. Hopefully, he would think her not being there to see them off merely a fit of pique on her part for being denied the right to go with them.

The earl turned away again, and the figures disappeared into the darkness of the night. Their horses should be waiting, they would be mounted in only minutes and riding out of the cobbled yard. Good.

She dragged on the cloak over the green merino she had once more donned. She'd rather have her jeans, but that would make the grooms question her story. No, she'd have to manage as she was. She tucked her shawl about her neck like a muffler and set forth.

Her sneakers made as little noise as did the satin slippers as she hurried across the hall. She checked for stray footmen and butlers, then ducked into the long ballroom. It took her a moment to adjust to the darkness, then she ran across the marble tiles to where velvet drapes concealed the French windows. She unlatched one and let herself out into the freezing night.

Icy wind cut through her, and she huddled into the woolen folds of her cape and trudged toward the stable. Next time she had an adventure, she'd have to do it during the summer. January was no time to go haring about in the dead of night.

Nor were her sneakers waterproof. Snow clung to their leather surface, melting slowly, penetrating the heavy wool of her socks until her toes numbed. If only she'd been wearing pile-lined boots when she went exploring that morning ages ago—in the future.

Lights still illuminated the enclosed yard, though the horsemen had already departed. Lexie drew behind a tree to wait. To make this realistic, she had to give them at least a ten minute start. She hugged herself and wished for a pair of gloves. She could have waited inside where it was warm. At last, one of the lads began extinguishing lanterns, and she sprang into action.

"Wait!" she called, and hurried forward.

One of the men—the undergroom, she saw, as he crossed beneath the beam from a light—strode up to her. "Yes, miss?"

"Have they left? Yes, of course they must have. Oh, dear. I must go after them, then. I've thought of something they must know. Please, can someone saddle a horse for me?"

"Don't worry yourself, miss. I'll go," the groom offered. "What is it you want to tell them?"

Lexie swallowed, momentarily taken aback. "I—it's too complicated to explain. Please, it will be faster if I go."

He shrugged. "Want someone to go with you, miss?"

"No, that's all right. It shouldn't take me long to catch up to them. If you hurry." She pretended impatience, pacing the yard, thereby keeping herself warmer in the process. She wanted to give them time to get safely inside the cavern before the noise of her arrival alerted them to her presence.

Five minutes later, the groom threw her onto the side-saddle on the bay mare. Her skirt proved more of a hindrance than she'd expected, but she managed to hike it up sufficiently to hook her knee safely in position. Her cloak covered her legs, but did little to warm them. Settled at last, she turned the horse through the gate.

For the first three miles she followed the road, then slowed, suddenly uncertain of the way. There was a turnoff along here somewhere—or was it a mile farther? It had been snowing that night she and Wyndham had gone to search for Vaughn. Now, everything looked different, dark and unrecognizable. She urged the mare into a trot, scanning the shrubbery to her left.

A movement caught her eye, a shape merging deeper into the night shadows, too large to be a harmless animal on its nightly prowl. She tensed, and her mount threw its head in protest. The shadow shifted again, and Lexie caught the outline of a huddled figure, a dark cloak wrapped about a shapeless body.

Her horse sidled as she started to turn away, but she couldn't leave, not if someone were in trouble. She bit her lip, gathering her courage. Hers was the advantage, being on horseback, if the person tried to attack her. Still, she kept her distance.

"Do you need help?" she called.

The figure stiffened, then a pale face emerged from the enveloping cloak. "Miss Anderson? Is that you?" a soft trembling voice called.

It took a second for Lexie to place it. "Miss Langley?" she cried, and nudged the horse closer. "Are you all right? What are you doing out here? We're miles from the Priory."

"I've *got* to know the truth!" the woman cried. "I cannot believe Mr. Stoke guilty, not until I see the evidence for myself. If he's there—" She broke off and dabbed at her eyes.

"How did you know about the meeting tonight?" Lexie demanded.

"I overheard Dr. Falkirk say something about it this evening." She sniffed. "Why aren't you with them?"

The corner of Lexie's mouth twitched. "They ordered me to stay home."

Miss Langley's head came up slowly. "They ordered you— Then why are you going?"

"To see for myself that nothing goes wrong—and help out

if it does."

Miss Langley rose, then brushed ineffectually at the snow which clung to her cloak. She raised a woebegone face to Lexie. "May I go with you? I don't think I realized how very far it would be, and how—how dark." She shivered.

Lexie brought the mare closer. "Here, think you can mount behind me? She seems to be strong enough to carry us both." She cast the woman an appraising glance. "No, neither of us is very big. Here." She held down her hand.

Miss Langley stared at it in apparent confusion. "What should I do?"

"Swing up here. No, I suppose I'd better." Lexie unhooked her knee from the pommel with care and jumped to the ground.

The governess, murmuring only a slight protest about not being properly dressed, allowed Lexie to help her into the saddle. She was forced, as Lexie had been, to hike up her narrow skirt in order to secure her knee over the pommel; but, as Lexie pointed out, her cloak covered her both for warmth and modesty. With a measure of uncertainty, the governess agreed.

Lexie then led the horse several hundred yards along the road until they reached a fence. After positioning the animal beside it, she climbed up, pulled her skirts to where they didn't hamper her, then swung her leg over the horse and eased herself down behind the saddle. The mare sidled, but accepted this added burden. Lexie patted her flank in mute apology, then tucked her cloak about her as quickly as possible. Settled at last, she instructed Miss Langley to proceed. This they did at a brisk walk.

"Thank you," the governess said presently.

"No problem." Lexie stared ahead. "Do you know where the turn-off is?"

"Just ahead." Now that she had a companion, the governess appeared to be recovering much of her equilibrium.

"What do you hope to accomplish?" Lexie asked.

The young woman before her let out a ragged breath, which hung before them in the freezing night air. "To see for

251

myself if there is any truth in the accusations against Mr. Stoke."

"And if there is? If he's there?" Lexie asked, though gently.

The governess sagged in the saddle. "I don't know. Leave, I suppose. But he won't be. There has been a mistake, some dreadful misunderstanding, and it will all be set to rights. Only I—I cannot ask him, can I? If I am wrong, and he *is* involved in this dreadful conspiracy, my confronting him might cause more harm to the Penrith family. And that I could not bear."

"For your sake, I hope I am wrong," Lexie said, and let it drop.

They reached the narrow lane to the left and followed it for just over a mile. Then Miss Langley turned their mount down another, and at last they left the road entirely to pass through a gap in the bushes. This led to a broad field, which they crossed slowly, the horse picking her way with care over the uneven ground. When they entered a spinney, the governess finally reined to a halt.

"We'd best get off here," she whispered.

Lexie nodded and swung to the ground, landing as quietly as she could manage.

Miss Langley followed. A twig snapped beneath her half-boots, and Lexie tensed, waiting for some reaction. None came.

"There." Miss Langley pointed toward a towering shape in the darkness, more a lightening of shadows than a definite form.

The ruins of the abbey. Lexie tied the horse's reins to a branch, then followed the governess from the sheltering underbrush. They had gone barely fifty feet before a low nickering sounded to their left. Lexie dropped low, but when no other sound followed she rose slowly and circled around through the shrubbery.

Miss Langley crept after her. "What is it?" the woman whispered.

Lexie made a hushing motion, realized it was probably too dark for her companion to have seen it, and inched forward until she reached a small clearing. Four horses stood in relative quiet, back fetlocks cocked, their reins fastened to various branches. The tall black she recognized as Wyndham's, the roan as Dr. Falkirk's. The chestnut must be Lieutenant Crewe's. And the gray—Wyndham's groom, she decided. That was why Huggins had not been in the yard to waylay her. She could only be glad that one of his men had insisted on coming along.

At least the men already had arrived and would be in position by now. That saved her the fear of being discovered—or worse, accidentally getting in their way. She was there solely for observation—unless, of course, the opportunity arose to grab the dagger and Vaughn. And what would she do with them, leave Wyndham forever with a casual wave of thanks for all the help?

She turned away, her heart aching. Whether their goodbye was long or short, it made no difference in the long run. Either way, he would be lost to her; they would be separated forever by the insurmountable barrier of time.

At least she had memories, of firelight dancing on his hair, of his deep, rich laugh, of the one night she had spent in his arms. She would relive these over and over again through the empty years ahead.

And they would be empty. How could she ever consider another man, now she had known Charles and his love?

Forcing the pain from her heart, she started forward. One hope remained to her. If the meeting *didn't* take place—or rather, if it took place somewhere else—then Wyndham would be safe, and she would be unable to leave him for a little while longer.

No, she couldn't be so purely selfish. For the sake of England, for the sake of *history,* they had to catch the conspirators. She had to concentrate on being silent, not on the loneliness that seeped into her.

Besides, if nothing came of this venture, that poor nervous lieutenant would be terribly disappointed. And worse, Wyndham would have the authorities out for his blood.

Lexie and Miss Langley reached a clearing that had once been a lawn, but hesitated at the line of trees. Beyond rose the ragged silhouette of the ruined abbey. Beyond, they would be exposed.

Or would they? Only the faintest moonlight penetrated the heavy cloud covering. The ruins were more a suggestion of fallen walls rather than any concrete shape. Lexie gestured for Miss Langley to duck low, as she did herself, then ran lightly across the snow-covered grass toward the shadows of the tumbled stones.

Twigs snapped, and Lexie hugged her new shelter, peering across the clearing. A rustling followed, then a horse stamped in impatience. Lexie swallowed, her throat uncomfortably dry. The conspirators were already here, their mounts tethered close by.

Her knees buckled, but she forced them to cooperate. It hadn't seemed real before. Last time she visited the caverns, when she and Wyndham searched for Geoff Vaughn, they had been empty. Now they weren't.

Miss Langley drew a shaky breath. "Let us go see." The words came out on a broken sob.

Lexie nodded, then bee-lined for the one wall which remained standing. The door leading to the passageway stood a few inches ajar, as if someone feared the noise it might make if the rusty hinges were forced. "You can't make any sound," Lexie whispered to her companion, then eased the door open just enough to allow herself to slip inside.

A faint light greeted them, illuminating the shallow chamber in which they stood. Lexie turned to the right, from where the flickering glow emanated, then rounded the corner to find a guttering torch thrust into a metal bracket on the wall. She walked more easily, able to see her way, knowing she would not collide with anything that might betray their presence. She threw Miss Langley an encouraging smile and began her cautious descent.

Here, the snow didn't reach, but the walls remained slippery and cold from the continual moisture from the ocean below. Lexie's foot skidded on the slick surface, she caught her balance against the wall, and grimaced as the rough-hewn rock bit into her hand. She'd never cared much for spelunking, even at the best of times.

They followed the switch-back route with care, slowing at

every hairpin curve to assure themselves no one lurked just out of sight. At last, after they'd descended perhaps two hundred feet, the subdued rumble of the waves reached her from where they crashed against the side of the cliff below.

Was this high tide? No, that wouldn't make sense, not with a meeting. It must be low, with the smugglers bringing their boats close into the sheltered cove. Close, for a rapid and easy departure to France, carrying the fateful information to Napoleon . . .

Another rumble reached her, of voices raised in argument, and her heart skipped a beat. Miss Langley's hand caught her arm. For comfort, Lexie realized after a quick look at the woman's drawn face. That made two of them who were scared.

Again Lexie inched forward, with the governess sticking close to her side, and they rounded the next bend. Ahead of them, gathered at the turning, stood four men. Lexie's worried gaze sought out Wyndham's tall figure, and she barely bit back a sigh of relief. He was safe, at least for the moment. That was all that mattered.

Next to him, the eager young lieutenant leaned intently forward. In one hand he clasped a pistol, which did nothing to steady Lexie's own nerves. From the set of his back, he seemed nervous. He probably hadn't really believed he might come face to face with genuine spies. He would have hoped, though. He must be near frantic with excitement. Lexie shrank back, knowing the folly of startling a man in so obvious a state of nerves—particularly one in possession of a gun.

"Which route should we tell 'em to take?" a rough voice demanded from the cavern beyond, barely audible to Lexie's straining ears.

"You must be more familiar than I with the landings along this coast."

The second, muffled voice sounded eerily familiar to Lexie. That supercilious tone, that slight sneer in the words. . . . Lexie closed her eyes and could see the masked man standing over her once more, threatening.

"Aye, o'course we does. But them Frogs ain't goin' to just

sit 'ere and look 'round the countryside." This was followed by a derisive laugh on the part of several men.

"Not like they're not," agreed another deep voice.

"'Ow'er we to tell 'em to get from 'ere to London?" the first pursued.

Lexie gripped her hands together to keep them from trembling. Now the authorities *had* to believe Wyndham. The plot would be prevented—if they got out of this to carry the message to the lieutenant's superiors.

An unwary boot scraped against stone behind them, and Lexie spun. For one endless moment, she stared, incredulous, into the bewildered face of Mr. Grenville Stoke.

A gasp escaped Miss Langley as Lieutenant Crewe, his hands trembling, spun about. His finger clutched the trigger and the pistol went off with a resounding explosion.

The ball ricocheted off the roof of the passage and rock fragments cascaded about them. Lexie ducked low, covering her head and neck as sharp shards rained upon them as the ball struck a wall, then the floor. Stillness followed for perhaps one stunned second, then a flurry of booted footsteps sounded as the conspirators and smugglers burst upon them.

Chapter Twenty

Trapped. Lexie drew back against the slimy wall as chaos broke loose about them. Wyndham ducked low and launched himself into the midriff of a bulky man who bore down on him. Miss Langley screamed, Mr. Grenville Stoke lunged forward, and everywhere men struggled, fists swinging. Lexie gasped for breath, then looked about. If she could find some weapon, some club. . . .

She grasped the heavy wooden base of the torch above her and dragged it free of its bracket. A rough dressed man staggered back into her and she brought it down on his head with a sickening thud. He dropped, and Lexie looked up to meet Wyndham's shocked gaze over the man's inert body. She grinned, and knew it a poor attempt.

Then another smuggler dove in, fists flailing, and Wyndham closed with him. Lexie swung once more and a second of their opponents collapsed in a heap at her feet. More took their places. Dr. Falkirk battled another—was it Mr. Walling, from the inn? Lexie plowed forward, torch swinging, but couldn't reach them.

A heavy-set man thrust her backward into Lieutenant Crewe, knocking askew his right hook into the jaw of a man who looked familiar—the ex-barman from the Crown Inn, she realized. So the trio hadn't gone far. Another smuggler knocked the torch from her hand, then with one sweeping blow threw her against the wall. Her head struck stone and she slid to the ground, stunned.

There wasn't room in here. No one could fight in so narrow a passage. The damp stones beneath their feet provided slick footing, and the men slipped, their punches going wild. Wyndham worked steadily forward, thrusting the smugglers from his way, forcing his passage toward the cavern. Lexie raised dazed eyes to the opening. Grenville Stoke stood there . . .

No, he was beside her, his body shielding Miss Langley as he struck a smuggler. With one swift movement, he pulled a gleaming knife from his boot. Lexie's breath caught in her throat . . .

The wrong knife.

Lexie turned back in time to see Wyndham stumble over a fallen man—his own groom—and close on Sir Thomas Stoke.

Dear heaven, she'd been after the wrong man. A shaky laugh, of mingled horror and consternation, escaped her. Sir Thomas Stoke, not his brother Grenville.

She rose on unsteady legs, pushing against the back of one of the men to keep her balance, then a shot rang out and she ducked once more for cover. When the last of the ricochets died away, she again forced her way to her feet.

And stopped as a wave of disorientation left her trembling, her knees too weak to support her. She stumbled as the cavern shimmered about her, spinning, men everywhere, even above and below her. The sounds of the struggle echoed hollow in her ears, as if they came from a great distance—across the ages.

She stood alone in the corridor, while hazy images, holographic in their insubstantiality, fought about her. Wyndham swung at Sir Thomas, who merely stepped back, dodging with ease. In Sir Thomas's hand . . .

The dagger gleamed, bright and solid, the only other substantial object in this hazy between-worlds she inhabited. Every chased line of the silver handle glittered, stark and clear. The star sapphire winked, blazing with a light of its own, as it turned in Sir Thomas's grasp. Then it plunged downward, toward the earl's shoulder blades.

"Charles!" Lexie screamed, and surged forward, only to

258

collide with Lieutenant Crewe. She staggered, once more firmly in the past—and firmly in the midst of the struggle.

She shook her head to clear her reeling vision. Wyndham still stood, and the dagger . . . Sir Thomas clasped it in his hand, and Wyndham gripped the wrist, forcing it back, away from himself. Behind them in the main cavern, just watching, his expression unreadable, stood Geoff Vaughn.

The dagger clattered to the stone floor, the sound distinct over the other noises of fighting to Lexie's ears. An exclamation of satisfaction escaped Wyndham, and at last he closed his hands about the throat of the man who had murdered his younger brother.

Lexie ducked away from a smuggler's flailing arm, darting forward to reach for the dagger. It continued to glow, as if with an inner light of its own. As her fingers neared it, a booted foot, sliding over the damp stones, kicked it from her grasp.

She lunged after it, only to collide with the man's leg. He grasped her hair, jerking her head back, and she stared up into the glowering face of the ex-barman. He flung her aside, then turned, swinging, and his massive fist landed squarely on Wyndham's jaw. The earl's hold slackened on Sir Thomas, who followed up the advantage, striking Wyndham in the stomach. The earl doubled over.

Again Lexie dove for the dagger, but the ex-barman caught her about the waist, pinioning her arms, lifting her from her feet. She kicked, her foot struck his knee, and with a yowl of protest, he spun her about and hit her across the face, sending her staggering backward.

"Enough!" Sir Thomas's deep voice carried over the din of the struggle. His left arm clamped across Lexie's shoulders as he dragged her against himself.

Lexie barely noticed. Her world spun crazily and she sagged, limp in his grasp, the only solid sensation the stinging prick of the dagger point against her neck. That she experienced with vivid intensity, like acid on a raw nerve. Yet time remained solid about her, not dragging her into that dreaded *between*. Why didn't it?

Wyndham stopped in mid-lunge, barely recovering his

balance. "Let her go," he gasped, the words hoarse in his throat.

"I think not."

Lexie closed her eyes, fighting the waves of dizziness. Perhaps if she concentrated, she *could* go now, back to her own time, away from all this—if only she could be sure Geoff Vaughn would come with her. She moved her head, trying to catch a glimpse of him, but he remained out of sight, probably behind them.

Or *could* she go home? Her senses reeled, but her surroundings did not. The nearness alone of the dagger should have produced that dreaded effect. Yet now, even with it actually *touching* her, it didn't send her hurtling through time as it did once before when it brought her back to this era.

Because Sir Thomas Stoke held it. The realization struck her like a blinding flash. In the cavern, when she'd first found herself in this alien time, when *he* held the dagger, it hadn't affected her. And now *somehow,* his presence held her here, because *he* possessed it again—or because *it* possessed him.

"You." Sir Thomas gestured at Wyndham. "Against the wall. And your men." He punctuated the command by pressing the blade more firmly against Lexie's throat.

She winced at the sting, then something warm touched the spot, seeping down the cold flesh of her exposed neck. Blood.

Wyndham, his expression haggard, remained frozen. The others, Lexie saw, had stopped their various struggles and now stood motionless, watching.

Except Grenville Stoke. He took a step forward. "You can't do this, Thomas."

Lexie's captor gave a short laugh. "Can I not? The cards, for once, appear to be all in my hand."

"Don't hurt her." Grenville Stoke took another cautious step toward them.

Again, Sir Thomas laughed. "Lord, what a fool you are. You always were, though, were you not? Playing with your fool collection while opportunities slipped through your grasp. And now you're clinging to the skirts of women."

Grenville shook his head. "It was you I followed this night. You haven't been quite as clever as you believe, dear brother."

The sneer sounded in Sir Thomas's voice as he answered. "Did our talk last night finally alert you to the true reason I've sent you on those trips? I didn't think you could be such a simpleton, believing those journeys innocent, never realizing you carried messages."

Grenville stiffened and his eyes narrowed, becoming mere slits in the wavering light of the remaining torches. "How long has this been going on?"

"Years, 'dear brother.' We have laid our plans well, with your unwitting aid. Napoleon will be in London before spring."

Grenville advanced again. "Let her go," he said, his voice oddly calm.

The dagger never wavered from Lexie's neck. "No, do you think we can let any of you live? Yes, 'dear brother,' even you? We have kept this little conspiracy of ours very quiet, the only ones who have learned of it have carried that knowledge to their graves."

Lexie met Wyndham's frozen stare and her heart sank. He would do nothing to escape, nothing that might cause her harm, not while she remained a hostage. He wouldn't risk her, even though death faced them all. She had to free herself somehow . . .

She allowed her shoulders to slump, as if with despair, her head dropping and her knees buckling. Sir Thomas muttered something near her ear and shifted his grip on her. His wrist brushed her chin, his hand touched her mouth, and she bit as hard as she could.

With a cry he released her, and she lunged forward, only to have her head jerked back by her hair as he caught her once more. His arm fastened about her throat, choking her, as Wyndham spun on the smuggler nearest him, flooring him. Grenville followed suit, and the struggle resumed about them.

Suddenly Wyndham dove for the rocky floor, then he stood slowly, a pistol in his hand. "Let her go, Stoke."

261

The two men faced each other across Lexie for a moment that rivaled eternity.

A soft laugh shook Sir Thomas. "I believe we are at a standoff, my dear Wyndham. You cannot shoot me while I hold her, nor can I kill her—at the moment. I believe it is time we called an end to this farce, do not you?"

He stepped back, dragging Lexie with him, the knife once more at her throat, until they entered the main cavern. The ex-barman ducked after them, followed by Walling. Sir Thomas barely spared them a glance. Wyndham followed slowly, keeping pace, the pistol still raised.

"Bring him." Sir Thomas jerked his head toward Geoff Vaughn.

Vaughn started. "What the hell—" He broke off on a cry of startled pain as Walling jerked his arm behind him, twisting it.

"To the boats," Sir Thomas directed. He waited while his two henchmen forced the protesting Vaughn down the twisting passage, then dragged Lexie another step backward. "They are yours, men," he shouted.

The remaining smugglers erupted into the cavern. One took Wyndham down in a flying tackle. He rolled, but the man landed on top of him. Lexie cried out in warning as another joined the fray. Sir Thomas's grip shifted on her, and she pulled free.

He swung, and pain exploded through her temple. As she fell, darkness swarmed through her, obliterating her senses.

Chapter Twenty-One

Nausea stirred in Lexie's stomach, dragging her back from black oblivion. She shivered, cold to the bone, unable to move. Darkness engulfed her, making it impossible to see anything, to discern even the faintest outlines of her surroundings. Her world tipped and swayed, as if the rough wooden floor beneath her possessed a life of its own. Several minutes passed before she realized it actually *did* move, rising and falling in an uneven rhythm.

She repressed the groan that rose from the depths of her being and shifted, trying to ease the ache just below her shoulders. She couldn't bring her arms in front of her. They felt heavy, flaccid, with the numbness of having the circulation cut off for too long.

She rolled to her side, removing the pressure from them, and seconds later an inept acupuncturist went to work, jabbing thousands of tiny, sharp needles into her hands and wrists. She gritted her teeth against the piercing stabs, only to encounter the rough folds of a rag. That explained the foul taste in her mouth. Someone had gagged her. That also explained her inability to move; ropes bound her wrists. She tested her ankles and found them restricted, as well.

The floor continued its unmannerly rocking, and at last, with a fresh onslaught of the queasiness, she identified the dull roar and thuds accompanying the movement as the ocean, and waves hitting a hull. She must be lying in the bottom of one of the smugglers' crafts.

Memory flooded back, unwelcome and painful, and she closed her eyes tight, trying to block the horrifying images which assailed her. Charles . . .

Again, she saw the smuggler slamming into him, knocking him to the rocky cavern floor. Dear God, was he even still alive? How could he have fought his way free, with so many enemies? She huddled down against the rough-hewn planks, her heart as frozen as her body.

From somewhere on the deck above her head, a hoarse, guttural voice called out a sharp order. The thudding of boots reached her, followed by several more *sotto voce* commands and responses. The pitching of the boat slowed to a gentle rock, and only a soft lapping of wavelets reached her ears. They must have entered a sheltered cove . . . But where? How long had she been unconscious?

Well, she might find out at any moment. She tensed, waiting, holding her breath. Minutes passed, and though movement sounded above her, no one descended to her dark, dank prison. She forced herself to relax, to ease the knotting tension of her muscles—to conserve what little energy she possessed until an opportunity for escape presented itself.

Another shout, louder this time, reached her, and muted voices came from a distance in answer. More creaking sounded, as of lines pulling taut, then silence surrounded her except for the soft slap of the water. Lexie lay quiet, straining her ears for any sign that someone remained on board.

If not . . . Had she been abandoned? Had the smugglers just walked away, leaving her to die? Panic welled in her, and she struggled, tearing the skin about her wrists and ankles until tears of fear and frustration slid down her cheeks.

No, she had to get a grip on herself, she couldn't go to pieces like this. She had to think, to be rational. She drew a deep, steadying breath, then another and another, until her racing heart steadied to a more normal rate.

Fighting only tightened her bonds. She'd have to try a different approach. Gathering her strength, she curled her legs under her, stretching to reach the ropes about her ankles, but the gropings of her numbed fingers failed to find the knot. Nor could she work her wrists loose enough to enable her to maneuver her arms beneath her and to the front. With a muttered oath, she collapsed, panting. She was stuck.

And what did she do now? Wait to die? No, that didn't make sense. Why would the smugglers abandon a boat? If Sir Thomas wanted her dead, he could have just shot her once he was free of the cavern. That must mean he intended to keep her alive—unless he meant to dump her overboard in the middle of the Channel. That, unfortunately, seemed like a real possibility.

And what did Sir Thomas plan to do about himself? He would hardly dare return to his home, for he must know the authorities would be waiting for him. If, of course, Wyndham or any of his companions had survived. But Sir Thomas hadn't waited to see. Which made it most likely he intended to cross the Channel and go to France. With herself as a hostage in place of Kester, perhaps?

Lexie groaned. Of course. Perhaps Sir Thomas hoped to buy Wyndham's silence with her life. Even now, he might have gone ashore to discover whether or not the earl lived. If he didn't, Sir Thomas would probably have her killed at once.

And if Charles didn't live, would she even care what Sir Thomas planned for her?

She didn't know how long she had lain there, but subdued voices mingling with the creak of boards and lines roused her at last. She tensed, listening, trying to count the number of men who once more boarded the craft. What had they learned—or what had they done? She tried to pull herself into a sitting position, but her cramped muscles prevented her every bit as much as did her bonds.

Rusty hinges creaked only feet from her, and she jerked her head about to stare at a dim rectangle opening to the night above. The next moment a dark shape filled it. Glaring fire sprang to life before it, casting leaping shadows on hideous features.

Lexie swallowed the scream that welled in her throat.

Only a lantern, she told herself. Someone, it appeared, deigned to visit their captive.

The light lowered, illuminating the wood timbers which formed her prison, dancing across the barrels and bales stacked against the sloping walls. And across the buckskin breeched legs and gleaming top boots of her jailor. Sir Thomas Stoke.

Lexie drew back, scraping her shoulder against something hard and sharp she couldn't see. That now familiar prickling sensation crept through her, playing havoc with her equilibrium. He must be carrying the dagger on him.

Now, the hazy thought drifted through her mind, would be a really excellent time for her to return to her own era. Perhaps if he came near enough, but didn't actually touch her . . .

"Good evening, Miss Anderson." Red and orange light flickered across Sir Thomas's sardonic smile as he towered over her, a figure out of demonic nightmares. His voice, though, remained smooth and suave, as if they met at a ball or *soiree.* "Yes, your Mr. Vaughn has told me you are *not,* as we believed, Wyndham's cousin. Ah, I forget, you are at somewhat of a disadvantage, are you not? Have no fear, I shall have that disreputable rag removed from your mouth in a trice."

He balanced the lantern on a barrel, and dropped to one knee at her side. She stiffened, but suffered his touch perforce as he pulled her to a sitting position. Nausea swept through her, followed by ripples of dizziness, but that sweeping sensation of drifting between times eluded her. With every ounce of her will she strove to find it, opening herself to the tingling that danced along her flesh as she reached for her way home . . .

She sank back, exhausted, only to find Sir Thomas still supporting her.

"I don't believe we'll be needing this again." He pulled out the rag which had been stuffed in her mouth, and cast aside both it and the one which had held it in place. "And now, Miss Anderson, are you thirsty?"

An uncomfortable dryness constricted her throat, and an

unpleasant taste lingered on her tongue from that foul cloth. When he held a flask to her lips, she took some of the liquid tentatively into her mouth.

And spit it out. It burned, tasted worse than her gag. "What—?" she managed to gasp.

Sir Thomas grasped her hair at the nape of her neck and jerked her head back, pulling her off balance. She fell against him, and the dizziness returned, wave after wave of it. Even though he released her hair, she couldn't move, couldn't struggle . . .

With a sense of drifting away, she felt him pinch her nose. She gasped for breath, and he tilted the vile contents of the flask into her mouth. She tried to spit it out, but his hand clamped over her lips. He held her trapped until the aching need of her lungs decided the issue with a reflexive gulp. Fire burned down her throat, and she gagged, but the damage had been done.

Sir Thomas shoved her aside as if she were a sack of potatoes, and he laughed—a chilling sound. "Sleep now, my dear." He picked up the lantern.

Her surroundings blurred. Sir Thomas seemed to float above her as the dizziness returned with unsettling force. The dagger . . . No. Her burgeoning hope faded. Only the effect of whatever he had forced her to swallow. Hazily, she wondered what he had given her as her senses slipped away.

During the innumerable hours that followed, she drifted in and out of consciousness, never fully awake. Only impressions reached her, of a lightening of the gloom about her, the rocking motion, the creak of the aging timbers, the pungent odor of pitch and tar. Occasionally she became aware of the shouts of the men above deck or the rattling of a chain. And the gulls, squawking their noisome challenges to one another.

Then brilliant light surrounded her, and vaguely she realized someone picked her up, carried her, tossed her onto something soft and yielding. The ungentle hands of a man forced more of the repulsive drink down her throat, but she couldn't command her arms sufficiently to struggle. She lay there, limp and helpless, hazily disgusted with herself for not being able to fight, until unconsciousness once more claimed her.

She roused again, this time to uneven motion which lurched rather than rocked. The salty tang of the sea had faded beneath dust. The drumming in her brain settled briefly into hoofbeats, then crescendoed once more until it pounded through her very being. Hours must have passed, she realized. Impressions settled into tangible reality, then faded only to return once more. The drug must be wearing off . . .

The icy draft seeping through the doorway helped steady her reeling senses. She lay still, eyes clamped closed, welcoming the chill as she willed her stomach to settle. She couldn't bear another dose from that flask. But if she appeared unconscious, perhaps Sir Thomas would leave her alone.

The movement slowed, and the carriage in which they rode swayed to a stop. A horseman pulled abreast of them, and Lexie partly opened one eye as Sir Thomas let down the window. A freezing blast of air hit her in the face.

"What is it?" Sir Thomas demanded.

"Them Froggies ain't there," a coarse voice answered.

Sir Thomas swore softly. "Delays," he muttered.

"Weren't as if they was expectin' us today," the other man pointed out.

Sir Thomas's jaw clenched. "And what should that matter? They knew the message would come soon. They should have been prepared." His fingers tapped against the leg of his buckskin breeches. "We will go to the rendezvous point and camp there."

He shouted to the driver to proceed, and threw the window back up against the weather. Hunching down once more in his corner, he muttered something Lexie couldn't quite catch. Prudently, Lexie closed her eye again. A rendezvous point with the French . . .

The reality of being in France struck her like a mallet. How could Wyndham reach her—if indeed he were able to follow at all? He might already be dead. . . . No, she couldn't think about that. History *knew* the third earl of Wyndham

268

helped prevent Napoleon's invasion plans. He *must* be alive.

But what of her being in the past, her being held hostage by Sir Thomas in that cavern so Wyndham didn't kill him? *Had* her mere presence in this time contaminated events, changed the course of history?

No, this got her nowhere. If anything had happened to Wyndham because of her, if he were unable to fulfill his role, then it was up to her to repair the damage she had done. She had to block out the pain of her fear for Charles and think. If they were on their way to rendezvous with Napoleon's army of invasion . . .

No, he assembled that force not far from the coast, near Boulogne. Her research had told her that. And unless her senses were more messed up than she thought, they had been in this carriage for hours. They must be headed to some private appointment. Perhaps to meet someone with whom Sir Thomas could demand considerable money for his role?

The carriage pulled off the road and onto a rutted lane. They lurched along this for some time, then came to a halt. Lexie lay still, concentrating what little energy she possessed on keeping her muscles limp. She *had* to convince Sir Thomas she constituted no threat to him. Unfortunately, it was all too true.

The vehicle swayed as her companion stood, and it took a conscious effort on her part not to cringe as he leaned over her. He shook her arm, held it a moment, then released it.

The door opened, gusting damp, freezing wind inside. Lexie shivered, but luckily Sir Thomas looked over his shoulder at the intruder.

"Bring her," he said, and climbed down.

The other man—probably one of the smugglers from the unpleasant collection of odors hovering about him—took his place. He grasped Lexie and heaved her over his shoulder in much the manner of a farm laborer hefting a sack of grain, and clambered down from the carriage.

Damn, she wished they'd take the precaution of wrapping her in a blanket so she wouldn't be seen or couldn't get away or whatever reason they could come up with. Then at least she wouldn't be so insufferably cold. How could she

269

maintain the pretence of being unconscious when her teeth chattered?

Again, she opened one eye and tried to get a look at their surroundings. Early night made it impossible to see details, but she gained the impression of a forested area with towering trees and a great deal of underbrush. Presumably, there must be water of some sort nearby, but though she strained her ears, she could hear nothing but the sound of hammering.

A deep, uncouth voice gave a sharp command, two more answered, then canvas flapped against rope as the men erected a tent. Lexie closed her eye, blocking out the unwelcome sight. Just what she needed, to go camping in the middle of the snow. If the prisoner got a tent, of course. Given a choice, she'd rather stay in the carriage.

Her bearer halted, and Lexie waited, gritting her teeth against the cold. She wanted a drink of water—hot, preferably—but didn't dare alert her captors to the fact she was aware and thinking. Why couldn't this be in the middle of August, and a balmy, summer's eve?

With the tent lines secured, one of the men threw an armload of bedding inside. This her bearer apparently took to be sufficient preparations, for he unceremoniously dumped Lexie within. She sprawled across something hard, rolled, and settled finally on her stomach, her face half buried in a mildewed bedroll. Better than on snow, she told herself. With an effort, she remained limp.

The man left, and voices sounded outside her door. Apparently Sir Thomas set a guard on her. Great. She didn't know if she dared move, she might make a noise.

She compromised by wriggling into a more comfortable position—one that covered her enough to avoid a case of frostbite—and lay there, awaiting developments. With her ankles bound and her arms still tied behind her, there wasn't much else she could do, except listen and learn what she could. And try not to think about Charles and what might have happened to him.

Time passed—incredibly slowly—then more footsteps sounded just beyond the canvas flap as two men approached, then paused.

"In here?" Vaughn's light voice sounded haggard.

"No, Mr. Vaughn. A wise jailor does not put his prisoners together where they can plan an escape." Sir Thomas sounded amused, completely in control.

Lexie cringed. So, the conspirators had taken Vaughn prisoner, also. How many hints had he already dropped—and worse, how much more would he tell the French in hopes of saving his own life? He could betray the British, history, everything they knew, up to and including the balance of power in the modern world.

Vaughn's story would never be believed, of course, but enough of what he said would be remembered at critical moments. Napoleon might well invade and capture England. And if warned of the inherent dangers awaiting him, he might also make a conquest of imperial Russia. Nelson hadn't even faced the combined Spanish and French fleets at Trafalgar, yet. Without mastery of the sea, the Peninsular Campaign might never succeed . . .

If the French heeded even just a few of Geoff Vaughn's words, there soon might be one Europe, under one ruler. How long could the infant United States stand against such power?

The smell of cooking meat drove those horrendous thoughts from her mind, replacing them with what for her, at that moment, loomed as the most momentous matter of all. Food. Her mouth watered, and her stomach cried out a plaintive complaint. Didn't Sir Thomas believe in feeding his prisoners? Well, maybe not his unconscious ones, she supposed. Perhaps that act of hers hadn't been such a good idea after all. At this moment, she was willing to risk being given another draft of that drug in exchange for a single mouthful of something chewable.

Was that a potato roasting? Maybe her guard would check on her, just to see if she had come around and might fancy a bite. Finally, unable to stand it a moment longer, she rolled over so she could call out the tent's flap to whoever stood watch. He might be sympathetic . . .

He wasn't there. At least her attempts to attract his

attention brought no results. Maybe he had gone for his own meal. And left her unguarded? She considered that. Maybe they didn't think her much of a risk.

Well, they were right on that point. And they must be shorthanded. A scream of frustration welled in her, and she savaged her wrists against their bonds, trying once more to free herself. The knots held, but her temper didn't. For one moment, she honestly longed for her gag back so she'd have something to sink her teeth into for a good gnash.

The tantalizing aromas from the fire continued to assault her senses, and she forced her mind from them, back to escape. No, that impossibility only tied her empty stomach into a tangle of spaghetti.

Good grief, couldn't she get her mind off food? Exercise was supposed to help. She repositioned herself so she lay on her back—wincing as her hands dug into the hard ground—and pulled her protesting muscles into a sit-up.

It didn't help, she decided at last. It just made her hungrier. Gradually, the noises from the camp quieted, even the tantalizing smells faded on the icy wind. Lexie closed her eyes, not so much tired as physically and emotionally drained.

An eerie cry, followed by absolute silence, brought her fully awake. She tensed, every nerve alert against she knew not what, her heart pounding. Some time had passed since she'd heard any noises in the camp, she realized. She must have been dozing.

The new sound came again, slower—like the tearing of a heavy material. Like the tent fabric, perhaps? She turned her head, trying to still her pulse so she could hear over the throbbing in her ears, and peered into the blackness. Nothing.

The tearing continued, slow and steady. Was that a lightening patch, a hole in her prison, the forest beyond? Shadowed movement . . .

She found she held her breath, and forced it from her lungs, replacing it with cold, stimulating oxygen. Could it be . . . A shape, charcoal against black, pushed through, blocking the opening.

"Lexie?" The deep voice spoke her name, barely a breath of sound.

Relief, joy, incredible love surged through her at the welcomingly familiar whisper. "Charles!" He lived, he had come for her . . .

She struggled, but before she could reach a sitting position, he dropped to his knee beside her and dragged her into his arms. His mouth covered hers, and she lost herself in the haven of his embrace, returning the caress of his lips with a fierceness wrought by her fears for him.

"Oh, my love," he murmured against her hair, and his hands slid down her arms until they reached the ropes about her wrists. His fingers clenched on her already scraped and raw flesh. *"Confound* them! Could they not have released you in here?"

He set her from him, then eased the point of his knife into her bonds. In another moment, her arms fell limp to her sides. He had freed her ankles before sufficient feeling returned to her hands to allow them to regain a measure of use. He drew her close once more, and eagerly she turned her mouth to his. Instead she encountered his ear, as he leaned to whisper in hers.

"Can you walk?"

"I'll crawl if I have to," she assured him—though at the moment she had doubts about being able to accomplish even that.

"Come, then." He took her hand and drew her toward the slit he had cut. He stuck his head through first, checking, then slipped out.

Lexie followed, giving a pep talk to her aching muscles. Once free of the tent, Wyndham drew her to her feet, then held her until her wobbly legs accepted her weight. She made no objection when his arm lingered about her waist for support.

"Come." The gentle whisper barely sounded in the stillness. He took her hand and led her toward the underbrush, away from the camp.

Lexie held back. "We can't." She stood on tip-toe to reach his ear. "Sir Thomas still has the dagger—and Vaughn."

273

The pale, filtering moonlight illuminated Wyndham's grim face. "It is not my intention to let that traitor reach the French camp with any more information. Nor with your Mr. Vaughn."

"No, you'd far rather strangle Sir Thomas," Lexie agreed, somewhat dryly.

"He murdered my brother. He—"

A twig snapped, and Wyndham broke off, alert, the grip of his fingers biting into Lexie's arm. She braced herself as a shadowy figure emerged from between the back two tents and approached.

Wyndham relaxed. "What did you find?" he asked.

The newcomer came a step nearer, and Lexie recognized the boyish, eager features of Lieutenant Crewe. He beamed at her, nodding, as if not knowing how to express his satisfaction that at least part of their mission had been accomplished.

"I've located that man Vaughn. He's in that tent." He gestured to the one next to Lexie's ex-prison. "There are three men with him—smugglers I'd wager."

Wyndham's brow lowered as he considered, then he nodded. "Stay here, Lexie."

"Oh, no." She started after the two men. "You two watch his guards while I cut Vaughn loose. It'll be safer that way, rather than just one of you watching three."

To that, Wyndham gave his reluctant agreement. He handed Lexie his knife, then glanced at the lieutenant. The young man nodded his readiness, and Wyndham drew the tent flap back enough to allow Lexie to slip inside.

The complete darkness brought her to a halt. Then dim outlines delineated three occupied cots in a line across the front of the tent. She strained her eyes, and made out another in the back.

Which sleeping figure was Vaughn? The one here, in the middle, with a guard on each side? Or the one blocked off from the entrance? She made her guess, crept through the front line, and peeked down at the man alone in the back. Familiar fair hair met her gaze, and relief left her weak. Of course, they still had to get him out.

He had been made more comfortable than she—probably

because he'd spoken up and demanded it. He not only had a cot, but a blanket wrapped about him and the rope about his wrists appeared to be loosely tied. Lexie bent over him, clamped one hand over his mouth, then caught him in the chest with the other as he bolted upright.

"Quiet," she hissed. "We're getting you free."

Vaughn fell back, silent. She could feel the tautness of his muscles as she slid the knife between the ropes. If she cut him and he yelled . . .

The soft snores and even breathing of the other men eased one fear, at least. Hopefully, they were all heavy sleepers. Biting her lip, she sawed, and the twined fibers separated, one at a time, taking forever.

At last, Vaughn pulled his hands free. "Help me up," he whispered.

Lexie put an arm about him, taking some of his weight to prevent the cot from creaking as he swung his legs free of the blanket and onto the ground. She cut through the bonds about his ankles, then helped him to stand. So far, not a sound. So far . . .

He limped with her to the tent flap, where he stopped, staring into Wyndham's angry countenance. For a long moment their gazes held, then Vaughn looked away and pushed outside into the icy night.

At least it didn't snow. She should be glad for that. "What now?" she asked as they retreated to a safer distance from the tent and its sleeping occupants.

"Perhaps you should ask your friend." Wyndham folded his arms, regarding Vaughn with barely veiled hostility.

Vaughn glanced at Lexie. "I want to go home. Back to my own time."

She tightened her lips. "What about all your great plans for buying land?"

He shook his head. "To hell with them. Life's safer in the future."

Lexie drew a shaky breath. "Then I guess we need the dagger."

Wyndham glanced at Crewe. "Have you found Sir Thomas?"

"Yes, my lord." He dragged his gaze from Vaughn. "What

did he mean by 'in the future?'"

"Just a figure of speech," Lexie said quickly. "He means safer than now." She threw Vaughn a quelling look.

Apparently Lieutenant Crewe accepted her explanation. He led the way around the back of the next two tents, to one that had been pitched almost opposite Lexie's. The camp had been constructed in a circle, she noted, with the large cooking fire in the middle.

Only one man stood—or rather lay—on guard. He reclined on the ground before the low-burning flames, his rifle clasped loosely in one hand across his stomach. As they watched, a rattling snore shook him.

"Keep an eye on him." Wyndham's hand rested on Lexie's shoulder. His lips brushed her forehead, then he gestured to Crewe to follow and he slipped inside.

"Watch the guard," Lexie hissed to Vaughn, and hurried after the other two.

At the flap, a wave of dizziness sent her reeling. She steadied herself, fighting for control. She mustn't make a sound—*none* of them could. Too many smugglers slept nearby who would overpower them easily. She cast an uneasy glance at the sleeping guard, then peered inside.

Wyndham stood just within, staring at the recumbent figure on the cot. His hands clenched at his sides.

"For the sake of England, we should smother him, my lord. While he sleeps so he doesn't make a sound." Lieutenant Crewe's whisper barely reached Lexie.

Wyndham's shoulders rose and fell with his deep, ragged breath. "No. I cannot stoop to cold-blooded murder. I would prefer a duel, but I would settle for a fair fight."

"You're not going to get one," Crewe pointed out. Yet he made no move, either, to kill the sleeping man.

"We'll take him captive," Wyndham decided.

"That we can, sir." Crewe sounded relieved.

"The dagger, first, I think." Wyndham looked about, rummaging silently through the few belongings in the confined space, then turned back to the bed.

Lexie's flesh tingled, and her surroundings began their eerie, swirling dance. The pale canvas shimmered, and she gripped the fabric, trying to hold on to the present. In another moment she might have the dagger—*and* Vaughn.

Slowly, her world steadied—and she caught her breath. Charles stood over the sleeping man. Sir Thomas must have the dagger on him, or near. If they roused him, it would take only one shout, and the smugglers would be upon them. Yet she couldn't want Charles to commit the silent murder, either.

The earl stooped and ran his hand under the pillow. Sir Thomas's head moved, then turned, and the faint light gleamed on his open eyes as he stared at the dark shape bending over him. With a lunge, Sir Thomas brought the dagger up from beneath the blanket.

His shout rang out, breaking the stillness of the night.

Chapter Twenty-Two

Sir Thomas, still enveloped in the blanket, jerked back his arm, and the pale moonlight glinted off the steel blade. Wyndham lunged at him, landing across his chest, and the camp cot collapsed. Lexie ducked inside, but could see nothing but a writhing heap of covers and bodies as the two men struggled in the near blackness of the tent.

Shouts sounded without, followed by running feet—which came to an abrupt halt. Bewildered voices demanded of one another what occurred, finding no answers. Lexie caught her breath, holding it . . .

Sir Thomas yelled, galvanizing his men once more to action. Their running footsteps resumed, this time bearing down on their tent. Crewe positioned himself just within the flap.

As the first of the smugglers bolted inside, the lieutenant swung, connecting with a sickening thud. The man dropped on the spot. Lexie saw the pale gleam of the young officer's grin as he swung at the next head to appear. He missed.

The smuggler didn't. Crewe doubled over, clutching his midriff as his breath exploded out of him.

Lexie looked about, frantic, searching for a weapon with which to help. Only a few feet away, Wyndham and Sir Thomas still rolled on the ground amid the remains of the cot and bedclothes, locked in deadly battle, their hatred too personal to allow anything else to interfere. The dagger . . .

As if her conscious search for it triggered the reaction, a

wave of dizziness swept over her. Her surroundings spun, and as the ground rose to meet her, a cry tore from her throat. She clung to rough canvas, desperately trying to retain her senses, as the fighting continued about her.

On hands and knees, she dragged herself along the side of the tent to get out of the way. As she reached out, groping for a clear path, her fingers closed over cold metal. A lantern? Her world steadied as she grasped the solid object.

Sitting up, she turned toward the fighters as Wyndham freed his elbow and closed with a punishing right. Sir Thomas ducked, twisting away. He drew his arm back, shaking it clear of the entangling blankets, and before Lexie could move, the knife flashed toward Wyndham's ribs. With a tearing noise that set her teeth on edge, it sliced through fabric—then lodged, as if striking something solid.

Lexie clambered to her feet, staggered forward, and swung. Sir Thomas's hand dropped from the hilt, limp, as he collapsed in a heap. Shuddering, she stepped back. Her gaze transferred to Wyndham. "What—?"

"My snuff box." The earl untangled himself from the bed-clothes and glared at Lexie. "I could have taken care of him myself!"

"Later," she snapped, and spun to face the immediate threat. Behind them, two more smugglers bore down on Lieutenant Crewe, who had managed to floor his last opponent. Lantern in hand, Lexie charged into the fray.

Wyndham grabbed the dagger free from his coat and slashed at the back of the tent. "Come on!" he shouted.

Grabbing Lexie by the neck of her cloak, he dragged her backward to the opening he had made. He shoved her through, landed a smuggler a leveler, and latched onto Crewe. He pushed the lieutenant toward the hole, then the next moment dove through after them.

"Over here!" Vaughn emerged from the trees, leading saddled horses.

Wyndham checked the girth of the first animal, then grabbed Lexie to toss her into the saddle.

"My skirt!" she protested. "I've got to—"

She broke off as, with a muttered oath, the earl slashed the

280

soft green merino with the dagger from thigh to hem.

Tingling, dizzy, Lexie clung to the horse, which faded in and out of tangibility beneath her grasping hands. Somehow, she managed to get her leg over as Wyndham boosted her into position. He moved away, taking the dagger with him, and her world settled. She pulled herself erect and took the reins in fingers that still trembled.

Vaughn and Lieutenant Crewe had already mounted, she saw, and Wyndham swung onto the last horse. Vaughn tossed him the reins, and the earl dug in his heels, sending the snorting animal forward into the darkness.

For a second time, Lexie realized, she escaped Sir Thomas's captivity in the dead of night, racing away on a horse. This was a habit she was going to have to break.

A dark shape loomed just before her and she ducked, dodging a low-lying branch. Damn, she wished she could see. What little moonlight illuminated the night didn't penetrate the forest canopy.

Her mount stumbled, jolting her forward, and she landed on his neck. The others raced on, her horse with them, but she managed to right herself and regain the stirrup she had lost. In a fleeting patch of light, she saw Wyndham remained in the lead, though Vaughn closed on his heels. Lieutenant Crewe kept his mount just to Lexie's right, as if guarding her.

She could only hope Charles knew where he went. It didn't seem possible, though. For all she knew, they might be riding in circles. How far were they from the coast, anyway? She hadn't been in very good shape yesterday during the carriage ride. Nor had she dared look out the window. They might have been following the Channel—or they might have been headed straight inland.

Her horse crashed heedlessly through the underbrush, clearing trees by fractions of inches. More than once, Lexie's knees scraped against hard trunks as her mount made no allowances for his rider. If she could just see the obstacles coming . . .

The next limb caught her right across the chest, sweeping her from the animal's back. She landed hard on her tail bone, the breath knocked out of her, and she gasped, choking. The horse, suddenly bereft of both weight and a firm touch on its mouth, first slowed, then dashed on after the others.

"Wyndham!" Lieutenant Crewe shouted. He pulled up and swung down. "Are you all right, miss?"

Lexie gasped again, and allowed him to help her to her feet. Her chest ached. "The—the *horse* ducked," she managed.

Wyndham, leading her mount, trotted back to them. "Lexie—?" Concern sounded in his voice.

"Don't get off, I'm all right." She allowed the lieutenant to help her back onto the horse, grimacing as she used her upper body muscles. "Just fine," she added, in a misbegotten attempt to convince herself.

"Hurry!" Vaughn, the urgency of his call in no way diminished by his hushed tone, rode into view. "Let's get out of here. I won't feel safe until we're back in England."

"Not our own time?" Lexie tried to find a more comfortable position on the saddle. There didn't seem to be one.

Wyndham glanced at her, and she managed a reassuring smile. He must have seen it even in the deep shadows, for he urged his horse into a trot, then a canter. With a sigh, Lexie allowed her horse to follow.

She nearly parted company with her mount once more as he jumped a ditch into a road. Yet they landed together, much to her satisfaction—though she had little time to congratulate herself. Wyndham directed them across the dirt path, and Lexie held on as they cleared the mud-filled trench on the other side. Once more they struck out through the underbrush. About a hundred yards later, Wyndham reined in and dismounted.

"What are we doing?" Lieutenant Crewe pulled abreast of him.

"Get off, and be prepared to silence your horse," the earl hissed. "Crewe, I want you to circle around to the left and have both your pistols ready."

"What's going on?" Vaughn demanded. "You don't really think they'll follow us, do you?"

"I am certain of it." A grim smile just touched Wyndham's lips.

"Why should they? Won't Sir Thomas just go straight to the French with his information?"

Wyndham shook his head. "He cannot risk our returning to England to raise the alarm."

"His brother will have done that," Vaughn protested.

"No, Grenville lacks proof, just as I did. Lieutenant Crewe is the one who provides the necessary corroboration. *Now,* if we once get back to England, we will be able to mobilize the authorities at last."

"That we will, my lord." Crewe checked his pistol. "There'll be no chance of any invasion succeeding, you may be sure of that."

"If we make it back. And Stoke will do all he can to make sure we don't. He will come to me." Wyndham's last words, barely audible, held deadly menace.

Lexie shivered. "You *want* to kill him."

He looked up, directly into her eyes. "I already would have, had you not hit him with that lantern."

"Or he would have killed you." She hugged herself. "Or none of us might have gotten away. I'm sorry I spoiled your fun, but right then didn't seem the moment to sit around and wait for the outcome."

A slight smile eased his tension. "Perhaps not."

"What are you planning, an ambush?" Vaughn watched him, intent.

"There are too many of them. No, we will do better to—" He broke off.

Lexie tensed, then she, too, heard the distant rumbling beat of many hooves. Steadily, the sound grew closer, louder.

"Get ready to clamp your hand over your horse's nostrils," Wyndham hissed to Lexie. "Whatever you do, don't let it nicker. And keep him silent." He jerked his head toward Vaughn. "Crewe?" The men crept a short distance away.

Lexie's mount's head came up, and she complied at once with Wyndham's instructions. The animal jerked away, but the action diverted it, and they stood in silence—at least for the moment. Lexie held her breath.

Someone crashed through the shrubs and low branches,

all too close, then others followed, spreading out on either side of the road, searching, coming much too close for comfort. Lexie counted the slow, tortuous seconds. Why didn't they give up? Why didn't they just go on?

One of the men stopped. He was so near, Lexie could actually see him as he peered into the darkness . . . right at them. . . . Her fingernails dug into the palm of her hand in which she clenched the reins. *Why didn't Wyndham do something about him?* Because, she realized, it would only alert the others. Let him just ride on. . . .

The smuggler kicked his mount and he forged ahead. After another minute, the last of the men in their thicket followed. For an interminable while, their small group waited, not moving, not making a single noise.

At last, Wyndham rejoined her. "I think it's safe now." He kept his voice low.

"Won't they figure out pretty fast they've passed us?" Vaughn demanded.

Wyndham regarded the other man for a long moment. "For you," he said at last, "it won't make any difference."

"You mean—?" Lexie tried to make out his features, but they blurred in the deep shadows of the night.

He touched her cheek with one finger, trailing it along the line of her jaw. "Crewe—" He tossed his reins to the lieutenant. "Hold them for a minute." He took Lexie's, as well, and handed them to the man. Grasping her arm, he drew her away from the others.

"Charles—" Her hand closed over his. The tingling sensation began at once.

He drew the dagger from his coat pocket. "We have this, and we have Vaughn," he said. He set it on a fallen log.

Lexie swallowed. "We—we have them both." For a long moment she stared at the handle, at the star sapphire which gleamed even in the darkness as if with a life of its own. The familiar waves of dizziness swept over her, unsettling, tugging at her. Nothing remained to keep her here. She could go home at any time . . .

Tears stung her eyes, and she blinked them back, refusing to give in to them. She looked up into Charles's face, and saw there a reflection of her own desire, her own heart-wrenching conflict. She didn't want to leave him, how could she go so far away, where she'd never be able to see him again, never hear his beloved voice, never experience the gentleness of his touch or know the joy of holding him in her arms . . .

"Stay." He spoke the one word so softly, it came out on the merest breath of sound. "Lexie—" His finger traced her lips, then his hand slid about the nape of her neck. "Forget the future. Stay here, with me."

"But Vaughn—"

"Send him back alone. I need you, Lexie. I want you to stay, to be my wife."

His wife. Unable to prevent herself, she moved into the encircling warmth of his embrace, holding him as silent tears of agony slipped down her cheeks and disappeared into the wool that covered his shoulder. To live the rest of her life with him. He offered everything for which she could ever long, and more. She choked on a sob. "Charles, if—if only I could."

"*Why* can you not? Lexie, my love, if it's what you want—"

She shook her head, only succeeding in burying her face more deeply in his coat. "I *can't,* Charles." She moved away a step, so her words weren't as muffled. "The future pulled at me even while we made love. Don't you see? Even if I tried to stay, my own time would drag me away from you one of these days. I *must* go to the era where I belong. Ours is a love doomed from the start." At that moment, the words didn't sound the least bit corny to her.

The brushes stirred, and Vaughn strode into their tiny clearing. He peered at them, then came forward slowly, as if compelled, his unwavering regard on the blade beside them. "That dagger," he breathed, elated. He couldn't seem to drag his gaze from the gleaming object. "You've got it, Wyndham!"

The earl drew a long, steadying breath. "Yes, I've got it." He continued to watch Lexie, his expression solemn. Only his eyes betrayed his yearning.

Vaughn shook his head, which seemed to break the spell

that bound him. "Well?" He looked from Wyndham to Lexie and back again. "What are we waiting for? Let's get out of here! Let's get back to our own time where we'll be safe! Look, if you don't hurry, Stoke's men might double back and find us."

Charles bent down and retrieved the dagger. Lexie's gaze lowered to his gloved hand, then she forced herself to look at the blade. After a moment, which seemed an eternity, he held it out to her. She took it in her trembling grasp, and the tingling sensation shot up her arms.

Vaughn grabbed her, making her wince as he latched on with a vice-like grip. She stared at the blade, at the chased handle, at the star which winked back at her. Hesitant yet compelled, she ran her finger over it. Cold, as cold as death . . .

She forced herself to maintain the contact, to not just feel it, but to *experience* it. Touch became no more than a peripheral sense, almost extraneous; for this she reached out with her soul. The shimmering encompassed every molecule of her being, the world about her reeled, insubstantial, of less impact than a dancing ray of light. She closed her eyes against it and concentrated, trying to capture that disorienting shift between times.

It eluded her. It tantalized and teased her, the sensation so near—yet remaining just beyond her grasp.

"I can't," she breathed at last. "The feeling—it just isn't strong enough. I—it's got to be the cavern."

As she spoke the words, the certainty of their truth grew within her. For both her and Vaughn to return to their own time, they would have to be in the same place where they started, where they first made the shift.

Relief flooded through her. She opened her eyes, and looked straight up into Charles's face. He stood before her, his expression strained, and she actually smiled. She could remain with him for a few precious hours more.

"The cavern," Wyndham repeated. He drew a deep breath and let it out slowly. "Or should I go after Stoke? There's a chance, if he cannot find us, that he'll abandon the hunt and instead carry a warning to the French along with his information. That might speed the invasion, make it imminent."

"I don't think so." Lexie held the dagger out to him, flat on her palm. "I think he'll come after this before he goes to the French. There's some link between this and Sir Thomas. As long as he touched it, it didn't effect me like it usually does. Like he served as a buffer."

"A *link* between them," Wyndham repeated. He took the dagger and turned it over in his hand. "Do you think it might draw him?"

"I don't know, but I doubt he'll willingly let it go. I'm surprised he let it out of his sight long enough for his brother to have been holding it at that ball. I think he'll be so desperate to get hold of it again, he'll keep following us—even back to England."

Charles glanced at Vaughn, whose avid gaze once more rested on the dagger, on the glowing star, and nodded. "It does seem to exert a certain power, doesn't it? Very well, we'd better reach the cavern before Sir Thomas."

The earl led them back to the clearing, to where Lieutenant Crewe awaited them, the reins of all four horses in his hands. "Mount up," Charles commanded. He relieved the lieutenant of Lexie's mount and held her stirrup while she swung onto the saddle.

Lieutenant Crewe scrambled onto his own horse. "What is your plan, my lord?"

"To head back up the coast."

"*Back* the way we came?" Vaughn, not quite settled on his saddle, set his mount sidling as he swung about.

Wyndham nodded, the movement of his head barely visible in the dark. "They're less likely to find us that way. They won't be expecting it—yet, at least."

"But what if they get ahead—get back to England first?"

"We'll just have to see to it they don't. They'll search for us for a little while longer along this route, I should think. If we move quickly, we should be able to reach the coast and locate a boat before they realize we are not to be found."

Once more they set off, staying clear of the roads, heading in the general direction of the Channel. Time slipped away, marked only by the beating of the horses' hooves and the

287

ache in Lexie's muscles. She had no other method of counting its passing. The frozen darkness continued to envelope them—but with the interminable night of the British—and French—winter, that could mean anything.

At last, they glimpsed ahead of them a collection of small cottages scattered across a wide area. Here and there a single pole rose high, like the mast of a ship. They *were* masts, Lexie realized. They had reached a fishing village. The Channel, at last.

They reined in. Charles signaled the others to remain where they were, tossed his reins to the lieutenant, and crept ahead on foot. Lexie peered after him through the blackness, continuing to watch even after his silent shape disappeared in the shadows. How long would he be . . .

"Why don't we just steal a boat and get on with it?" Vaughn demanded. His horse stamped and shook its head, its rider's impatience communicating itself.

"We can't just barge in, sir." A touch of wistfulness crept into the lieutenant's voice. "We wouldn't get as far as the beach. It may not be dawn, yet, but it's well into morning and you better believe there are any number of people up and about, getting ready to set off on a day's fishing."

"Oh, good." Only a slight touch of sarcasm colored Lexie's words. "Maybe we can pretend to be part of the group."

Lieutenant Crewe actually smiled. "Don't worry, miss. His lordship will hit on some plan."

Such faith. Lexie shook her head, and knew she shared it. If anyone could discover a way to spirit them through an enemy village, obtain a boat from under the noses of any number of hostile guards, and assure their escape, it would be Charles.

He returned twenty minutes later, his expression grim. "There's some activity, but it's not around the shore, yet," he told them. "We'll need a diversion. Load your pistol, will you, Crewe?"

"Going to take a hostage?" Vaughn asked.

Wyndham ignored him. "Lexie, take Vaughn and get as close to the boats as you can without being seen."

She hesitated. "What are you going to do?"

"Stampede our horses. Go on, we haven't much time. We want to be well into the Channel before the first light makes us an easy target."

She opened her mouth to voice any one of the innumerable fears which jostled each other in her mind, then gave up. She'd just have to hope the horses proved a sufficient diversion. She swung down and gestured for Vaughn to join her. "Come on."

Bending low, keeping to the underbrush, she headed in the direction Wyndham had taken earlier. She could smell the salt in the air, feel the sticky, freezing tang on her skin. The gentle slap of the wavelets hitting the sand reached her. But so did the hum of voices, of the fishermen preparing for their day.

She crouched by the last line of trees, the chill wind hitting her face. Already the sky paled toward a pre-dawn glow. If she peered really hard, she could make out the shapes of beached dories. Two men stowed something in the bow of one; she couldn't make out what.

About ten yards farther down, mostly floating, lay another, larger craft. Its sail remained furled, and a line secured it to a buoy, but it looked ready to go out.

Lexie nodded to herself, knowing she looked at twenty feet of pure escape.

The explosion of the pistol, followed by banshee-like shouts, tore through the stillness of the early morning. A frenzied whinny barely preceded the crashing of the shrubbery and the thundering beat of hooves that announced the onset of the stampede. The two men by the boat dropped everything and set off at a run.

Lexie didn't waste a moment. Grabbing Vaughn's arm, she raced across the soft, yielding beach, stumbling in her haste, to the more solid footing of the wet sand. Her anxious fingers found the securing knot.

In a minute, despite her shivering, she had it freed. Bracing her nerve, she waded into the freezing water. "Push it!" she called to Vaughn, and pulled at the stern.

Vaughn shoved on the bow, and slowly she felt the

wooden mass shift, then slide. Her slashed skirts swirled about her legs, then clung, impeding movement, but the craft came free of its resting place, gaining buoyancy as it moved into deeper water.

From up the beach, away from them, voices shouted, apparently occupied with catching the frightened horses. No one as yet paid them any heed. Lexie returned her concentration to the task at hand.

A dark shape emerged from the line of trees, and relief surged through her. No, it was two shapes, one lower, pulling ahead—a huge hound, secured on a lead, dragging a burly man equipped with a fowling piece.

The deep, vicious growl shot panic through Lexie as the animal, teeth bared, bore down on her.

Chapter Twenty-Three

Geoff Vaughn dove beneath the surface, leaving Lexie, up to her waist in freezing water and hampering skirts, to face the furious canine onslaught alone. The animal dragged its handler, who stumbled through the yielding sand, the leash looped over his wrist. She hoped it held.

With the sodden wool clinging to her legs, she could do no more than flounder through the wavelets. Frantic, she tugged at the boat, trying to dislodge it, to swing it between herself and the snarling beast. Dogs, she felt certain, could undoubtedly swim and bite at the same time, and be oblivious to the icy chill, as well. That same cold already had numbed Lexie to the point she might not even feel those wicked teeth tearing into her flesh.

The hound stopped short, its bark cut off on a startled yip, as his handler fell, pitching face downward into the sand. No, he'd been tackled, knocked unconscious—and off his feet. The dog spun around, letting loose a growl that sent shivers through Lexie's soul, but Charles scrambled to his feet and beyond the distance of the leash before the animal's massive jaws snapped closed like a steel trap. It strained, dancing at him, howling in its fury. The earl dusted the sand from his hands and breeches and ran toward the boat.

Lieutenant Crewe emerged from the line of trees and sprinted down the beach. "They'll be after us," he gasped as he splashed through the shallow water.

"Get in." Wyndham caught Lexie about the waist and

291

swung her to the deck.

Vaughn, water dripping from his hair, scrambled after her, leaving Wyndham and Crewe to drag the craft the last few feet. While the earl balanced the little sloop, Crewe climbed aboard, then set to work on the sail. Lexie ran a rapid inventory on boating supplies and found, to her immense relief, a set of oars. The wind might be blowing—at the moment—but knowing they had an emergency backup system made her feel better.

The craft rocked as Wyndham swung himself over the side. At once he went to Lieutenant Crewe's aid, and together they raised the sail. The sloop rode lower with the added weight, and the hull scraped bottom.

"Here." Lexie handed one of the oars to Vaughn. "Help me pole us free." She shoved her paddle over the side, into the sand at the bottom of the Channel, and pushed with all her might. After a moment, Vaughn followed suit.

Lexie cast an uneasy glance over her shoulder, up the beach to where the dog still leaped and strained at his leash and barked in fury. Any moment now, that poor man would regain consciousness and free the animal. So far, at least, none of the villagers had come to discover what caused the commotion. They would, though, and all too soon. If Sir Thomas came this way looking for them, these people would have a tale to tell.

Wyndham glanced at her. "He'll come," he said, as if sensing her unspoken thought. Immense satisfaction sounded in those two words.

He took the oar from her and thrust it deep into the sand. For a long moment he strained, then the sloop slid free, rolling gently. Lieutenant Crewe threw the boom until the icy wind caught the sail, and the sheet pulled tight in his hand as the little craft moved into it.

Lexie glanced over her shoulder again. "He's *got* to follow us." She swallowed. If Sir Thomas abandoned the dagger and went instead to the French with his information— No, it didn't bear thinking about. But there was more to it than that in Charles's tone. She cast him a reproving glance, and knew it wasted in the dark. "You're looking forward to fighting him again, aren't you?"

A laugh, no less menacing for its softness, escaped the earl. "Very much, my dear. Perhaps I flatter myself in thinking our personal feud will draw him every bit as much as will the dagger. He will come, even to England."

"Have you given much thought to *our* getting to England?" Lieutenant Crewe eased his hold on the sheet, adjusting the sail to keep it full into the wind.

Wyndham took it from him and settled in the stern, his other hand taking the rudder. The ready smile flashed in his green eyes. "We sail."

"In broad daylight—which you know full well it will be before we're out of sight of France. My lord, have you not considered the dangers inherent in crossing the Channel like this, when any patrolling enemy ship might spot us?"

"Not to mention our own Coast Guard," Wyndham agreed. "It appears we may have an eventful voyage."

"And a hungry one," Vaughn said. "I don't suppose there's any food around here?"

For possibly the first time, Lexie found herself in complete agreement with the man. She'd gone beyond the grumbling stomach stage; she honestly couldn't remember when she'd eaten last. Time had passed in such a blur for her, thanks to that foul drug of Sir Thomas's.

Well, she might as well see what she could find. She opened the door of the tiny cabin and descended the four shallow steps. Even stooped over, her head brushed the low ceiling. The beginnings of the faint dawn light seeped in from behind her and from the portholes on either side, allowing her to discern shapes.

Nothing fancy, she noted, just a few wooden chests. She checked them and found they held nets and floats. Maybe they could catch something to eat—though she'd never been a fan of sushi. But then, she'd never been this hungry, either.

She opened one more of the heavy boxes and found within it, to her utter joy, a basket covered in a coarse cloth. She ripped this off and revealed a broken loaf, a large yellow lump of cheese, and several apples. She broke off a piece of the bread and gnawed on it, savoring the coarse texture. It could have been fresher, but it was far from stale, and at the moment she wasn't making any complaints. To her, after her prolonged fast, it tasted like manna from heaven.

Next she gouged off a piece of cheese, and wrinkled her nose at the pungent odor. Goat, maybe? Oh, well, this was no time to be choosey. She bit into it and found it better than she expected.

With her stomach no longer quite as hollow, she covered her findings once more and carried them up to the others. Vaughn grumbled loudly, but accepted both cheese and bread, and stuffed an apple in his pocket for later. Lieutenant Crewe took his share with a nod of thanks, and Lexie turned to Charles.

That all-too familiar tingling sensation crept up her arms, and she shivered. He carried the dagger which would take her away from him at the end of this voyage—which suddenly seemed all too short. If only they could sail on like this forever, forget the future, forget Sir Thomas and Napoleon and the planned invasion . . .

But they couldn't.

Charles motioned with his head for her to join him on the bench which spanned the stern, and after a moment's hesitation, she did. His gaze rested on her, more a caress than a look. Longing welled in her, filling every part of her being. How could she bear to leave him, to be apart from him for the rest of her life, to have nothing but a few memories? But for her to stay was impossible.

But if he could come with her . . . ?

She swallowed. No, as much as she might will the invasion scheme to disappear, it remained, treacherous and deadly to the future of England. A definite task existed for Wyndham here, in his own time, something which he *must* accomplish, and he could not complete it within the next few hours. And then he had the rest of his life, filled with actions that might impact the future in who knew how many ways. No, people belonged in their own times. Hers would soon claim her, drag her back, separate her from him by so many years . . .

His gaze rested on her, his expression intent. "Between the rudder and the sheet, I don't seem to have a free hand," he said. The pain in his eyes belied the inconsequentiality of his words.

He knew, too, only hours remained to them, hours when they could not even be alone . . .

"I—I'd take over for you, but I can't sail. Here." She tore off a bite-sized chunk of bread and held it up to his mouth. His lips brushed her fingers, agonizingly sweet. She trembled . . . no, she *shimmered*. A wave of dizziness swept over her and she moved her hand away, breaking the contact between them.

"What—?" His gaze narrowed as he sought out her features in the greyness of early light, and his expression clouded. "That confounded dagger. Lexie, I'll throw it overboard."

"If only that would do the trick." Her throat constricted, and her eyes burned, but the ache in her heart went beyond mere tears. "Oh, Charles, I wish it would. But I'm afraid if you did, I'd be hauled back to my own time alone, and you'd be stuck with Vaughn."

He managed a half-smile for her weak attempt at humor. "That isn't quite what I had in mind."

"Me, neither." She fed him a bite of cheese, took one herself, then huddled into her woolen cloak. If only the bottom half of it would dry. She took a handful of the hem and wrung it out, but it did little good. The garment still clung to her legs, along with her skirts, soggy and freezing. It added another, purely physical, dimension to the misery engulfing her.

The heavy charcoal of the cloud covering lightened to a gold-tinged gray with the rising of the sun, but nowhere did so much as a patch of blue show through as the morning advanced. Toward midday the sky darkened once more, and the wind whipped an icy sleet into their faces, increasing their discomfort.

"At least it keeps visibility poor," Wyndham offered.

Lieutenant Crewe, who stood in the bow gazing before them keeping watch, nodded. "We'll see any other vessels before they see us, I should imagine."

Lexie peered overhead into the threatening clouds. "How

295

can you see to navigate? We could be going in circles, for all I know."

Wyndham shook his head. "The wind has been coming steadily from the north. I have only to keep it to our right, and we'll arrive in England. It won't be much longer now."

"But where?" Vaughn demanded. "We could end up anywhere from Ramsgate to Falmouth."

"I will endeavor to bring us closer to the mark than that."

"Not too close." Lexie laid her hand on his arm, then quickly removed it as the tingling raced along her flesh. "Can't we delay it just a little bit longer?"

His expression closed over. "I would give a great deal to keep you with me for even a few extra minutes, my love, but we must be at the cavern first. If Sir Thomas is ahead of us, he might arrange an ambush."

"But why should he think we'd go there, and not to your home?"

"There's a chance he might think that," he admitted.

"But you don't believe so?"

He shook his head. "Let us say I wouldn't want to count on it. I fear the dagger will bring him."

"Like a homing beacon." She gritted her teeth to keep them from chattering. "How did *you* find us? Did it draw you, too?"

He shook his head. "We used a far simpler means, I fear. We set off after you, almost at once."

"But how?" She cast her mind back, trying to remember what occurred. "You had been hit . . ."

"Knocked down, but not unconscious," he explained. "Between them, Dr. Falkirk, Huggins, and young Stoke managed to subdue the remaining smugglers. Even Miss Langley helped, tearing strips from her chemise to bind them."

Lexie stifled a laugh. "How—how appropriate. Though I thought all the best heroines did that to make bandages. Where did you get the boat?"

"It must have been one of the smugglers' crafts. It was anchored in the cove. Crewe and I set off shortly after Sir Thomas left with you. All we had to do was keep far enough back for them not to realize we followed them down the coast. Several of them went ashore at one point, but too many guards remained for us to try a rescue. Then we crossed the Channel." His hand tightened on the rudder, his knuckles whitening. "We appropriated horses and kept close enough to see where they took you, then waited until they made camp and went to sleep. Those were the longest hours I believe I have ever spent."

Lexie curled against him, resting her head on his shoulder, her hands clasped about his arm. The dizziness struck at once, forcing her to slide away. So many things she wanted to say to him filled her mind, jumbling over each other, impossible to voice, to know how to begin. She loved him . . .

She shied from contemplating the future. She couldn't, not yet, not while she could still see him, touch him, inhale the musky mingling of scents which were uniquely him. Despite the icy chill, she found comfort at his side, and her exhausted mind drifted toward sleep.

"There! Land!" Lieutenant Crewe, still in the bow, leaned forward, peering intently through the sleet.

Lexie swallowed and straightened up, rubbing her eyes. She must have dozed off—wasted precious minutes, perhaps even an hour or more, with Charles . . .

"Where are we?" Vaughn hugged himself, shivering in the cold. "Do either of you recognize this stretch?"

Wyndham tacked to the port, keeping the sail filled, and the icy wind drove them closer to the land.

Vaughn joined Crewe in the bow. "I don't see anything familiar," he said after a few minutes. "Haven't either of you ever sailed along here before?"

"Not for several years." Wyndham stared hard at the coastline. "I think we've come too far south," he said at last.

He changed tack, angling the sloop once more so they headed toward starboard, always closer to the beckoning shore. For some time they continued along the rocky coast, all gazes searching. An hour, perhaps two, crept past, before he at last nodded to himself.

"There it is," he announced.

Lexie leaned forward. "I don't see a cove."

"You can't, from here. It's just beyond that outcropping of rocks. We'll land up there."

They neared the ragged point, and Lieutenant Crewe leaned over the side, reaching for the boulders that formed the protective arm which sheltered the cove. They rounded it, and wave after wave of dizziness assailed Lexie. She clung to the boat and dragged herself away from Wyndham—from the one person she wanted to remain near.

About her, through the drumming in her ears, she could hear the men talking. The boat shifted beneath her as they steadied it, drew it to a spot where they could disembark. She closed her eyes, oblivious to all but that floating, insubstantial sensation of being somewhere lost between two times. She had to get inside the cave, with Vaughn, before she disappeared into the limbo she feared.

Someone scooped her up into strong arms, and she focused her hazy gaze on Wyndham's stern features. "Charles?" she whispered.

"I gave Crewe the dagger to hold," he explained. "You were shimmering again."

She buried her face in the soaked wool of his coat. "Hold me. Now, while we're still together."

His lips brushed her forehead, then her mouth. "Lexie—"

Vaughn's tense call interrupted him. With a muttered oath, Wyndham set her down on the rocks, then climbed over the side to join her. Crewe and Vaughn already started along the uneven path toward the cavern. Lexie grasped Wyndham's hand and followed.

With each step, the shivering waves of time increased. She would be torn from Wyndham in only minutes. Not a single doubt remained. The cavern, the dagger, Vaughn—all the ingredients were present. And she could wish them thousands of miles apart.

Her feet encountered sand, and Wyndham steadied her as she staggered. Her senses no longer functioned, everything blurred. With a concerted effort she gathered her wits together and clung to his hand as he led her up the beach. When he directed her toward it, she slid through the opening in the rocks, and the sound of the waves outside echoed about her. She shivered as she started toward the clammy corridors.

"Stay here." Wyndham gestured for Lieutenant Crewe to remain near the opening. The young officer at once drew his pistol and took up his post as guard, just inside the entrance. "Vaughn, take the dagger."

For once Vaughn acted without argument. He took the knife from the lieutenant, then started up the rocky tunnel through the darkness toward the main cavern, their path illuminated by the flickering glow of Wyndham's pocket luminary. When they reached the bracket, the earl kindled the torch, and they proceeded with more ease until they emerged into the chamber.

"Charles—" Lexie hung back, clinging to him.

Wyndham drew her into his arms. "My dearest love," he murmured, and his mouth covered hers.

For a long moment she clung to him, fighting the waves of dizziness, wanting only to remain here, in his arms, with him.

"Lexie, come on!"

Vaughn's words broke through the enchanted moment, and with reluctance she stepped from Charles's encircling hold. She gazed at his beloved features, memorizing the familiar lines of his face, filling the agony in her soul with memories of the love that filled his eyes. Green eyes, though the meager light denied her the chance to see their color once more. He was part of her, always would be, despite that terrible barrier of time . . .

From his right hand, he drew the emerald ring and slipped it over her thumb. "To remember me," he said, his words barely audible.

"How could I ever forget?" she whispered. With trembling fingers, she unfastened the locket from about her neck and placed it in his outstretched hand. His fingers closed about it, brushing her palm, touching her once more.

"Lexie!" Vaughn cast an uneasy glance down the passage the way they had come. "Let's get *out* of here!" He caught her hand and dragged her from Charles, into the middle of the rocky room.

A scrape echoed from above, their only warning. Lexie's head jerked up, and she met Charles's startled gaze in the dim light. He spun about as the orange glow of a torch flooded the chamber, coming from the upper entrance. A dark shape filled the gap, and light glinted off the barrel of a pistol. An explosion of sound filled the air, followed by the acrid smell of powder and the whining of the ricochets.

Chapter Twenty-Four

With the first flying fragments of chipped stone, Lexie ducked, covering her head and neck. One of the smugglers, his torch held high, charged into the room, followed by two more. Sir Thomas paused in the tunnel entrance, his smoking dueling pistol still clasped in one hand. The other held the matching gun.

He strode forward, his gaze leveled on the dagger Vaughn clasped. "I'll take that, I believe." His voice cut through the wavering darkness, as smooth and cold as polished steel.

Vaughn's grip tightened on the treasure, and his eyes gleamed in that shifting light as if with a madness. "No," he breathed.

Lexie caught his arm. "Give it to me."

Vaughn paid her no heed. His gaze riveted on Sir Thomas, then transferred to the dagger. In the flickering illumination of the smuggler's torches, the striated star in the sapphire gleamed. "No, it's mine, now," he breathed.

The chased silver handle glowed, as if with an inner light. Sir Thomas came a step closer, reaching for it.

Wyndham moved for the first time, lunging, unleashing taut muscles, ducking low as one of the smuggler's fired on him. The explosion echoed with deafening effect through the arched chamber. Another of the conspirators closed with the earl, swinging wide and hard as rock fragments rained from every point the deflected ball hit.

Sir Thomas crossed the remaining space between himself

and Vaughn in two strides, struck him with an upper cross to the chin, and grabbed the dagger from the man's loosened grip. Wyndham hurled his opponent from him, started toward Stoke, but another smuggler blocked his path. The earl's fist connected with a sickening thud, dropping the man where he stood, as another ball ricocheted about the cavern walls.

Sir Thomas stood over Vaughn, unmoving in the ruckus, clutching his prize. Awe filled his bemused features as he gazed at the gleaming sapphire.

Vaughn slouched on the floor, gasping, then looked up, his expression a contorted mask of madness. He regained unsteady footing and threw himself at Sir Thomas.

The two men staggered backward, ramming against the stone wall. For one long moment they locked together, Vaughn grasping to regain the dagger, Sir Thomas holding it just beyond his reach. Then the eerie lantern light glinted off the blade with a fiery iridescence as Sir Thomas swung, burying the dagger deep in Vaughn's chest.

"No!" The scream tore from Lexie's throat. Without realizing she'd moved, she reached Vaughn's side, falling on her knees and grasping his shoulders. About her, sound faded. Vaughn . . .

She swallowed, her mouth and throat as dry as a desert, and her hands slipped from him. Dead.

Stunned, she sat back on her heels. How could he be killed, so far from his own time? She'd never thought it possible. Now he would never go home . . .

His blank, staring eyes gleamed in the wavering light, and with a hand that trembled, she reached out to close them. And stopped, unable to touch him.

She couldn't just leave him like this. As the fight raged about her, she unfastened the hook of her cloak with fumbling fingers, then dragged off the garment and draped it over his body.

Dizziness engulfed her, wave after wave of unbearable disorientation. She turned about, staring at the dimming shapes of the struggling men. Wyndham swung, connecting with Sir Thomas's jaw, then closed on the man, his hands seeking his throat. Lieutenant Crewe, on the opposite side of the cave, struggled with a smuggler who wielded a knife.

Sir Thomas staggered backward, away from Charles's deadly onslaught, but before the earl could close with him once more, Sir Thomas drew a pistol from the voluminous pocket of his greatcoat. The explosion reverberated through the cavern and a sharp exclamation escaped Wyndham as he collapsed to the rocky floor.

Lexie cried out, her voice unnaturally loud in the stillness surrounding her. She reached toward Charles, desperate, but her arm remained frozen, immobile at her side. She struggled, but couldn't break free, couldn't shake off the tingling sensation which danced and prickled along her flesh. Her surroundings shimmered, grew hazy, and she screamed in anguish as Wyndham's beloved features blurred, then faded into nothingness . . .

Silence surrounded Lexie, a stillness so complete it penetrated the fog enveloping her like the roar of a freight train. She forced open eyes she hadn't realized she'd closed.

A dim glow illuminated the cavern, concentrated in a single spot of light against the wall before her. Her hand trembling, she picked up the flashlight, staring at it as if it were a foreign object. A *flashlight* . . .

Her own, in fact. She swallowed, but it did little to relieve the aching of her throat—or her heart. For a long moment she clutched the metal cylinder, seeking some measure of comfort from it. At last, steeling her nerve against what she might encounter, she eased the beam along the rocky walls.

The all-too familiar chamber stood empty, except for several pieces of furniture which lay tumbled about, mildewed with the dampness of ages. Just the way she'd seen it first, in fact—so very long ago, in her own time. She swallowed again. She really had succeeded in going back to where she belonged. And Wyndham, dearest Charles. . . . Nearly two hundred years separated her from him. She had lost him, forever.

Agony crept through her, leaving in its wake a raw,

unbearable wound. He was gone . . .

The icy coldness of the air recalled her at last. She had no idea how long she'd sat there, mourning, given over to that sick sense of grief which consumed her. She shivered. Why wasn't she wearing her coat?

Because she'd taken off her cloak. . . .

Her heart lurched, and with a tremendous effort of will she focused the beam before her, on the cavern floor. The star sapphire winked at her, and the chased silver handle of the dagger glinted in the light from where it protruded from torn, aging fabric. Not a blanket, as she had thought before, but a woolen cloak covering . . . Geoff Vaughn's body.

A wave of nausea left her trembling. She scrambled to her feet, sick with shock, and backed two steps away, her horrified gaze resting on the shrouded heap. She'd never liked him, but she hadn't wanted him dead. And she certainly hadn't wanted to see him die so violently, so far from his own time, in this dank cavern as cold as a—a tomb.

And Wyndham. . . . Thoughts of him, of her unbearable loss, drove all else from her mind as emptiness engulfed her once more. Again, in her mind, she saw him stagger under the impact of the bullet, then crumple. Had he died, too, here in this awful cave?

Dear God, she had to know, had to discover what became of him, what else happened that dreadful day. *Had* Charles survived? Or had he already succeeded in thwarting the invasion plans by luring Sir Thomas back to England? Had Charles played out his role in history—and died?

But the Penrith family continued, the title passed on. The current earl was living proof—no, he could be Kester's descendent, not Charles's. She hugged herself, cold and miserable. Had her presence in the past assisted in maintaining history as she knew it—or had it merely destroyed the man she had come to love?

Once more, she cast the beam about the cavern, the last place she had seen—and touched—Charles. The light flickered across something else that gleamed, and she stooped to find her camera, still in its case, the keys to her rented car still clipped to the leather strap.

A car. How odd that would be, after coming to rely on horses and carriages. Suddenly, she only wanted to escape, get out of here, away from Vaughn. What was she to tell the authorities? That a nearly two hundred year-old body belonged to a developer who could have been missing no more than two weeks?

She would tell them nothing, she realized. After all, it all happened so very long ago.

She swung her camera over her shoulder, and her fingers brushed light wool fabric rather than knitted yarn or a nylon parka. With a start, she turned the light on her clothes. She still wore her much mangled gown, drenched from launching the boat in the Channel, slashed by Charles so she could ride a horse, muddied and torn from her scrambling over rocks and fighting with smugglers. She would treasure it always, her memento, all she would ever have to remember Wyndham and the brief time they shared, those very few days that must provide her with an eternity of love.

All . . . She clutched at her thumb, and a racking sob shook her as her fingers encountered the cold metal circle. Charles's emerald ring. She still wore it. She had something of him, something tangible to touch when memory alone proved not enough. She had a horrible feeling that would be often.

She turned away and stumbled toward the entrance to the lower passage. Her skirt clung to her legs, still damp from almost two hundred years ago. Unsteadily, she descended through the twisting passages of the tunnel, until the roar of the ocean filled the entry chamber.

That was better than water, at least. The tide must be out once more. Relieved on that score, she climbed over the rocks and down to the beach.

And stopped.

Slowly, she turned about, gazing at the entry she had uncovered. In the past, it had been bigger. Someone had gone to pains to hide the cavern. The smugglers? Or Sir Thomas himself, to hide his murder? Vaughn's body had lain there for so very long, undisturbed. Perhaps it was for the best.

She set down her camera, then went to work, pushing the few rocks she could budge over the crevice, fitting them tightly, once more sealing off his tomb. For a long moment she studied it, assuring herself it would not easily be discovered again. If what remained of him was found now, he would be gone over by a team of forensic pathologists who would never be able to reconcile evidence of modern dentistry and medical techniques in so old a body.

Let him lie in peace, not become fodder for the supermarket tabloids.

For a long moment she stood in silent prayer for him, then whispered a last goodbye. She turned away and made her way along the sand, back to the steps leading to the walkway and abbey above.

The car stood where she had left it, under the protection of a giant elm. She was lucky it hadn't been impounded by now. As she unclipped her keys, the midday sun struggled to seep through the heavy cloud covering. Rain, though—or snow, if the cold was anything to go by—seemed more likely.

She retrieved her purse from the trunk, then opened the door and slipped inside. What would she do if the battery were dead? She switched on the key, and to her surprise the engine turned over at once, and its steady hum surrounded her.

After shifting into gear, she nosed it out onto the road. Definitely, this was easier to control than either a horse or a carriage—but she missed the charm. She missed *everything* . . .

She forced her mind back to the road. The speed bothered her, she realized, as she kept pace with traffic. Everyone moved so *fast*. If only she could sit beside Charles again in his curricle, plodding along at an easy trot. She wouldn't even complain about the cold.

She had pulled into the parking lot at the bed and breakfast before it dawned on her to wonder what to expect. If she'd been gone for two weeks, she probably didn't have a room anymore. Her luggage would be in the possession of the irate host, who must have assumed she'd skipped out without paying her bill.

She closed her eyes. Two weeks. Her lifetime with Charles.

No one raced out to meet her, so she locked the car. She started for the office, then stopped. The thought of explanations left her ill. She just wanted to get out of the cold, rest for a bit, and *then* she could face everything. And the key to her room—her ex-room, more likely—still hung on her ring. She might as well give it a try. If no one currently occupied it, she might find sanctuary. She turned her weary steps across the lawn and up the stairs which led to the cozy apartment she'd occupied.

As she climbed, emptiness seeped through her, robbing her of inertia, leaving her drained. She should warm herself, get a cup of coffee, take a hot bath. She just didn't care, not with Charles gone.

She reached her door with only one person catching startled sight of her. A newspaper lay on her porch, and she picked it up without enthusiasm and glanced at the date. January seventeenth.

She blinked. The seventeenth? How could it be? That had been the date when she'd taken that ill-fated beach walk, two weeks ago. Unless . . .

What if no time had passed? What if she had been gone only hours, not weeks? How could her world, her life, have turned upside down in so short a time?

Somehow she unlocked her room and let herself inside. Everything remained as she'd left it; the covers on the bed still lay rumpled where she'd drawn them up over the pillow, not properly made for the night to come. The maid had not even made her rounds, yet. Lexie sank on the edge of the mattress, cradling her hand with the emerald ring, and stared unseeing into space.

The discomfort of cold finally disturbed her, penetrating her unhappiness. She pulled herself to her feet, set the pot to brew a cup of strong coffee, then forced her dragging steps into the bathroom for a long hot shower and hair wash. Memories of Charles, and the tub before the fire, tantalized her, renewing once more her longing for a time, for a man, who now remained forever beyond her reach.

She emerged at last, warmer and cleaner, but no happier.

The maid had been in, she noted; the untidiness had been straightened. She donned fresh jeans and a sweater knitted of dusty rose wool, then fastened her thick dark hair at the nape of her neck.

Three o'clock. She should eat something. She hadn't had any food for so long, except for that aging bread and the goat cheese . . .

Charles . . .

Yearning filled her to see Wyndham Priory. Even if she could never see him again, she could at least visit his home, wander through the halls, the familiar rooms. Maybe, if she willed it hard enough, she might conjure up in her mind an image of him standing before the hearth in his library, swirling deep red wine in his goblet, his smoldering gaze burning into her . . .

And she could learn what became of him. She needed that, to know for certain the end of their desperate tale. She grabbed up her keys, ran down the steps to her car and set forth for Wyndham Priory.

As soon as she pulled through the wrought iron gate, she could see the changes. The gatehouse stood empty, the asphalt didn't make the same crunching sound as the gravel. She parked her rented car on the circular drive, got out, then stood for a long while just staring at the facade, remembering how it looked nearly two hundred years before. The garden had changed, the ivy had been cut back. So many subtle differences . . .

Her heart ached. Still, Charles would be pleased to know his beloved home had been so well tended. Mustering her courage, she knocked. Several minutes passed, then the door swung wide and the butler—not Clempson, but the one she had met before, was it only yesterday?—stood before her.

He recognized her, and ushered her inside. "If you will follow me, Miss Anderson? His lordship is in the library."

The library. Lexie hurried in his wake down the carpeted hall, again noting the differences, seeking out the similarities. She glimpsed a tapestry, now much faded by age, but so welcomingly familiar. And a vase—

He opened the door to the bookroom, and Lexie braced

herself against the inevitable changes. She'd seen it before, she knew what to expect—yet she couldn't quell the pang of loss that swept over her.

A man's voice broke through the fog of memories enveloping her—not Charles's beloved deep tones, but lighter ones, of an older man, still familiar. The ninth earl.

He leaned back in a comfortable easy chair before the hearth, a cup of tea in his hand, a saucer on the round pedestal table at his side. Across from him on a loveseat sat an elegant lady of about sixty, her silvered hair swept high on her head. On a low table before her rested a silver tray and tea service, and a plate filled with tiny sandwiches. The woman looked up, her gaze rested on Lexie for a moment before traveling on to the butler, and her delicate eyebrows rose in a mute question.

"Miss Anderson, m'lady." The butler bowed first to her, then her husband. "M'lord." He withdrew.

Lexie threw a frightened glance at the door closing behind her. She shouldn't have come, it was far too painful. But since she had, she should have dressed more appropriately. She took a hesitant step forward.

"Miss Anderson." The earl set down his cup and stood. "How very pleasant. Will you not join us?"

Already, Lady Wyndham poured another cup of tea. "Of course she will. Milk and sugar?" she asked, her voice sweet and low.

"Yes, thank you." She never had gotten around to eating. She advanced another step, then paused. The earl waved her to a chair, into which she collapsed.

"We are having a little celebration," he explained as he resumed his own seat.

"Are you?" The events of the last few days filled Lexie's mind. But he couldn't be referring to any of that, for him it all happened so long ago, in the distant past. Where her heart remained.

"I believe you met Mr. Geoffrey Vaughn here yesterday?" The elderly man took another sip of tea, and smiled at her.

Guilty knowledge flooded through her. "He—" she began, then broke off, at a loss how to explain what happened.

309

"He will not be causing us any more distress." The earl beamed, his pleasure illuminating his entire countenance.

Lexie closed her eyes. Oh, God, here it comes . . .

"He seems to have disappeared," the earl went on, apparently oblivious to her reactions.

"And he has left massive debts," Lady Wyndham added. "He won't be able to pressure us into selling our land any more."

"Disappeared?" The word escaped her lips in a sound perilously close to a squeak. She picked up her cup with a trembling hand and gulped down a swallow of the scalding tea.

"We have had the police here asking questions," the earl went on, sounding pleased more than offended by what must be an unusual intrusion into his quiet world. "It appears Mr. Vaughn must have learned of their investigations into his dealings. They say he left his house at an unusually early hour this morning, but never arrived at his office. They found proof there that he has underworld connections."

"Underworld— I—I can believe that." Lexie kept her gaze on her cup, trying to blot out the mental picture of Geoff Vaughn, enshrouded in that icy cavern. A tomb, a mausoleum. . . . "It—you must be relieved," she managed.

"Indeed, and it has made me forget my manners. I do not believe you have previously met my wife?"

The woman turned to face her fully, and Lexie at last focused her gaze on the gently smiling countess.

And the blood drained from her face, leaving her clammy.

About her neck hung Lexie's locket.

Chapter Twenty-Five

The locket. *Her* locket. Emotion surged through Lexie, both pain and joy, mixing further with longing and relief. It took an immense struggle, but she managed to keep her countenance. She couldn't break down and cry, not here, not in front of these poor people. How could she ever explain what the sight of that simple piece of jewelry meant to her?

And she'd given it to Charles.

Her pulse pounded in her ears. The fact Lady Wyndham wore her locket meant that somehow Charles must have lived, must have escaped that cavern and returned with it to the Priory to pass along as an heirloom.

He had lived, even if only for a little while longer.

The earl drained the last of his tea from his delicate china cup. "And now, my dear, what may we do for you?"

Give me my locket back, she wanted to beg, but knew she couldn't. It had passed from her, she had to let it go, just as she had Charles. Besides, she had his emerald. She clasped her fingers about the ring which encircled her thumb. It would have to be enough.

And perhaps now she would be free of that dreaded nightmare. Did Lady Wyndham—or any of the current earl's ancestors—suffer from that sleep-destroying plague when they wore that haunted necklace?

The elderly couple before her watched her, their expressions gentle, expectant. They waited for her answer, she realized, and struggled to remember the simple question.

311

"I—I would like more information about the third earl. What happened to him, do you know? Did—did he survive his role in defeating the invasion plans?"

"He did, indeed," the countess assured her. "He married, had four children, and lived to a very comfortable old age. Come, would you care to see his portrait?" She rose, her smile warm.

"Yes . . ." Lexie's voice echoed hollowly in her ears. He married. The pain of his betrayal slammed into her, and for several sick moments her world spun once more. For him, she forced herself to remember, it all happened almost two hundred years ago, while for her it had only been that morning when last she kissed him.

She trailed after Lady Wyndham from the study in silence, across the Great Hall toward the stairs leading to the picture gallery above. She couldn't expect Charles to mourn for her all his long life. Memory would dim as the years slipped by. He had a duty to marry, for the sake of his title, for the succession. She could not expect him to shirk it just because one woman tumbled into his life for two short weeks.

Kester could have inherited, the thought flared in her mind.

She squelched it as unworthy. She wouldn't be jealous. She *couldn't* be. She should be glad he found someone who made him happy, who gave him a family to enjoy, an heir to inherit. He had found solace, she must be grateful for that. That she never would, she knew with a certainty that sprang from her soul. No man could ever take Charles's place in her heart, nor in her life. She had thought them soul mates . . .

She mounted the last few stairs, feet dragging, and looked up to see the countess awaiting her beside the first painting of a long-gone Penrith who had lived during the Reformation. Lexie remembered the striking pose, though she thought it had hung farther along the hall before, in one of the alcoves. "There—there are so many portraits," she managed.

The lady smiled in obvious pride. "The Penriths have a long and distinguished history."

Lexie nodded, and her gaze traveled over the line of huge

canvasses in their elaborate gilt-trimmed frames. So many *new* pictures—new, at least, since she last strolled down this hall. Almost, it looked like a fashion parade for the past five hundred years, the irrelevant thought flashed through her mind. And all of them either descended from or forebearers of Charles . . .

At her side, the countess provided names, an occasional date, a lengthy list of impressive accomplishments and government appointments. Charles's descendants had done very well for themselves, every one distinguished either in the political arena or in scientific or artistic pursuits. How very proud he would be . . .

"And here is Charles, the third earl."

Lexie braced herself. She wouldn't react, she wouldn't wear her heart on her sleeve. That was one of Charles's expressions . . .

With determined control, she faced the six-foot canvas, which depicted him in three-quarter length. Her gaze barely took in his rangy black stallion whose reins he held. She only saw *him,* his beloved features, that familiar smile as if he held a special joke, just for her, and knew she would enjoy it as much as did he . . .

In spite of her struggles to prevent them, tears misted her eyes. She should have brought her camera. She would get permission from the current earl, surely he wouldn't mind. Then she would have the print enlarged, transferred to canvas. And she could carry a smaller copy with her in her locket—a new locket, she amended.

"And this is his wife."

The countess's voice broke across her thoughts. Lexie swallowed, stealing her nerve. Then, with slow deliberation, she turned to view the portrait of the woman she couldn't help but think of as her rival. Perhaps she wouldn't be *too* pretty . . .

Her heart dropped through her stomach, all the way to the soles of her feet. She shook her head as shock left her light-headed, disoriented. She stared straight into painted translucent blue eyes set in an excellent rendition of her own face.

"Do you notice the locket she wears?" The countess touched her own—Lexie's own—suspended by its gold chain, resting on the soft blue wool of her jewel-necked sweater. "It has been lost for years."

"Twelve years," Lexie whispered, still stunned. The time it had been with her, in the present. It could not have been in both places at once . . .

"Why, yes." The elegant little woman laughed. "However did you know? It turned up quite by chance, only this morning. I am so glad to rediscover it."

Lexie's gaze strayed back to the portrait—*her* portrait?

Lady Wyndham moved a step closer. "She is lovely, is she not? Charles's wife? She—" The countess broke off, her eyes narrowing as her gaze rested on Lexie. "Why, you are almost identical to her. Even your pale eyes. They are quite a common feature among the Penriths, since Charles married Alexandra Falkirk. You must be descended from her, as well. How delightful, you're probably a distant relative of my husband's. He will be so pleased. He quite likes you, already."

A distant relative of her husband's. But how distant? Lexie stared at the countess for a moment, then back at the portrait. "Alexandra Falkirk." She repeated the name, sampling it on her tongue, awakening barely comprehended recognition from the depths of her subconscious.

The countess smiled, as if oblivious to Lexie's inner turmoil. "Yes, a lovely name, is it not? She was the daughter of William Falkirk. He was a doctor, I believe."

Lexie clutched the back of a chair, barely hearing the last words as a wave of dizziness engulfed her. About her, her surroundings shimmered, the elegant little figure of the countess fading. Transparent shapes hovered where the portraits in their elaborate frames should be on the walls. Her flesh prickled with that all-too familiar sensation of timelessness.

A hazy shape—a man in a white lab coat—came out of a room down the hall, assisting an elderly woman hunched over a walker. The rich carpet beneath her feet faded, and in its place appeared a smooth industrial rug. The walls, papered so beautifully, now displayed a coat of institutional green paint. Cheap, sturdy furniture replaced the beautiful antiques which had surrounded her moments before.

What happened? In rising panic, Lexie watched the changes taking place before her eyes. Wyndham Priory, as she knew it, grew less tangible, and this alternate reality took firmer shape. The countess, a puzzled smile on her sweet face, blurred, faded into intangibility. Lexie spun once more to face the portraits, confused and on the verge of panic. The painted rendition of her own face smiled at her, even as it grew transparent. *Why . . . ?*

And then she knew, with a certainty that filled her with an hysterical desire to scream and laugh at the same time. Her presence here, in what she had thought of as her own time, threatened to destroy the Penrith family, alter history in who knew how many ways.

She belonged not here, but in the past.

Blindly, she turned from the disintegrating scene about her. She had to get back to her proper time, to Charles, to fulfill her *own* role in history. Not just the present stood in danger, but all the preceding generations of Penriths, Charles's descendants—*her* descendants. Their myriad accomplishments and contributions to society and science would never have been made. Charles's home would be turned over to the government—which meant either his bloodline became extinct or his heirs became impoverished.

She *belonged* in the past . . .

The dagger. She had to get back to the cavern and the dagger.

"Miss Anderson . . ."

The thread-like sound of the countess's voice followed her, only to vanish into nothingness as Lexie ran along the Picture Gallery. She took the stairs two at a time, then darted across the Great Hall, brushing past efficient-looking men and women in white coats, elderly people sitting in those coarse wooden slat-backed chairs reading papers or staring into space. No one seemed to see her, be aware of her headlong flight.

She burst through the front door and ran down the asphalted drive. Her rented car stood to one side, the only tangible, unchanging object to meet her gaze. With a soft cry of relief she dove for it, then scrambled inside, fumbling with the seatbelt and the ignition. The engine turned over smoothly and she shoved it into gear, pointing it toward the gate.

Wave after wave of dizziness washed over her. She could barely hold the wheel, barely keep the car on the road. Only it wasn't a car in which she sat. She clung to the side of a wooden wagon, drawn by a sweating, terrified horse. Through a child's eyes, she looked up at the woman sitting beside her—her mother—as the shrieking, jostling crowd pressed against them. One man came so close, his torch extended. . . . Heat swept over her, burning, as the cart burst into flames.

And another man—horrified, Lexie recognized a younger Sir Thomas, his eyes possessed of a terrifying madness. He grasped her mother by the arm, and the flickering light of the flames glinted off the chased silver handle, winked in the eye of the star sapphire, as he plunged the weapon into her mother's chest. The reins fell from her hands, and the horse lunged wildly, out of control. The shaft gave way with a splintering crack, and the horse veered off, but the wagon continued straight. Lexie screamed as it slammed into a stone wall . . .

The seatbelt broke loose where she hadn't properly fastened it. As her car slammed into the wall, the door sprung wide and the force of the impact hurled her out, clear of the wreckage. Dazed, she struggled to a sitting position as the car burst into flame. Darkness, punctuated by blinding pinpoints of light, swirled about her, and she fell backwards into oblivion.

Sensation returned slowly. She ached all over, as if someone had picked her up and bodily thrown her into a

316

wall. Or as if she had been in an accident . . .

Memory flooded back and her eyes flew open. She dragged herself onto one elbow, her frantic gaze seeking answers. She lay in a bed—a familiar bed. She recognized the room about her, too. Her bedchamber at Wyndham Priory, still decorated as it had been when she'd left it nearly two hundred years ago—or only days?

"Lexie?" William Falkirk's gentle voice sounded at her side.

Slowly, easing her stiff neck, she turned her head, her heart swelling in relief. "Father?" And as she spoke the word—the name—she knew it to be true.

She reached out to him, and he clasped her hand, his touch warm and secure. "I—I survived that crash, when Mamma was killed. I've been in the future, which is why you couldn't find me."

His eyes narrowed, his gaze searching her face. "Sandra?" he asked at last, her name no more than a breath on his lips.

She nodded, unable to speak for the moment. Hearing her name again, in his familiar voice, brought a flood of lost childhood memories rushing back. The *al fresco* picnic when he'd taken her rowing, being curled in her mother's lap while he read from the morning's paper . . .

His hand tightened on hers. "But how—?"

"That—that dagger," she managed. "I relived it all, getting back here—the wagon, and those horrible men, and Mamma being—" She broke off, loathe to speak—or even think—of the dagger. "It was so much more vivid than just the nightmares, this time. I really *experienced* it. All these years, I've been an intruder in the *future,* but now I'm back—where I belong."

"Sandra," he repeated. A misty smile lit his pale blue eyes and he stooped to kiss her forehead. "You really are my Sandra. This is a joy I never hoped to find."

She caught his hand. "Charles. Is he—?"

"Resting, my dear. He sat with you for hours, but he is still very weak, himself. I sent him to his room only a little while ago."

317

"What happened? In the cavern, I mean. There were so many of the smugglers, and only Charles and Lieutenant Crewe."

"Help arrived. I had set Huggins to watch the entrance, just in case. When Sir Thomas and his men returned, he summoned me—and young Grenville Stoke. The three of us went in, prepared. The fight didn't last long."

Lexie shivered. "Then you cleaned up—and left Geoff Vaughn's body."

He nodded. "We decided it would be for the best if he simply disappeared as mysteriously as he arrived. There would have been so many questions from the authorities about who he was and where he came from. We thought it best to let him rest in peace."

"I—I came to much the same conclusion in the future." She swallowed. "So we succeeded, and Napoleon didn't—doesn't—get the information he needed. But—" She cocked her head to one side, frowning. "Why doesn't history point the blame for the conspiracy at Sir Thomas?"

Dr. Falkirk examined his hands with apparent interest. "Sir Thomas," he said, "died in a boating accident. He broke his neck when the tides dashed him against the rocks. A tragic occurrence, one fears."

She stared at him in dawning comprehension. "I see. He didn't have a single thing to do with the conspiracy, then? Officially?"

The doctor shook his head. "What good would it do to drag the Stoke name through scandal? If Sir Thomas had lived, of course, that would be another matter. There would have to have been a trial, an execution. An unpleasant business for all concerned." He shook his head. "Treason is a crime that could have serious repercussions for the rest of his family. Young Grenville may be something of a rake, but he does not deserve to live under that black a cloud—especially since he means to settle down and take a wife."

"Miss Langley?" How happy the governess must be. Lexie leaned back against the pillows, considering. "Yes," she said at last, "nothing could be gained by revealing Sir Thomas's

318

role. Let history remain vague. It's not worth destroying Mr. Stoke and Miss Langley. Oh, he must be *Sir* Grenville, now."

"I'm glad you agree." He sat back, his fond gaze resting on her. "My dear *daughter*," he said.

The door opened, and she looked from her father's smiling face to see Charles standing on the threshold, one arm strapped to his side. Her heart leapt, and she caught her breath. He really *was* alive, she *had* come back to him. They could be together. . . .

He remained where he stood, staring at her, not moving, as if he feared to break a spell.

Dr. Falkirk glanced at his friend, then his warm gaze returned to Lexie. "I'll come back later, my dear. We have much more to catch up on, you and I. But for now, I leave you in excellent hands." His fingers brushed her shoulder. "And you may be assured of my parental blessings," he added. He left the room, closing the door behind him.

Charles drew a long, shaky breath, and advanced slowly into the apartment. Then, as if his control crumbled, he reached her bedside in two strides, sank onto the edge of the mattress, and gathered her against him with his good arm. For a long while he said nothing, merely holding her so tightly she doubted she could ever break free. As if she'd want to. . . . His lips brushed her hair, her neck, sending glorious sensations through her.

"How long this time?" he demanded, and his voice betrayed the agony of their parting.

She snuggled even closer. "A lifetime," she promised.

At that, he set her from him, enough so he could see her face. "Are you sure?"

"Positive. I'll never go near that dagger again. And *knowing* I belong back here, with you—that's finally severed my ties to the future. It's not going to pull at me any more."

"You can be so certain?"

She nodded. "The future—" She broke off, her eyes widening as her hands tightened about him. "That's why I kept thinking I was getting lost in a limbo. I was trying to get back to a time—the *future*—where I shouldn't have been.

That's why I never made the shift on my own. It took the dagger to get me there completely."

He touched her cheek with a tentative finger, as if he feared she would evaporate before his eyes. "But what if you're wrong—what if you can't stay with me?"

The anxiety in his expression—his yearning for her—sent warmth flooding through her. "I *can*," she assured him. "And yes, I'm certain. You see, I've actually *seen* what happens to you—and to your descendants."

"And?"

Smugness settled over her, secure and happy. In all sincerity she said: "You can't do it without me."